G000164380

THE UNKNOWN

E.S. Taylor

East Ridge Publishing

This novel is a work of fiction. Names, characters, places, and incidents are either products of the author's imagination or used fictitiously. All characters are fictional, and any similarity to people living or dead is purely coincidental.

Copyright © 2015 by E.S. Taylor,
www.estaylor.com

All rights reserved. No portion of this book may be reproduced, stored in a retrieval system, or transmitted in any form or by any means – electronic, mechanical, photocopy, recording, scanning or other – except for brief quotations in critical reviews or articles, without prior written permission of the publisher.

Library of Congress Control Number: 2015944774

Copy Editing by Carol Davis,
www.caroldavisauthor.com

Cover Photo by Pavel Szabo/Shutterstock

Published by East Ridge Publishing
Tigerville, SC

ISBN-13: 978-0692476086

For Sharon,
Love you bad.

THE UNKNOWN

The only thing necessary for the triumph of evil is for good men to do nothing.

—Edmund Burke

Spring, 1865
Southern Virginia

Smoke was everywhere, hanging black and motionless like clouds in hell. The soldier screamed and whipped his horse. The steed ran faster and faster, flesh foaming with sweat, flanks quivering with each new blow. It tore into the ground of the countryside, throwing up loose clumps of earth in its wake, swerving and dodging the fleeing livestock.

The soldier was close enough now to feel the heat from the blaze. Glowing red ash swirled in the false breeze created by the fire and stung when it fell on his face and hands. He coughed and leaned low in the saddle.

Smoke spewed from the windows of the farmhouse like blood from a ruptured artery. Pieces of roof were scattered around the yard in smoldering lumps and had burned out most of the surrounding grass. The small corral alongside the house was empty, the fencing lying broken and pulled apart on the ground. There was no movement anywhere, save for the awful smoke streaming ever upward above the flames.

The soldier pulled hard on the reins. The horse sounded out from the sudden and unexpected jerk of its neck and ground to a stop twenty yards from the blaze. The soldier swung out of the saddle and ran toward the house. He fell, then struggled back to his knees. He searched the immediate area with his eyes and then began screaming their names. He screamed and screamed, but was answered only by the sound of the fire as it quickly and efficiently devoured the dry timber that had once been a home.

Nothing moved.

Nothing returned his call.

All was still.

Lost.

Then one of the bodies twitched.

The movement was negligible, a mere tic in the corner of the soldier's eye, just enough to draw his attention to the ground at the front of the house.

The nausea came then.

It was the smallest one who'd moved. And it was just a twitch, just a slight, seemingly insignificant jerk of the little girl's hand.

Tears crowded the soldier's eyes and he was back on his feet again, running into the confusion. Running to her.

She was still breathing, but in thin, shallow gasps. Her chest rose and fell in rapid, air-starved heaves, and the left side of her dress was mangled and soaked red and stuck to her body.

The soldier dropped to his knees and pressed a hand to her injured left side. Blood was everywhere and still coming. There were several puncture wounds in the fabric of her dress, small and ragged. Too many.

The soldier shook his head, as if that simple action could defy the inevitable, but his heart knew better and the tears broke. He swallowed and smiled down at her, then wiped the dust and ash from her face.

Every breath was an effort for her now, each one coming farther apart from the last. She managed a weak smile and touched his boot with two pale fingers. And for a moment, even through the pain, her eyes sparkled up at him just as they always had—shone bright, exactly as he'd remembered them.

Then they went out forever. Her chest contracted for the last time. The next breath never came.

The soldier lowered his head and closed his eyes. His body became suddenly warm and peaceful, his mind spilling over with memories of the past in bright, rapid flashes. He saw the girl, not as she was now—lying in the dirt beneath him—but smiling and radiant, closer to womanhood. Beautiful. From somewhere inside, he felt her embrace, knew she loved him, and recognized the scent that was uniquely her own.

Then it was gone. She was gone. The noise of the blaze returned to his ears like a blast of cannon fire. The smell of charred wood and death filled his nostrils.

He looked down at her, openly sobbing now.

"Libby, girl," he whispered, "you're so big."

He touched her eyelids but they wouldn't close. Tears clouded his vision and he cupped them away. He took her by the hand and discovered a silver coin in her palm. The coin reflected the failing sunlight as it spilled from her hand into the dirt below.

Then he was jerked away.

The soldier struggled to orient himself, tried to process the abrupt change of events. He was being dragged across the ground by both arms. He started kicking and flailing his feet. He caught a boot to the ribs, a hard and painful thud that blasted all the air from his lungs. He grimaced and tried to move his arms, but they were held fast. There were two men on either side of him. He could see them, but only as blurs in his peripheral vision, tugging and grappling with his wrists. And then another appeared in front of him.

This one with a shotgun.

The soldier was gasping for air now, staring up at the strangers in confusion and growing rage. More tears spilled off his cheeks.

"It won't supposed to go down this way," the man with the shotgun said. The man was thin and heavily bearded. He wore a disfigured, dirty black hat and, like his two comrades, was clothed in the familiar gray uniform of the Confederate army.

The man eyed the soldier for a beat, then gestured at the second dead body lying by the entrance to the house. "The old codger pulled a piece on me. We's only wanted the livestock, but the bastard wouldn't listen." The man's jaw set in anger and frustration. He shook his head and pointed at the girl. "The old man, he pulled that pistol, and, well … she was just right there beside him. She wouldn't get clear."

He spat. "It won't supposed to be like this. We's gonna carry the flag back at the Yanks. Just 'cause Lee gave up don't mean the fightin's over. Just look at you. They've disarmed you and sent you home like a little boy. Well, we's still got heart. We's still got weapons. We's still got the willing and able. We's just need supplies." He paused for a moment, looking over the soldier's uniform—a uniform nearly identical to his own—then added, "Brother."

The soldier spat at him and wrenched his arms, but the men had been expecting the move and held on. They leaned in opposite directions and pulled, stretching the soldier's arms to their physical limits, then each dropped a knee onto his wrists, pinning them to the ground.

The soldier gasped at the sudden pain.

"You know I can't leave you around now," the man said. "And I reckon it's safe to say you won't be joining our cause." He looked around and swore. "Damn, I wish you hadn't come around. We's really trying to do the right thing here."

He laid the shotgun down and drew his sidearm.

The soldier leaned forward and threw all his weight into a roll to his right. But the men dug their knees in and the roll never materialized. There was another, harder kick to his ribs.

The soldier bit back the pain and glared at the man in front of him.

"Hold him still, boys," the man said, and one of them kicked him again.

The soldier twisted and grunted with the new blow's impact, but again clenched his teeth and swallowed the pain.

The man drew back the hammer on his revolver and took aim at the soldier's chest. "It ain't personal, boy."

The two men got off their knees and stretched the soldier out again, leaning a safe distance away.

Their leader paused for a beat and met the soldier's eyes. There was remorse there, hesitance, uncertainty.

But then he pulled the trigger.

The soldier twisted to his left and the bullet took him in the lower abdomen. He screamed and wrenched against his captors, thrusting his legs aimlessly at the man to his right. The man gave him another swift kick in his side.

"Dammit, boys! Keep him still!"

The two men stretched him out once more, and the soldier screamed again. The scream erupted from him, a mixture of raw pain and pure rage. He continued to struggle, but his efforts were becoming futile, his strength waning.

The leader's eyes wandered to the ground below the soldier, where blood was beginning to pool. "Let him go," he said. "Just let the poor bastard be."

His two henchmen held on.

"He's finished," the man said. He picked up the shotgun and tossed it to the man on the soldier's right. "Go on and load up the cargo. We's need to be movin' on."

The henchmen dropped the soldier and walked away in opposite directions.

The soldier rolled over and clutched his side.

The leader watched his comrades go, then took his hat off and knelt by the soldier. He wiped sweat from his brow. "This won't how it was supposed to be," he said again. "I'm going to take your pain away. But first, I want you to know I'm gonna make this right. I'm gonna make all of 'em suffer, all of 'em that's caused us pain. Just when they're thinking they've won, I'm gonna bring Hades down on 'em. I'm gonna call down the righteous fire on those responsible for our sufferin'." He laid a hand on the soldier's shoulder. "That's my promise to you, brother."

The soldier looked up.

The man smiled and nodded. He slipped his hat back on and placed the pistol against the soldier's head.

The soldier closed his eyes as the hammer clicked back into position. He took a breath and held it, focusing only on the cool steel tip of the revolver against his flesh.

Then he took it.

In one quick, unexpected motion, the pistol was in the soldier's hand. The man's eyes widened and his lips parted to speak.

And then he died.

The bullet struck him in the forehead, leaving his face forever fixed in that moment of shock and surprise.

The soldier shoved him aside and struggled to his feet. Pain exploded through his gut like wildfire. He looked to his left where one of the henchmen stood by the broken corral. The man was leading a goat with one hand and cradling a chicken in the other.

The soldier limped two steps toward the surprised man and raised the pistol.

The man dropped the bird and dug for his sidearm.

The soldier fired and hit him high in the chest. The man's body snapped around like he'd been punched in the shoulder, but he quickly righted himself and freed his revolver.

The soldier fired again, but this time the man just stood there, wincing and taking careful aim as the bullet whistled harmlessly by.

The soldier was suddenly having trouble focusing. The world around him had begun spinning and oscillating. He staggered back a step.

The man fired and the soldier felt a tug in his upper left arm. He staggered again and squeezed off another round.

The man went to his knees, his weapon discharging into the ground. He slumped over and put both hands in the dirt.

The soldier heard yelling to his right, but it was a distant, hollow sound, like an echo in a faraway valley. He turned and saw the third man running at him, screaming, shotgun raised.

The soldier blinked, shook his head. Everything was becoming murky and slow, like the whole world was suddenly underwater. He saw the flash from the shotgun's muzzle just as he sighted the revolver and fired.

The spray from the ill-aimed shotgun blast spread up the soldier's right arm, slapping the pistol from his hand.

The man hadn't missed a step in the exchange and was still charging toward him like an angry boar.

Adrenaline seared through the soldier's body. He jerked the knife from his belt and lunged toward his attacker.

The two met in a collision that knocked the soldier to the ground. The man fell on top of him, shotgun still in hand, still screaming curses.

But it was already over. The blade had done its work in the fall, slipping delicately between the man's ribs and into his black heart.

The man pushed himself up on his knees and looked down at the reddening handle of the knife. He reached for it, then thought better. Instead, he rocked back and lifted the shotgun. He thrust the barrels against the soldier's chest and squeezed both triggers, but the hammers snapped down on spent cartridges.

He dropped the weapon and put a hand on the ground to steady himself. His skin was growing pale and blood was dribbling into his beard from the corner of his mouth.

The soldier shoved him away with a soft kick and stood up. He staggered to his left and dropped to his knees. He stood again, steadied himself, and looked around for the lost pistol. He noticed the blood then, and how it seemed to be all over him. He ignored it, picked up the revolver, and aimed the weapon at the man by the corral. But the thief was silent and motionless, slumped over in an uneven mass.

The soldier went back to the girl and knelt. And with that effort, all his remaining energy drained away into the earth beneath him.

He fell back beside her and the world began spinning again. But this time it wasn't altogether unpleasant. This time it was accompanied by a feeling like cool water, spreading first throughout his chest and neck, and then washing along his arms and legs. The fatigue in his limbs was glorious, and he wanted nothing more now than to sleep.

He cocked the pistol and slipped it under his chin, then closed his eyes.

He pulled the trigger.

It clicked.

Empty.

1

Fall, 1880

Jack fixed a cigar between his teeth, bit the end off and spit, then slid a match up the side of the column until it hissed and came to life. He took a couple of hard pulls to get the smoke going, then leaned back and looked across the front of the property. Thirty acres of fencing came together at a gate about forty paces from the front of Jonas Cantrell's homestead. The gate was closed but not locked.

"I don't reckon Jonas is going to make it," he said. "I mean, I don't reckon the cattle are going to make it."

Raymond was sitting beside him in one of the rocking chairs scattered across the front porch, his rifle lying across his lap. "They won't."

Jack pushed himself out of the chair. His joints were stiff—a consequence of the cool morning air. He was thankful the rain had stopped. Riding the property was, at best, difficult this time of year. The cold rain of early November made it nearly intolerable. He actually preferred the snow, once it arrived, since at least it didn't soak through his clothing so easily. Such things made a considerable difference when the temperatures made it into the awful mid-winter lows. Of course, at that point, rain was virtually impossible anyway; even the local rivers and streams ceased to be liquid. But even when the conditions were at their worst, fencing still failed and cattle still wandered. Just as they likely were now.

Having waited out the rain, he and Raymond were a little behind their usual morning routine. Still, Jack was in no hurry. He couldn't wait until the stiffness and body aches worked themselves out, because they *wouldn't* work themselves out. Only moving around would alleviate that problem. He had half the cigar left, though, and figured to spend at least a few more minutes nursing it before heading out.

He leaned on one of the columns supporting the roof overhanging the porch, hoping to get a better view of the looming cloud cover. But before he could get a good look, or the smoke back to his lips, a man broke out of the woods across the way in a dead run.

The man was moving with such urgency that a casual onlooker might have expected a party of Sioux warriors to come riding out behind him. He was holding his hat on with one hand and had vines and loose underbrush wrapped around one arm and both ankles. The foliage whipped out behind him like streamers, but he either didn't notice or didn't care.

Jack glanced to his left. Raymond was rocking slowly, still watching the woods across the way. He was tapping the stock of his rifle with one finger as if counting off each second as it passed.

In no time the man was at the gate fiddling with the lock. He was so edgy that he didn't notice the clasp was already disengaged and so, in his haste, locked it. His mistake registered quickly when he tried to run through it and promptly knocked the wind out of himself. The sudden impact caused his hat to drop off inside the fence, and for a moment he just stared at it through the gate, confused and holding his upper abdomen.

Jack started down the steps. It wasn't unusual to see Eli emerge from *any* point of the wooded area around Jonas Cantrell's place, or at any time, for that matter. He spent most of his time there. Neither was it strange to see him riddled with anxiety, as he apparently was now. That, too, was common. What bothered Jack was that Eli was trying to enter through the gate, whereas he normally slipped discreetly through the fence rails a hundred feet or so down the line en route to the barn where he kept his place.

Before Jack reached the bottom of the steps, Eli had given up on the gate and slid under the fence. He hurried toward the porch but then stopped and looked back at his hat.

Jack walked over and scooped it up. "Mornin', Eli."

Eli said nothing. He hurried over and took his hat, then looked nervously back over his shoulder at the empty early-morning horizon.

Jack rubbed his stomach, which suddenly felt like he'd eaten one of those green apples from back home. He unwound some of the loose foliage from Eli's jacket. "Take your time," he said. "Just take your time and get settled."

Eli looked at Raymond, then Jack. His face twisted up as if he intended to speak but nothing came out. He was wringing the brim of his hat to such a degree that Jack wondered if he'd pull it apart.

"Easy now," Jack said. "Just tell me what you saw."

Eli pointed behind him without looking back. "S-s-s-s-s," he started and shook his head. "S-s-someone's comin'."

Jack looked back in the direction Eli had come. He saw nothing, but that wasn't surprising. Eli often brought news of what lay ahead—or, in this case, what was approaching—well in advance. And he was always dead-on accurate. Always. But he was never this bothered over simple travelers.

Jack disentangled the last bit of underbrush and then slipped an arm around him. "Someone's coming?"

Eli nodded.

Jack felt the man's body trembling under his arm. "Coming here?"

"Yeah, Jack." Eli held up two fingers. "Ta-two riders ca-ca-comin'."

"Who do you reckon they are?"

"One ma-man wearin' pa-pa-purdy clothes an-and a na-new hat."

"Okay."

"An-and the other one is a, is a, a ..." Eli stopped and looked over his shoulder. "The other one is a s-s-soldier."

"A soldier?"

"Yeah, Jack."

"Alright," Jack said. "How far?"

Eli pulled on his crumpled hat and peered across the landscape. "La-less than four ma-ma-miles, ridin' qui-quick. Ma-ma-maybe a half-hour."

Jack patted him on the back and tried, to no avail, to meet Eli's eyes. "You're the best. Thanks for letting us know."

Eli grinned and then shuddered, like the attempted smile had caused him pain. He said nothing. And as soon as Jack removed his arm, he hurried back across the front yard, dipped under the fence, and disappeared back into the woods.

Jack watched until he was gone. He tossed the cigar. "Get any of that?"

Raymond shook his head.

"He says someone's coming with an armed escort, army escort."

Raymond reclined in his chair and stared out beyond the fence.

Jack stopped at the bottom of the steps and leaned on the railing. "Hell, Twin Pines is nearly a half-day's ride. Who'd ride through the night in this weather to come here? Reckon they're coming from somewhere else?"

"Not with a military escort."

Jack nodded. They'd heard of an army presence in Twin Pines, though they hadn't been in town in a few months. They almost never saw any military around Jonas's ranch, and when they did it was only smaller detachments chasing phantom Indians. So what would they want out here? Surely it wasn't legal business. Jonas had never cheated a soul, nor stepped on anyone's toes. In fact, some might say his honesty and high moral nature was his undoing, that a cattleman must be shrewd in order to be successful. But their employer never compromised if he thought it wasn't right. That was his most admirable quality. Besides, the army didn't preside over civilian legal issues. Did they?

Indians. The idea turned Jack's stomach over. The natives were wreaking havoc across the new northern territories. The government had turned away from treaties with the Indians, and that had inevitably led to clashes between the regular army and indigenous tribes of all kinds. Indians had been massacred, in some instances even women and children. In retaliation, settlers were being slaughtered. The stories were unsettling, to say the least. Travelers or patrons would stop by the ranch from time to time, some for a head of beef, some to sell their own. They were all different in every way but one: they all had stories of the Indian uprisings. And the stories only got more heinous with the passage of time.

The Sioux were the dominant tribes in the region, and the stories involving them were particularly disturbing. All Indian raids shared similarities, but the Sioux took it further. All tribes would move in quickly, with stealth and numbers, take what they wanted, and put down any men who opposed them. But the Sioux weren't stopping there. They often killed everyone: men, women, and children, it was said. Scalps were taken, preferably with the victim still alive. Homes were burned with families trapped inside. Some were tied to trees and skinned alive. Still others were cut and left to bleed out or, if death didn't come, left as offerings to the vaunted wolf and bear. And then recently, as if all this wasn't enough, Custer's cavalry had been utterly annihilated. The only settlers shown mercy were the women and girls the attackers found fair enough to take back to camp or sell off to slave traders. But those *mercies* were a matter of interpretation.

Jack could tell these stories were starting to bother Jonas. He had his three boys to worry about, and it was *him* that had brought them to this godforsaken place. Jack also knew some of the stories had been stretched, but the Indian raids were indeed very real and on the rise. And to say it had been on Jonas's mind would have been a gross understatement. In fact, Jack knew from experience, if one allowed his mind to wander long enough, the Sioux were behind every rock and every tree; they were every shadow on the evening landscape, every creak of the porch in the dead of night.

Would someone come this far to warn them of an Indian presence? In the dark and rain? Jack thought of asking for Raymond's opinion, but he already knew the answer. Nothing else seemed to bother him. Why should this?

He started up the steps. "Better tell Jonas company's coming."

Raymond kept rocking, said nothing.

The smell of coffee and overcooked beef met Jack at the door. The usual. Jonas was leaning against a counter in the kitchen. His boys were sitting around a table barely large enough for two, let alone three people.

Jonas's younger boys, Michael and Carl, were fighting for space at the small table. His older boy, CJ, was staring intently at his father.

"It's cowboys, Pa! Nobody says that anymore."

"I think I know what they're called, son," Jonas said. "And they're called drovers."

"Horsefeathers!" CJ said, using his own invented curse word—one that wouldn't get him into trouble with his father. "I'm tellin' ya, that newspaper you brought back from Twin Pines calls 'em cowboys. You'll see I'm right. I aim to be a cowboy."

With that, his brothers chimed in. "Me too! Me too!"

"You've got the boy part down," Jonas said. "But you remind me more of a mule than any cow."

Michael and Carl broke into laughter.

"Besides, you're already a cowhand," Jonas added, then cleared his throat. "I mean drover."

Before CJ could respond, Jonas pointed at the boy's half-eaten breakfast. "Finish up. There's work to be done."

CJ went back to his plate without another word, but his cheeks were flushed and he looked about to burst.

Jack was standing by the door, waiting for Jonas to look in his direction. Little Carl was the first to notice him.

The youngest boy gave a big wave with one greasy palm. "Hi, Jack."

"Mornin', little man."

Michael and CJ also greeted Jack. Jonas moved toward the coffee pot at the fire, but then stopped and looked back.

Jack knew he was wondering why he and Raymond weren't already gone. He met Jonas's eyes and gestured with a nod of his head.

"Finish eating, boys," Jonas said. He took off his apron and tossed it over a chair, and then walked over to the door. He lowered his head.

"Two riders," Jack whispered. "One well-dressed man with a military escort."

Jonas looked up.

"Maybe twenty-minutes," Jack added.

Jonas looked at the wall, expression blank, as if trying to work out some complex problem in his head. "An escort?"

"Want us to hang around for a bit?"

"I guess so," Jonas said. "Yeah, if you would." He turned and walked back toward the fire, pausing once, still in thought.

Jack lingered a moment, watching his employer, then eased out and pulled the door shut behind him. "I reckon we oughta mount up," he said.

Raymond slid his hat on and stood.

"He wants us to stay close," Jack said.

Raymond nodded.

2

Jonas was standing on the porch in anticipation of the visitors. He held his hands by his sides, then clasped behind his back, then in his pockets and out again. He was looking back across the landscape as if expecting Death itself to descend. Finally, he came down the first couple of steps and looked up at the sky and the now bright shining sun.

Jack watched him for a minute, then slung his jacket across his mare's saddle. He had positioned himself along the line of fence about thirty yards east of the gate, and roughly the same distance from the house. But even from there he could see the unsteadiness in his employer's hand, the concern on his face. Having grown fond of Jonas over the last couple of years, it was difficult to watch his once vibrant personality deteriorate so rapidly. But it was understandable.

Jonas had left Texas and everything he'd ever known a couple of years ago. He'd hired a crew and driven a thousand head of cattle into the territory, all his life savings would afford him. Like a lot of folks, he had been hooked by the prevailing propaganda: *The money will fall from the sky*.

There were maybe two hundred animals left. Maybe.

The winters had proved too much for the Texas cattle to endure. They had tried all they knew might work, and even some things they knew wouldn't, but there was just no way to keep that many animals warm with the resources they had.

Each of the last two cold seasons, they'd watched helplessly as the cattle died in droves. Winter mornings were greeted with dismay; first the barn would have to be checked for dead, and then the surrounding pastureland. It was a silent and terrible ritual that disheartened everyone involved, but none more than Jonas. The locals claimed this kind of cold was unusual, but, of course, that didn't matter. The damage was done.

Jack heard the front door open and close as he untied his mare from the fence. He towed the horse around by the reins until she was facing the gate, then mounted up. He was about to slip into his duster when he noticed Jonas standing beside him with two cups of coffee.

The mare, evidently as surprised as Jack, snorted and tossed her head, but recognition stopped her short of an all-out rear.

"It's not supposed to be easy to sneak up on a horse," Jack said.

Jonas extended one of the cups. "Or a soldier."

Jack took the coffee with both hands and held it to his lips. The fluid was thick and black as the night sky, a consequence of having hung over the fire too long. But that was okay. It was still liquid, at least on top, and it warmed on the way down.

"Much obliged," Jack said. "And I ain't been a soldier for a long time, but I don't recall it ever being too hard to get behind me."

Jonas leaned on a post in the fence and scanned the countryside. He blew across the rim of his coffee cup.

Jack glanced across the way to where Raymond was slowly riding along the fence into a position very much like his own, only west of the gate. He was taking sections from an apple with his hunting knife. The blade glistened and winked in the sunlight as he raised each piece to his mouth. Jack wondered where he'd gotten the apple.

"A fella once told me," Jonas said, "that upon coming home at the end of the war, he found himself suddenly alone in the midst of a thousand widows. Those were his words. But it just never seemed right to him. He said a handful of 'em took a shine to him in the years following; some even took the initiative. A couple of 'em really needed help—a man around, that is. But it just never seemed right to him."

Jack sipped the coffee. "I reckon that's understandable."

"Do you think she can see me?"

Jack turned in the saddle. Jonas was still leaning against the fence post, still staring at the empty landscape. He hadn't moved.

"What say?"

Jonas's voice came back hoarse and tired. He still didn't move. "Do you think she can see me?"

"Who?"

"Helen. Do you think she can see me? Right now?"

Jack sipped the coffee again. He believed she probably could. But he'd always felt that way—that loved ones gone could not only still see the world in its unfolding, but kept an interest in the things they'd left behind. It wasn't a belief he'd deduced from anything else, nor had it been taught to him in his youth. In fact, now that he thought of it, he couldn't explain it at all.

But Jonas hadn't asked for an explanation. The particular loved one he was referring to was his wife who, after a long illness, he'd lost to consumption three years ago back in Texas.

"I don't reckon I know," Jack said.

Jonas was silent. He continued to stare at nothing, apparently trying to work it out on his own.

Jack waited. It was his belief that, in the end, such things couldn't be worked out and were therefore better off left alone. He knew ideas alone could drive a man crazy if left unchecked. He'd witnessed it firsthand and, to some extent, had personal experience in the matter.

"I hope not," Jonas whispered.

Jack emptied his cup and laid it top down on the fence. He ran a hand along the mare's neck. "Jonas, you've done all you could do and then some. You couldn't have known it would be like this."

Jonas said nothing.

"And you've done a fine job with those boys," Jack went on. "I reckon they're as fine a young men as I've ever come across. You know, there's a lot worse things than—"

"Have you ever loved someone?"

"What?"

"You, Jack. Have you ever loved someone?"

Jonas straightened but still didn't face Jack.

"Well, yeah, of course I have," Jack said.

"I'm talking about a woman."

Jack looked away. He lifted his duster off the mare's back and slipped it on. "Won't you tell me what's bothering you?"

"Have you ever *been* in love?"

Jack didn't immediately answer. He shrugged into his jacket and then checked the inside pocket. He let his fingers linger on its contents for a moment.

"Once."

"You loved her?"

"Yeah."

"Where is she?"

"I don't know."

"Something happen to her?"

"I don't know that, either."

Jonas turned away from the fence. His eyes looked tortured and swollen. The lines in his face were wet and shimmering. He combed his hair back through his fingers. "Good lord, Jack, I'm sorry. It's just ... well, I don't know what it is. They say God puts men where he wants 'em to be. I reckon that's right, but ..." He trailed off in thought, absently wiping away tears with the back of his hand. He finally sloshed the rest of his coffee into the yard and started walking back toward the house.

Jack swung his mare around toward the gate. His heart ached for the man, and he felt like he should've said something more, but Jonas really hadn't given him the chance. He also knew that Jonas was probably looking for his own answers, that he might have been putting his questions *out there* so he could see them better. That was Jonas. But then, Jonas hadn't been Jonas lately.

God puts men where he wants them to be. Jack had certainly heard that said before, particularly during the war, and in at least half a dozen different ways. But was it true? How could it be? Would God place men in circumstances that could do them great harm?

During the war, a military chaplain had taught him a prayer. It had been the only time he'd ever spoken to a minister, and still was. The clergyman had claimed that men could not utter a more powerful prayer than this one. Jack had never forgotten it, though he'd also never employed it again after the war. But now he found it lying on his mind like a lead ball. He didn't like the feeling, because it was normally associated with great trouble, sometimes life and death. Which really didn't seem to fit the present situation.

But there it was.

The feeling.

He lowered his head and squeezed his eyes together—figuring this would ensure his prayer got through. He stayed that way for a second or two and then recited the prayer softly, quietly.

"God, please help."

He opened his eyes and angled his head to the left.

Just in time to see Raymond look away.

Just as Eli had said, about half an hour had passed when Jack saw horses approaching in the distance. Two riders.

Jonas, who was back on the porch, turned and mumbled something at the door—instructions to his boys, Jack figured. Then he came down the steps and started across the yard.

The riders reached the gate before Jonas and stopped. They surveyed the surroundings while they waited, probably wondering how they'd come to be expected.

Jack steadied his horse. Little of the travelers' appearance could be made out from this distance, but Eli's description seemed accurate enough. One man in well-kept civilian clothes, the other a soldier. It was the soldier part that had bothered Eli, Jack knew.

The well-dressed man dismounted when Jonas reached the gate. The two men evidently exchanged names, then shook hands and began talking. Jonas nodded and looked up at the sky as though agreeing with whatever his company was saying.

The soldier sat quietly aside while the two men talked, but even over this distance Jack could see the man's eyes searching him and then Raymond across the way. Jack looked away—no need to create tension. Cattle now dotted the landscape all around the ranch. Most were grazing, but a few were just lying around in the high grass. All seemed to be enjoying the sunshine. All seemed to sense it was one of the season's final offerings.

Jonas was waving when Jack looked back at the gate. Jack lifted a hand in return, but Jonas just waved harder, more persistent. It took a moment to register that Jonas wasn't waving, but motioning, motioning for him. Jack nudged his horse into a slow walk. He still wasn't sure he'd interpreted the gesture correctly until he arrived at the gate.

"It seems this gentleman is looking for you," Jonas said.

Jack dismounted and left his mare by the fence. He searched Jonas's face, but there was nothing there, nothing unusual, anyway.

The well-dressed man was young, maybe early to mid twenties, and wore wire-rimmed spectacles. His dark brown suit was still wet but lightening a shade around the shoulders. His hat was small and rounded at the top, and occasionally dripped moisture from the brim. It was the kind of hat Jack had seen bankers wear back east. It looked new.

"Jack Percy?" the young man asked.

Jack nodded.

The young man held out a hand. "Edward Heminger," he said. "Please call me Ned."

Jack shook his hand and glanced at the soldier, who was still mounted. He was cavalry. A captain, Jack deduced from his uniform.

The captain wore no expression, nor was he paying any attention to the gathering beside him. He was watching Raymond, who was slowly riding along the fence toward the group at the gate.

"I work for Richard Cavanaugh," Ned said.

Jack looked back at the young man, a bit taken aback. "Cavanaugh?"

"Yes, sir. I'm here on Mr. Cavanaugh's behalf. He sent me here to request a meeting with you."

"A meeting?"

Ned nodded. "Yes, sir. A meeting at your earliest convenience."

"What would Cavanaugh want with me?"

"I know this sounds odd," Ned said. "But I simply cannot disclose anything further. Mr. Cavanaugh would like to present his proposal to you personally."

Jack glanced up the line of fencing at Raymond, who was still approaching, and now returning the captain's stare.

The captain let the reins of Ned's horse slip through his fingers and drop to the ground.

"I ain't got time to ride into Twin Pines," Jack said. "Sorry you've come all this way."

Jonas grabbed Jack's sleeve and tugged him back a step.

"Jack, this is Richard Cavanaugh he's talking about."

"I know who he is."

"Do you?" Jonas asked. "I've heard he'll be appointed the next governor of this territory."

"And?"

"And you might want to consider that before turning him down."

"Why?"

"That's why."

Jack turned and faced Jonas. "He's as crooked as Stone Creek, Jonas. You know that."

"I don't know it for sure," Jonas said. "Neither do you. You've never even met the man. You know how that goes, folks talking. Hell, it must be pretty urgent; these two rode half the night to get here. It might even be something good for a change."

Jack pushed his hat back and rubbed his forehead. He was surprised at his employer's insistence. Jonas knew Cavanaugh's reputation as well as anyone. Aside from his commitment to put down the Indian threat, none of the locals ever spoke a kind word about the man. Except in his presence, of course.

But there was an element of truth in what Jonas had said. Jack had never met the man, and it was hardly rare to hear merely the worst tales about someone, only to find the opposite to be true later. He doubted this was the case.

Jonas stepped away.

Ned was standing by his horse, hands clasped behind him. Jack thought the kid must have undying patience. "Look, it's a long ride to—"

"I know, Mr. Percy," Ned interrupted. "Believe me, I know. Mr. Cavanaugh has instructed me to tell you there is one thousand dollars involved."

One thousand dollars. Jack's mind whirled at the figure. A man could work for years, save every penny, and still never see that kind of cash. Indeed, most men had never set eyes on that kind of money, much less held it in their hands. Some would kill or die for it, maybe more than some. Jack wasn't one of them. He had seen a stack of cash like that once. Confederate currency. Much more than a thousand dollars. He'd watched as it curled and blackened at the edge of a fire, worthless and abandoned.

"I don't chase bounties," Jack said.

Ned smiled. "Oh, no, Mr. Percy, he is not seeking a bounty hunter."

"What, then?"

"I'm really very sorry. Sincerely. But I just cannot go into any more detail here. Mr. Cavanaugh has given me strict instructions. He wishes to consult with you in person."

Jack looked to his left where Raymond had joined the group. He glanced up at his friend, who was still mounted, and then back to Ned. "Cavanaugh sent you through dark and rain to tell me he wants to talk? That's it?"

Ned took a breath, seemed to ponder something a moment, then said, "The issue is delicate, you might say, sensitive. He doesn't wish for details to get out."

Jack just shook his head.

"It's important, Mr. Percy."

"Why me?"

"Mr. Cavanaugh heard of your party from the survivors of Woods Fort. But again, I've said too much."

It struck Jack that Ned wasn't from around here, not that anyone really was. But the way he spoke, so proper and confident, was almost totally foreign in these parts.

Jack slipped his hat back on and stared off toward the woods Eli had disappeared into earlier.

"I think you'll find the offer quite attractive," Ned said. "The prudent man would at least consider it, if I may say so."

"The boys and I can handle things around here." Jonas's voice came from somewhere behind Jack, apparently reading his indecision. "Don't let that concern you."

Jack nodded, still gathering his thoughts. "I'll need some time."

"Of course you will, Mr. Percy," Ned said. "May I tell Mr. Cavanaugh to expect you this evening?"

Jack squinted at the sky. No clouds in sight.

"I reckon."

Ned smiled, looked relieved. "Very well, then. Gentlemen, very nice to make your acquaintance and thank you for your time. Good day." With that the young man tipped his hat, remounted, and swung his horse around.

The captain didn't move. He shifted in his saddle and faced Raymond. "Just one more thing," he said. "Who might you be?"

Raymond said nothing. He was looking down, fingering a nick in his saddle horn as if no one else was there.

"Oh, forgive me," Ned said. "Where are my manners? This is Captain Hardy of the Eighteenth Cavalry."

"Captain," Jonas said, and he and Jack tipped their hats.

Hardy likewise touched his hat, but he didn't look at them. Only Raymond.

"Got a name, mister?"

Raymond said nothing.

Hardy shifted again in his saddle and chuckled. He made a show of looking over Jonas's place, then began rolling a cigarette. "I've heard tale that Raymond McAlister frequents this ranch. Might there be any truth to that, mister?"

"I know you?"

Captain Hardy stayed focused on the cigarette, but he couldn't disguise the change in his posture. A grin touched the corner of his mouth. His face had well-defined lines and plenty of experience, and although he looked older, Jack figured him to be in his late forties or early fifties. He thought this not because of anything in the captain's appearance; rather, it was that generation of soldiers that would recognize the name Raymond McAlister.

Hardy lit his cigarette. "Heard you were dead."

"I heard that too," Raymond said.

An uncomfortable silence began to stretch. Ned broke in, "I suppose we should be heading back."

Hardy said nothing.

"Wouldn't you agree, Captain?"

Hardy ignored his young companion and, though the fence separated them, nudged his horse a step closer to Raymond's. "You'll be coming along, too, right?"

"Hell with Cavanaugh," Raymond said.

It was mumbled, barely more than a whisper, but the captain heard it. He grinned and laughed derisively, then looked at Jack. "I suspect you're a Reb too?"

Jack touched the brim of his hat. "We've moved on, Captain."

Hardy looked back at Raymond, who was still staring at the saddle horn. "There ain't no moving on."

Raymond said nothing.

"We really must be getting back, Captain," Ned said. "Mr. Cavanaugh—"

Hardy spun his horse around and had it loping back in the direction they'd come from before Ned could finish.

Ned just sat there for a moment, watching him go. Then he turned back to the others to tip his hat again. Only, this time, in his eagerness not to get left behind, he misjudged the quick gesture and the small hat fell off in the mud at Jack's feet.

Jack picked it up—not the first time he'd done such a thing today— and took a shot at brushing the mud off. It only smeared across the brim. He shrugged and handed it back.

"Thanks," Ned said in a distracted voice. "I look forward to making your acquaintance again."

Jack nodded and watched as the young man put the spurs to his horse and quickly fell in behind Captain Hardy.

Jack lingered at the gate as the visitors became small against the horizon. Ned's words echoed in his mind: *He heard of your party from the survivors of Woods Fort.* There was no telling what

Cavanaugh had been told about Woods Fort. More than half of the stories that made it back to Jonas's place were fiction, and no two exactly the same. Besides, it was rumored that Cavanaugh had been granted a unit of cavalry for the protection of Twin Pines, as well as himself. That rumor had been confirmed today. At least, the cavalry part had. So why would the old man be interested in Woods Fort?

Raymond was already moving back down the fence, into his usual routine.

Jack climbed on his mare and caught up. "What was that all about?"

Raymond shrugged.

"You know him?"

"I don't reckon."

Raymond didn't look at Jack when he spoke, seldom did. Instead, his cloudy blue eyes searched the area immediately in front of them, just outside the boundaries of the property.

Jack was used to this, but many weren't. In fact, many took Raymond's disposition as challenging and, in some instances, threatening. But Raymond had never seemed either of these to Jack. He seemed more detached than anything else. A quiet soul.

They rode a short piece in silence.

"What do you think of this whole Cavanaugh business?" Jack asked.

"Wouldn't take a nickel from him if I was starving."

"Yeah, I figured you'd say that."

Jack pulled up and looked back toward the house while Raymond continued down the fence. Jonas was standing out front, watching them across the distance. Jack reluctantly turned his horse and headed back.

Jonas met him several yards from the house. "Forgive me, Jack. It was wrong to interfere in your business like that."

"You didn't."

"I shouldn't have said—"

"I appreciate your advice."

Jonas just nodded. "What do you reckon he wants?"

"I really don't know," Jack said. "Can't make sense of it. Thought he might be looking for someone to do some ranging, scouting for Sioux. I believe Joe Phillips was doing just that a few months back."

"Joe Phillips is dead."

"Yeah, I heard."

"A thousand dollars for ranging?"

"I know. Can't figure it."

"What does Ray think?"

"You know what Ray thinks."

They were both silent a moment. Jonas was running his hand down the nose of Jack's horse. Jack was thinking about what he had to do before he left.

"I'd like to ask a favor, if I might," Jonas said.

"Of course."

"I'd like you to take CJ."

Jack sighed.

"I know what you're thinking," Jonas said. "But I figure it'd be good for him. He's got to get out of here sometime, and he'll do whatever you ask. You know that. You know how he looks up to you."

Jack shook his head. "That's not it, Jonas. We don't even know what this is about. It could be anything. Hell, to hear folks talk, the ride into Twin Pines ain't even safe anymore."

Jonas said nothing.

"Besides, there ain't no telling how long this might take, or which way I might be heading after I leave town. There may be no time to bring him back."

"You ain't following me, Jack. I'm asking you to take him *with* you."

"You can't mean that," Jack said. "A man ain't even secure on his own ground anymore." He waved a hand at the horizon. "And heaven only knows what's out *there*. You've heard the same stuff as me. Even if only half of it's true—"

"That's why you're the only man I would let him go with," Jonas said. "I trust your judgment."

Jack shook his head.

"Forgive me, Jack. I don't mean to press it. I really don't." Jonas paused. "Look, the boy just ain't been the same since Helen died. It's like he quit growing, quit maturing, I guess. It's like his mama took a part of him with her. His brothers, they screamed and cried and got it all out, but it wasn't the same for him. He and Helen were tied together, really close, you know. They were joined in a way I can't get my head around."

Jack understood. A boy and his mother. He looked toward the house. CJ was standing at the bottom of the steps.

Jonas followed his gaze. "I think he needs to get shed of this place for a spell. He needs something else to think about, something other than cows and cowshit to look at."

Jack stared at the young man. He was an average sized seventeen-year-old boy. He had sandy brown hair, a lanky frame, and a quick wit. He was always looking for adventure, perhaps even a little too high-strung. To Jack he was everything a seventeen-year-old boy was supposed to be.

He was a good kid.

Good lord. Jack motioned for him.

CJ came running.

Jonas patted Jack on the knee. "Thanks. I'm indebted to you."

"Don't thank me yet."

3

Jack was alone at the gate again, waiting. He was thinking of Captain Hardy's strange interest in Raymond, the way he'd grinned after getting Raymond's name, the way he'd lingered when his companion turned to leave. Odd, but not altogether surprising.

Raymond was a war hero. Or better put, he would've been a war hero had he not been on the losing side. Jack had heard of Raymond's legend from the battle of Sharpsburg long before he ever met him, but he hadn't mentioned it until they'd ridden together for a while. Even then Raymond offered little in response. He'd said the earth had opened up that awful day and hell had spilled out. And that was it. Nothing more. Jack never brought it up again.

They had ridden together for some time, their camaraderie coming through a series of chances neither of them would ever comprehend, or cared to. Having gone here and there after the war, taking odd jobs where available, they had simply joined together on the well-worn trail leading out of the broken South, and had been together ever since.

Jack glanced up and down the fencing. There was no sign of his friend now. In fact, Raymond hadn't been seen since the short meeting had broken up an hour ago. He obviously had no interest in Cavanaugh, and leaving Jonas out here alone might be more than he could stomach. Jack wondered if he would sit this one out. It made perfect sense, was probably even a good idea. But the thought of Raymond not being around left a hollow feeling in his gut. A lonely feeling.

Down at the barn CJ was trying to get away from his little brothers, who were hanging on to him with everything they had. Jack leaned against the gate. He thought the whole thing touching until he heard Michael screaming, "You're not taking Major! He's mine!"

Major was Michael's horse.

Jack sighed and glanced at the sun. Time was fleeting.

With the help of Jonas, and by using the grazing cattle as an obstacle course, CJ eventually mounted his brother's horse and evaded his siblings. He hurried up to the gate and stopped beside Jack.

Jack surveyed the boy's mount. The saddlebags bulged and strained against the tie-downs as if ready to burst, giving the animal the absurd appearance of an oversized pack mule.

"What've you got in there?"

CJ was sitting in the saddle, stiff and proud, like a victorious general. "Just my stuff."

"A horse will tire awful quick with a load like that."

CJ patted the horse on the front quarter. "Not Major," he said. "Nah, Major can go like the wind. You know, the wind's been known to move entire houses from one place to another."

"Yeah, but never very far," Jack said. He mounted his mare. "And usually in pieces."

CJ said nothing, clearly unconcerned.

Jonas finally made it up the gentle slope to bid them farewell. He grabbed CJ by the leg and pointed at Jack.

"Whatever he says."

CJ nodded.

Jonas took Jack's hand in a firm grip. "Godspeed."

"Thanks."

The ride into Twin Pines took about six hours, which got them there just before dark. They kept a brisk pace without conversation. Although, every hour or so, as if he couldn't help it, CJ would recite a couple of dry jokes he'd picked up from travelers passing through his father's ranch.

The boy fell silent, however, as the town came into view. Jack noticed the young man's eyes, now wide and alert, taking in the looming picture before them.

Twin Pines was not very big, only mildly populated, but for this part of the world it might as well have been a metropolis. It was of typical frontier design, one wide street leading straight through the middle of town. Buildings—mostly small businesses, various trades, at least a couple of saloons—lined either side of it. There were a few new houses on the outskirts, along with a livery stable. The smell of fresh paint hung weak in the air. Whether this new cow town had a future was anyone's guess, but the locals were determined it would be the Deadwood of the north.

Jack's uneasiness only grew as they entered the outskirts. The ride in had given him plenty of time to roll the whole thing around in his head. But the more he thought about it, the questions simply compounded. He would hear the man out. That's why he was here. All the thinking was only causing anxiety he didn't want or need. He heard Jonas's words again: *It could be something good for a change.*

They had traversed less than half of the small town's main boulevard when Jack pulled his mare up and stopped outside a small supply store. A sign overhead read simply *Supply*. The name *Miller's* had preceded *Supply* at one time, Jack remembered. And if one looked hard enough, its ghostly outline could still be seen bleeding through fresh white paint.

Jack dismounted, tied his mare outside the shop, and instructed CJ to do the same. He stared at the sign for a moment, curious over the change.

CJ wasn't paying the sign any attention. His eyes were still big and round, soaking up the surroundings. The side-by-side businesses, the fancy covered wagons parked along the street, the people walking up and down the sidewalks.

"Ain't never seen so many folks dressed so nice at the same time," he said. "Everybody here must be rich! Or headed to a funeral!"

Jack chuckled. There weren't many people out, little more than a handful, really. And the great majority of them were headed out, headed home. Nightfall dropped like a curtain in these parts, particularly in the winter, and was long. It was a strange phenomenon that had taken Jack some time to adjust to. Very different from the

South, where days and nights varied little from season to season. "Come on, there's someone I'd like you to meet," he said.

They paused on the first step of the sidewalk and waited as a middle-aged couple walked by. CJ took off his dusty hat and held it against his chest as they passed.

"Howdy."

The lady slowed and dipped her head, but the man just kept walking, gently towing the woman along.

CJ stood on his toes and watched the couple proceed up the walkway until they entered a coach farther up the street. He started leaning in that direction.

Jack took the boy by his shoulders and steered him into the supply store. The door creaked and a little bell jingled as they went inside.

Shelves upon shelves greeted them inside the door, lining the walls with what seemed to be anything anyone could ever want or need—everything from heavy ranching equipment to cooking utensils. There were new hats, chaps, boots, and even a few shirts hanging behind the counter at the back of the store. At the counter, two men were inspecting a bone-handled hunting knife.

"That's Randy Miller," Jack said.

"The bald fella?"

"Yeah."

"We're here to see him?"

"Yeah, he owns the place," Jack said. "He and his wife founded it five years ago."

"He knows Mr. Cavanaugh?"

"No, I need to inquire something of him."

"Where's she?"

"Who?"

"His wife."

"She passed on about a year ago."

"What happened to her?"

Jack thought about it. "Don't really know. She just suddenly got sick and then she was gone."

CJ looked away, nodding.

At the back of the store, the shopkeeper turned his back and began coughing violently. He went on for a long time, coughing and coughing, sometimes gasping for breath. He finally fell silent and leaned against the counter, breathing heavily and dabbing at his chin with a dirty handkerchief. When he turned back to his patron, he was visibly fatigued.

The patron took a step back.

"Your pa could use some of this stuff," Jack said.

CJ was watching Randy. "He runs this place by himself?"

"Here all the time," Jack said. "Lives somewhere in the back, I think."

"Ain't he got no kids to help him out?"

"They had a son."

"Had?"

Jack picked up a shovel and turned it around in his hand. "He died back in the spring."

"Dern it! What happened to him?"

Jack leaned close to the boy and whispered, "The reason I'm telling you all of this is so it don't get brought up later."

CJ said nothing.

"You know what I'm getting at, right?"

"'Cause talking about it makes him think about it."

Jack nodded, feeling a bit foolish trying to explain something to a young man who had firsthand experience in the matter.

CJ waited.

Jack glanced back at the counter. Randy had the knife out of its sheath, pointing out something about the blade. He hadn't yet noticed them.

Jack put the shovel back in its place. "Randy cut a deal with his suppliers some time back. They asked him to meet their supply team a day's ride back to the east. In exchange, they offered to discount the inventory. Make it worth his while, and keep them out of Indian territory."

"Was it a good deal?"

"I don't know the specifics. I reckon it was. He took it, anyhow."

"His son went with him to get the stuff?"

"His son went *alone* to get the stuff. Had to after his mom died."

CJ frowned. "He didn't come back, right?"

Jack glanced back toward the counter. "He never came back."

"You mean they never saw him again?"

Jack sighed. "Sheriff Murphy found his wagon the next day, or what was left of it. All the cargo was gone."

"What about him?"

"His body was in the woods."

"He was dead?"

"He was dead."

"What happened to him?"

Jack checked the counter again. "It was bad."

"You was there?"

Jack said nothing. He stared at a pair of saddlebags sagging from a nail in the wall.

"Indians?" CJ asked.

"That's the majority opinion."

"You don't believe it?"

"Don't reckon it matters what I believe."

"What do you think?"

"I don't."

CJ sucked in a breath, evidently accepting that Jack would go no further. "What was his name?"

"Brody."

CJ mouthed the name soundlessly, apparently committing it to memory.

Jack glanced toward the back of the store. It looked like Randy was finishing up with his customer. "Come on."

While the young cowpoke was walking out with his new knife, Randy turned his back to the counter to record his sale. Jack started toward the back of the store but had gone only a few steps before the old man was bent over coughing again.

Jack stopped at the end of an aisle and turned away, waiting for the shopkeeper's ordeal to end.

Randy finally rose and braced himself on the wall. The paperwork from the sale was still in his hand but had been thoroughly pulverized during the coughing fit. He leaned on the counter, his breathing slow and difficult.

"No way that knife was worth the price," Jack said.

"Don't matter anyhow. I'm gonna be dead before it's paid for."

"That's no kinda talk. I reckon you're in the prime of life."

Randy grunted a laugh. He extended his hand and Jack took it in both of his. "It does my soul good to see a friendly face around here."

"How are you?"

Randy cleared his throat. "Well, I'll tell you, Jack, I'm still here. And that's about the best I can say anymore."

Jack smiled warmly at the old shopkeeper. He looked worse than last time. A lot worse. "Just make sure you stay here. I'm a bit picky about who I deal with, you know."

"Don't suppose I have much say in it," Randy said. "But I'll tell you what: if the Lord comes back tomorrow, I aim to be near the front of the line." He coughed again, heavy and wet, but not as bad this time. He wiped his mouth with the handkerchief from his front pocket and then quickly replaced it, but not before Jack noticed the red smears.

It was happening so quickly. Only a few months had passed since Jack's last trip through here. He'd heard of consumption but had never witnessed its power firsthand. Was this what Jonas's wife had gone through? CJ's mom?

"Might I trouble you for a favor?"

The older man's brow furrowed. "Come now, son. No need to ask. Tell me what you need."

"Much obliged," Jack said. "This is CJ."

CJ stepped closer to the counter and pulled his hat off.

Randy extended his hand.

CJ hesitated but then shook the older man's hand firmly.

Randy was obviously used to the hesitation. He leaned back against the counter and squinted at the boy, scrutinizing his facial features. "Jonas's boy, I'd guess. Is that right?"

"Yes, sir."

"Well, he certainly won't be denying you," Randy said, then paused as if a thought had struck. He shrugged it off. "It's a pleasure to meet you. Your father is one of the better men I've known."

"Thank you, sir."

"Mind if CJ hangs around here a bit this evening?" Jack nodded toward the north end of town. "Got some business up the hill."

"Mind? Well, it'd be my pleasure."

Jack gave CJ a pat on the back. "If you need help with anything, CJ here is a fine hand to have around."

Randy looked mortified. "That ain't no way to treat a guest, Jack. Won't be none of that kind of talk." He turned to CJ. "I'd bet this young gentleman's quite knowledgeable in the finer points of cattle ranching. And that just happens to be my greatest interest at present."

"He's certainly full of stories," Jack said.

Randy disappeared into a back room and came back with a worn wooden stool. "This seat is reserved for only the most honored guests." He patted the stool. "Make yourself comfortable, young man."

CJ slid onto it. He looked relaxed enough, considering Jack hadn't warned the boy of his plan to leave him here.

"I'm very much obliged," Jack said. "I should be back shortly."

Randy shooed Jack away with his hands. "Go on and see to your business."

Jack nodded and moved back to the front of the store. He stepped through the door and closed it gently behind him. He felt a pinch of guilt over leaving CJ with a stranger, but there were no other real options.

He went a couple of steps up the sidewalk then stopped and peered in the storefront window. The boy was already into one of his long monologues, hands and arms moving as much as his lips.

Randy was smiling broadly, willingly along for the ride.

Jack eased away and leaned against the wall. He looked toward his destination, somewhere ahead in the purple dusk.

The house on the hill.

The air had turned bitter.

He flipped up his collar and started walking.

4

Nightfall was descending and only a handful of stragglers were still outside—mostly stumbling in and out of the competing taverns. Loud, drunken lies carried outside the walls of the nearest pub, followed by the echoes of fake laughter only sporting women could manage. But it was clearly winding down. No one wanted to be out at night, not even the heavy drinkers.

One man lay in the street. The drunk turned his head as the sidewalk creaked under Jack's footfalls.

Jack avoided eye contact. *Three too many*, he figured. Instead, he looked ahead at the large white house sitting just outside the commerce section of town. It was a fairly new place, or at least recently renovated. It sat on the side of a well-manicured hill, elevated just enough that nearly the whole town could see it—or perhaps, be seen by it.

The evening wind was fierce and bit into exposed flesh like splinters of ice. Jack slipped his hands into his pockets and lowered his head, using his hat to deflect as much of the frigid breeze as possible.

He caught a glimpse of another man then, this one across the street, a lone figure sitting in the shadows of the vacated barbershop. The man's face was down, hidden by the brim of his hat. He wore a dark, ankle-length duster, the wooden handle of a long hunting blade just visible at the front of his belt. A Winchester repeater lay across his lap. He was tapping the rifle's stock with one finger.

Jack watched him as he passed but Raymond never looked up. Jack stepped off the boardwalk and began ascending the hill.

There were two soldiers standing outside the house as Jack approached, one on either side of the door. Jack stopped twenty feet short, suddenly unsure of the next step. One of the bluecoats stepped forward, looked down the length of the house and then at Jack.

"You expected?"

Jack took a breath, but before he could reply the front door creaked open. The profile of a man appeared in the doorway, speaking softly back into the house.

Both of the soldiers stiffened and corrected their posture. The one who had stepped forward eased back into his original position by the door.

The man in the doorway wasn't paying them any attention. He stood in the threshold watching or listening to something inside, something out of view. He finally nodded and stepped out.

The man paused as the door closed behind him and took his time adjusting the buttons on his coat. He glanced up, saw Jack, and spat. His contempt was obvious, clear in the dark, narrow slits of his eyes, and he was making no effort to hide it.

Captain Hardy.

The captain moved to a horse tied to a nearby tree, mounted up and swung around in Jack's direction. He kicked the steed into a trot but slowed as he approached, eyes connecting with Jack's. He looked very much like he wanted to say something, but didn't.

Jack pushed the brim of his hat back so he wouldn't have to look up, and then waited until Hardy's mount came even with him.

"Something on your mind, Captain?"

Hardy said nothing. His horse moved several paces beyond Jack, then stopped.

Jack turned his head, keeping the man in his peripheral vision.

The captain was facing away, his horse pointed toward the town below. His body swelled under his coat like he was taking a deep breath, like he was about to respond. He didn't, though, nor did he turn. But he didn't move on, either.

Although his face was hidden from view, Hardy was clearly thinking something over, obviously grappling with some private decision.

"Care to share it?" Jack asked.

Hardy's hands moved out of view, fumbled with something only he could see, then there was the hiss of a match and the orange glow of a cigarette. The captain tossed the match on the ground and exhaled blue smoke to the side. He huffed, shook his head, and then nudged his horse into the darkness toward town.

Jack looked on, said nothing.

"Are you expected?"

The question came from behind him, from one of the soldiers by the door. But Jack didn't turn; he watched as Hardy's silhouette slowly blended with the night.

"Yeah, I think so."

"Name, please?"

"Jack Percy."

"Your name, sir?"

Jack faced the soldiers. "Jack Percy."

The older of the two soldiers nodded and stepped inside.

Jack glanced back in the direction Hardy had gone, but the captain was no longer visible. It was almost completely dark now. Dim candlelight flickered in some of the windows throughout town. No doubt some of the proprietors lived in their stores as Randy did.

Jack squinted, trying to see farther out. Weaker lights came in and out of focus, shimmering and wavering, reflecting flames from the homes on the outskirts. Whether the distant lights were from fireplaces or candles he didn't know. But they were coming from the area where he'd observed the newer houses while riding in. His earlier hunch was right. All could be seen from this hill.

Jack turned to the remaining soldier, a young man. "I suspect it's tough taking orders from a fella like that."

The soldier said nothing.

Jack understood the silence. "Where you from?"

"Eighteenth Cavalry, Second Division, sir." The young man didn't move. His face stayed locked forward.

"No, I mean, *where* are you from?"

"Pennsylvania, sir."

"Reckon you're used to cold, then."

"Yes, sir." The soldier's eyes remained frozen forward, expression unchanged.

Jack nodded. He might as well have been talking to the door. The young man was obviously new to this. A new recruit. The way he had referred to Jack, an unremarkable civilian, as "sir" was something his superiors would sooner or later wash out of him—sooner if they knew he was extending the salutation to an ex-Confederate soldier.

The front door opened and the first soldier emerged. "Mr. Cavanaugh will see you now."

The older soldier moved aside as Jack squeezed by and then closed the door behind them.

The warmth in the house was like a slice of heaven, quickly restoring circulation to Jack's extremities. He had forgotten how cold it was.

"This way," the soldier said.

Jack fell in behind him. He peered into the room at the front of the house as they walked by. Red carpet blanketed the floor and was very well kept, very clean. Several archaic-looking lanterns with polished silver bases were scattered about, a couple of them burning, most not. A huge bricked fireplace roared in the back wall.

A young girl dressed in a maid's outfit was dusting in the corner of the room. Very young. She turned, met Jack's eyes, but quickly went back to work. He tipped his hat, but she either hadn't seen or didn't care.

The bluecoat led him toward an open door at the end of a small corridor. The short hallway was surprisingly well lit, despite receiving its only light from a small candle above the hall's entrance. The light didn't carry to anything beyond the open doorway, however, and although there were voices coming from the room ahead, nothing intelligible could be heard.

The soldier stopped short of the room and stood at attention against the wall.

The voices fell away.

Jack looked at the soldier.

The bluecoat nodded without losing his stare on the opposite wall.

Jack got the impression that his were not the only eyes on the soldier anymore. He stepped inside.

Richard Cavanaugh was leaning back in his chair, hands resting on his stomach, fingers entwined. Casual. Several papers were scattered across the desk in front of him, some face down. The room, small compared to the rest of the house, was made up mostly of bookshelves—two and a half walls. Most of it was just empty space, however, devoid of any reading material. Competing for the rest of the wall space were various game trophies, some familiar and others not from this part of the world.

To the right of Cavanaugh's desk was another soldier, this one of much higher rank. A colonel, Jack knew, by his decorations, also a war veteran.

Cavanaugh stood and extended a hand across the desk. "Mr. Percy, I presume?"

Jack took it and squeezed softly, matching only the effort offered by the older man. He nodded.

Cavanaugh slumped back in his chair. "Kind of you to come with such little notice." The old man spoke slowly—*pro-nounc-ing ev-ery word*—with a hint of accent Jack didn't recognize, and was dressed like a typical businessman. A politician. His tie seemed to be cramping his neck. He ran a finger underneath it.

Jack noticed the colonel looking him over. "Mr. Heminger made out it was urgent."

"Ah, but it is *very* urgent, Mr. Percy," Cavanaugh said.

"I'm listening," Jack said, but then he turned and faced the colonel, who was openly staring.

Cavanaugh wearily rose to his feet again. "Forgive me, gentlemen." He gestured to his right. "This is Colonel Benjamin Asheworth of the Eighteenth Cavalry. And, Colonel, this is Jack Percy."

Jack touched his hat. "Colonel."

Asheworth didn't return the gesture.

"Corporal!"

"Yes, sir, Colonel."

"Why was this man not disarmed before entering this office?"

Jack glanced down at his revolver and then at Cavanaugh.

Cavanaugh folded his hands and rested them on the desk. He gave Asheworth the kind of look a patient adult would give an interrupting child.

"Ye-yes, sir. My apologies, sir." The corporal moved in front of Jack. "Please raise your arms away from your body."

Jack complied reluctantly, eyeing the colonel.

Asheworth was watching his subordinate.

"Mr. Percy, they tell me I will be appointed the next governor of this territory. And as a potential federal official, the government of this fine union is taking measures to ensure my safety." Cavanaugh paused as the corporal removed Jack's sidearm. His eyes seemed to twinkle at the scene. "As you can see."

"You figure me a threat?"

"Not at all, Mr. Percy. Just formalities, is all. Just formalities."

The soldier returned to his post by the door.

"Your weapon will be returned upon your exit," Asheworth recited to the wall in front of him.

"I understand you were an officer at one time," Cavanaugh said.

Jack watched Asheworth a second more, but the colonel no longer seemed interested in him. "At one time."

"Unfortunately, our dear colonel here doesn't recognize the legitimacy of that particular uniform. The years, I'm afraid, have narrowed his thinking."

"I don't reckon that's why you wanted to see me."

"Indeed not, Mr. Percy. Indeed not." Cavanaugh leaned back and placed his hands behind his head, apparently choosing his words. "I heard of your party's heroics at Woods Fort. That is why I called you here this evening."

"I don't understand."

"I have a missing person on my hands. I want you to go get him."

"Missing person?"

"I received a telegraph from Washington two days ago," Cavanaugh went on. "The federal government has offered a five hundred dollar reward for this man's safe return. President Hayes says he would consider it a personal favor if I deliver him in one piece. That's why

I'm contributing an additional five hundred dollars to whoever brings him back."

Jack ran a hand under the band of his hat. "With all due respect, Mr. Cavanaugh, you've got the wrong man. We're not Indian fighters. Woods Fort was altogether different." He shrugged. "We're just ranch hands."

"That may be, Mr. Percy, but your party is nonetheless the most qualified we have. The most experienced we have. We simply do not have time to wait for others. Time is our foe, I'm afraid. We must act with the greatest speed or failure is all but certain."

Jack glanced at Asheworth—steel gray hair parted neatly to one side, decorations hanging from his breast, boots polished and reflecting the light. The hilt of his sword quivered almost imperceptivity, like the colonel had the shakes.

Asheworth didn't notice Jack's appraisal. He stared straight ahead, eyes fixed on the same spot on the wall in front of him.

"I know what you're thinking," Cavanaugh said. "And I understand. But we feel it would be a mistake or, better put, downright foolish to send a dispatch of uniformed cavalry into this particular area. Most of this region is still uncharted territory, unmapped and undiscovered for practical purposes. It would pose too great a risk to our soldiers. Think about it, Mr. Percy. The savages would love nothing more than to see our troops all lined up, riding in a tight little formation through a narrow valley. It would be like a gift. You have heard of Custer, haven't you?"

Jack nodded.

"Besides," Cavanaugh continued, "this unit's objective is to ensure and protect the well-being of Twin Pines." He grinned sympathetically and leaned forward. "There's no guarantee the primitives would give trouble to civilians passing through the area. But they are certain to attack a military dispatch."

Jack chuckled, couldn't help it. In all honesty, he knew very little of the Sioux, or Indians in general for that matter. But he did know they were not long on patience, particularly when the pickings were easy. And they were showing favor to no one. But the notion of the cavalry drawing a lot of attention and thus an attack was realistic. On the other hand, the military faced such propositions all the time. Danger was intrinsic to any mission involving army regulars, cavalry or otherwise.

Jack cleared his throat. "Sheriff Murphy—"

"Is an old man now," Cavanaugh interrupted. "He's worn out. I have no confidence that if we sent him out of town he'd be able to find his way back, never mind locate a missing person. And if he did happen to make it back, he'd likely be dragging his good-for-nothing entrails and missing his scalp." Cavanaugh pursed his lips and looked down at his desk, apparently regretting that last part.

"Who's missing?" Jack asked.

Cavanaugh started to speak but then hesitated. He fingered the paperwork on his desk. "I don't wish for this information to get out to the townspeople, Mr. Percy."

"Alright."

"The folks in town have missed him," Cavanaugh said. "But they don't know he's overdue yet. If we bring him back, this would be an excellent opportunity to show the settlers that the government is in control."

Jack swallowed another laugh.

"According to the telegraph, his name is Thomas J. Morris," Cavanaugh said. "He's a preacher of sorts. A missionary would be the correct term, I suppose. He came through Twin Pines about a month and a half ago, hung around a couple of days, and then proceeded north. He informed us he'd be returning here before moving on to the west. To 're-supply and reconnect' were the terms he used."

"Reconnect?"

"You know the song and dance, Mr. Percy," Cavanaugh said. "He charmed the usual following while he was here: preaching, saving, baptizing, and all that other stuff. He supposedly even works with the savages, speaks their language, if one can imagine that." He laughed sarcastically. "A lot of good that has done him."

Jack rubbed his head. A small headache was gaining momentum. "How overdue is he?"

"When he left, he said he would return in two weeks. You can do the math."

He's dead. The thought flashed through Jack's mind as quickly as any he'd ever had.

"Where'd he go?"

"Jones Mine."

"Jones Mine?"

Asheworth cleared his throat. "It's a small settlement three or maybe four days' ride north of here. Only the fool could miss it. Point your pony at the brightest star, as they say, and your arrival is inevitable."

Cavanaugh glared at the colonel. It wasn't clear whether he was surprised or annoyed by the interruption. What did seem clear was his apparent impatience with the man. The earlier look of a tolerant adult was slowly transforming into something akin to annoyance or weariness.

Jones Mine? Jack rolled the name over in his head. Well traveled through the years, there weren't many places he didn't at least recognize by name. But this one eluded him. North of here? There was life *north* of here? The way he understood it, there was nothing at all noteworthy between here and the border. *Trees all the way to Canada*, it was said. And Sioux, of course.

"Never heard of it."

Cavanaugh's cold stare toward the colonel broke slowly. "Most folks haven't," he said. "And that's exactly how the Jones Mine populace wants it. They used to send a couple of wagons every other month or so to pick up supplies, but only what they absolutely needed, only what was necessary. They felt if they indulged too much, then their great plan for self-sufficiency would fail, or at best be delayed. They told us if there was something they wanted, they would grow it themselves or build it with their own hands." He grinned. "They were a spirited bunch to be sure, but not very smart. We warned them, getting out that far from civilization is just asking for trouble. Wouldn't you agree, Mr. Percy?"

Jack nodded. The question struck him as odd, considering what the old man had warned the Jones Mine folks of was exactly what he was now proposing to him.

Cavanaugh glanced at Asheworth through the corner of his eye. It was a subtle gesture. Just a quick, barely perceptible movement of the eyes. "That was several years ago," he said. "Much of it before my time. They stopped sending their wagons; there were no more riders. All communication was lost. This led us to believe they were managing on their own now. Self-sufficient, after all."

He's dead. The thought reemerged in Jack's psyche.

Colonel Asheworth was slowly shifting his weight from one leg to the other. He closed his eyes and let out a long, quiet breath through his nose. A slender, well-crafted cane leaned against the wall beside him. He was uncomfortable, perhaps in pain. More than likely he'd been standing in the same spot since before Jack arrived.

Somehow this brightened Jack's mood. His day had been long as well.

Everyone was tired. It was getting late. It was getting cold. They were getting nowhere.

"I guess I'm a bit confused," Jack said.

Cavanaugh waited. The lines sprawling away from his eyes seemed deeper with each passing minute. He waved a hand. "Go on."

"Well, a thousand dollars, the president … a preacher?"

"Ah, yes," Cavanaugh relaxed back into his chair. He lifted his feet up on the desk and lit his pipe. He puffed on it three or four times until he was satisfied with the fire. "I guess it would seem odd. But you see, Mr. Percy, Morris is no run-of-the-mill church house preacher. He's what you might call a scholar of sorts, a learned man. He spent a great deal of time in Europe, studied there, earned himself quite a reputation, it seems. Obviously he has attracted a few friends in elevated positions. As I understand it, he turned down some—how should I put it?—*lucrative* job offers, some from inside Washington, others from the country's more prominent universities. Apparently he traded a considerable career and income for wilderness and savages."

"Why?" Jack asked.

Cavanaugh took a quick pull from his pipe. "You know the type, Mr. Percy. He's convinced it's his *calling* to run around the countryside chasing and collecting the lost. Whatever that means. If you ask me he's a fool. We tried to warn him about venturing too far away from civilization, just like the fools from Jones Mine, but each time he would just go on and on with something or other about the Lord and that was the end of it."

Jack understood. He had met those types in his time. During the war he had even seen them cut down in the heat of battle, most having never fired a shot or even bearing arms. There was something inherently crazy about them. Still, Jack had a deep sympathy for them, even admiration. Their bravery, he thought, was unparalleled.

"This is what concerns our great president," Cavanaugh said. "As you know, the Indian contingent in this area has become more and more concentrated as our regular army has pushed them up from the south. There are said to be as many as six tribes now in this general vicinity. Under normal circumstances this would work in our favor. Normally, they'd be fighting amongst themselves. We would just go in, pluck out our missing man, and return. But instead, the Sioux have united, sending their raiding parties where they will and killing as many of the white man as they can. They are terrorizing the settlers, Mr. Percy. I'm sure I need not point out what this has done to the poor souls in this region. Many are missing. Many more are dead."

"I've heard the stories," Jack said.

"They are savages. Primitives, you could say. They take life without conscience. They cannot be made civil as our government has attempted to do. Our leaders are becoming delusional on this point, I'm afraid, reacting too slowly." Cavanaugh gestured toward Asheworth. "I had to supply this unit with the latest repeating firearms myself—after continual, *ignored* requests." He shook his head, turned solemn. "You know what they did to Randy Miller's boy, don't you? You know what the savages did to him?"

"I heard."

Cavanaugh sighed. "Alas, it is our desire to prevent this from happening to Morris, our president's desire. Will you help us, Mr. Percy? Will you help your president?"

There was a window in the back wall behind Cavanaugh's desk. Jack stared through it into the darkness. He'd known clergymen of all sorts, and when they felt they were needed in a place, they stayed, regardless. Of course, that assumed there was a place at all. Could a small settlement have survived these last years of aggression? Under present circumstances, it seemed unlikely. It was largely believed the Indians had concentrated themselves in the mountains directly north of the budding northern territories. Some said they were even holed up across the border in Canada, though no confirmation had ever been brought to Jack's attention. But if it were true, what were the chances that this Jones Mine settlement had crafted a defensible position and was holding out? Holding on?

Jack knew he was reaching, but the thought tugged at him. What if they really were holding out, the town and the preacher? Wouldn't word have made it back to Twin Pines of a settlement in distress? Someone hearing shots? Hunters, trappers … anyone? Or maybe there was no distress; maybe Jones Mine was thriving in the face of it all.

"Will you accept, Mr. Percy?"

Jack stood numb. The preacher couldn't still be alive, could he? And what if he was? What help could Jack be? He had no particular talent for this. He'd just be kicking a hornet's nest. The whole thing was no good. Bad idea.

"No, thanks."

Jack saw Asheworth stiffen from the corner of his eye. "A colleague once told me the only safe escape from the South is a cautious retreat backward."

Jack glanced at the colonel. "Never heard that one before." He turned to go.

"Two thousand," Cavanaugh said.

Jack stopped and leaned against the doorjamb. "With all due respect, Mr. Cavanaugh, this just isn't—"

"That's fifteen hundred from my own pocket," the old man said, "payable in the denomination of your choice upon Morris's return. That is regardless of the state you might find him in."

Jack said nothing.

Cavanaugh's face reddened. His feet dropped to the floor. "Damn it, man, we are talking about a man's family. The savages know no prejudice when it comes to their depraved ways. It's not just men being targeted, but women and children, as well. Children, Mr. Percy. Children! You're acting as if there are choices here. For God's sake, there's a woman and child in those godforsaken hills."

Jack felt the first thud in his chest. An empty, cold feeling swam through his gut.

"Family?"

"Yes, yes." Cavanaugh waved his hands in disbelief. "Morris has his wife and daughter with him."

Jack shook his head. Of all the reports they'd heard, it was the stories of the women that made his heart ache the most. The men were killed, sometimes in the most painful, grotesque manner imaginable, but for the women it was often worse. Much worse. Just the thought of it stirred emotions he scarcely knew he had.

"And you think he's still in Jones Mine?"

"That's our greatest hope, Mr. Percy. Probably our only hope. That's why you're here."

Jack said nothing for a long time, his conscience and reason warring against one another.

Cavanaugh watched him, matching his silence but clearly suppressing impatience. Finally, he said, "Mr. Percy, what more do you—"

"I'll take a look," Jack said. He nearly stuttered the last part, not believing his ears, not trusting his lips.

"Good man," Cavanaugh said. He set his jaw. "Remember, I want him retrieved, regardless." His eyebrows furrowed and he pointed with the stem of his pipe. "Do you follow?"

Jack nodded. He wanted a live man or a dead body.

"Even if it means altering your course," the old man added.

Jack didn't respond to that.

Cavanaugh turned to Asheworth. "Have you got it?"

The colonel slipped a hand in his breast pocket.

Cavanaugh glanced at the hallway. "Mr. Heminger?"

There was no response.

"Mr. Heminger!"

Silence.

Cavanaugh looked at the corporal by the doorway. "I need Mr. Heminger."

The soldier got an apprehensive look on his face and he looked to his colonel. Asheworth gave him an *okay* nod, and the bluecoat ran off in search of Cavanaugh's assistant.

Maybe it was the fact that his power didn't extend as far as he wanted, or perhaps he felt his ego had been damaged in front of a stranger; in either case, Cavanaugh's anger would have been easy to discern even by someone who'd never met him. The shade of his face darkened and he shot Asheworth a poisonous stare.

The colonel kept his head down, ignoring his boss, and handed him the folded paper he'd retrieved from his pocket.

Cavanaugh opened a drawer and unfolded a pair of spectacles. He spread the paper out on his desk, glanced at it, then passed it to Jack. "It's a crude map of the area north of here. It shows the believed location of the Jones Mines settlement. The colonel here obtained it from our most current military intelligence."

Jack gave it a quick once over, then turned for the door.

"Just a moment." Cavanaugh glanced down the empty hallway. "There's one more thing."

Jack leaned back on the doorframe.

"You remember Mr. Heminger, I presume?"

"Yeah."

"He's going with you."

Jack was shaking his head before the old man finished his sentence. "With all due respect, sir, that's just not possible."

His bluntness obviously stunned Cavanaugh, but didn't dissuade him. "I'm afraid this is not negotiable, Mr. Percy. Consider it part of your fee."

Jack had a strong urge to remind the old man who was asking for help. He suppressed it, however, something he was beginning to feel he had done too much of this night.

Ned Heminger entered the room. He smiled a greeting at Jack and then faced his superior.

"He will only be an observer," Cavanaugh said. "He won't get in your way, I assure you." He turned to Heminger. "Isn't that right, Ned?"

"Mr. Cavanaugh—" Jack interrupted.

Cavanaugh held up a hand. "I insist."

Young Heminger was apparently not only ambitious but a quick learner as well. He was already visibly shaken, catching on fast to the unfolding conversation and his role in it. "Mr. Cavanaugh," he said with open apprehension. "What are you talking about?"

Cavanaugh looked at Jack. "When will you depart?"

"Sunrise."

"He'll be ready."

Jack abandoned formalities and gave the man a long, frustrated stare.

Cavanaugh matched it. "Something you wish to add?"

Jack let the silence make his point, then stepped into the hallway.

"Mr. Percy," Cavanaugh called after him. "Colonel Asheworth will also be riding out tomorrow. He'll be checking on a small family settlement about a day's ride northeast of here. That is, should you need any assistance."

Jack turned to the corporal. "You have something of mine."

The corporal peeked in at Asheworth, but the colonel was occupied with the growing exchange in the office. Apparently a silent quarrel had broken out. He gestured with a nod of his head. "C'mon, I'll give it to you outside."

On his way out of the house, Jack heard Ned Heminger's muffled pleading and then Cavanaugh's booming voice. "Do you want my recommendation?"

The cold hit Jack like a horse in full stride. He could see his breath before he was fully through the door. Outside, the corporal returned his revolver and even gave him a sympathetic smile.

Jack checked the loads, holstered the pistol, and then started down the hill into town.

5

The darkness was engulfing. No visible moon. Even the brilliant stars high above struggled to penetrate the night. The soft, wavering lights from town were mere pinpoints now, small and insubstantial in the dark.

The two soldiers—the corporal who had led Jack through the house and the younger man from Pennsylvania—still stood at either side of the door. It was only from the light of the windows that they were able to see each other at all. That light, however, wasn't necessary to alert the two men of each other's presence; the constant sniffling and occasional swearing took care of that.

The light from the fireplace inside cast out about thirty feet from the closest window, flickering and playing about the brown lawn like a thing alive. Although its power to illuminate anything outside was nil, the light was nonetheless comforting, in its own way.

Thirty feet. The three shadows were at roughly that distance when they slowly began emerging into view. Coming closer.

The Pennsylvanian was shuffling his feet now, running in place, trying to trigger whatever mechanism in the body produced heat.

The corporal backhanded him in the gut. "*Shhhh!*"

"What?"

The corporal said nothing. His hand slipped to his side, fingered the grip of his revolver. He squinted ahead and started to point out the approaching shadows to his younger comrade. Then froze.

"What?"

The shadows were becoming clearer, taking shape, more like silhouettes. Details were forming. Arms. Legs …

"What?"

The corporal drew his pistol, and the confused Pennsylvanian dove for cover behind a nearby hardwood.

"Don't shoot! Don't shoot!" a voice sang out.

Then laughter.

The corporal lowered his sidearm, but only slightly. "Who's there?"

Three men came into view. One in front. Two behind. All uniformed cavalry.

The corporal's relief.

"Jeez, you nearly scared the life outta me," the corporal said. "Don't be sneakin' up like that."

The soldier at the point was bent over, hands on his knees, laughing. He looked up and grinned, revealing two incomplete rows of green teeth. "You was gonna shoot us—" he started, but was overcome by laughter again.

The two soldiers behind him were breathing heavy, eyes wide. They were not laughing. In fact, at that moment, they might have been the only men in the territory who were sweating.

"And where was you?" Greenteeth went on through his laughter. "What was you gonna do behind that tree?"

The Pennsylvanian emerged from the darkness and returned to his station by the door. He said nothing.

"Don't be sneakin' up like that!" the corporal snapped. "You might've been Sittin' Bull for all I knew."

Greenteeth laughed harder. "If I'd been an enjun ..." He paused to breathe and then pointed to the ground in front of the corporal. "If I'd been an enjun, you'd be as dead as that stone."

The corporal looked at the rock at his feet, then thrust a finger to his left. "Just get over there and relieve Henson on the side of the house."

Still snickering, Greenteeth straightened and waved a hand in mock salute. Then he spun on his heels, clicked them together, and started along the front of the house.

"And don't be sneakin' up like that," the corporal yelled after him. "I could've killed you!"

More laughter.

Henson was shivering from head to toe. At least, he thought he was. Any sensation resembling feeling was lost from the knee down. He checked his boots. Still there, but there was no way to know if feet still occupied them. He sighed, trying to wiggle lifeless toes while watching for movement at the tip of his boot. He looked up just as the next shift rounded the corner.

"Hellfire," he said. "It's about time. I thought I was gonna freeze to death over here."

Greenteeth stopped and spat. "Well how in tarnation you suppose I'm gonna keep warm?"

"Don't know, nor care."

The voices from inside the house were audible, albeit barely, through the window on the side of the house.

Greenteeth glanced up at the frost-tinted glass. "What are they yappin' about in there?"

"Do I look like their ma?"

"I don't know about theirs, but you're gonna be mine if they aim to keep me in this frozen Hades much longer."

Henson gave Greenteeth a long, disgusted stare. "I oughta just shoot you now and put you out of my misery."

Greenteeth patted the stock of his rifle. "You just go on and try it, little lady."

Henson glared, thinking it over, but the sound from the window drew his attention away. The voices inside were a lot louder than usual, almost clear.

The two soldiers eased to either side of the window frame. Greenteeth blew Henson a kiss. Henson spat on the ground between them. They leaned closer. The voices inside were growing louder by the second. No, only one of them was.

"I was told—"

"I'm not interested in what you were told!"

Silence.

"And Heminger?"

"He's driving me crazy, anyway."

Silence.

"Do you follow?"

"He got 'em here."

"Then he's fulfilled his purpose!"

 Silence.

"Do you follow?"

"Understood."

"This obsession ends now, Colonel. Do not trouble me with it further."

Silence.

"Do you understand?"

"Yes, sir."

"No more favors."

"Yes, sir."

"Leave me."

"Yes, sir."

6

Jack wasn't sure if he'd adjusted to the cold or if his body had gone numb. He was walking back through town, wondering if he'd ever agreed to anything more foolish in his life. It wasn't too late; he could easily climb back up the hill and refuse. And he wondered why he wasn't doing just that. It seemed the only rational thing to do. Still, he moved on, away from the house on the hill, thinking. He was sympathetic to the preacher's plight, but that wasn't all of it; there was something else, something more than the money, something just out of reach.

He passed a break in the buildings and stopped. He stared through an alley and out into the dark countryside. Except for the occasional gust of wind, there was no sound. The street was empty, and he found the silence made it both easier and harder to think.

He was struck by how alone he felt. The emotion was strong and sudden, and it called to mind those lonely nights during the war, when all one had for company was himself and God—even when surrounded by hundreds of men. He'd never really known how to talk to God, and had never cared for the counsel of his own pessimistic thoughts, so silence and solitude had become a friend. An ally. A comforter.

But not now. Now it seemed like an intruder, attempting to reopen wounds of pains long past. He resisted and the memory of the war faded—that was a power it had taken him many years to refine. But it was replaced with the face of his grandmother. Not the woman's strong, confident eyes of his youth, but the tired, gray eyes of her deathbed. It was, regrettably, those eyes he remembered most. In the days before her passing, she'd told him to face life, stand up to it, outwit it when he could, and when that wasn't possible, to fight it. She'd instructed him to always do the right thing, whatever the cost.

That last part—*to do the right thing*—had been spoken to him in his adolescence, years before the war, and had strangely engrained itself. It had brought him much pain, yet seemed virtually irresistible.

Something bumped the side of his foot and he looked down. There was a small glass lying in the dust beside his boot, the kind used for quick shots of liquor. A tool for a speedy drunk. Since it had made it into the street, he figured it must've worked. How far had he walked?

It was then he noticed the night was no longer quiet. The air carried with it a new sound, a shuffling sound, echoing faintly off the adjacent buildings. He turned, searching for the origin of the noise. It wasn't coming from the street, but nearby. And it wasn't exactly shuffling, but hard thuds in sequence, one after another. Footfalls. No question. And fast.

Someone running.

He remembered the alley.

Someone was running through it. Had to be. But who? And at this hour?

The blood went cool in the small of his back. One word swirled in his mind.

Indians.

Then another.

Sioux.

Then his mind really began to betray him. Everything he had seen and heard came crashing into his head like an invading army. Unlike many other things in his past, the images of Sioux handiwork still held a vividness that time seemed powerless to expunge. These, as well as the stories, all joined together in one coordinated assault on his psyche, with one sinister message.

He struggled to clear his mind, to focus. He had to see them first, had to have that advantage. His hand moved toward his pistol and he took a slow step back. The glass broke under his foot. The thin snap rang like gunfire in the silence. He quickly looked to the boardwalk for cover and then darted behind a column and pulled up to it. The cold wood pressed against his face. He pulled his revolver and drew back the hammer. The cylinder rotated and clicked.

The sound was bearing down now, echoing from one side of the street to the other, impossible to pin down. He closed his eyes, narrowing his senses. The noise seemed to be on both sides, but that couldn't be right. He turned his head, listening, eyes still closed. The echo was dying out behind him; the source was definitely in the street ahead, the ground he'd already covered. Still coming. Maybe fifty feet.

Then forty.

Thirty.

Silence.

Jack held his breath. His pulse roared in his ears. Cold perspiration trickled down the center of his back. He glanced back. Nothing. All had gone quiet.

And then he felt it, that primal and trustworthy sense of being watched, that prickle of hairs on the back of the neck.

Whoever was out there knew where he was.

He squeezed his revolver, aware of its heft and cool wooden grip in his palm. His fingertip felt raw against the trigger.

A hand touched his shoulder.

"It-it's ma-ma-me, Jack."

Jack didn't turn, didn't speak. He lowered the hammer on his sidearm and holstered it, then leaned his head against the column. His hat fell off and hit the wooden walkway with a hollow thump. He stayed that way, silent and unmoving, waiting for the pain in his chest to subside. He finally swore and pounded his head against the column. He regretted that instantly.

"Why'd you sneak up on me?"

"Di-didn't want you to sh-sh-shoot me," Eli said. He offered Jack's hat back.

Jack rubbed the sides of his head. The headache was approaching intolerable.

"How'd you get behind me?"

Eli pointed at the darkness. "I wa-wa-went around."

Jack sighed, took his hat.

"Sa-sa-sorry, Jack."

"No, no, it's okay. I'm just a bit edgy, is all." He patted the old scout on the back. "I'm really glad to see you."

"You in tra-tra-trouble?"

Jack's head throbbed more and more with every beat of his heart. The pain was robbing his power to think. He considered the question. Truth was, he didn't know. "No," he said. "At least, not yet."

Eli spun around and glanced at the street behind him. He studied the buildings across the way for a moment, then looked at Jack and shook his head, confused.

"The old man wants me to find someone," Jack said. "A preacher and his family. They left here headed north and … apparently lost their way."

Eli nodded.

"Ever heard of Jones Mine?"

Eli shook his head.

"Yeah, me neither. I wonder—"

Eli walked away, headed back up the street.

"Wait a minute," Jack said.

Eli looked back. "Yeah, Jack?"

"Where are you going?"

"I'm ga-going with you."

Jack wondered if he was missing something. "I'm headed back to Randy's place, where it's warm. It's this way."

Eli stood there a moment, as if waiting for more, then nodded and continued up the street.

Jack went a couple of steps after him. "Don't you want to come?"

Eli stopped. "Nah, I like to la-la-look at 'em wa-when we're na-not home."

Jack was suddenly tempted to check his surroundings. "Who?"

Eli laid his head back and pointed at the sky. "Angels."

Jack looked up. In every direction the sky seemed near capacity with endlessly winking stars, each one as immaculate and brilliant as its neighbor.

"Tha-that's heaven," Eli said. His usual anxiety and nervous disposition seemed momentarily suspended. He looked up again, grinning, pointing. "Up there."

Jack nodded. "Just don't get yourself killed."

The scout chuckled. Then he ran off and disappeared.

"I'm serious!" Jack yelled after him.

But Eli was gone.

Jack shook his head. He still hadn't adjusted to the fullness of the old scout's eccentricities.

Eli had run across Jack and Raymond's path a couple of years ago. Literally. They had been traveling north into the new territory when he just popped out in front of them like a stray dog. He'd looked sickly and appeared to be starving, so they'd fed him and let him bed down in their camp for the night. He never went away. But he never stayed, either. Rather, he'd pop up now and then—much like he had the first time—to warn them of some obstacle far ahead or suggest a change in direction. They had initially thought him mad, but, to their amazement, he was always right. A first class scout.

It was quite a while before Eli ever just sat and talked, and then it was only to Jack. But even then, though he'd sometimes talk for an hour at a time, very little communication took place. Nonetheless, Jack did learn that Eli had ridden with John Mosby during the war. Mosby, known by his detractors as the "Grey Ghost," had commanded some of the most elite scouting divisions in the Confederate army. It had been during one of his clandestine raids into the North that Eli and several of his comrades had been ambushed, betrayed by one of their own. Apparently, only Eli survived the massacre. But survival had been a mixed blessing. He was captured and, in his words, spent "a long time" in a federal prison camp.

When Jack asked how he'd gotten out, Eli told him abbreviated stories of prisoners smearing themselves with coal and walking out with the colored laborers, and still others who'd successfully feigned death only to get up and walk away when the grave diggers had their backs turned. When Jack asked again how *he* had gotten out, Eli grinned as though embarrassed, and said, "I ju-just left."

His "sickly" look never changed. And in time, they realized it was just his normal appearance. Jack privately wondered if it was the prison camp that had taken such a toll on him. Eli couldn't remember his age, nor could he tell you his last name. He wore the same worn-out clothes every day, but—and Jack swore a man could set his watch by this—every evening, just minutes before the sun went down, he could be seen down by the creek, scrubbing and wringing his old garments in nothing but his long cotton underwear. Unless, of course, it was one of those evenings when he was washing them, as well.

Jack laid his head against the column again and closed his eyes. The cold wood temporarily eased the throbbing pain in his head. And for a moment, he wished he could just remain there, alone in the stillness. But life wouldn't have it that way, he knew. Like a cruel, invisible taskmaster, life had a way of forcing him on just when he was beginning to get comfortable, just before he could relax.

The column's anesthetic effect didn't last long—not nearly long enough, anyway—so he pushed away and slipped his hat on. He clamped it down tight. The heavy burning behind his eyes was returning in force. He needed rest.

The figure across the street startled him—a solitary soul standing in the shadows of the opposite boardwalk. Just a silhouette, really, an outline created by the lamplight of a nearby window.

"Change your mind?" Jack called. But the words had barely left his mouth when he realized it wasn't Eli standing across the way. Nor was it Raymond.

Jack stared. Having his eyes closed the moment before had improved his night vision, but the distance and weak light made it difficult to discern details. It was a man, however. He could tell that by the figure's proportions, or lack thereof.

The man tilted his head.

"Sorry," Jack called out. "Thought you was someone else."

The man said nothing.

Jack started up the sidewalk.

The man did too. A fast, parallel adjustment to Jack's own movement. Just a quick step or two.

Or did he?

Jack stopped. The man appeared to be standing in the same place now, the exact spot as before, but at the same time he didn't.

"You alright?" Jack called. He didn't like having to raise his voice like he was, but neither did he want to cross the street. In fact, he felt a strange impulse to step back, or move on entirely. The feeling was intense and wholly internal, abrupt and instinctual. He resisted it.

The man tilted his head again. A curious gesture, reminding Jack of the way an animal would angle its head at a strange noise.

Jack still couldn't tell if the man had actually moved or if his own angle had just changed. But he could see better now, some detail, though murky in the shadows.

The stranger appeared to be dressed head-to-toe in all black—long, coal-black hair slick against his scalp. Something like a priest, minus the collar and frock. He wore no jacket, no gloves, no hat. But his body didn't seem to react to the cold. He didn't seem to mind it. He didn't shiver.

Jack did. And it wasn't because of the cool night air, but the man's deathly pale complexion and watery gray eyes. Focused eyes. Penetrating. How the hell could he see the man's eyes from this distance, the lifeless gray, the excessive moisture?

Then he couldn't.

The stranger was gone.

Jack blinked, looked up and down the street, searched the sidewalks, squinted at windows.

Nothing.

"Hello?"

Silence.

Raymond was sitting on a bench outside Randy's store, hat tilted over his eyes.

Jack stopped short of the door and sat beside him. He rubbed his head wondering if he was going mad or just exhausted. "Seen anyone on the street?"

Raymond pushed his hat back. "Eli's out there."

"You saw him?"

"No."

"Anyone else?"

"No."

They sat in silence for a bit. Finally, Jack unpacked the specifics of the meeting and his decision to go. He left out the black-clad stranger.

Raymond nodded once as Jack spoke, but otherwise remained quiet.

Although no outward expression suggested it, Jack knew his friend thought it was crazy, maybe thought *he* was crazy. And he wasn't alone. Jack agreed. But still, something about the whole thing nagged at him, something he couldn't put his finger on.

"I reckon he got what he deserved," Raymond said, referring to the preacher.

Jack said nothing. The words stung a bit, but Raymond wasn't one to pull any punches. Jack lowered his head and squeezed his temples again. He needed to get some sleep.

Raymond also had his head back down, eyes wandering over the rifle in his lap.

Jack got up and gave the door a gentle push. It creaked and dragged against the floor. It wasn't much warmer inside, but it would do. The place was dark and quiet, so he eased behind the counter and peeked into the back room.

CJ was sleeping on a cot along the back wall, while Randy snored from a rocking chair at the youngster's feet.

Jack backed out. It was later than he'd thought. He scanned the store for a hospitable place to lie down.

A pair of blankets and pillows were stacked by the front window.

Jack made a mental note to thank Randy for his kindness tomorrow.

As he lay down and closed his eyes, his mind began replaying the events of the day, untangling and dissecting them. He pushed the thoughts away.

Tomorrow.

7

Jack woke to the sound of Randy coughing from somewhere in the back of the store. He sat up and shaded his eyes from the window. The headache hadn't gone but had eased considerably. His body was urging him back down, however, but he knew that could never be. In fact, judging by the amount of sunlight filling the shop, he was a little worried he'd overslept. He came slowly to his feet and waited for the ache in his back to let up. It didn't.

"How'd you manage on that cold floor?" Randy asked.

Jack glanced out at Raymond, who was sitting alone outside the door. "It was fine. I'm very much obliged."

Randy grunted. He was sitting behind the counter in the same spot as yesterday and probably the day before and so on. He was thumbing through a stack of papers and, despite the chilly temperature of the room, had beads of sweat on his face. A quiet wheeze slowly grew in his chest until it finally forced him into another coughing fit.

Jack folded the blanket and dropped it, along with the pillow, on top of the other set Randy had left out. The other set lay exactly where it had last night, undisturbed.

"Come now," Randy said, clearing his throat. "By the way you're standing, I would guess it weren't very fine at all."

Jack walked over to the counter and eased onto a vacant stool. "Always a bit stiff in the morning. Slept like a dead man, actually."

Randy grinned. "You've got the rigor, then." He leaned to his right and glanced at the front window. "He out there all night?"

"Couldn't tell you."

"One of them that don't need much rest, huh?"

"I wonder if he sleeps at all."

Randy settled back on his own stool. "So tell me, how—"

Then he was coughing again. It was a hard, wet cough this time that took him mercilessly and held him through several ragged breaths. The shopkeeper slumped over and pounded his chest.

Jack turned away.

Randy noticed and held up a hand. "No, no, it's alright. It's always the worst in the morning." He managed a weak smile. "It'll pass."

"You holding up?" Jack asked.

Randy blinked. "Well, it hurts like hell," he said. "But afterwards I see these little orange lights." He waved his hands around and wiggled his fingers. "They're really pretty, but the damnable thing is I can't focus on any of 'em. They just twinkle around the edges, taunting me, sometimes for a full minute or two. But none of 'em ever comes to the middle where I can get a good look at 'em." He frowned. "It don't do to move my eyes, either; they just run away then."

Jack grinned, feeling both sympathy and admiration. The two emotions, he had noticed, often came together.

Randy blinked again and wiped sweat from his brow. He looked at Jack. "Holding up? Why, I'm having a time." He gestured at the room. "I'm sitting here with you, ain't I? Listen, once a man is alone for a while, he learns right quick the value of honest friends and fine conversation. And also how hard they are to come by. They're a treasure, Jack, not to be taken lightly. They're come and gone in a blink."

Jack nodded.

"That youngster back there," Randy went on, "you sitting here, it just does an old soul good to be around solid folk. He don't say much, but even having ole Ray out there is nice."

Jack chuckled. "You must be one lonely man indeed."

Randy laughed, then coughed. "Horsefeathers," he said, and pointed at the back room. "I ain't never. Where'd he pick that up?"

"It's from his own head, I'm afraid. I wanted to thank—"

"Listen here, now," Randy interrupted. "I know I've got this thing inside me, eatin' me up. I know I ain't got long left, and it don't matter. No, it don't matter. I ain't got to face no affliction that ain't common to man. If it ain't this way, then it'd just be something else.

Besides, I'm getting tired of this dirt-hell anyhow. I've been blessed, had a fair life, I reckon, but now everyone's gone, and ..." His voice trailed off.

Jack said nothing.

"I just want to tell you," Randy said, "your leaving that boy with me was the best time I've had in a long while. I laughed some, cried some, then went to sleep happy. It means a lot that you think enough of this old man to have left him." He cleared his throat. "So don't you go thanking me for nothin', you hear?"

Jack nodded.

"You hear?"

"I do."

"Good."

Randy looked down at the counter and shook his head. "Horsefeathers," he said quietly. "So, what business you got with Cavanaugh?"

Jack ran a hand through his hair. For the briefest of moments he'd forgotten what had brought him here and what still lay ahead. With more than a little reluctance, he went through the essentials with the shopkeeper, abbreviating much and skipping more.

Randy listened. He occasionally turned his head to one side, as if stretching out a sore muscle, but never for long, and never far enough to lose eye contact.

Jack finished by telling him that Cavanaugh didn't want the townspeople knowing about Morris's present situation.

Randy didn't immediately speak. He looked at the counter, thinking it over. "He's dead, Jack."

"Yeah," Jack said. He glanced at the window, wondering when Ned Heminger would show and then if the young man even knew where to look for him.

"Listen, Jack, I know you can handle yourself and all, probably better than any man in this town. I know all about Woods Fort."

"It ain't what you think."

"Maybe it is. Maybe it ain't. It's just ... well, it just ain't wise to get that far out by yourself. Especially north. God only knows what's north of here. And you'll be huntin' a dead man. You know it, same

as me. You might as well be chasing a ghost through those hills."
Randy waved a hand in the general direction. "Hellfire, you can't
even trust the settlers anymore. I hear tell that some of 'em's even
making deals with the savages. They're giving each other up. And for
what? Their lives? What kind of life is that? And what good is a deal
with devils?" The shade of Randy's face darkened. His eyes glazed.

He hit the counter.

"They're devils, I tell you! Them godforsaken Sioux heathen are
ever' bit as demon as the dominion below us."

Jack hadn't seen this side of Randy but had expected it eventually.
The man had done more than most to suppress his pain, but, of
course, everyone had their limits.

Still, the shopkeeper fought it. He focused on his fist and for a
moment didn't appear to be breathing. He finally relaxed his grip and
turned his hand palm down, fingers splayed. His eyes welled as he
watched something only he could see. A single tear slipped from the
corner of his eye. "If you ever were to happen across the ones who
done it," he whispered. "You'll let me know."

"Of course I will," Jack said.

Randy nodded without looking up. "I just want 'em to remember my
boy."

Just as Jack reached across the counter and squeezed Randy's
shoulder, there was shuffling in the back room, followed by a couple
of deep thuds against the floor.

Randy kept his back turned as CJ emerged. He pulled a fresh
handkerchief from his pants pocket and dabbed it across his face.

Jack was glad to see the boy, and even more thankful Randy had
seen him. He knew the conversation—if it could be called that—
would change now. It wasn't that he was disinterested. He just didn't
know how to speak to the shopkeeper's pain. Had no idea how. And
remaining silent, offering little or no support, made him feel awkward
and useless. He had been in this position before, sometimes with
friends, sometimes not, and every time he felt their pain, sensed its
power. And there was always the impulse to lessen their suffering.
Like now. But he never quite knew how and, in his eyes, never
succeeded.

CJ raised his arms and yawned in a deep breath. He shivered. The cold air didn't take long to bite. He blinked at Jack and grinned. His hair was all pushed to one side, evidence of a good rest, the kind of sleep where one wakes in the same position they laid down in. The grin faded, however, when the youngster's eyes moved away from Jack and surveyed the rest of the room.

Unfamiliar.

Jack understood. The boy was facing his first real case of homesickness. There was no crackling fire he could pull himself up to, no ready-made breakfast awaiting his attention. The accustomed smell of boiling coffee was absent. No Carl. No Michael. No Jonas. Everything CJ encountered on a daily basis was missing, and though he'd probably never admit it, it was telling on his face.

He shouldn't be here, Jack thought. And he certainly didn't need to be in the untried country north of here, chasing after someone who might no longer exist. A ghost, as Randy had put it.

Not only was it no place for a boy, it was no place for *this* boy. Jonas's boy. Jack couldn't bear even the idea of some harm befalling CJ, let alone being responsible for it. Jonas had insisted, but had he known his son might be wandering around Indian territory, hunting a missing person, he would've thought differently. Wouldn't he?

"Howdy," CJ said, still wiping sleep from his eyes.

"Mornin'," the two men said together.

"Sleep well?" Randy asked.

CJ yawned again and collapsed on the nearest stool. "Like a wet log."

"What do you think about hanging around here a few days?" Jack asked.

The boy studied Jack like he wasn't sure he'd heard him correctly. "Well, I …"

It occurred to Jack that he hadn't consulted Randy before bringing this up. He gave him a slow, questioning look.

Randy nodded.

CJ stared out the window.

Jack knew the boy hadn't forgotten his father's instruction: *Whatever he says*. But that gave little solace. He knew it was breaking

CJ's heart, and that was a consequence that bore heavy. He wondered if he was overreacting.

"I'd like to go with y'all, Jack."

"I know," Jack said. "You remember when we talked about not getting out in the open in small groups?"

"Yeah."

"That's why I'd like you to stay here a spell. Not long; few days should do it."

"Where you going?"

"North."

"Why?"

"Looking for someone."

"Somebody's lost?"

"That's what I'm told."

CJ went quiet while he thought about it.

Jack glanced at Randy, who was studying the counter like he was suddenly fascinated by its contours.

"What's north of here?" CJ asked.

"That's just it," Jack said. "Don't really know. The way I understand, not many folks do. I reckon it ain't much to see either way."

CJ nodded, said nothing.

Nor did Randy.

In fact, the room was suddenly so devoid of sound that it left Jack's ears ringing. He glanced again at the boy, who was staring at the floor.

Jack got up and leaned the stool against the counter.

"Wait!" CJ shouted.

Jack saw Randy's body shudder from the sudden outburst.

Apparently CJ had, too, because he flushed. But he wasn't deterred.

"I can cook a little," the boy said quickly. "You know I've whooped up a few things before, when Pa was busy and all."

Jack rubbed the back of his neck.

"I can track some. I found that heifer that slipped the fence. Remember the heifer that slipped the fence?"

Randy produced a pocketknife from somewhere and began digging into the countertop.

Jack watched him.

"And hunt too. You know I can hunt, Jack."

Jack said nothing.

"And … and … I can ride. Heck, give me a couple of sticks and I'll build you a—"

"Get your stuff ready," Jack said.

CJ didn't wait to see if he'd heard correctly. He didn't pause to consider which line had been the deciding one. He didn't hesitate. He turned and took the shortest route to the back room and disappeared.

Randy held a handkerchief to his mouth and coughed into it. He looked at Jack, perplexed.

"If it gets bad, we'll just turn tail and run," Jack said.

"Yeah, but—"

"I know," Jack said. "What do you get for them smokes?"

Randy grabbed a handful of cigars from the shelf behind him. He dropped them on the counter.

Jack went for his pocket.

Randy held up a hand. "You'll pay me when you get back."

Jack smiled. "Much obliged." He slipped into his duster and dropped the cigars in one of the pockets. "Will you send him out when he's ready?"

Randy nodded and Jack turned for the door. He was halfway across the room when he stopped and turned back.

"Know anyone around here that dresses in all black, kinda like a priest, and ain't got much color to him?"

"Don't know," Randy said. "What's he look like?"

"Strange eyes, pale as a dead man," Jack said. "That'd be enough if you knew him."

"Nah, don't know anyone like that," Randy said. "Hellfire, I thought I was the ugliest one around these parts."

Jack grinned at the shopkeeper. "I reckon this fella would give us both a run at the money."

Randy started to laugh but was quickly coughing again. "Competition's good for the circulation," he managed between wheezes.

Jack walked outside. "Thanks for everything."

Randy's voice chased after him as the door closed. "Dammit, I told you not to—"

Except for a different jacket, and the look of a man who hadn't slept very well, Ned Heminger looked very much the same as he had the morning before. He was riding an impressive brown gelding with U.S. branded on its hindquarter. His saddlebags were packed and tied down neatly, a small leather bag attached to one side. As appearances went, he looked well prepared. Very well prepared, Jack thought, except ...

"Where's your rifle?"

Ned pushed his wire-rimmed spectacles up the bridge of his nose. "Rifle?"

Jack stepped around the horse and glanced through town. A lone cavalry soldier sat horseback at the far end of the street, veiled in the long early-morning shadows from the buildings. Jack raised a hand in his direction, but the soldier didn't return the gesture.

Ned's gelding tossed its head and snorted, obviously uncomfortable with Jack's movement.

Jack looked at Ned. "Didn't you bring a firearm?"

"I did not, Mr. Percy. I am only an observer."

Jack studied him, wondering if he was serious.

Ned looked like he'd just enlightened Jack in some way. He reached down and extended a hand.

Jack took it and squeezed. "You're really unarmed?"

Ned tapped the side of his head with a finger. "My weapon is here, Mr. Percy."

Looks more like a target, Jack thought. "Alright, but I have to tell you, I don't think heading out of here unarmed is in your best interest."

Ned tipped his hat. "Noted."

"This would be your last chance to reconsider."

Ned said nothing.

"Alright." Jack turned toward his horse. He saw Raymond then, already mounted and waiting at the northernmost edge of town, where the first of many hardwoods formed the forest's edge. The trees were peculiar to this area and almost totally unseen anywhere else in the territory.

Raymond had noticed the bluecoat as well and was watching him from under the brim of his hat.

Jack had just gotten a foot in the stirrup when the faint scent of flowers caught his attention. The gentle breeze carried the aroma all around him, like a slow, invisible river washing past. No, not flowers. The scent was too sweet, too artificial—pleasant, but unnatural. Familiar.

He looked at Ned. "You wearing perfume?"

"It's cologne, Mr. Percy."

"There's a difference?"

"Cologne is non-layered, not as strong. Doesn't last as long. It's relatively new, actually."

Jack just stared.

Ned didn't notice. He'd removed a leather-bound notebook and pencil from his jacket pocket and was scribbling something inside.

"Listen," Jack said, but before he could finish his thought, the door of Randy's shop exploded open, spilling CJ out. The boy was pulling on his jacket with one hand while trying to get into a boot with the other. A strip of jerked beef dangled from his mouth like a long, withered tongue. He stumbled toward Major but stopped when he noticed Ned.

"Who's this?" Ned asked.

Jack wanted to laugh at the spectacle CJ was, but didn't. Ned, he thought, was no less a spectacle, just in a different way. He pulled himself up onto his mare. "This is CJ Cantrell," he said. "And CJ, this is Ned Heminger. He'll be coming with us."

Both of the young men tipped their hats as CJ struggled into the rest of his clothes.

Raymond was already moving north. Jack watched him as he waited for CJ. Raymond was going against his own judgment by coming along, Jack knew, perhaps his better judgment. He was here only because Jack was, and that fact pained Jack a great deal. But, on the other hand, seeing him out in front brought a measure of peace this outing wouldn't otherwise have had.

"Isn't he a little young, Mr. Percy?"

Jack turned.

CJ had just slid into his saddle. He pulled his hat down tight and tore a bite from the jerky. His neck and cheeks flushed and his eyes grew hot. Jack figured if Ned were any closer he might've disappeared in a cloud of smoke.

Jack grinned at the boy, at the anger in him. "I reckon he's old enough." With that he swung his mare around and started off in the direction Raymond had gone.

Ned fell in behind him, with CJ in the rear.

They had ridden only a couple hundred yards when CJ called up from the back.

"What is that?" the boy shouted. "Smells like someone herded a passel of womenfolk through here."

Jack said nothing, giving Ned the chance to answer for himself.

He didn't.

"And what's with the soldier?" CJ hollered.

Jack slowed and looked back. The cavalryman, who'd been watching from the street only minutes earlier, was now in front of Randy's store. The bluecoat dismounted and stood by his horse.

Because of the distance they'd covered, it was impossible to tell exactly what the soldier was doing, or if he was doing anything at all. He appeared to be just standing there beside his horse. But before Jack could pull his mare to a complete stop, the soldier had tied his mount to the hitching post and walked inside the shop.

"Probably needs an edge on his knife or somethin'," CJ said, answering his own question. "Randy says he can sharpen any kind of blade."

Jack thought about it and then glanced at Raymond, who was slowly pulling away. He reluctantly loosened his grip on the reins; the slack slid through his fingers, and his mare resumed her earlier pace without prompting.

He said nothing.

8

"So how old are you?" CJ blurted.

Ned looked up. "Me?"

"Yeah."

"Twenty-three."

"Well, I'm seventeen."

Ned only nodded. He was twisting the cap off a small wooden bottle he'd retrieved from his saddlebags. He carefully applied a little of the container's contents on a strip of jerked beef and took a bite.

"And?" he said to CJ.

"And I was born on horseback," the boy said. "That's seventeen years in the saddle, chewin' dirt, spittin' mud, and wrangling everything on four legs or two."

Jack had been mostly staring at the ground, lost in thought, but he looked up as the tension rose from his right. If the boy glanced to his left, Jack was ready to give him a discouraging nod. But CJ didn't look left. He glared at Ned.

"Mind getting my canteen?" Jack asked.

Ned looked at Jack, but CJ didn't respond, didn't move.

"CJ?"

The boy turned, softened. "Yeah, Jack?"

"Mind fetchin' my water?"

"Sure thing." CJ jumped up and started toward Jack's horse.

Jack broke off a piece of hardtack and folded jerky around it in a vain attempt to give it flavor. He looked up as he chewed. Even at its highest and most productive position, the sun seemed to have little power to warm the earth below. Cold wind rushed through the forest in sporadic bursts, curling around trees and foliage with a sound like a distant tide.

This bothered him. Regardless of the sun's seeming inadequacy at this point, he knew the nights would be worse. A lot worse. And though he was no stranger to cold nights in open country, he also knew this was not the same cold he'd grown accustomed to in the south. This was cold that brought death.

The first half of the day had passed quietly, without conversation. Even the forest was mostly silent. This Jack considered a blessing. The small group had pressed hard and covered a lot of ground. This was also good, but unsustainable. If they pushed too hard, the horses would tire and a good start would be rendered meaningless later in the day.

So they'd pulled up at the first creek they came to—which wasn't much, little more than a jagged, muddy line through the forest floor, shallow and thin. But it was wet. And passing up a water source in unfamiliar territory was tantamount to shooting yourself in the foot.

CJ and Ned had dismounted quickly and dropped grain for their horses, then went about unpacking their rations and resting saddle-weary legs. After a casual look around, Jack did likewise, finding an accommodating rock and joining the young men on the ground.

Raymond's horse was tied to a tree upstream, going through the feed he'd left her. But there was no sign of her rider. The area around the mare was just the same empty forest.

Jack took a bite and looked at Ned. "So, what do you do for Cavanaugh?"

Ned was watching CJ, who was still at Jack's horse looking for the water

"I'm an apprentice, of sorts."

"What's that?"

Ned slid around on his rump, trying to improve his seat on the forest floor. "It's an understudy, I guess. For the type of work I want to get into, I need experience, hands on with the trade, you might say."

Jack nodded. He had no idea what an understudy was either.

"You see, I studied back east for a few years and took a degree in economics," Ned went on. "But it didn't take long to discover that wasn't enough. Not just the degree, that is. So, in short, I'm kind of learning the trade from Mr. Cavanaugh. How I got way out here is a long, drawn-out affair, involving friends of friends of friends."

Jack finished his jerky and tossed the remaining hardtack in the direction of Ned's horse.

"Anyway," Ned said, "the bottom line is, I'm seeking a letter of recommendation from Mr. Cavanaugh."

"What'll that do?"

"It'll help me break into public office, I hope. Or at least it'll make it easier."

"You're aiming to be a governor too?"

"I wish to go all the way, Mr. Percy."

CJ dropped the canteen in Jack's lap. "All that learnin' ain't worth a fart in a whirlwind out here. Out here it's guts and nuts or moans and bones. Ain't no place for catheads."

Jack glared at the boy, but CJ wasn't paying him any attention.

Ned's eyes narrowed. "Just as stone to sword, is education to mind. Ever shaping, ever honing, ever perfecting. The fruit of which is like a fine edge. Those without will be inexorably pulled into the void, the blackness, oppressed by their own ignorance. They are loose sand in a rising tide…" He trailed off, abandoning the quote and waving a dismissive hand at the boy. He began writing in his ledger again.

CJ's face was pink and darkening. It was clear he hadn't understood what Ned said. But he knew he'd been insulted.

"*You're* the fruit!"

Ned ignored him. He closed his ledger and sprinkled more of the little container's contents on his lunch.

"What's that?" Jack asked, hoping to change the subject.

"This?" Ned asked. But as he looked up, his gaze fell over Jack's shoulder and fixed on something in the woods beyond.

Jack turned. Raymond was approaching from the north, dead leaves and sticks snapping under his feet. He was looking around, apparently taking in everything except his traveling companions.

Ned and CJ watched in silence.

Raymond stopped between Jack and CJ and took a swallow from his canteen.

"You were saying?" Jack asked.

Ned looked back to the container. "Yeah." He held it up for all to see. "It's an old family recipe handed down from my grandmother. I'm told she got it from her longtime Mexican maidservant. Anyway, it's a powder spice. It can be used on any kind of meat." He grinned. "Really adds to the flavor."

"Uh-huh," Jack said.

"I would gladly offer you some, Mr. Percy, but unless you've got a pretty strong stomach, I wouldn't recommend it. Takes some getting used to."

Jack held up a hand. "None for me." He'd tried the stuff before, during a brief stay in Texas years ago, or at least something like it. Mexican Pepper, they'd called it. He'd figured it more like gunpowder. It had taken three days to get it out of his system.

"I'll take some," CJ said.

Ned grunted.

CJ reached for it. "Ain't nobody scared of a little dust in a bottle."

Ned started to say something, but didn't. He twisted the cap on and tossed it to CJ.

CJ rolled the small container around in his fingers, then lifted the cap off and sniffed.

Jack was thinking of intervening, but figured the boy had to start making his own decisions sometime. This seemed as good a time as any. Besides, it couldn't be as bad as the Texas stuff.

No harm.

CJ sprinkled a little on his jerky and glanced around at his audience. He took a bite and chewed, eyes thoughtful. "It's alright, I reckon."

Jack noticed moisture forming at the corner of the boy's eye.

"Can you taste the spices?" Ned asked.

CJ swallowed. "Don't taste nothin'. Like chewin' on ashes."

"That's probably because you didn't get enough."

Jack gave Ned a sharp look.

Ned laughed and reached for the bottle. "No, no, you really don't want to overdo it."

CJ was breathing with his mouth open now. He poured on more powder. A lot more. He flashed a quick, defiant look at Ned and took a bite.

Jack grimaced.

CJ tossed the bottle back to Ned. He made a show of stuffing the remaining jerky in his mouth, kneading the meat slow and deliberate between his teeth, like a cow working her cud. Then, with one quick swallow, his mouth was empty. He licked his fingers.

Ned went back to his ledger, grinning like a schoolboy.

Jack shook his head.

CJ wiped his eyes.

Jack had noted the boy's toughness in the brief time he'd known him, and figured he was calling on every bit of it now. He also knew one thing for certain: CJ was determined not to reach for his canteen.

Jack grunted and looked up at Raymond, who was still standing beside him. But Raymond was preoccupied, looking off into the heavier brush opposite the creek.

Jack shifted, trying to follow his gaze. But nothing looked unusual. All was quiet. He gave Raymond a questioning glance.

But Raymond wasn't paying Jack any attention. Instead, he knelt, picked up CJ's canteen, and thrust it against the boy's chest.

Jack followed Raymond upstream. They stopped at a spot where the creek was deep and moving well, and Raymond knelt to fill his canteen.

"Something wrong?" Jack asked.

Raymond shook his head.

"You see something back there?"

"No."

Jack stepped back to give him room and looked out at the endless timber. He'd been studying the so-called map Cavanaugh had given him throughout the morning, and each time he'd folded it back up frustrated. There was no clear trail to Jones Mine. If there ever had been, time had long since erased it.

"I figure we oughta get as far as we can today before it really gets confusing."

Raymond stood. As he came to his feet, he winced and pressed a hand into his lower abdomen.

This wasn't new. Jack had seen him do it before, many times, even as Raymond tried to hide it. But it had been worse this year, more frequent.

"You alright?"

Raymond said nothing. His hand slipped back to his side.

"You hurtin'?" Jack pressed.

Raymond placed the top on his canteen. "It always hurts."

"What does?"

"The past."

"The war?" Jack asked. "You were hit?"

Raymond didn't answer, didn't say yes, didn't say no. But Jack thought he detected a nod, perhaps an involuntary one, but a nod nonetheless.

His mind wandered back to events he had no desire to revisit. Screams, like nightmarish echoes. Soldiers pleading, crying. Makeshift doctors groping, digging, cutting. Reluctant comrades holding down their friends. It had been a kind of necessary torture, with the only means of relief sloshing around in the bottom of a whiskey bottle. And even that was a luxury toward the end of the war. The procedure alone had killed some; others had not been so lucky.

"They get it out?" Jack asked.

Raymond took a breath, looked out at the forest. "Went straight through," he said finally.

Jack shook his head. "Good lord, Ray."

"Doc said I must have something left to do."

The last part of the day was a slow and steady uphill climb. The grade was easy and gradual but had taken a toll on the horses. Despite numerous stops to rest, the animals were showing real fatigue now: dangling tongues, irritability, flesh cool and wet with sweat. They were slowing with each passing minute.

Still, Jack was pleased with the progress they'd made. He figured they might have cut a half-day off the trip by pressing on as they had. But now time was fleeting. The barren trees were casting longer and longer shadows as the sun retreated on a low plane to the west. Also from the west, the cold breeze still came and went, now stinging any exposed skin like a burn.

He pulled up at the first level spot they came to, dismounted and looked around. It wasn't much of a clearing; in fact, it wasn't a clearing at all. Cold, gray trees crowded together in scattered clumps, allowing only thin streams of the fading sunlight to reach the forest floor. The ground was thick with dead leaves. But that was a good thing. Anyone attempting to set an ambush, or steal around in the night, would be easily detected in the brittle foliage.

Ned slid from his saddle. He stretched and took slow steps around his gelding, bending and cracking his knees. The young man had impressed Jack. Not only had he ridden the length with them, but had kept up—and without any hint of frustration or grumbling.

Jack walked over to CJ and put a hand on his shoulder. They both looked back at Ned, who was already busy writing in his journal.

Jack spoke quietly. "He ain't that bad, and he's going to be with us the whole way. So you need to stop letting him get to you."

"Horsefeathers!" CJ whispered. "He's the one being ornery! And I've seen lots of folks smarter than him. Just because he's got all that studyin', don't mean he's the biggest toad in the puddle."

"He ain't the only one being ornery," Jack said. "Just try and get along. This ain't a contest, and we don't need bickerin' or any other distractions out here." He squeezed the boy's shoulder. "I need you to do this for me."

"It ain't me."

Jack squeezed again.

CJ huffed, set his jaw

"Alright?" Jack said.

"Alright."

Jack looked around. "We're gonna need a fire. Won't you see if you can dig up some kindling?"

CJ nodded. But his body had begun a subtle, perhaps unconscious, sway—one leg to the other, side to side, to and fro. His eyes narrowed, focused inward, like something sinister had just occurred to him. He stiffened and placed a hand on his stomach.

"You alright?" Jack asked.

"Yeah." CJ said. "It's just … well … it's just, that stuff … it's been kinda—" He ran off and disappeared in a nearby stand of shrubbery.

Jack shook his head and fished out a cigar. As he glanced around the would-be camp he saw Ned standing alone among the horses and trees. The young man was shivering and rubbing his hands, apparently not knowing what ought to come next.

"You can gather up some of these rocks, if you like."

Ned looked confused.

"CJ will clear a spot for the fire when he gets back," Jack said.

Ned just stared at Jack. A hesitant, uncertain grin formed at the corner of his mouth. "Are you serious?"

Jack said, "You're free to sit and wait, if it suits you. We'll see to it in a minute."

Ned held up a hand. "No, no, Mr. Percy. It's not that. I mean, what about the Indians? Wouldn't they see the light from a fire?"

Jack lit his cigar and nodded sympathetically. "No choice. Won't be able to take the cold without a fire."

Ned looked away, obviously bothered by that conclusion.

CJ came back into camp loudly, crashing through the dead leaves. He was cradling a bundle of sticks and dry brush in his arms. "Ain't no kind of Indians worth freezin' to death over." He dropped the kindling in a heap at his feet. "Besides, the gol-derned Sioux already know we're here anyhow."

Ned kept his distance, said nothing.

CJ went to work in the middle of the small clearing, ridding it of leaves and brush, then hauling rocks back one by one.

In only minutes the boy had the woods glowing around them. Shadows danced and played off nearby trees, wavering in and out of existence like nocturnal spirits of the forest.

Ned backed up. A hiss rose from the damp sticks as moisture bled away. The leaves and kindling crackled and spat. But it was the slender column of smoke, advancing steadily upward through the trees—and growing thicker and thicker by the moment—that had Ned's attention.

Jack understood the young man's reservations; they were common sense concerns. But there was really no choice in the matter, and probably nothing he could say would still the doubts in Ned's mind. So he walked into the woods, a short piece away from the camp, where a massive but long-dead hardwood lay on its side. The once mighty tree had been opened up along the length of its trunk by a quick and powerful lightning strike long ago, and had leveled a couple of smaller specimens on its way down in what must have been a spectacular crash.

Jack sat on one of the smaller trees and drew on his smoke. He could hear the fire gaining strength behind him in the camp. It sounded nice. He'd always liked the solitude of the woods, even *these* woods, though he knew things could change here in an instant. But he didn't want to think about that now. He slipped a hand into the inner pocket of his jacket and came out with a small, folded piece of paper. The page was old and stained with age, and he used great care unfolding it. He took another long drag on the cigar and began scanning the text. There were hardly more than a couple of lines, so finishing didn't take long. Still, he studied it for a few minutes, carefully reading through it multiple times before full dark cut him short.

He felt that old familiar tug, the urge to curse the night, the world in general. But he swallowed it down. There was no use in it. He'd tried that years ago. But life just kept moving, cold and indifferent, whether you approved or not.

He gently refolded the page and tucked it away. There was talking around the campfire now. He stood and glanced up at the sky. What seemed like a thousand stars were already visible and winking down from the darkening canvas overhead. They were nothing short of spectacular in this part of the world.

Eli's angels.

The thought made him smile.

"I said, what were you guys talking about?"

CJ looked up from the flames. "Who?"

"You know who," Ned said, impatient. "I saw him whispering to you earlier."

"We weren't whispering."

"Well, I for one couldn't hear."

"Your ears are bad too?"

Ned paused, then said, "No, my hearing's fine. What do you mean by 'too'?"

CJ pointed at his eyes.

"Oh, these," Ned said. "These are strictly for reading and writing. My vision is fine."

CJ snorted.

"What?"

"If your seeing's so good, then how come you wore them spectacles all day on the trail?"

"I forget they're on sometimes," Ned said. "That's all. And I don't remember seeing any trail today."

"Like I said."

Ned stared at the teenager for a long time, face reddening. He finally took a breath and tried again. "Since I'm on this expedition as well, I think I deserve to know about any discussions pertaining to the task at hand. And that would include what you guys were talking about back there."

CJ looked back at the fire.

"What?" Ned insisted.

"Indians."

"Indians?"

"Sioux."

"What about the Sioux?"

CJ cleared his throat and looked around. "We were wonderin' if you'll wet your britches when they drag you away."

"You're impossible," Ned said. "You know that? Why are you so difficult?"

CJ spat in the fire.

Ned opened his journal and shifted to catch the firelight. He started writing. He went on for a full minute, scribbling and erasing and scribbling some more, pausing only once to adjust his glasses and chuckle at something on the page. He concluded his entry with an audible thump of his pencil, then leaned back and scanned over the material.

"Don't be writing nothin' about me in there," CJ said.

Ned ignored him.

"I'm serious."

Ned said nothing.

Jack stepped into view and tossed his spent cigar into the fire. He gave CJ a long, disapproving glare.

CJ looked back at the fire, probably wondering how long Jack had been standing there.

Ned's pencil was back to the paper. "What does CJ stand for, anyway?"

Jack sat down. Raymond was reclining against a tree not far from the fire, but not close either. His hat was over his face, so it was hard to tell whether he was sleeping or not.

Jack knew he wasn't.

CJ jabbed a stick at the fire. "Nothin'. Just CJ, that's all. And don't be talkin' about me in there."

"No way," Ned laughed. "It's an abbreviation, obviously. No one's name is just two letters."

CJ started to get up. "I'll show you a gol-derned aberration."

Jack put a hand on CJ's shoulder and forced him back down.

"*Ab-bre-vi-a-tion*," Ned said slowly. "Not *ab-er-ra*—"

"Are you still bothered by the fire, Ned?" Jack asked. But it wasn't a question.

Ned got the hint. He put away the journal, but not the smirk.

The boy stared at the fire, working his jaw.

Ned yawned and stretched, a shiver visibly running through him. He held his hands to the fire. "It's okay, Mr. Percy. I'm just a little edgy, I guess. I was assured your group could handle any surprises the redskins might throw at us."

"This ain't my group," Jack said. "And what was that? You were assured of …"

"The Sioux," Ned said. "Mr. Cavanaugh told me how you encountered the natives a couple of years ago and were able to drive them away. Woods Fort, right?"

Jack shook his head. He glanced at Raymond, who hadn't moved.

"That's just a couple days south of Twin Pines, right?" Ned asked.

"That's right."

"Well, he told me the survivors reported that you guys saved their lives. That you were heroes."

Jack stared at the fire. "He did, did he?"

"Yeah," Ned went on. "He said you guys rode up in the nick of time and ran the savages off. That they fled like the true cowards they are."

Jack said nothing. He just watched the flames as they quickly reduced the lifeless hardwood to ashes. He felt the chilly night air biting into his back.

"He told me …" Ned paused. "Is something wrong, Mr. Percy?"

"We weren't heroes."

Ned leaned down, trying to see Jack's face. "Say again?"

"We were late."

"Late? Well, you couldn't have been late. If you had been delayed any, those people would have died."

"They did."

Confusion washed over the young man's face. "But I was told—"

"Sioux don't run," Jack said.

"But what about Emmit Browne and his wife?" CJ's voice came out soft and hesitant, like he was unsure of himself, unsure if he was out of line.

Ned glanced at CJ. He seemed surprised by the question; surprised the boy didn't seem to know any more than he did.

Jack took out another cigar and bit the end off. He dragged a half-burning stick from the fire and lit it. "What about 'em?"

"Weren't they there?" CJ asked. "Wasn't that the Brownes that went back east?"

Jack held the cigar at eye level and rolled it between his fingers. "There were eight of 'em in all," he said, "in a couple of wagons.

Migrants crossing the territory. They had already come a long way. A *long* way. Everything they had was in those wagons, their whole damned life hitched to a pack of horses."

Jack drew on his smoke and sighed. "But the Sioux were waiting. I reckon they'd scouted 'em miles before and ascertained their route. I figure they came down from the hills, hard and fast, wanting the cargo. The settlers turned their wagons back toward the old fort in Johnson Valley. They made it, but the Sioux cut 'em off before they could get inside and mount a defense."

Jack looked across the flames into the dark forest beyond, watching the scene unfold in his mind's eye. "They just needed another minute or two," he said quietly.

Ned shifted uncomfortably. "But where were you?"

"Due west of the valley," Jack said. "We were headed north when the first shots went off. And then the screaming started, that god-awful screaming. We rode hard and got there in time to see firsthand what it's like for a man to be held down and scalped. The whole valley echoed his screams, but the Sioux wouldn't silence him until they had their trophy. There were already five dead scattered about the wagons and along the edge of the fort."

Jack stopped and took a long, hard drag on the cigar. He drew the smoke painfully deep into his lungs and then exhaled over the fire. He watched the heat snatch the smoke away into the night.

"We came out above 'em, behind an outcropping of rock and brush. There were four raiders, a small group in all but more than enough. Ray started down toward 'em, behind the rock and scrub. I managed two or three carefully aimed shots before they saw me. One fell. The other three returned fire and pinned me down."

Jack looked at CJ. "When the shooting stopped, only Emmit and Renee Browne were still alive. They were clinging to each other under one of the wagons, weeping like infants. Their two eldest boys lay dead only a few feet away from them. Mutilated."

CJ lowered his head.

For a few minutes only the sound of the fire filled the camp, popping and hissing.

Ned was staring at the ground, shaking his head. Finally, he looked at Jack. "What happened to the other three Indians?"

Jack glanced at Raymond, who still had his hat pulled down, still hadn't moved from his spot under the tree. Ned and CJ followed Jack's eyes.

"They were dead too," Jack said.

9

Jack walked up the hill and sat down on a large, moss-covered rock. He took a long drink from his canteen. The water was a thick, icy slush. He opened the map again, though it was no real help. There were no landmarks of any kind, nor was there any way to determine the distance they had covered or had left to cover. It was essentially a piece of paper with an X by Twin Pines and another X, slightly northeast, with Jones Mine scribbled beside it. There was little about the terrain, no water markers, and nothing noteworthy regarding the surrounding area. Basically useless.

He dropped the map beside him on the surface of the rock and shook his canteen. The container was half-empty now, so he screwed the cap back on and placed it on top of the map.

The sun was already pouring thin streams of light back into the forest. He had slept well. *Too well*, he thought, since he hadn't stirred or heard a single thing all night.

Back down the hill, CJ and Ned were still sleeping in heaps around the smoldering remains of the fire. A broken tree limb lay in the leaves beside CJ, evidently used during the night to keep the fire going.

There was, as usual, no sign of Raymond.

Jack's mind returned to the man they sought and the chances that he was still alive. Given the time since he'd last been seen, along with the strong possibility that he was unarmed, and the absurd fact that his family had gone with him, the preacher's odds were lowering considerably by the minute.

Jack shook his head, almost angry, as he thought of the way folks had thrown caution to the wind in these parts. So many had paid dearly, yet so many more were still undeterred. He thought again of Woods Fort and how seemingly unnecessary it all was.

The thought was interrupted, however, by something back down the hill, something to the west of camp. From this distance it was hard to tell what it was, but something was standing perfectly erect, shrouded behind a clump of trees and thick underbrush.

Jack shifted around on the rock. Whatever it was appeared to be about six or seven feet high, perhaps taller, and was completely still. Solid, maybe. Possibly a tree stump. The thing was rounded off at the top, giving the eerie impression of a man's head. Light peered around one side as if exposing an arm.

Jack continued to stare. And the longer he watched, the thing almost seemed to move. He remembered experiencing a similar sort of thing as a boy, lying on his back and gazing at clouds as they crept by overhead. The more he lay there, the more images and likenesses he saw.

But, of course, clouds *did* move.

Now light was leaking around the other side.

Another arm?

Jack started at the sound of rustling leaves to his left. Eli was approaching from the east, farther up the hill. The scout was coming in hard, in an all-out sprint. He tripped over a branch but never broke stride.

Jack grinned and picked up the map.

"Where've you been hiding?"

Eli was already shaking his head as he stopped beside Jack. He bent and put his hands on his knees, then pointed back to the south.

Jack glanced behind him at the cold, empty forest. He patted Eli on the back. "Just take your time and get settled."

Eli snatched his hat off in a quick swatting motion, then stood, eyes wide. His thin, stringy hair was plastered to his forehead, dripping little rivulets of sweat down his cheeks and neck. He was still holding a trembling arm toward the south.

"S-s-soldiers."

Soldiers? Jack thought for a moment. "Oh, yeah. They're headed for some small settlement east of here. Supposed to be about a day's ride northeast of town, if I remember right." He sighed and squeezed Eli's shoulder. "I'm sorry, I just plain forgot to tell you. Cavanaugh said they'd be coming out behind us, but they oughta be breaking off to the east soon. Probably already have."

Eli studied Jack's face, blinking, looking genuinely puzzled. His eyes moved to the ground thoughtfully, and then he began shaking his head as if in conversation with himself. Finally, he looked up.

"Na-na-no."

"No?"

Eli pursed his lips, took a long look over his shoulder. He was shaking his head again when he turned back. "Ain't na-no settlement."

"To the east," Jack said again, wondering if maybe the scout hadn't heard him correctly.

"Yeah, Jack."

Jack said nothing, his turn to puzzle.

"Na-no settlement."

"You're sure?"

"I la-la-looked."

"You looked?"

Eli nodded, quick and confident. He pointed back to the east. "I la-looked. Na-nothin' east."

Jack took his hat off and rubbed his head. As he thought about it, he looked back down the hill for the curious tree stump, but couldn't seem to locate it. When he turned back, he bumped into Eli, who was also leaning and straining to get a better view of something.

Jack followed his gaze back toward the campsite where Ned was up and slowly walking up the incline toward them.

Jack noticed the apprehension rising in the scout and stepped into his line of sight. "You're sure?"

"Yeah, Jack."

Eli peered around Jack at the stranger coming up the hill.

"He's alright," Jack said, but he knew no amount of reassuring could lift the old man's anxiety.

Eli shuffled back.

Jack handed him the map. "Take this. I ain't got no use for it. Maybe you can make heads or tails of it."

Eli snatched it away and hurried off in the direction he'd come from.

"Thanks!" Jack called.

"Who was that?" Ned asked.

Jack watched Eli zigzag in and out of the trees and then finally melt away in the early morning shadows.

"A friend," he said.

"He's with you?"

"He's with us."

Ned glanced in the direction Eli had gone. "Where's his horse?"

"He ain't got one."

"Well, heaven's sake," Ned said. "I can probably get him a deal on an older mare or gelding when we get back to Twin Pines. Mr. Wilkins at the livery stable has—"

"He don't want one."

Ned started to finish, but didn't. He studied Jack as if waiting for the rest of a joke.

"You've got perfume on again," Jack said.

"Cologne, Mr. Percy."

Back down the hill, Jack saw CJ jump out of his bedroll and run awkwardly into a nearby stand of underbrush. "Come on," Jack said. "We gotta get moving."

The terrain leveled off around mid-morning. They had pressed hard again and were making good progress, but were now halted at another creek, this one much wider than any they'd encountered thus far.

Even on horseback, the stream was too wide to jump, and the water too deep and cold to wade across. So they were forced to ride upstream until the creek narrowed sufficiently.

Raymond rode across first and dismounted on the other side. He left his horse to drink while moving farther upstream to refill his canteen.

Ned swung down from his saddle and motioned for Jack and CJ to go on ahead. He then hurried off and vanished into the privacy of the trees.

CJ eased his reluctant horse in next, with Jack following close behind. Sunlight came down unmolested through the cloudless sky, and the air was much better than it had been the previous day. More tolerable. But it was still anything but warm. And the ice-cold water hadn't changed a bit. It stung Jack's flesh, even through his clothes, as the horses hustled across and splashed up the bank on the other side.

Once across, Jack and CJ followed Raymond's lead, watering their horses and topping off canteens.

Ned reemerged from the woods a few minutes later. He walked toward the bank, then stopped and looked around. He glanced at the wooded area behind him and then back down the creek from which they'd come. Then, just as he was starting to look exasperated, he found what he'd been searching for.

His gelding—sharing the cold water with the other three animals on the opposite side of the creek.

Jack noticed the young man's predicament and laughed. "Must've followed us across," he said. "Couldn't wait, I reckon."

Ned smirked.

"Just whistle for him," CJ said.

Ned said nothing. He frowned at the horse as if angry with it, as if the animal had violated some understood protocol. Finally, he squeezed his lips together and made a couple of odd squeaking noises. The sound reminded Jack of an injured rabbit.

The cavalry horse didn't respond.

"You're suckin' in," CJ said. "You're supposed to blow out."

"He's not a dog," Ned said.

"Can't you whistle?"

"Of course I can."

"Well, that ain't no kind of whistlin' I ever heard. Sounds like you're trying to blow him a kiss or somethin'."

Ned glared at CJ, then at his horse. He repeated the same sound a couple more times, but the gelding never lifted his head.

"Whistle!" CJ insisted.

Ned ignored the boy and stepped forward. He peered over the riverbank, sizing it up.

"Just sit tight and we'll bring him back across," Jack said.

Ned was still surveying the gap. He was nodding to himself and looking more and more confident every moment. "I think I can make it."

Jack shook his head. "Ain't worth the risk." He motioned for CJ to lead the horse back across.

"Just hold on," CJ said. "Ain't no way you make that jump."

CJ started toward the horses, but Ned had already stepped back and lowered himself into a sprinter's position.

Jack held his hands up. "Just wait a—"

The young man exploded out of the crouch and bolted toward the riverbank at a dead run. He planted his foot at the edge and, with a short, barely-audible grunt, leapt with all he had. His momentum carried him immediately airborne and into an upward angle above the creek. He soared beautifully, even gracefully, like a natural athlete.

Jack cringed. The young man had given it a heck of a try. For a moment, it even looked like he'd pulled it off. In fact, he probably would have pulled it off had he not slipped, ever so slightly, in that last critical step.

Ned must have concluded the same thing, because at the top of his arc, he began flailing and pumping his arms and legs. His mouth opened in a silent scream, and then the muddy bank on the opposite side received him with a thick, slushy thud.

Jack took his hat off and rubbed his temples. He eased over to the bank.

The young man was covered head-to-toe with the dark clay of the creek bottom. He was back on his feet, but standing motionless, as if frozen, watching the sludge drop lazily from his arms and torso into a heap at his feet.

Jack braced himself and extended a hand.

Ned reached for the offered hand slowly, like the mere act of moving his limbs was challenging now. And then the ground gave way underneath him, and he slid back into the water in a reverse belly slide.

Jack lowered his head, no longer able to watch.

Ned jumped up and high-stepped out of the freezing water. He shook his head, genuinely disgusted now, even angry, and then he looked up. But not at Jack.

CJ was curled up in a ball at the horses' feet. His laughter was so intense that it had passed beyond the point of producing sound. In fact, it was only when the boy had to stop and breathe that he made any noise at all.

Ned just watched him, refusing to move, until CJ finally popped up and struggled over to a stand of young pines farther up the creek. As the boy slipped out of sight his laughter became audible.

Ned waited until he'd fully disappeared before taking Jack's hand.

It took more than a little effort to liberate him, but after a couple of tries Ned was on solid ground again.

The young man stood by the bank, shivering and looking himself over. Since the lower half of his body had gone into the water, his pants and boots were now mostly free of the mud and silt. Mostly. His upper body was a different story.

Jack handed him his hat, which, ironically, had completed the journey across. "You still smell nice."

Ned frowned and took the hat with two careful fingers.

"Just giving you a hard time," Jack said. He pointed upstream. "Go on and get yourself cleaned up. There's probably a spot up the way where you can get to the water and get this stuff off. We'll wait."

"I'll be fine," Ned said.

"Your pride got you dirty, Ned. Don't let it keep you that way."

Ned looked at himself, then up the creek. He shook his head. "I'm fine."

"Suit yourself." Jack turned away.

CJ came out of the pine trees, grinning like an idiot, and Jack couldn't help but smile back at him. It wasn't until then that he noticed Raymond was nowhere around. Nor was his horse. Jack glanced around the immediate area and, when he still didn't see him, took his mare by the reins and led her up the gentle rise to the west.

He spotted his friend from the top of the slope, dismounted and standing by his horse some thirty yards away. Jack called out to him but got no answer. He waited, sensing he shouldn't raise his voice, then finally mounted up and eased his mare down in Raymond's direction.

Raymond was standing near the front of his horse, staring out into the deeper woods.

Jack stayed in the saddle, trying to interpret the look on his friend's face.

Raymond didn't acknowledge him. He was looking straight ahead, carefully probing the forest with his eyes. His head was turned slightly to one side, like he was listening to something.

"Ray?" Jack whispered.

Raymond said nothing, though he did turn his head faintly in Jack's direction.

Jack took the hint. He looked ahead, searching the woods, trying to determine what had his friend's attention. But the forest was calm and silent before them. Even the endless breeze was momentarily at rest. There were no animals stirring, no leaves rustling, and, other than the young men's voices carrying over the hill behind them, there was no sound.

The silence lingered with neither man speaking, and then Raymond's posture finally relaxed a bit. He moved back alongside his horse but continued to watch the woods to the west.

The sound of disturbed leaves rose behind them and Jack turned.

CJ and Ned were just coming over the rise. CJ was looking straight ahead, smirking, while Ned was chipping the drying mud from the sleeves of his jacket.

Jack looked back at Raymond. "What is it?"

Raymond exhaled as he watched the others approaching. "I reckon nothin'."

"You see something?"

"No."

Jack remembered Eli's earlier concerns about the soldiers. But before he could mention it, CJ and Ned were beside them.

The two were apparently just concluding their latest quarrel. In fact, Ned had now completely turned his back to the boy and was digging through his saddlebags, likely for the journal.

CJ was still laughing, still smiling broadly. But as his eyes met Jack's, the amusement began to fade. The corners of his mouth turned down. His lips tightened.

The two held each other in curious stares for a beat, and then looked out at the forest over each other's shoulders.

CJ was turning pale.

Jack eyed the boy, then Ned. The slosh of dead leaves underfoot was still there, still as clear as the bright shining sun. Only, now, no one was moving.

Jack looked at Raymond, who was already pulling his rifle from its scabbard.

In the woods directly ahead, the slope turned up sharply about twenty yards out and then climbed steadily upward. The sound was there, somewhere, but hard to locate. At moments, it seemed to be everywhere in front of them, echoing from the trees and uneven terrain. Then it would shift, turn east, then west, then nothing.

Then everywhere again.

Raymond smacked the hindquarter of his horse and moved up against a tree. His mare quickly bolted away and disappeared.

Jack turned in his saddle, hoping the source of the noise wasn't somehow behind them too.

The horses reared in an explosion of panic, and Jack saw Ned thrown to the ground.

Jack spun around so fast that pain splintered through his lower back. He winced and looked up just in time to see someone streaking down the hill in front of them.

Coming in and out of the trees, dodging, jumping, weaving—disappearing and reemerging. And then clearly, the unmistakable long, dark hair of an Indian.

10

The Indian came down the hill with the speed and grace of a young deer. She darted through the brush at the foot of the slope, leapt over a fallen tree, and landed flat-footed directly in front of Jack and the others.

She immediately recoiled and cried out when she saw them, and then backpedaled and thrust out a hand to shield herself.

Jack sat motionless in his saddle. Tense. His pistol was drawn but held low, beyond the view of the intruder. He eased the hammer back.

The young woman's eyes flicked nervously from one man to the next until she'd taken in the whole group. Then she twisted around and searched the area behind her, and the steep rise leading back into the forest from which she'd come. Her distress was palpable when she turned back and faced Jack. Her reddish-brown flesh was a shade lighter than it should've been, and the thick white lines painted along each side of her face had been smeared considerably by tears.

Raymond was still standing by the tree, his rifle pointing at the ground. His eyes weren't on the woman, but the hill behind her.

Ned groaned as he slowly collected himself from the ground.

Jack raised his free hand toward the young men at his left. "Easy, now."

The woman took a hesitant step, stopped, then looked back up the hill. Her eyes were big and round and focused. But there was an unmistakable urgency there, too, a rigidness in her wiry frame impossible to miss.

Jack noticed crimson splotches peppered and smeared on her legs and feet, and how they were multiplying and thickening with each rapid pump of her heart. The blood was coming from an open gash in her upper left arm and was dripping off her fingertips with severe consistency.

He also noticed the knife scabbard attached to her waist. Empty.

She was clinging to something in her right hand. It wasn't the missing blade, but some sort of round object with a stick running through the center. The stick was adorned with a handful of smooth, gray stones, each of which carried various markings that meant nothing to Jack. At the bottom of the circular object, four or five loose feathers swung freely and quivered with each tremble of her hand.

Again she looked back, apparently more concerned with what lay unseen behind her than the four white men. She raised an unsteady hand and pointed at the hill.

"*Wackhan sica!*"

Jack holstered his pistol and held both hands out in front of him.

She squinted and studied his hands, as if trying to interpret the gesture, then leapt in place and thrust a finger behind her. "*Wackhan sica!*"

"I don't understand," Jack said.

"*Okiya!*"

Her voice was raw emotion. Fresh tears slipped off her cheeks. She touched her hands together and held them out to him, perhaps trying to mimic his own gesture. Blood dripped audibly on the leaves at her feet. She pointed at the forest beyond and then slowly brought her hands up to her chest. She met his eyes.

"*Omakiya yo.*"

Jack saw movement from the corner of his eye, either from CJ or his horse.

"Nobody moves."

He turned his palms up toward the woman. "I don't understand," he said. "Is that your name?"

Another tear. She patted her chest and tugged at her coat.

"*Okiya.*"

Jack said nothing, didn't know what to say.

The woman finally lowered her hands and looked away. And what Jack saw in her then broke any and all barriers imposed by spoken language. What he saw at once tore at his heart and sent tremors through his spine.

He pointed at her arm. "You'll be needin' help with that."

She looked at the object in her right hand, massaged it gently between her thumb and forefinger. When she spoke again it was barely perceptible, only slightly more than a whisper.

Her voice was soft and young, almost enchanting. But her words were as unsteady as the rest of her being, bearing that same slight quiver. Only, these weren't just words this time; that was clear. They were lyrics, anguished and sincere. Piercing. A prayer, maybe. She closed her eyes, squeezing out more tears, and seemed to focus her senses elsewhere.

Jack watched her, inexplicably drawn in by her whispered song. He felt a sudden and powerful sense of pity and sorrow, a deep sadness and remorse over something he didn't understand. It was like watching someone wring blood from a raw open wound.

Then she was silent. When her eyes opened again, she was facing north. There were no more tears.

Jack saw something different then. He saw resignation. He saw defeat.

He started to speak, but she turned and jogged off to the north before he could. Just as suddenly as she had come, she was gone. Never looking back.

Jack swung down from his horse and unsheathed his rifle. He started toward the hill, but Raymond grabbed him firmly by the arm.

"Those damn cavalry boys are gonna get us all killed," Jack said. "Their scouts are out there messin' around, and if we leave 'em unchecked, they're gonna bring the entire Sioux nation down on us like a storm."

Raymond said nothing, nor did he relax his grip. He stared up the hill.

Jack took another step forward and Raymond's grip tightened. He could feel the power in his friend's fingers, the seriousness.

"What?" Jack asked sharply.

Raymond shook his head.

"What?" Jack asked again.

"Don't."

"Why?"

"Just don't."

"You know what she said?"

Raymond shook his head.

Jack glared at the woods, searching and listening. The Sioux woman was gone, vanished soundlessly into the thicket to his right. The hill from which she'd come was calm and still. The forest around them returned to normal, static and unremarkable.

Jack lowered his rifle.

Raymond let go.

Jack called over his shoulder to Ned.

Ned's voice came back with a hint of pain. "Yes?"

"You know what she said?"

"No."

Jack swore and returned the rifle to his horse. "You alright?"

"I'm okay," Ned said.

Jack knelt over the blood the woman had left behind. He took his hat off and squinted up the hill, replaying the scene in his mind. He stayed that way, watching and waiting, questioning.

The forest offered no answers.

The day pressed into late afternoon with everyone mostly quiet. They had all been a little shaken by the event earlier in the day. More than once it had crossed Jack's mind to call the whole thing off, to just do an about-face and head back to Twin Pines. But he didn't. He just kept riding, like the others, at a silent, intermediate pace, north.

Before dusk, the woods gave way to a large clearing, the largest they'd encountered so far. In fact, the empty landscape seemed out of place in the otherwise dense forest. It was wide open and inviting, sloping away gently back toward the woods to the east. It was level and mostly dirt but had a fair stand of grass as well. A welcome sight. And after being cramped in the claustrophobic wilderness for nearly two days now, it was like a glimpse of heaven. Even breathing seemed easier.

The clearing stretched out beneath a large, dusty hill that rose back into the forest to the northwest. Farther west, at the edge of the hill, a small creek dropped down sharply in a thin but eye-pleasing waterfall. The waning sunlight and shades of the surrounding area reflected in the waterfall, making it difficult not to stop and stare. The hiss of the water landing below, while faint, was calming.

But Jack stared at the hill. The fatigue of a long day was already heavy in his bones. And the hill was north, directly in their path. It loomed over them, long and steep, littered with jagged rock unearthed gradually by time and elements. At a glance, the large rocks seemed to be absurdly blooming from the dust-covered grade. A scattering of brush and the occasional tree also peppered the slope, but it was largely dirt and stone from bottom to top. It would take time to negotiate.

With maybe an hour of daylight left, Jack was tempted to stop and call it a day. He wanted to. The place was perfect for a campsite, wide open and unrestricting. But that also bothered him. It was too perfect. Too exposed. Too vulnerable.

He turned to CJ and Ned, who were shifting around in their saddles, taking in the scenery. "Let's get this over with."

Their exhaustion was obvious, but neither protested.

Raymond was by the creek with his horse, watching the water inch endlessly past. He knelt to fill his canteen as the others took to the hill.

It took time. The horses needed motivation, and there was more than a little shouting and swearing, but overall they navigated the daunting slope without incident. The top rewarded them with a view even more remarkable than the one below. Jack sat there while the younger men moved on, resting his mare and watching the sun dip toward the western horizon in its unique evening blend of oranges and purples.

Lengthening shadows and encroaching cold eventually beckoned him back to the woods.

He went reluctantly.

CJ busied himself with the fire, while Ned disappeared back in the direction of the creek—undoubtedly to get the rest of the frozen mud off his clothes.

Jack slipped away. He needed to think. He walked east for a while, familiarizing himself with the general terrain as he went. It was all the same—hardwoods, saplings, and scrub as far as he could see. Dead leaves crunched noisily under his feet.

Then the foliage abruptly ended and he was standing atop a huge rock. The rock was massive, gigantic, the very backbone of mountain beneath him, and probably as old as the world itself. It overlooked what seemed to be a hundred valleys, lying just below an early yellow moon.

Jack drank in a deep breath. His pulse slowed and his shoulders relaxed. The sensation was like emerging from a long, punishing run through a gauntlet. He slipped a cigar from his pocket and lit up, then just stood there, soaking in the serenity while it lasted. Because he knew it wouldn't last. It never did.

As if on cue, his mind wandered back to earlier in the day. The thought of Sioux being so close was no surprise, but seeing one had made their presence more immediate, more troubling.

And the woman. The desperate look on her face, the wounded arm, the regular *tick, tick, tick* of her blood on the leaves. Encountering her had aroused both sadness and, surprisingly, anger in him. He was convinced some of the cavalry scouts, riding far ahead of the main body of soldiers—and, consequently, their superiors—had been having their fun with her. But he knew that wasn't the only possibility. It was also possible that she was running from her own people. Breaking the law of the clan or crossing tribal lines could bring strong retribution, and could also go a long way toward explaining her panic.

But what was she trying to tell him? And why? After all, he was the enemy. Wasn't he? He recalled the surprised expression on her face when she stumbled upon them. The way she kept looking back into the forest, the way her eyes never stopped searching for the next place to run. The way she'd held out her hands to him.

It had been the look of desperation. The look of prey.

Red skin or pale, her humanity had spoken clearly.

She was afraid.

Jack saw movement to his left and turned to see Raymond approaching from the north. His friend was walking along the edge of the great rock, also admiring the view, and seemed oblivious to the fatal fall that surely awaited anyone who would lose their footing. He stopped beside Jack and smiled—not with his lips, as he seldom ever did, but with his eyes.

They both stood in silence for several minutes. Finally, Jack let out a long, reluctant breath. "I reckon you know the cavalry hasn't broken off yet."

Raymond tilted his head back and closed his eyes. "Yeah."

"Don't make sense," Jack said. "They should be a day southeast of us by now, if not more."

"Ain't no point in trying to make sense of them boys."

Jack faced him. "What was it back there with the squaw? Who was she running from?"

Raymond continued to take in the view. His eyes scanned over the numerous hills and valleys below and then out to the horizon. "I don't know," he said finally.

"Why'd you hold me back?"

"*Because* I didn't know."

Jack took a last hit from his smoke and scratched it out on the surface of the rock. He dropped the unused half in his pocket. "She seemed like ..." He paused, thinking it over. "That song, her eyes ... it was like she'd given up on something. It was like she—"

"She hadn't given up," Raymond interrupted. "But she *was* preparing to lose."

"Lose what?"

"All."

Jack shook his head. "No way those cavalry boys would kill her," he said. "Not out here. Surely they're not that stupid. They'd be calling down the thunder."

Raymond said nothing.

Jack started to continue but was cut short by a sound in the brush behind them. He turned.

The noise went on for some time: leaves shuffling, sticks snapping, bushes rustling, and then swearing. Finally, CJ staggered out onto the rock, pulling thorns from his legs and leaves from his hair. He straightened, brushed himself off, then looked out at the view.

"Whoa."

Jack watched the young man's eyes slowly go over the palette beneath them and then up to the yellow moon. He looked very young in the dwindling light.

"Ned's back there by himself?" Jack asked.

The boy shrugged. "He's got his pencil."

Jack grunted.

CJ gestured behind him. "Probably shouldn't go back that way," he said. "I mean ... uh ..." He cleared his throat. "You definitely don't wanna go back that way."

Jack cocked his head.

"'Cause I ... I wasn't really ... I didn't come out here lookin' for y'all."

"Thanks for the tip," Jack said. "Feeling better?"

"My arse quit burnin'."

"That's a start."

"I figure that's how Mexican folk knows it's time to eat again," the boy said. "When their arses quit burning."

Jack chuckled. "I reckon it takes a strong man to stomach that stuff." He looked around for Raymond, hoping to resume their conversation. But his friend was already walking back to the north the same way he'd come, along the edge of the rock.

Jack watched him go.

"Stronger man than me, anyhow," CJ agreed. "Like Ned's grandma, maybe."

"So what does it stand for, then?"

"It don't stand for nothin'. It's just CJ. Why's that so hard for ya?"

"Because you're lying. It's obviously short for something."

"Well, it ain't."

Ned laughed. "Must be *really* bad."

CJ was changing colors. "I'll tell you what's *really* bad, is being stuck out here in the wilderness with a grown man that still acts like he's knee-high to a mosquito."

Ned closed his journal; his body jerked as he continued to laugh silently.

"You clean up nice," Jack said, again hoping to change the subject.

Ned had spent a good deal of time at the creek, as was evidenced by his wet clothing, and had gotten rid of most of the mud. He nodded to Jack, taking the hint.

"Like blowin' flies off a turd," CJ mumbled.

Jack took his hat off and set it beside him. He was thinking about the next day and how much farther he was willing to go. He was already deeper into the thicket than he'd ever wanted to be. Asheworth had said it was three or four days' ride, and that was precisely why he'd pressed on so hard, determined to make four days' time in three. But how did the colonel know how far it was? Had he ever even *been* to this Jones Mine? Had he just been guessing?

Jack took a last bite from his supper and tossed the remaining hardtack toward his mare. He fished out the unused cigar from earlier and then glanced across the fire at CJ, who was ignoring everyone and everything. Jack knew he'd have to—

A rustling sound stopped him mid-thought. The noise was coming from the direction of the creek. A shuffling in the dead leaves, then nothing. Then the same sound again, only farther up the creek, and then silence.

Jack glanced at Raymond, who hadn't lifted his hat from his eyes. CJ turned in the direction of the noise, but, of course, couldn't see anything. Darkness had come quickly, as it often did in the woods, and visibility had been reduced to nearly nothing.

They all listened as the sound came and went again. And the more they heard it, the more difficult it was to identify. At one moment, it sounded very much like footsteps, treading through the leaves and brush. In the next, it was like the clatter of a bush shaken by the wind.

Jack could tell CJ and Ned were unnerved. Having seen an Indian earlier in the day wasn't helping. Neither of them, he figured, had ever laid eyes on a live in-the-flesh Sioux.

Jack wasn't immune, either. Deep down, he had no real confidence they weren't camped in the middle of a Sioux stronghold. The thought concerned him, but he still believed the cavalry scouts were out there stirring things up, and had played their part with the woman. He glanced again at Raymond, who still had his head down, his old black hat covering his face.

The noise subsided, and CJ's and Ned's attention slowly returned to the fire. CJ looked at Jack as if hoping for an explanation.

"It's the unknown that scares us, you know," Ned whispered.

CJ glared at him. "What?"

"The unknown," Ned said. "It's because you can't see it that it scares you."

"No, it's 'cause it might be another gol-derned Indian."

"That's right," Ned said. "But it might've been a squirrel too. You see, it's always the unknown. It's not the night that scares us, it's what might be *out there* in the dark, what we can't see. It's what we don't know that makes us nervous."

"Ain't no squirrels out here," CJ grumbled.

Ned looked at Jack. "I think everything we fear, even death, eventually comes down to the unknown. Think about it: we don't know if it'll hurt or how long it might last. We don't know if our loved ones will be okay when we're gone or what waits for us on the other side, or if there really is another side." He looked back at CJ and tapped the side of his head. "That thing out there worrying us may only be in here."

CJ sat quietly a moment, apparently considering it, then said, "I ain't got no idea what you just said."

Ned sighed. "Wouldn't you agree, Mr. Percy?"

"I don't know," Jack said, as he thought of things he knew very well, but which terrified him still. He looked at Raymond, who by all appearances seemed oblivious to it all. Jack figured there was some truth to what Ned was saying. Most men did fear the unknown. It seemed a natural thing, like all common fears and desires, just built right in from the womb.

But not Raymond McAlister. Jack had never seen fear in him. The things that made most men anxious, and some men flee, was precisely when Raymond seemed the most comfortable. Jack had always marveled at that part of him. The unknown, it seemed, was exactly what he longed for, the catalyst which gave him life. Not even death seemed to concern him.

CJ glanced sideways at Ned. "So you're sayin' if I hit you in the head, that noise will go away?"

The sound returned before Ned could respond. But this time it was different. This time it was coming from the south. The noise sounded far off at first, rising and falling and occasionally shifting direction. But that quickly changed. It started growing louder, clearer, gradually moving toward the camp. And not slowly.

Footfalls.

Ned rolled over and looked into the darkness behind him. The young man had been lying by the fire, warming and drying his damp clothing. He pushed up on one elbow.

Jack's gun belt was on the ground beside him. He slid his fingers over the butt of his revolver.

Raymond lifted the brim of his hat with one finger, shook his head at Jack, then dropped the hat back over his face.

The footsteps picked up behind Ned. This time they were close. Very close. Ned sat up and turned around.

A lone silhouette emerged from the blackness, running in from behind him. The figure broke into the firelight like a spirit from another world.

A sick moan escaped from somewhere inside Ned's body and he jumped up and stumbled backward. He apparently didn't realize he was standing in the campfire until the odor of burning cloth reached his nose. He immediately looked down and hopped in place, blasting a shower of sparks into CJ's lap, and then scurried out of the fire, dragging two smoldering logs with him.

"Sa-sa-sorry," Eli said. The scout hurried over, picked up the displaced firewood and tossed it back in the fire. "Sa-sa-sorry."

CJ leaned away to keep from being covered in ash again.

Eli stomped out the burning leaves at Ned's feet. "Sa-sa-sorry."

Ned watched in silence, hand over his chest.

Eli reached for him, but then hesitated and drew back. He hurried over to Jack and dragged him away from the others. "They're st-st-still there."

"Soldiers?"

"Yeah, Jack."

Jack looked back toward the fire. Ned was returning to his seat, inspecting the hem of his pants. "You seen any of their scouts up this far?"

Eli rubbed his arms. "Ain't s-s-seen 'em, bu-but they're out there."

Jack gave him a questioning look.

"I hear 'em," Eli said. The scout jumped at a noise somewhere out in the woods and turned toward the sound.

Jack waited.

"They're ga-ga-good," Eli finally whispered. "Keep ma-ma-movin', ka-ka-keep outta sight."

"Seen any Indians?"

Eli shook his head.

"You sure?"

"Yeah, Jack."

"We saw a squaw this morning," Jack said. "She was injured and acting like somebody was chasing her."

Eli's eyes narrowed. "Ain't sa-sa-saw no Indians."

Jack nodded but found himself wondering if maybe Eli could be misinterpreting what he was hearing, if perhaps whoever was moving around out there wasn't cavalry after all, but Sioux. The thought made him shudder.

"No Indians?"

"Na-na-no Indians."

"Any sign of 'em?"

"Ain't saw na-na-no Indians."

Jack sighed. "I figure there's a good chance the Sioux's north of here." He gestured back to the south. "And if the cavalry's back there, as you say ..." He trailed off and looked at the men around the fire. "I'm starting to wonder if it's worth it. I mean ..." He glanced back at Eli, but the old scout was staring deep into the dark, cloudless sky.

Jack smiled. "Won't you join us by the fire for a spell?"

Eli's head snapped around like he'd been slapped. He pointed south. "The s-s-s-s—"

Jack slid an arm around him and pulled him back to the campfire. He stopped at the place he'd been sitting and held a hand out at the empty space beside it.

Eli looked at Ned, then CJ.

"Howdy, Eli," CJ said.

Eli waved to the boy with a trembling hand. He inspected the area beneath him, ran his hands through the leaves, looked over his shoulder. He finally sat down and leaned back, peering up through the treetops.

Ned tore a sheet out of his ledger and folded it. He reached across the edge of the fire and handed it to Jack.

Jack took it with a curious look on his face. He unfolded the page and turned to catch the firelight. It read …

Wackhan sica.
Okiya.

"I think she was beautiful," Ned said, and then cringed, obviously waiting for a jibe from CJ.

None came.

"She was," Jack said.

"That's some of what she said. Or at least I think it was," Ned said. He was turning his pencil around in his hands. "I couldn't catch it all, but I recorded what I could, you know, in case you ever befriend an Indian."

Jack grunted. "Don't reckon that'll be anytime soon." He folded the paper up and slipped it into his pocket. "Much obliged."

Ned nodded and tucked the pencil in his ledger.

Silence returned, and Jack could feel Eli's discomfort, literally *feel* it. Aside from the occasional glance at the forest behind him, the scout was mostly keeping his head down now.

Ned rubbed his arms and slid closer to the fire. He was still shivering, still paying the price for his failed leap earlier in the day. "Good gracious," he said, "it's cold as hell out here. I don't think it ever gets this cold back east, even when it snows. We had a blizzard when I was a boy, but even then—"

"That's ignorant," CJ interrupted.

Ned stopped and rolled his eyes, evidently refusing to indulge whatever the boy was thinking.

CJ didn't need prompting. "Hell ain't cold," he said. "Just wait, you'll see."

Eli's eyes widened.

"It's a manner of speaking," Ned said. "But I wouldn't expect you to know what that is."

CJ huffed.

Eli watched the fire as if afraid to look up.

Ned folded his arms. "What would you say, then?"

"Me?" CJ asked.

"Yeah, you."

"I'd say it's colder than a witch's teat."

"A witch's teat?" Ned laughed. "And how would you know the temperature of a witch's teat?"

"It just makes sense," CJ said. "Think about it."

"I don't want to think about it!"

Jack sighed, shook his head. "I reckon y'all beat all I've ever seen."

"That's ra-ra-right," Eli whispered to no one in particular. "They are ca-ca-cold."

Everyone paused and looked at Eli.

The scout nodded confidently, eyes still on the fire. "I knew wa-one."

Jack chuckled, but CJ and Ned just stared at the old scout.

Still nodding and with complete sincerity in his eyes, Eli turned to Jack. "I na-knew wa-one, an-and her tee-tee-teats were ca-cold."

Jack smiled, but with a question in his eyes.

Eli kept nodding.

"You knew one?" Ned asked.

"Yeah," Eli said.

"A witch?"

"Yeah."

"When?"

"La-la-long time ago."

"What did she look like?"

Eli shrugged. "Pa-pa-purdy at first, bu-but changed."

"Changed?"

"Yeah."

"How?"

"She hay-hay-hated me."

Ned's eyes narrowed. He looked around the fire conspiratorially. "She do something to you?"

"Yeah."

"What?"

"She di-di-divorced me."

The woods erupted with the roar of Raymond's laughter.

Eli jumped as if snake-bit. The old man scrambled back on his seat and nearly toppled over.

Raymond went on laughing.

Eli collected himself, grinned nervously at Raymond, and then glanced around the campfire, where the two younger men had also joined in.

Jack reached for him, but Eli popped up and began backpedaling. Jack stood and put a hand on the scout's shoulder, trying to reassure him. Eli's body jolted at the touch.

"Ga-ga-gotta go."

"No you don't," Jack said. "At least get yourself warm before you set out."

Eli pointed to the south but didn't say anything. He looked up at the sky and began wringing the brim of his hat.

Jack watched as the old man struggled, watched as his remaining poise crumbled and fell apart. He said, "Your seat is always here."

Eli glanced at the firelight, then back to the south. "S-s-s—"

"Go on and keep an eye on 'em for us," Jack said.

Eli hurried away and disappeared into the darkness.

Ned was snoring in no time, which was no surprise considering the day he'd had. CJ held on, gazing wearily at the firelight, each blink of his eyes longer than the last.

Jack watched as the young man finally slumped over and drifted off. He wondered how Jonas would feel about the situation his boy was in—far away in the northern forest, with Indians likely nearby, and temperatures low enough to kill a man. The absurdity of the whole thing finally sank in. Deep down, Jack would've loved nothing more than to bring the preacher and his family back out. But deeper still he knew the clergyman had probably already met his fate.

He looked again at CJ, and then Ned. Neither of them belonged out here, nor did he or Raymond. He decided then, he would call it off in the morning. They would eat and turn back. Maybe the cavalry would provide them an escort. If so—if the cavalry agreed to take the young men out—then he and Raymond might continue on another day or so.

Maybe.

He lay down and put his hat over his face. Either way, he was going to get these boys back home.

Jack jolted at the scream. He lifted his hat off his face. CJ was still sleeping, but Ned was awake, eyes round and worried.

It came again, loud and high-pitched, and not too far off.

Jack felt chills run through him, and saw them run through Ned. The young man sat up.

Jack glanced over at Raymond, who hadn't lifted his hat but had turned an ear toward the sound.

CJ raised his head, squinting and blinking, and they all listened quietly.

Silence.

"Bobcat," Jack said finally, though he wasn't really sure if the animals even lived in this part of the country.

CJ nodded, but Ned was unconvinced. "How do you know?" he whispered. "Sounded like a scream to me. Like a woman screaming."

"I don't know," Jack said. "But that's what a bobcat sounds like."

That didn't help. Ned stoked the fire and stood up. He reached across CJ and grabbed an armful of fresh wood and added each piece until the flames were stretching up long and high again.

Jack watched him sympathetically, knowing he wouldn't sleep very much now. CJ, on the other hand, had already returned to his dreams.

Raymond hadn't moved. But he had raised his hat and was staring off into the woods.

The silence persisted, and Jack finally lay back down. He was awake for some time, never hearing anything more—aside from Ned occasionally adding fuel to the fire. And then slowly, almost stubbornly, he drifted back off.

11

Jack awoke to the ground moving beneath him. Sticks and loose stones twisted and gouged into his back. He opened his eyes to the dark underside of his hat and blinked. He was being pulled through the dirt and leaves. Someone, or something, had a hold of him, a hold of his jacket. Dragging him. He jabbed a hand to his side, searching for his pistol, found an empty holster. Adrenaline flooded his system, cold and then hot. He swatted his hat away and leapt to his feet.

There was a silhouette before him, obscured and backlit by the sun. Jack fell back a step. The early morning light besieged his eyes. He reached around his back for his blade. It wasn't there. It was still in his saddlebags. He dared a glance toward the horses. If he could—

"Sa-sa-sorry."

Jack deflated. Literally. All the energy that had coursed through his body so suddenly now stopped and hardened into burning knots. He lowered his head, drew in a breath and held it. It didn't help. His heart and chest were still pounding when he looked up and focused on the old scout.

Eli was bouncing on his feet, obviously agitated, but struggling to find words. He was pointing to the north with one hand and holding Jack's revolver in the other.

Jack watched him for a beat, still waiting to sober from the adrenaline high. He fought back a blind urge to swear at the man, something he knew he'd regret. Instead, he took his sidearm back and re-holstered it.

Raymond walked into the camp from the east and stopped beside Eli. He had whittled one end of a short hickory branch into a fine point and was picking his teeth with it. He paused, however, when he noticed the scout's desperation.

"Ca-ca-coming up the hi-hill."

Confused, Jack followed Eli's finger, which pointed north. The soldiers were south. Weren't they?

"Cavalry?"

"Na-na-no."

Jack glanced at Raymond, then back to Eli. He shook his head.

"They ga-ga-got her."

Jack reached out to the scout. "Just take your time and get—"

"Na-no!" Eli shook his head violently, as if trying to sling off whatever was clogging his power to communicate. He raised his hand again and stabbed a finger toward the north. "They st-st-stole her!"

Stole her? Jack thought. "A squaw?"

"Na-na-no." Eli dug into his pocket and came out with something small and silver. He handed it to Jack.

Jack turned the palm-sized item around in his hand.

"Compass?"

Eli nodded.

"Where'd you get this?"

"Ou-ou-outta their te-tent."

"Whose tent?"

Eli just pointed north again.

Jack tossed the compass to Raymond, who gave it a quick once-over and then offered it back to Eli.

Eli turned away from it.

"Ca-couldn't ga-get her. They ga-ga-got ra-rope around her na-neck."

"Good lord," Jack said. "Who does?"

Eli pulled his hat off, held it with both hands. "She's ga-ga-got hair la-like sunshine." He raised two quivering fingers. "Two ma-ma-men. She wa-was screamin'."

Jack looked at Raymond. Realization settled on both of them.

The bobcat of last night.

"Slave traders," Jack said.

"Yeah, Jack."

Jack looked back toward the camp. CJ and Ned were still asleep.

"Leave 'em," Raymond said.

Jack nodded.

They untied their horses and led them quietly away from the others. Eli ran ahead to the north and quickly disappeared from sight. After they were a sufficient distance from camp, Jack and Raymond swung onto their mounts and kicked them into a swift run.

They caught up to Eli at a clearing. The scout was peering down the crest of a small hill. The hill arched slightly near the top and then gradually sloped back toward the forest below, leveling out just before the first line of trees.

Eli pointed down the slope. "Here."

"What's here?" Jack asked.

Eli didn't answer. He took a step back and turned an ear to the woods below.

Jack listened as well, but heard nothing. He watched Eli take another step back, stop, listen, and then scramble up the slope behind them and vanish into the forest.

Raymond came alongside Jack as Eli disappeared. He spurred his horse lazily along the top of the hill, surveying the area below. When he reached the edge of the clearing, he dismounted and gave his mare a hard smack on the hindquarter. She loped off into the woods and Raymond stepped into the trees behind her.

Jack stayed at the top of the hill, still mounted and suddenly alone. Seconds turned into minutes, and the stillness of the forest stirred the growing feeling of solitude. His mind began sifting through possible scenarios, then more probable ones. And then the first faint sound of trampled leaves reached his ears from below.

At first, that was all it was, leaves and sticks, maybe the snort of a horse. But as the noise grew and came closer, the distinctive sound of voices emerged. The voices of men. Laughter. Shouting. But also, here and there, like a faint echo, the quieter and higher pitched sob of a woman.

Against his better judgment, Jack closed his eyes, hoping that by neglecting the one sense the others would sharpen. It had worked for him before. But the sounds from below were very close now, becoming clearer, and there was no more time.

He eased his mare back a few steps, removing her from the view at the base of the hill.

"Get on now! Ain't got all godforsaken day! And stop that golderned whining. You're giving me the headache."

The voice seemed directly in front of Jack, though he couldn't see anyone yet. The laughter that followed it was at roughly the same distance but farther to his left.

He waited.

The tops of their heads emerged first, followed by bodies, and then horses. Two men, traveling parallel to one another, with a space of about forty feet between them. Both on undernourished brown studs.

The one to Jack's left was middle-aged with a short, greasy brown beard. He was laid back in the saddle, head skyward, one hand holding his hat, the other tilting an unmarked bottle. Much of the liquid was missing its target, however, and instead ran evenly down his chin and throat and dripped from his snarled beard.

The other man was coming up directly in front of Jack, and was much older. He also wore a beard, but his was long and white. He held the reins of his horse casually in his right hand. In his left, the end of a rope was twisted securely around his knuckles. The rope was roughly fifteen feet long and sagged out in front of the old man's horse in a tight arc.

It ended around the throat of a young blonde-haired woman.

But barely a woman. She staggered in front of the old man's horse, goaded by his shouts and curses. Her head was down, arms lifeless by her sides. She looked to be in her mid to late teens and was smeared with dirt and leaves from head to foot.

The older man was the first to notice the lone rider stationed on the ridge. He pulled up and gave the rope a sharp yank, snatching the girl off her feet and hard to the ground. Her mouth opened to cry out, but there was only a whimper. She coughed and rolled onto her side, doing her best to restore the hem of her dirty brown dress, which had flown up in the fall.

The greasy drunk to Jack's left spat a stream of whiskey on the ground and ran a hand across his chest. He watched the girl until she'd covered her bare legs, then turned his eyes to Jack. They were wild eyes, malevolent, but unfocused.

"Howdy," Jack said. His pistol was drawn, hammer back, but lowered out of view. "What might you fellas be up to this fine mornin'?"

"Cut the shit, stranger," the drunk said. "You knows damn well what we're doin'."

The girl had climbed to her knees and had both hands around the rope at her throat. She appeared to be struggling to swallow.

"You a marshal?" the older man asked. His voice came out deep and throaty. He was wearing a fur-skin coat, buffalo maybe. The coat was backwoods but of fine craftsmanship, probably traded or taken from an Indian.

Jack looked back at the girl. She was coughing again but seemed to be breathing okay. Her wet, bloodshot eyes were fixed on him.

"I asked you a question, son!" the older man shouted.

Jack said nothing.

The drunk slid off his horse and stepped in front of it. He still gripped the bottle tight in his left hand but his right was tucked behind him; the holster at his side was empty.

"You ain't gotta talk," the old man said. "That's up to you. But if you know what's good, you'll just go on and move along. We got somewheres to be and won't be toleratin' no delay."

The drunk spat and came a step closer to Jack's mare.

"I reckon you're there," Jack said.

The old man shook his head impatiently, as if Jack were a child struggling to comprehend something.

"You reckon, do ya?" the drunk said. "You best not be thinkin' of nothin' silly now, mister. Ain't no heroes out here in the wilderness." He held up two dirty fingers. "Ain't but two kinds of men out here in the wilderness: there's the man that's breathin' and the man that ain't. That's it." He grinned and snickered through gapped teeth. "That's all there is."

He took another step toward Jack's horse.

"That'll be close enough," Jack said. He was struggling to keep one eye on the drunk and the other on the old man. "Just leave the rope and be on your way."

"I ain't gonna do that, son," the old man said. "Ain't gonna happen. Your time for choosin's running out. Last time now: you can either move aside, real nice like, or I'll be riding over your dead body. That's the deal. Plain and easy. Makes me no nevermind either way."

"They killed my pa!" the girl screamed.

The rope jerked again. Hard. She fell and rolled into the legs of the old man's stud, then lay gasping.

"We're done here," the old man said. He nodded to his comrade and began drawing his rifle from its scabbard. "You had ample warning, son. I ain't never been one to repeat myself, and I damn sure ain't gonna start now."

Jack tensed. He felt the drunk closing ground from his left, heard the mechanical click of a revolver. It was all happening too fast. He raised his pistol at the old man. Had to. Had to choose.

A single gunshot exploded like a thunderclap to his left. Jack ducked and swung his pistol around in time to see the drunk falling backward to the ground. The man landed like a stone, one arm folded beneath him and the other splayed lifelessly over his head. The unmarked bottle came to rest by his shoulder, gurgling and emptying its contents onto the ground. The drunk blinked once as if confused by the puddle of whiskey growing by his face. His lips parted, and then the light behind his eyes dimmed and winked out.

Raymond unloaded the drunk's pistol and dropped it on his chest. He stepped over the dead man's body and slapped the abandoned stud. The horse reared and darted back down the hill.

The older man was stunned. Having never gotten his rifle from its scabbard, he was defenseless. He held his hands out in front of him. "Whoa, now, fellas."

Raymond tossed something to him. The old man caught it with a bear-like paw and looked it over, confused.

His compass.

"How'd—"

"Leave the rope," Jack said.

The old man released the end of the rope and it dropped to the ground.

The girl immediately began trying to liberate herself, but the rope was obviously well woven and the knot sound. When she looked up, Jack saw the new tears and strain in her eyes, but also fresh determination.

"Leave the rifle, too, and be on your way," Jack said.

The old man began pulling his rifle from its sheath, but then hesitated. He glanced at his fallen comrade, then, while holding Raymond in his peripheral vision, turned his head slowly in Jack's direction. His grip on the rifle tightened. The knuckles on his hand paled.

Jack nodded toward the dead man. "Only two kinds of men out here in the wilderness."

The old man studied Jack for a long moment, then finished drawing his rifle and dropped it to the ground. He scanned the forest around them. "You fellas don't know what you're doing," he said. "They won't like you taking their prize."

Jack said nothing. He holstered his pistol and watched as the old man turned and eased his horse back down the hill and into the woods below. His rifle lay on the ground but that alone probably hadn't disarmed him. Jack had a strong urge to stop the old man, take him back to Twin Pines if nothing else. But the man disappeared and he just looked on. Jack satisfied himself with the thought of reporting him to the cavalry on their way out. It was their job to clean up the trash of this territory, not his.

The girl continued to grapple with the rope. She'd managed to widen the loop a bit but had also tightened the knot. It still wouldn't slip over her head.

"Can I help you, miss?" Jack asked.

She paused a moment to dry her eyes, but then attacked the rope again. She said nothing.

Jack leaned back in the saddle and gave her space. He watched as Raymond departed back into the woods to retrieve his mare. Finally, after she'd made no more progress, Jack reached into his saddlebag and withdrew his hunting knife.

The girl's eyes widened. Apprehension washed over her face. But Jack didn't remove the blade from its sheath. Instead, he tossed it on the ground in front of her.

"For the rope."

She scurried over on her knees and yanked the blade free, then wedged it between the rope and her throat.

Jack grimaced. It was a tight fit. But in slow, cautious, sawing motions, she began getting through.

Jack tried not to stare. He felt awkward sitting idle on his horse while the girl tried to free herself, but, not wanting to alarm her any more than she already was, he remained.

"Who were they?" he asked.

She stopped and stared down at the knife. A tear wet the blade. "They killed my pa," she whispered.

Jack lowered his head. "I'm sorry." The small consolation sounded ridiculous in his ears. It always did. It was true, of course, but it ultimately didn't matter. Nothing he could do or say could repair the deep wounds inflicted upon this young lady. They were, he knew, already hardening into twisted, painful scars that no physician could ever heal.

He had some too.

She jolted at the sound of approaching horses and quickly went back to work on the rope.

"It's alright," Jack said. "They're with me."

Not listening or not impressed, the girl never looked up. She broke through just as Ned and CJ arrived and then leapt to her feet and bolted for the line of woods to the west. She hesitated for a heartbeat to look back at the knife lying by the severed rope, but continued up the hill without it.

Ned and CJ stopped and watched her. They turned confused looks to Jack.

Jack took his hat off and rubbed his head. He sighed. "Will you get her back, Ned?"

Ned looked like he'd just been asked to assassinate the president. He didn't move.

Jack looked him over, then CJ. "You look the least threatening," he said to Ned. "If we don't bring her back, she'll get herself killed." He glanced back at her as she labored up the slope and closer to the forest. "Or worse."

Ned hesitated, apparently thinking it over, but then kicked his horse.

Raymond emerged from the north on his mare. He stopped and looked on as Ned rode beside the running girl, shouting down to her. The girl never broke stride. Instead, she leaned forward and lowered her head, pressing on harder toward the woods.

Evidently realizing it was going to get difficult if she made the trees, Ned jumped from his horse and tackled her.

Jack cringed and closed his eyes. *That's not what I had in mind.*

They struggled. Ned's pleading echoed throughout the clearing. And in no time at all, the girl was on top of him, jabbing and swinging her fists violently. Ned screamed and waved his hands in front of his face, desperately trying to intercept the blows. His feet kicked wildly at the empty air behind him.

Jack just watched, stunned, hoping the young man could salvage some of his dignity. But with each passing second the onslaught only worsened, and it was quickly becoming clear that more than Ned's dignity would need salvaging.

Jack nodded to CJ and then spurred his horse into a swift lope. He thought he heard Raymond's laughter as he rode up the hill.

Jack jumped from his horse without pulling the reins. He grabbed the girl from behind and hauled her off of Ned. He picked her up and held her off the ground. She thrashed, fists, elbows, and feet whipping back into her new opponent. Jack squeezed, pinning her arms to her sides, and adjusted his footing to avoid being kicked. She went on fighting, using her head, heels, fingernails, anything she could, until exhaustion finally overtook her. It didn't take long. She tried to scream then, but all that came out was a dry, raspy sob.

Jack said, "If we wanted to hurt you, we could've at any time."

The words came out harsher than he'd wanted.

The girl didn't respond, but neither did she resume her struggle.

Ned sat up slowly. Along with numerous red splotches about his face and neck, his nose was bleeding. He ran a hand across his mouth and stared at the blood as if amazed by it. He finally picked up his hat and stood. He slapped the dirt and leaves from his pants and shot Jack a hateful glare.

Jack spoke softer this time. "I'm going to let you go, miss. I know you've been through a lot, and I know it's hard, but I need you to trust me. Just catch your breath and get settled. We'll get you out of here if you'll let us. You have my word on that."

The girl stiffened.

Jack held on.

"There's nobody to run from," he said. "Those other fellas are gone. They'll not harm you again, and neither will we. I promise. But if you take off into those woods, you're liable to get hurt a lot worse and maybe never come back."

He let the words hang there a moment.

The girl said nothing.

He let her go and backed away.

She stood there, eyes to the ground, unmoving. The tears returned.

Ned prodded his nose with the sleeve of his coat, now frowning at the blood.

CJ pulled a handkerchief from his saddlebag and dismounted. He approached slow and easy and stopped beside Ned.

Ned glanced at the handkerchief.

CJ offered it to the girl.

She eyed the cloth, then CJ, then the handkerchief again, but didn't move.

The rope had opened up a couple of nasty gashes around her neck. The blood, now mostly dried, had run down her throat and crusted at the fringes of her dress. She probed the wounds with the tips of her fingers.

CJ gave her a warm, reassuring nod.

She snatched the handkerchief and held it to her eyes.

They made their way back to camp at a slow pace. The girl was riding Major as CJ led her along on foot.

Ned was alone, way out in front of the group.

Jack fell in beside the girl. "What's your name?"

"Angelina." Her voice was hoarse and whispered, still burdened by her ordeal with the rope. Jack hoped it wasn't anything serious or permanent, but he was glad she was speaking.

"Well, ma'am, if I may say, that's a very pretty name."

"Sure is," CJ added.

"I'm Jack, and we call this fella here CJ."

Angelina sniffled and wiped her nose. "I'm sorry."

"Nothin' to be sorry about," Jack said. "Not a single thing. Just try and make yourself comfortable and we'll see to those wounds presently."

She nodded but kept her head down.

Jack moved up alongside CJ.

"We're going home."

12

CJ rebuilt the fire. He kept it small by adding only the driest and smallest of kindling but, nonetheless, managed to generate the heat of a much larger blaze.

Angelina kept her distance. She was eating with both hands, chewing only as long as necessary to get the dry meat down, then swallowing hard and reaching for more.

CJ kept it coming.

The girl's long blonde hair fell straight down, spreading around her face like a protective yellow veil, and for a while she seemed determined to stay behind it. But her exhaustion and the warmth of CJ's fire eventually drew her in, first with a slow, inconspicuous shuffle of her feet, and then a step, then another. Finally, she was sitting by the flames, leaning in close and massaging the heat over her exposed arms.

Satisfied she was in good hands, Jack walked away to the south. He paused by Ned, who was packing up loose items around camp in preparation for leaving, but the young man wouldn't look at him. Jack moved on. He went a short distance into the woods and sat down. He lit a cigar and pulled on it a few times, then took the old piece of paper from his pocket. He unfolded it carefully but then just held it a while. He didn't read it this time; he didn't need to. The page took him away from the cold, gray forest as reliably as it always did, just by holding it. The present melted away into scenes and images of a world gone by. Another world. The memories of that world felt like something from a different lifetime now, someone else's life, like an old story handed down from a generation past. They had become like memories of memories, vivid but hard to trust. But they were his. They were who he was, or had been.

He laid the paper in his lap and looked down at the lifeless, withered leaves at his feet. In a strange way he felt he could relate to them, that his spring had also come and gone, and the long, hard winter of life was slowly hardening him as well. He picked one up. It was cold and brittle, easily broken, easy to crush.

Something touched his shoulder.

He looked up and saw Raymond standing beside him. Raymond was tapping his shoulder with the knife he'd left back on the hill. Jack folded up the paper and returned it to his pocket. He took the knife and stuffed it in his belt at the small of his back.

"Thanks," he said, then gestured back to the north. "And thanks, Ray."

"You need a shave," Raymond said.

"Yeah, I reckon I do."

"What's wrong?"

Jack took his hat off and ran a hand through his hair. "Just thinking."

"You ought not do too much of that," Raymond said. "Ain't no good in it."

Jack nodded and put his hat back on. "You bury that fella back there?"

Raymond was watching Eli now, who was storming in through the brush from the southwest. "That fella got the grave he deserved."

Eli stopped in front of them, panting and grasping his knees. He craned his neck toward the girl sitting by the fire.

Jack glanced back at Angelina, whose face was still cloaked behind the curtain of blonde hair. "She's alright," he said. "I reckon she owes her life to you."

"They ought not st-st-stole her."

Jack nodded but said nothing. He and Raymond were quiet while the scout watched the girl eating by the fire, perhaps relishing his accomplishment—or, at least, as much as he would allow himself to. A small grin touched the corners of the old man's lips.

It dawned on Jack that he'd never asked Eli if he had any children, just as he'd never inquired of the man's marital status. It just never seemed the right time with Eli. The man stayed almost exclusively to himself, appearing only when he thought it absolutely necessary, and then only long enough to pass on that which he deemed important. Jack *had* asked his age, however, some time ago, and Eli had tried to answer that question, just as he would when anything was asked of him. But after much thought, Eli had shrugged and said he didn't know. He was a brilliant scout, Jack had honestly seen none better, but the scars he carried from the war ran deeper than most.

Eli's eyes came slowly back to Jack. "They-they …" He shook his head. "S-s-soldiers."

"Still south?"

"Yeah, Jack." Eli took a breath. "They wa-was playin' with their na-na-knives and askin' ba-'bout Ray."

"Ray?"

"Yeah, Jack."

Jack looked at Raymond, then Eli. "Where are they?"

Eli pointed back to the south. "In that pa-pa-purdy place."

Jack knew immediately it had to be the clearing at the bottom of the steep, boulder-strewn hill. The creek and open area would make a great campsite but would also leave them vulnerable to Indians. Strange, he thought, but they were never supposed to be this far north anyway.

"What were they asking about Ray?"

"Talk la-like they wa-was lookin' for him."

"Looking for him?"

"Yeah, Jack."

"How close did you get?"

"I ca-ca-could hear 'em."

"How many's there?"

Eli looked at him curiously. "All of 'em."

Raymond walked away in the direction of his mare, which was tied to a nearby tree.

"You sure they didn't see you?"

"Yeah, Jack."

Jack stood up, thinking about it. He put a hand on Eli's shoulder and looked back for Raymond, who was at his horse and appeared to be mounting up.

"Where are you going?" Jack called.

Raymond climbed into his saddle.

"To see what they want."

Jack hurried back to the campsite as Raymond followed Eli to the south.

"Where are y'all going?" CJ asked.

"Down the hill a piece," Jack said. "Just sit tight. We'll be back shortly." He looked at Angelina. "You get enough?"

She nodded.

"More water?" Jack asked.

She sniffled and cleared her throat. "Cynnamon got me some."

"Did he now?" Jack glanced casually to his left.

Ned opened his journal and began writing. His lips spread into a wicked grin, probably the closest he'd been to a smile today.

CJ didn't notice.

Jack chuckled. *That was quick.* Young or old, nothing could change the behavior of men like the entrance of a pretty lady. He doubted even Raymond knew CJ's given name. "It's spelled with a 'y'," he said to Ned.

Ned nodded, but never looked up from the ledger.

Jack untied his mare and swung into the saddle. He lingered for a moment, just watching the motley group of youngsters. They were all in their own world. The differences were striking. So were the similarities.

He rode off in the direction Eli and Raymond had gone.

Jack caught up just as Raymond and Eli began navigating the underbrush at the western side of the creek, where the waterfall started its descent.

As the slope began to sharpen, Eli turned and whispered, "No ma-more horses."

Jack and Raymond eased off their mounts and secured the horses to nearby trees. They retrieved their rifles and continued on foot.

The clearing came into view about halfway down the hill. On the other side of the creek, where they'd been just yesterday, there was a small but well organized tent city. Cavalry soldiers meandered around from tent to tent. Some talked, some played cards, a few others already had fires going in anticipation of the night's meal.

Jack was amazed at how the day had gotten away so quickly. Still, it seemed awful early to be setting up camp. He figured the commanding officer had decided to put off the intimidating rocky slope until morning. *Not too wise*, Jack thought. The place was way too open for his taste, too hard to defend. He shook his head, wondering why he was even thinking such things, especially while stealing down their flank.

And why the subterfuge, anyway?

Eli grabbed him by the sleeve and pointed to a single tent by the creek's edge. The tent was much larger than its counterparts in the clearing, and wholly isolated.

Raymond continued down the hill, easing away to Jack's right and toward the tent by the water.

Jack went left.

They moved slow and quiet, paralleling their approach and taking care not to give away their position. Eli, however, went only a few yards, stopped, looked at both of them nervously, and then started back up the hill.

Jack leaned against a tree and watched until Eli made it to the top and slipped into a knot of pine saplings. Then he shot a hard look at CJ, who was crouching in the foliage forty feet behind him.

CJ froze, eyes wide.

Jack put a finger to his lips and pointed at the ground in front of him. The boy eased down the hill quietly, pausing a couple of times to assess his route, and then finally stopped in front of Jack.

"What are you doing?" Jack whispered sharply.

CJ opened his mouth, then thought better of it.

Jack could tell the boy knew he'd made a mistake, but he partly blamed himself for not making the point more clear when he'd had the chance.

"There's a fine line between bravery and stupidity," Jack said.

CJ said nothing.

Jack waited.

The boy nodded.

"You left the girl alone with Ned?"

CJ flushed, looked down.

"She's liable to kill him before we get back," Jack said.

A grin tugged at the corner of the boy's mouth, but it didn't stick.

Jack put a finger in his chest. "Stay behind me."

CJ nodded.

"You understand me?"

"Yeah."

Jack turned. Raymond was still to the right, but farther down the hill now, closer to the creek. Jack made up the lost ground, still keeping his position roughly parallel to Raymond's. They both stopped about twenty feet from the water's edge.

It was mostly quiet. Any noise from camp was largely drowned out by the slender waterfall and the gurgling creek. The tent Eli had pointed out was stationed ten feet from the creek's edge on the opposite side, and was even bigger than it had looked from a distance. There was a small portable table sitting by the entrance, a large piece of paper unrolled across its surface. From this distance it looked an awful lot like a map.

A detailed map.

Surely not. Jack's mind swam back to his meeting with Cavanaugh as he stared at the table. If that was a map of the northern territory, then why …

A soldier walked in from the camp and stuck his head inside the tent. Jack noted the sleeve and profile as the soldier backed away, saluted, and then headed back toward the main body of troops.

Captain Hardy.

The man who'd escorted Ned to Jonas's ranch.

Hardy was barely out of sight when the tent flap peeled back and another soldier stepped out. This one was leaning heavily on a cane. The man limped down toward the creek, not more than thirty feet from where Jack and CJ were squatting in the brush, then dropped his cane and proceeded to relieve himself.

Jack shook his head in disbelief. But there it was: the cavalry—equipped with its highest-ranking officer—spread out right there before him in a place they were never supposed to be.

For the sake of the man's dignity, Jack waited a few seconds. Then, with his rifle held down in a non-threatening manner, he stepped out from behind his cover.

"Colonel Asheworth."

Asheworth stumbled back and nearly fell from the surprise. He shot a quick look over his shoulder in the direction Hardy had gone, and then squinted at the stranger, searching for recognition. When it came, his face lit up in obvious surprise.

"Mr. Percy," he said. "Well, what ... Where did ..." He looked back toward the camp again.

"Figured y'all would've broken off to the east by now," Jack said.

"Yes," Asheworth said. "Yes, indeed." He knelt to retrieve his walking stick, and it was easy to see that the simple act was causing him real pain. He recovered quickly, though, snatching up the cane and standing resolute with it by his side.

Jack was impressed at how swiftly the man rebuilt the officer's façade.

In an obvious delay to answer the question, the colonel took a breath and surveyed the forest around his visitor. He didn't notice CJ, who was still hidden in the growth behind Jack. What he did notice, however, as his eyes panned to the left, was Raymond, who was leaning casually against a tree by the creek, his rifle hanging through folded arms.

Asheworth's eyes narrowed, then glistened. His lips quivered as if to speak but instead spread into a twisted grin. And right then and there, his countenance underwent total and complete transformation. He leaned on the cane, ignoring all else, and took a tender step toward Raymond.

"Well, well," he said. "Raymond McAlister, in the flesh. The great war hero." His voice had become deep and hateful. "Oh, forgive me, that's not right, is it, McAlister? You're no war hero; you're no hero at all. Know why that is?" He raised his voice. "Do you know why, McAlister?"

Raymond said nothing.

"Because you lost!"

Asheworth's face had reddened with absolute hate. He took another step toward Raymond. "You know what they say: 'To the victor belong the spoils.' Take a good look, McAlister. These are the spoils." Without losing eye contact, the colonel pointed to the various decorations sewn and fixed on his uniform. "The spoils, you see, that's why you're on that side of the creek instead of this one. It's why at this very moment you're hopelessly pinned down and outnumbered. And this time there's nowhere for you to run, no rock to climb under. No retreat.

"You're all alone in these godforsaken woods," Asheworth went on. "And now, McAlister, you're going to lose again, lose all."

Raymond didn't move, hadn't moved. His posture and disposition were unchanged.

Asheworth raised his walking stick and jabbed it in the air. "I saw what you did, you unholy bastard. I saw what you did to those boys. Those good boys. I was there when they cried their last. I tried to put them back together. But you made damn sure that would never happen, didn't you?" He took another step forward. "Oh, yes, that's right, I was there. I sent them in there, you see. I ordered them into those woods *personally*."

"You should've led them," Raymond said.

Asheworth spat at him. "They were boys! All of them, just boys!" He glanced at Raymond's belt. "Is that the blade, McAlister? Is that the blade you used on my brother?" The colonel tapped the side of his knee with his cane. "Is that the same pistol that gave me this?"

Raymond said nothing.

Asheworth straightened. "Oh, if you only knew how I've waited for this day. If you only knew the promises I've made. I never forgot you. No, I always knew you'd slither from your hiding place someday.

Now your arrogance has led you to me. God has led you to me. You chose not to fight as a gentleman, McAlister. And for that, you shall not receive a gentleman's death. For that, you shall be put down like the rabid beast you are."

"Big talk for a man who can't even piss without a walkin' stick!"

Jack turned toward the new voice at his left, as did Asheworth.

CJ had risen from the brush, faced equally flushed with anger. "You must not be afraid of dyin', old man."

Asheworth grunted, looked back at Raymond. "Dying? Why, I don't know. I've never tried it."

"I have," Raymond said.

Asheworth's eyes flicked to the top of the hill as a number of dismounted soldiers swung in behind his intruders and began taking up position.

Jack spun around, stunned by the sudden change of events, and cursed himself for having trusted Cavanaugh. "You mean that's what this was all about? Revenge? You're mad, Colonel. The war is over."

Asheworth wasn't listening. His smile had stretched to the point of absurdity, like he had a direct view of the gates of heaven themselves, or maybe hell. He began to laugh, one eye on Raymond, the other on the hill.

Jack turned again.

Three soldiers were already digging in behind them, maybe more. The waterfall blocked any hope of retreat to the north, while to the south, the slope dropped off sharply toward the creek. It would take way too much time to run in that direction, and then they'd only be pinned in the valley. The view to the east, over the creek, opened up into the heart of the cavalry encampment.

Jack yearned for a moment to think, but there was none. He thought of the young man behind him and his heart began to race. Charging the three up the hill was sinking in as the only real option. But it would have to be perfect. And nothing was ever perfect. Jack knew as soon as any shots were fired, or on the colonel's orders, the remaining men in camp would converge on them. He also knew the soldiers above would have no trouble holding them in place until help arrived.

Asheworth shifted the cane to his left hand, freeing his right to hang by his sidearm. His fingers twitched by the holster.

Raymond watched the colonel. He hadn't yet lost his gaze on him, hadn't yet turned to survey the blockade behind them. He hadn't looked to the north or south. He just stared straight ahead, at Asheworth.

Asheworth returned it. That earlier glint had come back to his eye, as well as a slight tic. The two men had entered a place that only they were privy to. A silent exchange passed between them, clear and palpable and wordless.

The colonel grinned.

Raymond rocked off the tree and leapt across the creek.

Asheworth dug for his pistol.

Jack went a second after Raymond, dragging CJ out of the brush behind him. CJ swung alongside and they both reached the creek bank simultaneously. They hurled themselves over the water as one and came down ankle-deep in the mud on the other side.

The rifles behind them came to life in three successive explosions. One of the shots slapped into a tree to Jack's left, another found the creek, spraying water on the back of his neck.

Asheworth raised his pistol, but Raymond snatched it from his hand as he ran by on an angle to the north. Jack fell in behind him, CJ in tow.

The colonel screamed orders from behind them as if he were in pain.

More shots rang out from the hill to the west, but the trees were giving them momentary cover.

Raymond switched his rifle to his left hand and fired Asheworth's pistol into the camp until it clicked empty. He dropped it and bolted for the foot of the slope—the same one they'd navigated not twenty-four hours before.

The camp was buzzing with surprise. Two dozen soldiers ran about, checking their loads and trying to discover what was happening. Captain Hardy walked in the midst of the troops, unfazed, barking orders and pointing his finger.

Raymond ducked behind a rock at the bottom of the hill. Jack followed, jerking CJ in behind them.

Raymond put a hand on Jack's shoulder and pointed at the boy.

Jack nodded.

They peered around the rock and watched as the soldiers assembled into two units. A smaller group mounted up and rode off to the east, away from them. The remaining troops formed into a skirmish line and began advancing toward the hill.

Raymond stepped back and lowered his head. He pressed a hand into his side and winced. He took a breath, let it go, then looked up at Jack.

"Go."

Jack tore up the hill, dragging CJ, boots slipping on the dirt and gravel. He looked back and saw Raymond step out and fire at the approaching line of soldiers. The shot was high, but the line broke and scattered to either side.

Jack stopped behind the first large rock they came to. CJ fell but quickly gathered himself and pressed his back against the stone. Jack glanced around the rock. The bluecoats were moving out at wide angles to the boulder Raymond was behind. He saw a couple of them pause to check the target through the sights on their rifles.

Raymond hadn't moved.

Jack swore, still not believing what was happening. He grabbed CJ by the front of his jacket and pointed at the top of the hill. "Don't stop for nothing!"

CJ looked up the hill.

"For nothing!" Jack screamed.

The boy flinched, set his jaw and swallowed.

Jack looked back down the slope. One of the cavalrymen was easing up the eastern side of the hill and, as best as Jack could tell, was almost in position for a shot.

Raymond still hadn't moved. He was still standing behind the same boulder at the foot of the hill, still facing the backside of it. His rifle was gripped firmly in both hands but pointed at the ground.

CJ began crawling up the hill, carefully staying in the rocks and brush along the way.

Jack raised his rifle at the gunman on the eastern side of the slope. The man had his eyes on nothing but the boulder Raymond occupied. Jack watched the soldier's movements down the barrel of his rifle, struggling to see through the foliage between them.

The bluecoat stopped, locked his firearm against his shoulder and lowered his head.

Jack took a breath, held it, and fired.

The soldier twisted and went down on one knee, but then swiveled and fired in Jack's direction.

Jack ducked in behind the rock, cursing.

Another shot went off. Close. Then another. Then silence.

Jack brought his rifle back around, took aim, but then noticed that the bluecoat was unarmed. The soldier was staring at his hands in shock and disbelief, blood dripping between his fingers. There was a long, jagged rip in the breast of his uniform, the cloth around it growing moist and dark. He staggered once and dropped out of sight.

Raymond was moving up the west side of the hill now, wiping his blade on his pants.

The troops behind him began reforming.

Jack pushed off the rock and ran. The slope was punishing. His chest burned and his legs ached. The ridge was only twenty yards ahead. He realized his back was exposed as he passed the last tree, and he knew if he stopped now he would never make it. He heard the report of another rifle and stiffened, but felt nothing.

He pressed on. Another shot rang out as he dove over the long rock formation at the top of the hill. He dropped down and pressed himself against the rocks, waiting for the pain. None came. He looked down at his chest, heaving. No hits. No blood.

CJ was farther down the rock formation, not more than ten yards away from Jack. Farther still, to the east, were Ned and Angelina. Angelina was crying but not making a sound. Sadly, staying quiet in a moment like this was a trick no girl her age should know anything about, Jack thought. Ned looked like he could join her at any moment. And yet, at the same time, he seemed out of sorts. Confused. Jack watched him, silently wondering if Cavanaugh's apprentice had known this was coming all along.

More shots exploded, this time from the east. Jack rolled into a ball, pressing himself painfully into the rocks. Dirt and little bits of stone sprinkled down on his neck.

CJ looked at Jack down the line of rocks. The young man was obviously shaken, but his eyes were focused and sharp. He held up his rifle and pointed to the east.

"They're flanking us," Jack yelled.

More shots came in from the bottom.

CJ looked down, thinking, then glanced back to the east.

Jack knew it all too well. The soldiers at the bottom would hold them down with cover-fire while the group to the east moved in beside or behind them. Standard procedure. He looked back at CJ and briefly wondered how the boy had retrieved his rifle. The young man had always been resourceful. He would need all of it tonight.

Jack took his hat off and looked back down the hill. With dusk already upon them, only the twinkle of scattered firelight could be made out in the camp below. But the two soldiers coming up the west side of the hill were clear enough. Jack was stretching out, trying to improve his view, when the muzzle flashes erupted in unison from the bottom.

The sound was deafening, pounding and echoing through the rocks and trees like a god-awful storm.

Jack rolled onto his stomach. The same two soldiers were midway up the slope now, open and exposed. But before Jack could get his sights on them, they fanned out and stepped into the heavy foliage near the waterfall.

Silence followed. And for a glorious moment, there was only the hiss and murmur of the creek. Jack's ears rang in the false stillness.

Then there was a flash and a single rifle pop inside the brush by the falls.

At first, there was only the echo, rolling away across the surrounding hills and valleys. But then one of the bluecoats fell backwards out of the bushes, writhing and holding his chest. Raymond emerged next, dragging the second soldier's lifeless body by the back of his collar. He sheathed his blade and let the dead man fall, then picked up the first soldier's rifle, unloaded it and put the shells in his pocket.

The remaining cavalryman rolled over once and fell silent.

Raymond tossed the empty weapon on the ground beside the fallen soldier. He stared at the man for a long time, eyes blinking and unfocused. He finally took his hat off and laid his head back against a tree.

That was when Jack saw another soldier not more than twenty yards away. The bluecoat was on the eastern side of the hill, directly opposite Raymond, moving silently closer. The soldier stopped and leaned against the tree Jack had passed on the way up, and then took aim at Raymond.

Jack swung his weapon around, placed his sights more or less in the center of the soldier's uniform, and pulled the trigger.

Nothing. Not even a click.

The cavalryman moved around the other side of the tree, putting the obstacle squarely between himself and Jack.

Jack swore, remembering he hadn't chambered another round after firing earlier.

The tip of the soldier's rifle came up again, poised in the same direction.

Jack looked back at Raymond, who had moved to the left and was now kneeling. His maneuver, unbeknownst to himself, had momentarily blocked a clear shot from the soldier. But as soon as he stood up, or turned north, it would be all too easy for the bluecoat.

Nightfall was descending like a blanket, and the end of the soldier's rifle was beginning to blend with the darkness. But it was still there, and Jack could still see it. He saw Raymond move slightly and wanted to call out to him. But he knew that would be a death sentence for his friend.

The rifle inched forward as the would-be sniper dialed in. But only the rifle. The soldier's body was still thoroughly concealed behind the tree.

Jack pulled the lever on his Winchester. Time seemed to speed up, pressing against him like a force. He quickly considered his chances of scoring a lucky shot, maybe hitting the barrel of the soldier's weapon, and figured they were roughly nil. So he took a breath, jumped to his feet, and ran toward the tree.

He tried to make his steps light and soundless, and thought he had. But a second before he reached the tree, the tip of the rifle dropped and disappeared.

The soldier had heard him.

Jack tried not to breathe. Perspiration swelled on his face and neck. He heard shuffling from the opposite side of the tree, boots scraping the ground, and then a long, quiet exhalation. The trooper was still there, still on the other side, not more than a few feet away. Were it not for the tree, the two men could've reached out and touched each other.

Jack knew he had to go, and go now. But which way?

The guns opened up from below. The blasts flooded the hillside in a tidal wave of sound.

Jack moved, committing himself to the left side of the tree, praying the soldier was expecting different. He went slow, dirt and loose stone threatening every step. He felt the Winchester cold against his hip, heard his pulse throbbing in his ears. His progress exposed more and more of the tree, and the bottom of the hill, but nothing else.

The rush of footfalls behind him came next.

And then the blast.

Jack went to his knees, ears ringing. He dropped his rifle and rolled to the ground. Everything went dark and unfocused. He could hear only his own breathing now, which roared like thunder in his head. His hands went out blindly through dirt and rock, searching for his fallen rifle, finding nothing. He gave up and groped for his pistol.

He saw the soldier then. The man was on his knees in front of him. He looked surprised, or maybe confused. Their eyes met for a beat and neither moved. And then a viscous line of blood and spit spilled from the corner of the soldier's mouth, and he fell lifeless in the dust in front of Jack. The earth immediately began to darken around him.

Jack stared at the dead cavalryman, dazed. The soldier's body shuddered once, then stilled. Jack absently searched himself for wounds, found none, felt none. He glanced up when the soldier's rifle hit the ground.

"You'll be needing these," Raymond said.

Jack took the cartridges from Raymond's hand, and then Raymond pulled him to his feet.

Jack stared at his friend, but couldn't find his voice.

Raymond pointed at Jack's rifle, still lying in the dirt, then turned and disappeared in the darkness.

13

Heavy cloud cover advanced overhead like a great black veil, seemingly encompassing the whole sky. Jack watched as the moon and stars winked out one by one behind it. The sudden absence of light made the darkness nearly complete.

He was still hunkered down at the top of the hill, still behind the west side of the rock formation. Farther to the east, CJ huddled against the cold, Ned and Angelina to his right. Ned's head and arms were tucked between his legs, while all that could be seen of Angelina were a few strands of loose hair poking through gaps in CJ's coat.

Raymond was somewhere on the eastern end of the ridge, apparently anticipating a flanking maneuver from Asheworth.

Every so often, and totally at random, the soldier's rifles would ring out, sometimes starting from the bottom, sometimes from the east. The shots from the east seemed to be getting a little closer each time. Occasionally, a couple of lucky rounds would find their way in close and punch away at the rocks around them, forcing them all into tight balls and amplifying the whimpering from the young lady under CJ's coat. CJ and Ned jolted with each new discharge, and Jack realized the suppressing fire was serving a dual purpose now. A tired opponent was a half-beaten opponent.

Jack dug in his pocket and retrieved the rifle cartridges Raymond had given him. There were three. The rest of the ammo was on the horses, which could be anywhere by now. He drew his pistol and spun the cylinder slowly, checking each chamber.

The soldiers would probably make their run at first light. And if Asheworth was willing to give up a few troops, and it seemed clear that he was, the cavalry should overrun them easily. Jack wondered why Raymond hadn't just killed the colonel when he'd had the chance. It would've been so easy. But then, losing those few precious seconds could have cost them everything in their flight to the bottom of the hill, and, in the end, probably wouldn't have made any real difference anyway.

Jack looked to his right, where he knew CJ and the others were, but could no longer see them. He hurt for them, likely more than they did for themselves. More than likely. Hope was always stronger in the young, and sometimes blind. *So young.* And for what? Asheworth's revenge? The whole thing incensed him. The whole idea of it. The whole thing just an elaborate setup.

Shots exploded into the night again, this round startling Jack so bad it hurt. They started from the bottom this time, and then the east came in, ever closer. Angelina's muffled cries grew louder and louder. And then her resistance finally broke, and she sobbed openly into the night.

Jack thought of intervening, thought of asking CJ to intervene, but he didn't. What did it matter now? Instead, he listened.

The sound awakened a thousand ghosts in his mind—soft echoes of spirits trodden and crushed, trapped in a past that would never die. It was the mother's tortured animal wail as her son was lowered into the ground before her. It was the widows, shaking, screaming, inconsolable, whose husbands were no more and never would be again. It was the little girls clinging to ankles, daughters, sisters, when father or brother was forever lost. It was the naked and tormented pleading to a cold, empty sky that remained cold and empty.

A single tear slipped down Jack's cheek. He wiped it away and put his head back against the rock.

It was a young woman, her love headed off to war, holding on tight, resisting his every movement away. Just one more kiss, one more embrace, one more look into his eyes. *Just one more …*

The tear returned and dropped into his lap, this time unabated.

The guns came in again, the east followed by the bottom. Angelina was hysterical now. She called out for her pa.

Jack wondered if Asheworth would give the others safe passage if he requested it, or at least the girl. Surely the girl. But the thought was cut short.

It started out faint, only barely audible, and then increased slightly. The noise was directly behind their position, on the topside, to the north.

The sound of scattered leaves. And then nothing. Then again, to the northeast and northwest, and then silence.

Jack shifted the rifle to his left hand and drew his sidearm. He stared into the blackness.

Angelina had gone silent.

The leaves sang out again, all around, everywhere alive.

Jack tensed, his ears suddenly filled with the sound. He drew back the hammer on his revolver.

Silence.

Jack closed his eyes, trusting the greater sense to guide him. He raised the pistol, aimed it into the night, and listened.

And listened.

But there was nothing more.

The night went quiet, almost perfectly quiet, an ominous and uncanny stillness that disturbed Jack worse than anything thus far. And then the air began moving in a gentle breeze. High overhead, treetops moaned and creaked, unseen. And then, as if hesitating, the unmistakable song of rain began, stopped, and came again.

Jack put his hat back on at the first few drops. He pressed himself against the rock and kept listening. But there was only the rain now. He filled his lungs with the scent of the cold rainwater and watched the darkness through heavy eyes. He eventually lowered the pistol and rested his head on top of his knees.

The same heavy cloud cover that had first hidden the moon and stars, and then dropped this slow, soaking rain, had also warmed the air a bit. It wasn't much, but probably enough to keep them all from freezing to death in the night.

Jack felt the rifle slide off his lap. He left it and tucked his free hand under the crook of his knee. His eyes burned, but he resisted and tightened his grip on the pistol. The night continued at an agonizing pace.

The rain drummed straight down against the leaves on the forest floor, a chorus of sound not unlike a mother's soothing voice. Jack's shoulders began to relax and his heart rate started to slow.

Jack flinched at the sound of the voice. He jerked his head up and was immediately blinded by the early light of dawn. He was still rolled up in the same position he'd fallen asleep in, his body panging with stiffness. He squinted ahead, hearing the voice again.

"Get down!" he said.

"I bra-bra-brought the hor-horses." Eli was on his toes, peeking over the rocks at the valley below.

Jack cursed himself for falling asleep.

"Dammit, Eli! Get down!"

The scout looked around and then knelt.

Jack noticed his mare then, standing behind Eli, who was holding her reins. Where had he found the horses? And when had … Jack shot a quick glance down the line of rock to the east.

"Where's Ray?"

Eli didn't seem to hear the question. He was staring at the ground between quivering hands, his mind elsewhere.

"Eli, where's Ray?"

Eli pointed east.

Jack stretched his legs and then rocked into a squatting position. Blood slowly returned to his extremities, bringing only more stiffness and pain. He put a hand against the rocks and swore at himself again for falling asleep.

To his right, CJ and Ned were also sleeping in similar masses. Angelina was beside them, huddled under CJ's rain-soaked jacket. Her bloodshot eyes met Jack's, and he felt an urge to nod at her, to attempt a reassuring smile, but he couldn't. He looked back at Eli.

"Did they get behind us?"

Eli met the question with a blank expression. His lips parted, then he flinched and looked back at the forest. He stared for a long time and was pale when he turned back.

"I think they were moving around up here just before the rain," Jack said.

"They was … they … they're ga-ga-gone."

"What?"

"Ga-gone."

Jack searched the scout's face, trying to process the information. He finally got up and peered over the rocks.

The valley below was empty. There were no tents, no fires, no horses. The camp was gone.

Just gone.

"Where did …" Jack looked around blankly. "When?"

"Da-da-don't know."

The way Eli was shaking was starting to bother Jack. He put a hand on the old man's shoulder and squeezed. They both looked on as Raymond emerged in the valley on his horse.

"They pulled out?" Jack asked.

Eli said nothing. His eyes stayed on Raymond for a time, then flicked to the forest surrounding the valley below.

Jack waited for an answer that didn't come. He decided not to ask again. Instead, he nodded at the others. "Will you keep an eye on 'em?"

"Yeah, Jack."

Jack grabbed his rifle and took his reins from Eli. He mounted up, groaning as he did, and started down the slope as quickly as the damp ground would allow.

He pulled up by the tree where the soldier had lain dead hours before. The bluecoat was gone. Just the slightest hint of blood still clung to the tree's spider-like roots above the ground. Jack examined the area around the tree for footprints, a sure indication that the fallen soldier's comrades had retrieved him in the night. There were none. He looked to the west, where Raymond had encountered the two troops in the brush by the falls. The dusty ground was still dark from the brief rainfall earlier. But that was it. The bodies were gone.

Jack gave the mare her slack and let her navigate the rest of the hill at her discretion. She took him to the bottom, expertly dancing around rocks and foliage, and then loped into the open valley.

The clearing was void. Asheworth's tent by the creek was gone. Only ash remained from the fires the previous night. The grass was pressed down in tight circles where the cavalry had laid out rocks to contain the fires. But the rocks were nowhere around. There were no half-burned logs or kindling or brushwood, no charred timber of any kind. Just scattered ash.

Jack turned his mare toward Raymond, who was sitting on his horse some forty yards away, and rode over to him.

"What's going on?"

Raymond shook his head.

Jack glanced around the valley. "When did they pull out?"

Raymond gestured toward the ground. "They didn't."

Jack looked down at the uneven color of the valley floor, then back at Raymond. He dismounted slowly, still studying his friend's expression, then swept a hand through the grass. It came back wet and streaked red, blood sticky between his fingers.

Raymond waved a hand, indicating the rest of the valley.

Jack walked a few paces. More blood. He looked out at the rest of the clearing. The high grass was winter-blond, but with irregular red blotches all over, in every visible direction. He went back to the bottom of the hill where the skirmish line had been. Rainwater sat in scarlet puddles on the stony ground, gradually receding into thin cracks to the earth below. A chill raced up Jack's spine.

"It's the same to the east," Raymond said. "Where the flankers were."

Jack looked at his friend. The irony of it all was settling in. Cavanaugh had said that sending soldiers into this area would be foolish, that the Sioux would love nothing more than to discover a uniformed dispatch all lined up in some valley. It would be "like a gift," he'd said. That night, in what was now an obvious chorus of lies, there had been one truth, perhaps one even Cavanaugh and his colonel hadn't fully believed, or appreciated. Still, even if the Sioux had executed the assault perfectly ...

"I never heard any shots."

Raymond gestured toward the forest. "There's more."

Jack followed Raymond to the edge of the woods. Raymond stopped at the line of trees, and when he didn't dismount, Jack stepped around him.

Then he stopped as well.

Sitting inside the edge of the woods, just before the foliage really began to thicken, were two stacks. The first was a mound of rifles. Each of the weapons was placed neatly and methodically on top of one another, forming a small cube. A second and smaller mound of revolvers lay alongside in a similar pile.

Jack handed his reins to Raymond and picked up one of the cavalry rifles. He worked the lever, ejecting an unspent shell from the top, then cycled through the remaining load. Ten cartridges hit the ground.

"Still loaded," he said.

He dropped the rifle and grabbed another. Same thing. Fully loaded. He tossed it back on the pile and looked at Raymond. The two exchanged a long, thoughtful stare.

"They haven't been fired," Jack said blankly.

Raymond said nothing.

"Why would Indians leave the rifles behind?"

"They wouldn't," Raymond said. He was staring into the depths of the forest now, a look of uncertainty on his face. A look Jack had never seen before.

Jack glanced back at the hill. Ned was carefully directing his gelding down the slope. CJ was still up top, standing on a tall boulder, whooping and pumping his rifle above his head in victory.

"Who the hell did this?" Jack asked.

Raymond shook his head.

Jack felt an empty pit growing in his gut. "Why are we still here? Why didn't they take us?"

"They were too spread out," Raymond said. "And they knew we were waiting for it, but the soldiers weren't."

Jack stared absently at the forest, mind swimming.

"There's something they're protecting," Raymond added. He turned his attention to the top of the hill. "Or something they want."

Jack followed Raymond's eyes. CJ had climbed down from the rock and was standing beside Angelina now. They were both looking down the hill at him and Raymond.

"They'll be back," Raymond said.

Jack's pulse quickened at that last thought. "We need to get back up there."

He grabbed one of the rifles from the pile, then took his reins from Raymond and mounted up. They both kicked their horses and started back toward the hill. They were only halfway across the clearing, however, when Jack veered off.

Ned was easing his horse through the center of what had been the cavalry encampment when Jack pulled up and slid off his mare.

"What ... what happened?" the young man muttered. He didn't look up as Jack approached, seemed almost incapable of tearing his eyes away from the ground below. "Where did they go?"

Jack walked directly to him, pulled him off his horse, and threw him to the ground.

The young man landed with a thud that immediately snatched the air from his lungs. He rolled onto his side, holding his chest, looking around in confusion.

Jack climbed on top of him, forcing him back down. He pressed the army rifle against Ned's chest and put his weight on it.

"Mr. Percy—"

Jack spoke through clinched teeth. "Were we all supposed to die in this field, Ned?"

"Mr. Percy—"

"Did the preacher ever even exist?"

Ned stared up at Jack, eyes wide. "Yes," he said. "Yes, we were supposed to be looking for a preacher. I don't know why they ... I don't understand what ..." He swallowed. "Colonel Asheworth was supposed to be checking on a settlement in the east."

Jack leaned on the rifle. "There ain't no settlement east."

"That's all Mr. Cavanaugh told me. I swear it, Mr. Percy. I swear it on my father's grave."

Jack pushed harder. He felt Ned's body trembling beneath the rifle, felt his chest shudder. Jack searched his face, but there was only fear in the young man's eyes, only confusion.

On my father's grave.

"That's all. That's all I was told, Mr. Percy. I don't …" The young man's voice was starting to break.

Jack got up and spat to one side. He cursed himself silently, knowing already he'd made a mistake. Cavanaugh had had no more interest in his apprentice than he'd had in anyone else in this party. That had been easy to see back in Twin Pines. Plain.

Jack looked away, swore again. He saw Raymond standing behind him in his peripheral vision.

Ned rolled off his back and sat up. Jack reached for his hand. Ned hesitated, but then took it and came to his feet.

"I'm …" Jack started. "I had to know."

Ned nodded.

Jack handed the cavalry rifle to him.

Ned took it quickly, as if failure to do so might result in another toss to the ground.

Jack sighed. "You can use that, right?"

Ned looked at the weapon, then at the forest. He nodded.

Jack wasn't convinced, but he turned back to his horse. "Come on. We gotta get back."

"Who did this, Mr. Percy?"

Jack stopped and leaned against his saddle. He took in the ground around him. "I don't know," he said finally. As he mounted up, he saw Raymond was already at the foot of the hill and climbing. Jack sat for a moment trying to gather his thoughts, wondering what the next step was. He heard a voice and tugged his mare around to face Ned.

"What say?"

Ned didn't answer. The young man had turned toward the forest, face pale. He was awkwardly trying to rub his arms while cradling the rifle. His eyes went from the woods to the ground, there and back again. He finally closed them altogether and took a long, deep breath. As he exhaled, he nodded to himself and whispered, "The unknown."

Part 2

14

...They won't like you taking their prize.

The old man's words rushed through Jack's mind like an unexpected gust of wind. He glanced over his shoulder at Angelina, who was sitting alone, silently working on a small piece of jerky. The young girl was still gathered up inside CJ's coat. Her hair was wet and stiff, standing out in tangles across her shoulders and back. But it was her red, swollen eyes that struck Jack. He wondered when she'd last slept. He thought again of the old man's threat, but he couldn't get his mind around that now. There was too much to do and precious little time.

CJ was asking questions he had no time or answers for. Raymond had said *they'll be back*. And if that was so, they had to act quickly. Timing was everything. It was painfully obvious they would have no chance of repelling the sort of an attack that could blot out an entire unit of cavalry.

Raymond whispered over Jack's shoulder, "They've gotta go."

Jack nodded. He was looking at Major now. CJ's horse was tied off twenty feet away, sifting through a knot of foliage.

"What've you got in there?"

CJ looked up at the sound of Jack's voice.

"Huh?"

Jack pointed at the horse's bulging saddlebags.

"Oh, just extra stuff," CJ said.

"Such as?"

CJ shrugged. "Some extra clothes, cartridges, a blanket. Uh ..."

"An extra pair of britches?"

"Yeah, there's some in there."

"Get 'em," Jack said.

CJ blinked, confused, but then hurried over to his horse.

Jack knelt beside Angelina. Her green eyes were large and suspicious, still crowded with tears.

"I need you to trust me again," Jack said.

She nodded.

"Can you do that?"

Angelina said nothing, but she didn't look away.

CJ returned with the pants. Jack took them and grabbed the boy's hat off.

"I need you to put these on," he said to Angelina.

Her eyes narrowed as she took in the clothing, but it was a gesture of confusion, not unwillingness.

"I'm sorry," Jack said. "I really am. I know it seems strange, but there's just no time to explain."

She looked at the woods and shivered.

"And when you put the hat on," Jack said, "I need you to stuff all that pretty hair up underneath it. All you can manage."

A tear broke and slid down the base of her nose.

"Will you do that for me?"

Her lips parted and her voice cracked, but still there were no words. She took the clothes, tugged CJ's coat over her exposed neck, and turned toward the forest.

"Please don't go in the woods," Jack said. He grabbed CJ by the shoulders and spun him around, then looked at Ned with raised eyebrows.

Ned followed suit.

"No one will look," Jack said. "You have my word."

Jack slipped an arm around CJ. "Don't stop for nothing," he said. "Ride like you've never ridden before. If you need to sleep, don't. If she needs to sleep, she can do it on the back of your horse."

"But—"

"For nothing!" Jack snapped. "Take her straight to your pa's or get Doc Lewis to look after her, then go find Sheriff Murphy."

The young men were nodding uneasily, fear and indecision in their eyes. Ned had moved closer to hear the conversation, but was mostly staring at the ground and wringing his hands.

"Just don't stop," Jack finished.

They stood in silence, waiting for Angelina to give them the *okay*, if she would.

CJ asked, "What are y'all gonna do?"

"We're going north."

"North? Why would y'all go north?"

"We're gonna make a little noise."

"But they'll come after you."

Jack took a breath, offered the boy the best smile he could manage. It was the first time he'd seen real anxiety in him. "It'll be alright."

CJ threw his arms around Jack and squeezed.

Jack returned it.

"Please don't stop," he whispered.

Jack stood with the three of them—Ned on his U.S. cavalry steed, CJ and Angelina on Major. Angelina had done exactly as he'd asked. With CJ's pants and coat, she looked as much like a man as was possible, given the circumstances. She had the hat pulled down tight and the collar raised on the jacket. There were still a few sprigs of the girl's long hair escaping through gaps in the disguise, but Jack knew it wasn't going to get any better.

Raymond was behind them, tending a small fire he'd built using the wettest wood he could find. He was adding leaves and anything else that would put off a solid stack of smoke.

"Remember?" Jack asked.

CJ nodded. "But what about—"

Jack smacked Major hard on the hindquarter. He stepped back and watched as CJ and Angelina bolted down the hill to the south.

Ned brought his horse alongside Jack and looked down, eyes trying to speak what the mouth couldn't.

Jack extended a hand. "Pleasure riding with you," he said. "And my apologies."

Ned took the hand and squeezed.

Jack smacked the gelding, and Ned had to release Jack's hand to gather the reins. The young man looked back several times before disappearing down the hill.

Raymond's voice came over Jack's shoulder. "Go with 'em."

Jack said nothing. He stood in silence until he could hear them no longer, then turned and surveyed the fire. A thick column of smoke was climbing straight up through the trees and still air. Just as they had hoped.

Jack mounted up and drew his rifle. He chambered a round.

"Ready?"

Raymond took a breath, and they both dug in their heels. The horses lunged forward and they sped northward, firing their rifles into the air as they went.

15

Jack pulled up. Had to. The mare was slowing with or without his consent, and he couldn't afford to have her exhausted now—or worse, to come up lame.

They had been riding at intervals nearing full gallop for a few hours now, slowing only to refresh the horses or when their northern course was impeded by heavy brush or thick forest. They had also continued discharging their rifles at a regular clip, but, in the interest of conserving ammo, those intervals were widening now.

Raymond eased up beside Jack.

The sun had rotated well beyond its high point for the day and was now deep into its descent. It seemed rushed in its downward arc to the west, and the air was already starting to attain that painful quality. The approach of nightfall, the events of the day, and their predicament began to work on Jack. He and Raymond had done their best to draw attention to themselves, and likely had. He hoped they had. But the whole thing had been done in a wave of emotion, and now the cold and bitter logic of their circumstances was biting in like the wintry air.

It had been the right thing to do, perhaps the only thing. Jack was as sure of that now as he had been then. But only now was the outworking of their decision beginning to sink in. Thoughts of Custer entered his mind and he sympathized. But he and Raymond had more time to think about it, more time to ponder their annihilation.

But annihilation at whose hand? What's hand?

Jack chuckled, then wondered what he was laughing at.

He looked over at Raymond, whose eyes were set forward, no noticeable expression or emotion. There was nothing in his face that would indicate the kinds of thoughts Jack was having. He was still

Raymond. The same man who preferred to sit alone on the front porch at Jonas's ranch; the same man who, night after night, slept upright against a tree, hat down, deceptively oblivious to the world around him. The same one who'd killed the kidnapper and cavalry troops as though there were nothing to it. He was the enemy that Colonel Asheworth had loathed to the point of obsession. He was Jack's most loyal companion. His truest friend.

All at once, a wave of guilt rushed through Jack. The man beside him, his friend, was only here because Jack had bought, or been duped, into this. And now they were being hunted by possibly the most efficient Indian tribe they'd ever seen or heard of. Or worse still, being sized up by some unknown or yet undiscovered predator. God only knew. The identity didn't matter; the results were the same.

They pushed forward in silence, allowing the horses their own pace, and eventually came into a small clearing.

Jack stopped.

The lay of the land was now leaning from west to east. The clearing, however, was level, and held only a few trees and scattered underbrush.

The top of a large boulder was exposed to the east, where the slope resumed its steep, downhill slant. Centuries of runoff had partially unearthed the large stone while at the same time eroding its crown into a smooth, flat surface. Back to the west, at the edge of the clearing, the forest tightened back up and continued its gradual ascent. More of the same.

But Jack's attention was on a particular hardwood, a single oak, wide and ancient, with several scuffs etched into its trunk. From a distance, the abrasions looked recent, fresh. It wasn't the tree, however, that had snagged his interest, but what was lying at its base. He started to point out the object to Raymond, but Raymond didn't seem to be paying attention. In fact, he had his head down, something Jack rarely saw in the saddle.

Jack dismounted and walked over to the foot of the tree.

Then he lowered his head too.

Lying on the ground, among the blood-sodden leaves, was a circular object, a small stick running through the center of it. The polished gray stones attached to the stick had various markings on them, but only a couple were still clear. Dried blood obscured the other impressions. Two were stuck together. All but one of the feathers that had once been attached to the bottom of the circle were now stripped away.

Jack picked up the object he'd seen the Sioux woman carrying only a couple of days earlier, the once beautiful relic she'd been gripping so tight. The look on her face still haunted him. Her song still rang in his ears.

Jack turned a broken feather between his fingers. The leaves and ground beneath him was still moist with blood, a lot of it. But, just like the field that had once hosted Asheworth's troops, there was no body.

He laid the feather back down and gently covered it with a handful of leaves.

"I'm sorry," he whispered.

"She had a warrior spirit," Raymond said.

Jack noted the sincerity in Raymond's voice. He stood up. "Who would do this?" he asked. "And why?" He motioned back to the south. "Hell, who *could* do this?"

Raymond shook his head.

"She knew who it was," Jack said. He looked to the south, trying to recall anything from that day that might help them now, any clue they might've overlooked or misunderstood. Nothing came. "It has to be Indians," he said finally. "It's gotta be the Sioux. But why in hell's name—"

The sound of sticks breaking and leaves rustling sang out from the hill above them.

Jack looked up the slope and drew his pistol without thinking. Raymond, who already had rifle in hand, only watched, keeping the firearm pointed at the ground.

More noise behind them, to the north. Jack whirled around in time to see a young pine tree swaying from side to side.

Leaves shuffled to the south. Jack spun again and saw a stand of dry underbrush quivering as if blown by the wind.

Then nothing.

Jack gripped the pistol. He scanned the forest ahead with eyes and ears, but the silence stretched on. He realized he was holding his breath.

"Maybe you asked the right question," Raymond said.

As Jack turned his eyes toward Raymond, a shadow crossed through his peripheral vision. A blur. He swung the pistol in the direction of the movement, already applying the first bit of lethal pressure to the trigger.

And then the sound came.

It was a distinct hissing noise, not unlike that of an angry snake. But it was traversing through space, starting at some point *out there* and coming closer. In an instant, one ear was full of the sound, and then both. All in less than a second or two.

Raymond dropped to his knees. There was a soft, wet slap, and then fine splinters of wood came down on the top of Raymond's hat. He rolled out from under the tree and grabbed the reins of his horse.

Jack fired in the direction he'd seen the shadow a moment earlier. The report echoed loudly in the silence. He saw nothing. He looked back at the tree where Raymond had been and saw a shiny steel bolt protruding from the hardwood.

Raymond grabbed the back of his jacket and pulled him into the clearing. Jack stumbled, recovered his balance, and turned. He saw Raymond was already mounted and shouting something down at him. He also saw something standing about fifty feet beyond.

Jack raised his pistol at the distant form, stealing a precious second for careful aim. He saw a blurred movement of gray an instant before the hammer connected with the firing pin.

Raymond's horse reared at the explosion from the revolver, blocking Jack's view. Jack moved away from the mare and dropped to one knee as Raymond brought his rifle around. They both took aim.

But there was nothing there.

The forest was empty in front of them.

Everything fell silent again. The two men held their firearms frozen before them, triggers halfway home. A bead of cold sweat started down the side of Jack's face. And then the sound of sloshing leaves and snapping limbs rose behind them.

Jack holstered the pistol and leapt onto his mount.

The hissing returned.

Raymond's horse screamed and reared as a steel projectile bit deep into her rear quarter. Raymond held on, struggling to control his injured mount. He cried out and smacked the mare violently, sending her surging forward toward the large boulder at the crest of the hill.

The noise was all around them now. Jack lay down on his mare's back and dug in his heels. The horse covered the ground in an instant. She hesitated a beat where the slope turned down beside the boulder, and then leapt down the hill.

Jack hit the ground, thrown off by the unexpected jump. Air rushed from his lungs and pain exploded in his abdomen. He clawed at the ground and rolled over, gasping. He swung a hand up and caught the reins a second before his mare bolted down the hill. The slack tightened and the horse jerked him thirty feet down the slope before she stopped and reared.

Jack rolled over and coughed. He looked back toward the top of the hill for Raymond.

His friend's wounded horse had just reached the edge of the sharp grade. And had stopped dead.

Jack's heart raced. He tried to call for the mare, to coax her into that final step over the rise, but there wasn't enough air in his lungs to make the sound. Instead, he watched helplessly as the hissing sound returned.

Raymond dove from his saddle and slapped into the rocky earth with a groan. He bounced to his feet, reins still in hand, and threw his momentum against the mare's harness. She stiffened and tossed her head back. Raymond gathered himself and pulled again, digging his heels into the hill. But the horse was locked up tight.

Then she reared hard and cried out. The mare hopped and bucked and swung her head around, snapping her teeth as if she were trying to ward off a swarm of angry bees.

Jack was up and moving and screaming for Raymond. He'd noticed a deep depression underneath the massive boulder and was struggling to bring his own horse back up the hill.

Raymond was easing to his left, toward the rock, but he didn't look back. He was still talking to his mare, soothing and reassuring her.

She was tossing her head relentlessly, straining to get a look at the strange things sticking in her side. But even in her painful confusion, her ears repeatedly flicked toward the sound of Raymond's voice, and her eyes continued to come back to him.

Jack made it to the entry of the cavern and realized they weren't making the only noise on the hill anymore. He swung his pistol around and fired blindly into the forest.

"Dammit, Ray! Come on!"

Raymond turned, scanned the woods farther down the hill, then reluctantly broke for the rock.

Jack led his horse inside. The area under the rock was only about seven feet high, and no more than fifteen feet deep. But at the moment, it was like a safety net dropped straight from heaven.

Raymond followed him in. He knelt and pressed a hand into his lower back, grimacing, then leaned his rifle against the dirt wall of the cavern and drew his pistol with one hand and his blade with the other.

Jack pulled his horse around sideways and lowered his rifle across the saddle. He sighted at the entry of the cavern and held his breath.

The sound was coming, near the entrance.

At the entrance.

Jack's finger slipped inside the trigger guard.

Raymond's mare limped inside.

16

"We have to stop."

CJ sighed. "You heard what Jack said."

"We can't even see where we're going," Ned went on. "For all we know, we might be heading north again."

"We're still going downhill, ain't we?"

"And?"

"And if we're still going downhill, then we ain't headed north."

Ned huffed. "I've never seen such naiveté."

CJ looked around for whatever Ned was talking about, but then just decided to ignore him. He was confident they weren't heading north, but he also knew Ned was right. A light drizzle had begun falling and the accompanying cloud cover was making it nearly impossible to keep their bearing. The arrival of clouds and rain had reduced their line of sight to only a matter of feet. It wouldn't be hard for anyone to lose their way in these conditions, even if they knew the terrain. But for three youngsters trying to *feel* their way through the foreign wilderness, it was almost guaranteed.

Angelina hadn't spoken since they'd separated from the others. She was wrapped in one of CJ's blankets, head against his back, hiding from the cold and terrible forest that had taken so much from her. Her light breathing and intermittent tears had left a lingering warm spot on his back.

He didn't mind.

Ned pulled up. "Here. This is a good place."

CJ stopped. They were in a clearing, really only a gap. But the small opening was mostly void of the familiar and tiresome undergrowth and scrub. The ground was level, and even visibility seemed better. It *was* inviting, but …

"Horsefeathers," CJ said. "Anybody in creation could see us here."

"But we could see them too."

"You're dull as a wagon tire," CJ mumbled.

"What?"

"Look, if we gotta stop, we need cover." CJ glanced around the immediate area, hoping to spot a hospitable place, but the darkness was too great. He swung his horse around.

"Help me find some bushes or somethin'."

Ned grunted another protest, made a show of tugging at his reins, but then stopped.

The sound was faint and quiet, its origin impossible to pin down through the trees. It was there, and then it wasn't.

A slow, broken, hissing noise.

CJ lifted his rifle from its saddle boot and listened. He slowly drew back the hammer until it locked in place. The click was like a roll of thunder in the quiet.

Angelina slid the blanket down to her shoulders.

Ned fumbled out the spare rifle, apparently following CJ's lead. He laid it across his lap and placed both hands on top of it. CJ wanted to ask what he was doing, and if he had cocked the firearm, but he didn't dare break the silence.

Sssssssssss

A tremor rippled down CJ's back. Both his arms tingled. He slid out of the saddle as quietly as he could and then helped Angelina down. He led her over to a nearby tree where she sat and proceeded to re-cocoon herself in the wet blanket.

CJ patted her shoulder, hoping she understood the gesture to stay put, and then looked back at the horses.

Ned was still mounted, still in the open, still holding the rifle down like it would jump away. Rainwater dripped from the brim of his hat.

CJ took a step toward him.

Sssssssssss

Ned went pale. His body visibly stiffened. He sat motionless, eyes round with fear, not daring to turn his head in the direction of the sound.

CJ knelt, senses raw. He aimed his rifle into the darkness, searching for something more concrete than noise, hoping to find nothing.

He heard leaves rustling behind him and swallowed into a dry throat. He didn't move. Twigs snapped somewhere in the woods beside him. Then silence.

He remained still.

The sound came again, but this time in a whisper, and not two feet from his ear.

"Sssseeee-ja-jaaaay."

CJ lowered the hammer and set the rifle down. He put a hand on the ground to steady himself. He hadn't realized how badly his chest was burning.

Eli crept closer until the faint moonlight unveiled his face. "Di-didn't wanna sc-sc-scare ya."

CJ nodded. "Yeah. No. It's alright. I'm really glad to see ya." He picked up the rifle and got to his feet. "Where's Jack and Ray?"

Eli looked down, suddenly lost in thought. He said nothing.

CJ waited, but the scout stayed that way, unmoving and silent. CJ finally touched his sleeve. "Eli?"

Eli jerked and his head snapped up. For a moment he just stared at CJ like he'd forgotten who he was, like he'd suddenly awakened in a strange place. Then he turned and walked away, motioning for the boy to follow.

CJ started after him but then stopped and looked back. Ned hadn't moved. He was still in the center of the clearing, still astride his horse, still facing the opposite direction. Angelina, however, was watching them through a small opening in the blanket.

Eli's voice came from the darkness to CJ's left. "Ca-ca-come."

CJ held up a finger to Angelina and silently mouthed, *Back in one minute.*

She blinked.

Eli was moving quickly and CJ had to hurry to keep from losing sight of him. The scout glanced back occasionally but kept up the brisk pace. Like a practiced dancer, he ducked, leaned, and soundlessly skipped over any undergrowth in his path—some of which CJ would never have seen without his guidance, never mind avoided.

Eli finally stopped by a large stand of scrub and looked around.

CJ used the pause to catch up. He figured they had gone at least fifty yards by now, and he was already growing uncomfortable at being that far away from the others. He was also sure *"one minute"* had passed. But when he stopped beside Eli and started to give voice to his concerns, the scout grabbed him by the sleeve and pulled him into the underbrush.

Dry, wiry fingers grabbed and pulled at their clothing as they waded through. And though the rain tapping into the brittle, lifeless earth gave them plenty of cover, CJ couldn't help feeling uneasy about the noise they were making.

Still, Eli went on, crashing through the brush, no longer able to avoid the obstacles the forest threw at him.

CJ grabbed the back of Eli's jacket and ducked in behind him. It seemed like a good idea, a good way to avoid getting separated in the thicket, but it wasn't enough to keep him from colliding with a tree when the scout veered suddenly to the left.

CJ rolled backward into a knot of loose foliage and briars. The thorns immediately bit into the exposed flesh of his face and hands. He twisted around, trying to untangle himself. But before he could make any real progress, Eli was standing over him, cutting, pulling, and forcing the worst of the barbs down with his foot. He took the boy's hand and pulled him to his feet.

"Sa-sa-sorry."

"It's okay," CJ said. "It was my fault." He started picking thorns from the sleeve of his jacket. "I don't think we should go any farther. Feels like we're getting a long way from—"

Eli was moving again.

CJ caught up and tucked in behind him again, this time keeping his head up. "Eli, I think we're getting too far from the others."

Eli said something, but CJ couldn't make it out through the noise.

"We gotta go back, Eli."

The old scout kept moving.

CJ was getting desperate. He decided the only thing left to do was grab the back of Eli's jacket and dig in his heels. Eli stopped before he could.

They were standing in a small oval break in the thicket. The space was just large enough that three, or maybe four, could sit down comfortably, wholly isolated from the surrounding forest. The delicate foliage would also act as a sentry of sorts, an early warning, sounding out if anything attempted to intrude from the outside.

"Here," Eli said.

CJ nodded. "It looks—"

"Sta-stay here 'til ma-ma-mornin'." Eli tilted his head back and closed his eyes. "The-they's a ra-ra-ridge," he said, pointing to the west. "Ten ma-minutes yonder. Sa-soon as you ga-get there, ga-ga-go south." He opened his eyes and looked at CJ.

CJ nodded.

"It'll ta-ta-take you ho-home."

CJ took Eli by the sleeve. "What are you telling me this for? You're staying with us, ain't ya?"

"Ca-can't."

"Eli—"

"Ca-ca-can't." Eli looked away. Looked north.

They both stood in silence for a moment. Eli's eyes probed the darkness as if seeing. His bottom lip quivered, matching the tremble in his hands, and CJ could only wonder at the thoughts that were swirling in his mind.

The scout finally looked down and rubbed his hands together. "Go on, na-na-now, and ga-ga-get your fra-friends."

CJ knew he had to do just that. His worry over Angelina was coiling in his gut like a restless snake.

"Who's out there, Eli?"

Eli looked up at the night sky. He twisted his head around, looking this way and that. He seemed to be searching for a hole or break in the clouds. There was none.

"Bad," he finally said.

"What is?"

Eli's eyes came back to the black forest, and CJ saw concern in them. He saw doubt.

"Get on na-now."

They had to leave the horses. There was just no way to get them into the hideout. CJ and Ned reluctantly hitched them to a couple of trees a safe distance from the thicket. They slung their canteens over their shoulders and grabbed a handful of food and anything else they thought they might need from the saddlebags.

CJ slipped an extra box of rifle cartridges into his jacket pocket. He found it difficult to separate from the horses. In fact, it felt like amputating an important body part. He knew the rule as well as anyone: *always stay close to your mount.* But there were no other options.

Eli stood by until they were all safely inside, more patient than CJ could ever remember. Then, as though satisfied, he started walking north.

CJ followed him a few paces through the brush, resisting an urge to grab him by the arm. "Please be careful," he whispered.

Eli stopped and turned. He nodded at CJ and smiled.

CJ smiled back. "And thanks."

Eli glanced once more at the cloudy night sky, then turned and made his way into the darkness.

Ned was sleeping in no time, snoring loudly, and then Angelina shortly after. But CJ sat up, listening to the subtle sounds of the forest, the light patter of rain. He was surprised at how tired he was, and was sure if he only closed his eyes he'd be gone in a blink. He had no urge to try.

Still, the camouflage Eli had provided brought a measure of peace he hadn't known for a couple of days now, and his body was responding to it in a slow wash of relaxing muscles he found hard to resist. His eyes burned, felt dry and scratchy. His head ached.

His will weakened.

The noise of the forest went on, oblivious to the young man's plight. The rain, lighter and lighter. The wind through barren trees. A falling branch from somewhere above.

A distant crack. The swish of leaves.

17

Little pellets of ice hopped and danced about the entrance to the cavern, at first melting away but then starting to accumulate. The night had come, bringing freezing rain with it.

Jack and Raymond had been slumped at the rear of the small, dark pocket for what seemed like hours now, their backs pressed against the cold, damp, muddy wall. The darkness was thick and palpable, suppressing their range of vision to mere feet beyond the cavern entrance.

There had been no attempt by anyone or anything to enter their safe haven. No leaves rustling or trees bending from beyond. There had been no more blurry shadows or hissing sounds, just silence.

But *they* were still there, Jack knew, still not satisfied. He knew this not from any kind of evidence, but from something inside, something in his gut— a place that warns of danger long before there's anything external to fear, a place where trustworthiness is proven but often ignored.

He was holding one of the bolts that had struck Raymond's mare. The other one was lying somewhere outside, where Raymond had slung it after pulling it from the horse's flank. They had each taken turns inspecting the thing before darkness set in. The projectile was only about seven inches long, just a little longer than Jack's hand, and had two rear stabilizers on the blunt back end. The smooth, polished shaft was about an inch in diameter and shined all the way up to its razor-sharp tip. The whole thing was apparently one piece, easily the finest craftsmanship Jack had ever seen, easily the most lethal arrow ever pointed in his direction. The weapon gave rise to both terror and awe.

Jack tossed it aside and it clinked against the rocky, mud-covered ground. He hoped he would never see such a thing again, but felt certain he would. He leaned farther into the back wall and laid his rifle across his lap. It was then he noticed a vaguely circular object lying a few feet away. With some effort, he leaned forward and picked it up. The sticky gray stones and single feather brought instant recognition. Jack had no memory of how it had gotten into the cave. He guessed it had still been in his hand when the disturbance broke out, and he'd unknowingly carried it inside during the confusion. Or maybe he'd dropped it into his coat pocket as he drew his pistol, though he didn't recall that either. Whatever the case, here it was: one more cruel reminder of the mistake this whole foray had been.

He took out his matches. They were damp, but after a couple of tries he managed to get a cigar lit. He closed his eyes, enjoying the sweet flavor and, at present, the only source of happiness available. He slipped a hand between the folds of his jacket and pulled out the worn, folded page that had become the companion of his evening smoke. He didn't open it, as the darkness would never allow him to view its contents, but just held it, drawing calm from it. It always did that for him. Though, in truth, the page should have been a source of sadness rather than strength. And that had been the case once, but time had slowly taken away its edge. So now what used to cut perfectly and deeply, only had the power to pierce. But pierce it did. Sometimes.

Raymond groaned as he tried to find a more comfortable position on the cavern floor. He stretched out his right leg and released a long, even breath.

"Who was she?"

Jack glanced at the corner where Raymond was sitting, but only an obscure profile was visible.

"What say?"

"No one spends that much time with anything unless it has to do with a woman."

Jack said nothing. He pulled on the cigar and stared at the cavern entrance for a while. He watched the ice and rain spreading on the ground outside, freezing, melting, refreezing, or at least what he could see of it. And then his mind swam slowly backward, and he didn't see the cavern anymore.

"She was beautiful," he said. "My heavens, was she beautiful. Like nothing I've ever seen." He looked down and went back to the smoke. "Those eyes … those big, round, green eyes. The way they looked back at me. The longer I stared into them, the drunker I'd feel. The more nothing else mattered, or existed.

"There was something right away," Jack went on. "Something that connected us. She was the first woman I ever kissed, the only one I ever loved, I mean, really knew I loved. Everything changed when she was around, everything else became unimportant. It was like the world stepped aside for her."

"What was her name?"

"Rikka," Jack said. "I don't remember her last name, never really did for that matter. It was one of those long, hard to pronounce names, like a foreigner or something." He marveled at how sharp her memory still held in his mind. That lively green shade in her eyes, the tint of her hair in the sunlight, the curves of her face and jaw, the power in her smile. The touch of her hand. It was all still there, still intact, still fresh.

"What happened?"

"War," Jack said. "I signed up like everyone else. Hell, I reckon her father was glad; he'd never cared for me anyhow. He was just like the rest of those business folk types, wanting better for his girl than a farm boy. Don't reckon I blame him now."

Jack went silent a moment, and Raymond let it linger. He relit his cigar and stared outside.

"She wept when it was my time to go—clung to me, crying and pleading and fighting me to stay. I've never forgotten what it felt like to have someone care that much. I think it's what got me through the war alive, what kept me from losing my mind." He held the old letter up in front of him. "She still gives me peace, still keeps me going."

"Where is she?"

"Don't know. I wrote to her several times while I was gone, but I never got anything back." He handed the letter to Raymond. "A friend of hers gave me this when I got home."

Raymond unfolded the page and struck a match. Jack could see the scribbled words in the wavering light ...

All I know is we are going west. Will wait for you always.
I love you.
Rikka

"I never knew if she got any of the letters. I found out later that her father took off chasing gold. I searched for two years, all the way to the sea, until I couldn't keep myself up anymore. No one had seen or heard of her." Jack ran a hand down his face and sighed. "I heard all the stories, the god-awful stories, read the papers from town to town—all about the victims of the so-called gold rush, folks that set out for riches only to find Indians. I finally gave up and came back east. It was, and still is, the hardest thing I've ever done. Harder than anything I went through in the war."

Jack tilted his head back and drew on the smoke. "Those eyes," he said. "I still remember 'em so clear." He glanced at Raymond. "Ain't that funny, I can't remember what I ate for breakfast yesterday, but I still remember those big green eyes from some twenty years ago."

Raymond handed the letter back. "That's because those memories live in a different place."

Jack nodded.

"And it was jerky," Raymond said.

Jack grunted. "Yeah, I reckon it was."

"Let's go find her."

Just the sound of it stirred emotions Jack hadn't felt in years. He swallowed them down. "Twenty years is a long time," he said. "A lifetime. Besides, she's still alive in here." He touched his chest, echoing Raymond's sentiment. "Hell, if she is still alive, I reckon she's long married by now."

"So?"

Jack grinned at his friend, though he doubted Raymond could see the gesture. He noticed the shimmering blanket of ice then. The moon, having evidently found its way through the clouds, had lit up the frozen ground outside and, with it, had awakened a myriad of sparkling pinpoints of light, all of which were winking back up at the great glowing mass hanging somewhere high above. It was a thing of beauty.

"If we get out of here," Jack said, "I might just take you up on that."

Except for the hollow sound of wind blowing across the cavern opening, all remained still and quiet. The freezing rain had stopped and the thin mantle of ice it had left behind was still glowing and reflecting the moonlight. The ice— deceptively illuminated the world outside, as if enticing the cavern occupants to a peek beyond their earthen prison. The lure was strong and Jack nearly went for it, but his muscles protested at even the slightest movement. He was tired. He hadn't slept well since they'd entered the forest, and nearly not at all in the last couple of days. He knew the idea was beyond foolish, anyway, but the temptation was nonetheless great.

Raymond continued changing positions, still favoring the area below his ribs. A couple of hours had passed, and his periodic groans had lessened, but his discomfort was obvious.

Jack glanced to his left. The newfound moonlight had opened up the cavern a little, revealing more of his friend's shadowy profile, but little else.

"Is it always this bad?"

"No."

"How'd it happen?"

Raymond didn't answer, so Jack looked back at the cavern entrance. The fatigue was getting hard to bear now, and a part of him wished *they* would just come and get it over with. But still another part of him was terrified at the mere thought of it. Then he wondered if anyone was out there at all. It hadn't, until now, occurred to him that their unknown adversary might have sniffed out the misdirection and doubled back in pursuit of the youngsters. And they were all alone.

Raymond cleared his throat and shifted around again. Jack wondered if his friend was trying to mask his discomfort now. All he could make out through the darkness was Raymond's lowered head. Unusual, considering the circumstances. Jack tried taking solace from

it, knowing that Raymond was seldom—no, never—surprised. If he
didn't feel it necessary to stare at the cavern entrance, then maybe it
wasn't. But perhaps it was something else. Maybe he was hurting
pretty bad. The thought of it started the flow of guilt again, guilt for
having dragged them both into this thing. And now ... now, he didn't
know what to do.

"I'm sorry," Jack said.

"What?"

"Why'd you come?"

"Where else would I be?" Raymond said. "You're the only family I
got."

Jack sighed. "If I could go back ..."

"If you could go back, then there's no one to block those hillbillies
from finishing what they started with the girl."

"I reckon," Jack said. "But look where we are now."

"Yeah, I know. But the question is, how much would you be willing
to give up for the sake of someone else?"

The question surprised Jack, especially coming from the perpetually
quiet Raymond McAlister. He pondered it. Would he have come just
for Angelina's sake? If that had been the only deal, to bring her out of
the woods, no money involved? He was pretty sure he would have. In
fact, something inside was telling him he would've been even more
eager. But was that enough to justify this dark, wet hole in the side of
the earth? It was a question no one could answer for him.

The cave went silent again as neither of them spoke. Jack was
thinking about what Raymond had said earlier.

"Don't you have any family back home?"

"No."

"No big eyed-lady whose last name you can't pronounce?"

Raymond shifted again, let out a breath. "Just Libby."

"Libby?"

"My sister."

"Back in Virginia?"

"Yeah ... Virginia."

Raymond's voice had gone thin, almost a whisper, like he was
standing at the threshold of a door he didn't want to open.

Jack decided not to push.

"My father was a bastard," Raymond said. "He married my mother when she was young, then abandoned her in the first year when she turned up pregnant with me. She always struggled."

Raymond's horse whinnied and tossed her head, and Jack's fingers tightened around his rifle. He glanced at the entrance to the cavern, but he knew it was probably the mare's pain and growing discomfort that had aroused her.

"I was told he'd come around from time to time," Raymond went on. "But never long and never often. I never knew him; I was too young then. But I do remember the last time he came. He knelt beside me, told me he was my pop, and gave me a silver coin. I cursed him for a coward, swore I'd repay to him all the ills he'd visited on my mother. But it all stayed in my head; none of it made it past my lips. I was too scared, I guess. He patted me on the head and went in the house. I remember the boots he was wearing that day and the creak of the porch, but nothing else, nothing about his face. That might've been the last time I seen him."

The wind rushed across the entrance of the cavern, spilling a wash of freezing air inside. Jack shivered.

"I heard 'em fighting from where I was playing behind the house, then he was riding away, gone again, chased off by my mother's screams. She wept for two days after that." Raymond paused. "Libby was born that winter. Mom held her, named her, and then, with the last bit of her life, she kissed Libby's forehead and whispered something in her ear."

Raymond stopped. The tone of his voice was very quiet now, barely audible, almost as though he was talking to himself.

"I'm sorry," Jack whispered.

Raymond cleared his throat. "We lived with Uncle Devin then, my mom's brother. He was a good man, like you. He had loved his sister, and he loved his sister's children. He had a small farm, never married, always did the best he could. We always ate but were always hungry too. Uncle Devin was one of those that regularly went on about the goodness of God, trusting the Lord, and such as that. But it never did him any good. He was mostly blind when I left for the war."

Jack nodded.

"She took her first steps in my direction, Libby, that is, and never let up. It was the worst sort of nuisance at first, having a young'un constantly underfoot. But she wouldn't go away. Try as I might, and I did try, I just couldn't shake the little thing, couldn't even pass her off to Uncle Devin. She wouldn't go to anyone else, wouldn't have it, and that was that." Raymond stopped, then said, "And then a time came when I didn't want her to go away. There was a moment in the field when it struck me that she was as much me as I was me. But she wasn't me. Far from it. Oh, God, Jack, she just wanted to play, even when we were sick and hungry. She just wanted to laugh … She was my mother. And she wasn't my mother."

Jack noted his friend's use of the past tense but remained quiet. He took the Indian relic from his lap and began absently chipping away the dried blood with a fingernail.

"When Lee laid his sword down in sixty-five, the Yanks swore that if we surrendered our weapons and promised never to bear arms against the Union again, then we could go home. So we did. Most of us did." Raymond changed positions again. "We were all kinda numb for a bit. It didn't seem real. Most of us were thankful, thankful to still be alive, and some of us didn't know what it meant to be alive anymore. But we disbanded and went home. I stayed in camp an extra day, helping those who needed it, then I left too. That one extra day cost me everything."

Jack looked at the profile of his friend. Raymond sat unmoving, the brim of his hat pointing down. A shape in the shadows.

"I stopped by a creek ten minutes from Uncle Devin's place," Raymond said, "just long enough to scrub the worst of the blood and dirt from my uniform. That's when I heard the distant thunder in the south. But it wasn't thunder, and I knew it wasn't. Then I saw the smoke. Uncle Devin was already dead when I got there, and Libby was on her way. Her whole left side had been ground up by a scattergun. I got to see her off; I even felt her go. She had grown so much …"

Jack felt tears welling. He ground his teeth. "Who?"

"Bastards," Raymond said. "There were other places, other folk, all left in the same state around the area. All on the outskirts. All defenseless."

Jack shook his head; he had heard the stories. Confederate holdouts who didn't want the war to end, terrorizing their own in order to drum up support or supplies. Yankee cavalry units, suddenly finding themselves riding behind the lines, uncontested by Southern regulars. Some only took what they needed or wanted and moved on. Others would burn the homes, barns, and stables of their victims. Some wouldn't light the fires until the families were locked firmly inside. Demons, all of them. The very angels of hell. They were men who would've been in prison or at the end of a rope had there never been a war.

"The burial was three days later: Uncle Devin, Libby, and myself last. Whoever I was back then went in the ground with 'em. I stopped caring for anything. It's the last time I remember crying." Raymond lifted his head. "I could've been there," he said. "If I hadn't stopped by the creek, I could've been there. If I had left the army when they released me, I would've been there." He paused. "Just like you and that Rikka, it's all I've ever wanted, just to be there."

Jack rested his head on his hands. He couldn't bring himself to say sorry again. It was just so trivial, so inadequate. He became aware of the cold again, surrounding and invading the small space like a thing alive. Water dripped somewhere.

The twinkling ice had lost its magic.

"I'm sorry," he whispered.

18

Jack winced at the pain in his back and neck. He placed his hands on his knees and forced his legs out. They felt dead and threatened not to work. He groaned and looked to his left, trying to blink away sunlight, hardly believing he'd dozed off. The space beside him was empty, both Raymond and his mare gone. The Indian relic was lying on a rock where Raymond had been sitting. It was clean and dry. Jack slipped it in his pocket and got to his feet.

He led his horse up the hill slowly, allowing time for blood to find its way back into his extremities. Raymond was walking his horse in the clearing where they'd been surprised yesterday. She had a marked limp, but was moving. And though she'd be limited to short intervals and a much slower pace, it appeared she would make it.

Raymond looked up as if reading Jack's thoughts, and nodded.

Jack scanned the forest. The woods around them, once alive with movement and sound, were quiet now. Whatever was out there had either moved on or was waiting.

But waiting for what?

And why?

Jack turned to Raymond. "What say?"

"North."

"North?"

"We can't go back the same way," Raymond said. "They'll be expecting that. We'll have to keep 'em unsteady. Going north then doubling back through that valley to the east will force 'em to think a bit. And each minute they stop to think is a gift to us." He paused, then said to himself, "There has to be a creek down there."

Jack looked north. The thought of taking a route different from the others was a little unsettling, but not as much as riding back into the teeth of another ambush. Besides, the idea made sense: if there was a creek in the valley, it would enable them to move both faster and quieter, under the camouflage of moving water. At least ...

"If they ain't watching us," Jack said.

Raymond just nodded, said nothing.

They continued north, stopping every so often to rest Raymond's wounded mare. The ride had become easier. The underbrush that had slowed them earlier had receded considerably—still there, but thinner and more spread out. The early sunlight was flowing through the forest in brilliant, thin streams of yellow light, and was softening all but the thickest stands of ice from the previous night.

Just seeing the sun was enough to lift Jack's spirits, as though somehow the light brought protection. He knew in his gut this wasn't true, but he didn't have the energy to listen to his gut. He didn't want to. He would take whatever peace he could get, no matter how limited or irrational.

They moved on, watching and listening, roughly following the forest wherever it led them. Every breath from the horses was visible now, as well as their own. In fact, as the cold went, the days and nights were getting harder to tell apart.

Jack lifted a cigar from his pocket, then thought better of it and put it back. He looked across at Raymond. "What was the deal with Asheworth? The woods? The boys? Why'd he hate you so bad?"

Raymond shrugged, shook his head. "There were a lot of woods, a lot of boys."

Jack just nodded. He was thinking now of their conversation last night, the last thing Raymond had said about his dad. "You said it *might've* been the last time you seen your father?"

Raymond turned his head in acknowledgment of the question, but didn't speak.

They rode on in silence.

Jack regretted the question. Raymond had always been reluctant to visit the past, and last night Jack had seen the pain it caused him to peel the flesh back on those old wounds.

Jack had no such wounds. He'd lived a charmed life during the war, and he knew it. He'd not only survived the conflict but had also risen in rank—to captain—even after fighting on the western front, where defeat and retreat had been commonplace. He had no family to speak of, save for his grandparents, who'd died almost as one just as the war was beginning. He'd never known his parents. There had been no one left at home to find suffering after the war. No one except himself. He'd been shielded.

He'd been lucky.

"I think I killed him," Raymond said.

"What?"

"My father. At Cold Harbor in sixty-four." Raymond shifted in his saddle and grimaced. "We came out to collect the fallen during the ceasefire. The cessation was long overdue, so the man was already swollen and pale. But he looked like me. Just like me. Like I was staring down at myself. Only this fella was older and wearing blue. He was lying on his back in front of the trench I'd been defending, and there's a better than average chance I put him there."

"You seriously think it was him?"

Raymond's eyes wandered off, like he was revisiting that distant place in the past. Then his voice came likewise, soft and quiet, as if from far away. "I reckon that'd be alright."

Jack glanced ahead. He'd become distracted by a subtle, yet evident, change in their surroundings. The soft black soil, so prevalent thus far in the forest, had gradually changed over to a grainy dirt and clay. The trees were still all around, but no longer in front of them. There was no more underbrush impeding their path. Their course was turning slightly eastward, just as they wanted.

Their course?

Jack stared forward through tired eyes, trying to process what he was seeing. It certainly wasn't that the trees weren't growing as thick in this particular locale. They were. Nor was it the case that the familiar foliage and scrub hadn't taken in this place. It had. What was striking, however, was that all of these things seemed to have been removed from their immediate path. The area ahead seemed to have been beaten down at some point. The underbrush was there, but it was small and unmatured. Where there had once been trees, there were now stumps. The ground below, underneath a plethora of leaves, was firm and rutted.

Could it be?

Jack's mare reared violently. Before he could react, or even register what was happening, he was sliding down the animal's back. He instinctively grabbed for the saddle horn, desperate to hang on, but couldn't get a hand on it. Couldn't find it. He tried again, reaching, stretching, but only succeeded in snatching a handful of the horse's mane. He held on. Several strands of the animal's coarse hair snapped in his fingers. But the majority held, as did he.

Then a dark smudge swam through his peripheral vision. It had been just a smear from the corner of his eye, but it had been moving. And it had been large. And now, Jack deduced quickly, it was in front of his horse.

He groped for his pistol and nearly lost his balance. The mare was still on her hind legs, still kicking and screaming. He found the saddle horn, stood up in the stirrups, and leaned into the animal's panicked rear. He managed to free his sidearm, but not before the mare twisted to the left and came down hard facing the flank of Raymond's empty horse.

Jack swung his pistol around and drew the hammer back.

Her eyes met his, and even through the rush of adrenaline, he shuddered.

A woman. An old woman.

She was dressed in a long, dirty gray cloak that flowed out behind her in a snarl of dried mud and leaves. Matted gray hair sprung wildly from inside the hood of the cloak, covering most of her face and neck.

But not her eyes.

Her eyes penetrated. They bore into him, large and lifeless. Emotionless. Like nothing existed behind them. She didn't blink.

Jack did.

He struggled to clear his mind, to form words, but nothing came.

"You have offended them," she said in an airy, quiet voice. "They are the Watchers."

Sweat was forming under the brow of Jack's hat. He realized he was squeezing the handle of the pistol and tried in vain to relax his grip. He noticed the woman was clutching a cane in her right hand, but she wasn't leaning on it. Then he saw the bottom had been honed to a sharp point.

Where the hell was Raymond?

Jack tugged at his mare's reins. Her breathing was deep and ragged, like she was recovering from a long, exhausting run. She pawed and tossed her head, responding little to his attempts to settle her.

Jack leaned toward the woman.

"What say?"

The left side of her mouth curled up, forming an absurd half-grin, and she tilted her head slowly to one side. Her gaze seemed to intensify then, drilling into him through dead gray eyes.

"You have seen but you have not seen," she said. "The trees move; the bush gets up and runs. Shadows live; the snakes are hissing. The Grigori have come. The Nephilim are growing."

"What are—"

"You have offended them. They are the Watchers." Her head straightened. "Now you go the way of the soldiers."

Her head suddenly jerked to the right. The turn was quick, unnaturally fast, almost like something outside herself had suddenly snatched her head to one side.

She raised the tip of her cane at Raymond, who had appeared from behind a tree to Jack's left, his rifle pointing at the ground. Her head tilted again to one side, then the other, then back again.

"None can resist," she said to Raymond. This time her voice was not quiet, but seemed to emanate from her bowels, raspy and sick. She slid a step back and waved the stick like a weapon. Like a challenge. The grin had left, but her eyes were unchanged—hollow, unblinking spheres, dark and vacant. Jack saw them flick between himself and Raymond.

Or did they?

Raymond didn't move.

"None!" she hissed. And then, abruptly, she swung around and limped into the forest.

Jack sat motionless, stunned. He looked at Raymond.

Raymond didn't turn. He watched the woman's movement through the trees until there was nothing left to see.

"Ray?" Jack whispered.

Raymond said nothing.

"Ray?"

Raymond looked up.

Their eyes met, but neither spoke.

The surroundings were turning cold again, threatening. Jack looked back at the forest where the woman had gone.

"Hey!" he called.

Nothing.

"Lady!"

Silence.

Jack holstered his pistol and looked at Raymond. "We might oughta turn back." He meant it, but the suggestion came out with little conviction. Truth was, he hadn't a clue what to do. There were no good ideas. No more misdirections to try. There was just no way to know where *they* were. Who *they* were. He had an impulse to chase the woman down, to get answers even if it meant standing on her throat. But he didn't. He glanced at the woods. Where had she come from? And who the hell was she? Certainly not an Indian, for her flesh was as pale as his own. More so. Much more so.

And those eyes.

Raymond screamed and lunged onto his horse.

"Go!"

Jack whirled. He saw a tree branch quivering in the distance. The sound of snapping limbs and crushed leaves crawled up his spine like something alive. He bent low in the saddle and fell in behind Raymond's limping mare.

They were moving downhill, following the slow, gradual turn of the track between the trees. Jack's stomach burned. He looked back, saw only trees speeding by on either side. Nothing jumped from the forest's edge; there was no one in pursuit. He heard nothing except the pounding of the horses' hooves.

Raymond suddenly pulled up and spun his horse around.

Jack jerked his reins to avoid a collision and sped several yards past before he was able to swing his own mount around. Confused, he yanked his rifle from its scabbard and drew alongside Raymond. He saw the blood collecting below Raymond's mare then, and understood why his friend had pulled up. He'd had to.

Raymond faced the ground they'd covered. His face was beaded with perspiration and locked in a grim, determined glare of anger.

They would make their stand here, Jack knew. And that was fine. He swung his mare around so her head wouldn't interrupt his aim, and then sighted his Winchester at the eastern edge of the forest. Raymond, he knew, had the west.

They waited.

A gust of wind poured through the woods. Trees roiled and creaked. Leaves fell. Air hissed along the ground. The whole forest was abruptly alive with sound and movement.

Jack swore. His rifle flicked from one tree to the next, from quivering bushes to swirling leaves and back again. But nothing was coming.

Nor did it.

The wind died away. There was no more sound. No more movement.

Jack spat. "What are they waitin' for?"

Raymond said nothing. His blue eyes combed the landscape with the grace and skill of a predator. But, like Jack's, they found nothing.

Minutes passed. Jack finally lowered his rifle and felt the blood returning to his arms. His fingers tingled. He glanced back, paranoid of their unguarded rear, but saw only more of the same. He allowed his mare to fall back a few steps toward a knot of grass she'd been eyeing. From there he could see that the woods to the north were sloping down into what was probably a small valley or ravine. And then he saw something else.

Out of the valley behind them, just visible through the trees, was a gray, angular structure. It was large and unnatural, and having spent the last several days with only trees and scrub, it took Jack a moment to register what he was seeing. He pulled his reluctant horse away from the grass and moved closer to the valley.

"Ray."

Raymond looked over his shoulder. His expression had softened but was still lined and hard-edged.

Jack gestured with a nod of his head, and Raymond swung his mare around. Jack grimaced. Even from several yards away, he could see the puddle of blood the horse left behind.

Raymond pulled up beside Jack. He located the tin roof immediately. His eyes narrowed.

"Reckon it's a house?" Jack asked.

"No."

"What, then?"

Raymond shook his head and nudged his horse down the hill.

The path widened and then flowed into a larger open area below. The tin roof didn't belong to a house, but a building of some kind. And not just one. As they came farther down the hill, they saw two other buildings beside it on the north side, and two more directly opposite to the south. The structures were separated by a broad, empty street, lined with dirt-filled troughs and empty hitching posts. Everything was stained with the loose dirt from the street, and obviously had been for some time.

They eased down the grade, passing a small sign in the brush to their right. The sign was nailed to a couple of thick support posts and had been almost completely overtaken by vines and foliage. The words were small and worn, nearly unintelligible. Jack leaned from his saddle to get a better look.

JONES MINE.

This was the entrance to the town. Jack was surprised the place even existed. He had automatically assumed that since the rest of Cavanaugh's story had been lies, then all of it had. But here it was: Jones Mine.

Jack moved into the street. There was a dangling sign attached to the first building on the north side. Considering the state of the place, the word *Blacksmith* was surprisingly clear. The structure beside it, in the middle, had no such sign. Its door hung outward, the top hinge snapped away from the frame. The lone window beside the door had been broken inward. The final building in the sequence had a large sign on the roof that simply read *Trade*.

Across the way, on the south side, stood what had probably been a makeshift schoolhouse and post office.

Jack looked back. There was a large church on a hill to the west, overlooking the town. The place of worship was nestled back in the trees and had once been grand. But now its white-paneled sides were tan with dirt and neglect. All the windows, which were numerous, were either shattered or missing entirely. A long steeple lay broken on the ground by the entrance.

Jack's mare tugged at the reins, instinctively pulling him toward one of the barren troughs. He gave her the slack she wanted. Raymond's horse was already there, sniffing into the dust of the empty basin.

Raymond dismounted and looped his reins around one of the hitching posts. He stepped into the unmarked building with the busted door and broken window.

Jack did likewise, tying his horse to a separate beam, but then stopped on the connecting walkway. He searched the forest surrounding the town. There was nothing unusual there, no movement or sound. But he could feel it, something uneasy, something stirring within.

He walked inside.

The floor creaked; broken glass snapped beneath his feet. The room smelled damp and stale. Sheets of linen were strewn liberally around the place, discolored by the dirt from outside. Long-dried contents of a dozen or so broken bottles stained the floor. Most of the shelves were broken or pulled down. Those that had survived were empty, save for a couple of books and a few rolls of gauze. A small desk sat in the middle of the room, dividing the space into two partitions, while a long, narrow table sat flush against the wall in the back.

Jack picked up a little wooden nameplate lying among the debris at his feet.

Arthur Watts, M.D.

He held it up. "I reckon the town doc used to be here."

Raymond was standing behind the desk holding a piece of paper, his eyes working from side to side. He nodded at the floor behind the desk.

"He still is."

Jack stepped around the desk, all the while eyeing his friend. The thin sound of glass still popped under each footfall.

Raymond went on reading.

The desk was pulled up against the wall, presumably to allow easier access to the examining table in the back. As Jack rounded the doctor's old workspace, he found himself thinking about all the life and death this room had likely seen.

Probably none like this.

The body was sitting upright in the wedge between the desk and the wall. Jack knelt. It wasn't a body anymore, but it had been. All that remained now was coarse, gray bone, peering through gaps in the man's clothing. There was a puncture in the doctor's vest, and a long, life-ending fracture along the left side of the skull. One of the fingers on the right hand was broken off.

Jack shook his head.

Raymond handed the paper to him, then moved back to the broken window and looked out.

Jack stood and leaned on the desk. He looked down at the page.

... all the symptoms of classic dementia, but only the persons who had taken up with him were exhibiting the signs, which was largely the youth of the populace. This was most puzzling indeed. I have never observed the disease in a youth and never seen the onset so quickly take hold of a victim of any age. But yet, there it was before me: detachment, memory loss, disorientation, all typically associated with the loss of cognitive function. Many could not remember names or places; some could not tell me their own names. None could tell me where they were, not even the country they were in. Some would become disoriented in only an instant, not knowing how they got in the room or why they were here. This was totally random, never a pattern. There were occasions when a few patients momentarily regained function that had only moments earlier seemed lost. Memory

was suddenly and completely restored, disorientation relieved, detachment gone. The patient was just as they would be normally. But this never lasted; the illness would always return, sometimes the next day, sometimes in minutes. This was all in the beginning. As time passed the sudden recoveries diminished, until finally gone for good. Except for those brief, positive relapses, this is precisely what one should expect from progressive dementia. What did not fit, however, was that the sufferers never displayed a loss of motor skills. Indeed, their physical aptitudes were only more pronounced. Reflexes were the most responsive I have ever observed or studied. They possessed an extraordinary ability to react. Strength and speed of motion were phenomenal, unparalleled by anything I have heard of. I could never make this fit into the model of understood dementia.

He would return periodically as the years passed, and again they would follow him into the forest, sometimes for days, before finally returning with their mental states only further deteriorated. Eventually, they were completely unresponsive to anything: friends, family, things they once treasured, evoked no emotion; their reason was no longer present. They had lost that which made them human.

In due course, the elders, parents, and those who were just generally concerned formed a posse and waited incognito until he came again. He did, and when he and his subjects were a day into the forest, the posse went in as well. The rest of us, those who were left, waited several days before forming our own small search party. We entered the woods on the same path the others had taken, and searched all that we could in a day's light. Blood was spread without prejudice: on trees, in the leaves, drifting in the creek and mud; wherever they had fallen, there was blood —, but no bodies. All we were able to locate were their firearms, which were all laid neatly in a pile, stacked meticulously on top of one another; all of which were fully loaded. None, so far as we could surmise, had been fired.

Except for us (the search party), no one who entered the forest that season ever returned. Well, that is, until now. They have killed everyone, and now they wait for me, the last, letting me wither away. My great hope, perhaps my last hope, is that …

Jack flipped the page over only to reveal the blank back side. He pushed off the desk and scanned the area around him. "Where's the rest of it?"

Raymond spoke from his position by the window. "That was it. It was lying beside him."

"You read it?"

"Enough."

Jack pulled on the desk's top drawer. It resisted, but finally slid open with a whine. There were pencils, papers, and various other stationery scattered around inside. A couple of small, unopened bottles—presumably medicine of some sort—rolled around and came to rest in the back. But there was nothing else. No more of the letter.

Jack knelt beside the doctor's remains. The body was resting against the bottom drawer of the desk. Jack wondered if he could move it without it coming apart. He wondered if he wanted to. He decided to look through the pockets first, hoping the doctor would have kept the rest of the letter on his person. That would make sense; lots of folks did. But it wasn't there.

Jack sighed and stood up reluctantly. He gently lifted the body by the shoulders, elevating it only an inch or two above the floor, and slid it away from the desk. The wall where the remains had been was black with dry, decomposed blood. The dark fluid had also hardened in a ragged oval under the desk.

Jack felt a pang of guilt for having disturbed the remains. He wasn't sure why, but something just felt wrong about it. He laid a hand on Dr. Watts' shoulder as if to apologize, then opened the bottom drawer. It slid open easily, with almost no effort. And it was empty—save for a handful of unsharpened pencils and rat droppings.

Jack swore and stood. He slipped the letter into his pocket, figuring to deliver it to Doc Lewis back in Twin Pines. He moved back around the desk slowly, sifting through scattered mail as he went.

"Everything's several years old," he said absently. He scanned the rest of the room. "I reckon we oughta get moving. Need to be in that valley by nightfall."

Raymond said nothing. He was still looking out the window, but had moved to the far side, closer to the door.

Jack dropped the mail on the desk.

"Ray?"

Raymond remained silent. He didn't turn, didn't nod, didn't acknowledge Jack at all.

He stared outside.

19

The wind had come again, twisting about chaotic brown spirals of leaves and dust in the street. It swam through the abandoned buildings of Jones Mine, provoking eerie creaks and moans from the neglected structures.

It also lifted the edges of the gray, hooded cloak, shrouding the figure on the hill behind the school.

The cloak appeared to be long and heavy, and although the breeze tossed the fabric about, it unveiled nothing of the shadowy form beneath it. The hood drooped low over the figure's face, but even from a distance of some seventy paces, it seemed to be silently communicating with Raymond, returning his stare, beckoning him.

Jack pressed a shoulder against the doorjamb and peered out at the rifle sheathed in his saddlebags. He swore and slid back against the wall.

"We've gotta get out of here."

Raymond didn't respond, didn't move, didn't break from his private conversation at the window. His gaze was locked on the hill, eyes narrowed like those of a boy whose long-awaited dance had finally arrived.

Jack watched him, noting the absence of anxiety in his friend, the life in his eyes. He looked back out the door.

The gray shape moved and in a blink melted into the cover of the trees.

Raymond followed, moving away from the window, around Jack, and out the door.

Jack followed, hand on his pistol. He was scanning the opposite edge of town, but thinking of nothing now but the rifle. His back met

Raymond's, who seemed to have stopped. But Jack kept moving, twisting around Raymond and quickly reducing the distance between the mare and himself.

Then he froze.

Another figure. Standing less than ten feet away, at the corner of the building. And just like the one on the hill, the long, hooded shroud revealed nothing of the presence behind it.

The horses grunted, strained at the hitching posts. They tossed their heads and pawed the ground. But Jack was eyeing the familiar shiny, steel bolt loaded in the stranger's crossbow. The stranger made no attempt to raise the weapon but, rather, seemed to be watching Raymond, who was the closest. It slowly tilted its head to one side.

Jack's pulse quickened. A tremor shuddered through his hand as it moved closer to his holstered pistol.

They stood there, in silence. Three of them. Close. No one moving for what seemed like an eternity.

The air stirred.

Leaves scraped across the walkway.

Raymond's hand slid over the handle of his knife.

The shrouded figure straightened its head.

Jack went for his pistol.

In a heartbeat, Raymond was down. His blade slid across the walkway and slapped against the doorjamb of the doctor's office.

Jack fired. He held the trigger and worked the hammer, loosing four shots in quick, rapid-fire succession. Two splintered into the side of the building, knocking a plank free from its framing. The other two found nothing.

Nothing at all.

The shadow was gone.

Raymond rolled over and pushed himself up to his hands and knees. Blood was already collecting in a shallow puddle below him. He dropped his pistol and leaned against the wall.

Jack looked around, saw nothing, then quickly knelt beside Raymond. The crossbow bolt was in his friend's shoulder, his left sleeve and hand already saturated with blood. Jack placed a hand on Raymond's chest to brace him and then reached for the bolt.

Raymond shook his head and pushed him away. He was breathing heavily and grinding his teeth. He closed his eyes and motioned at the corner as if to tell Jack a greater threat still loomed.

Jack went to the edge of the building and pressed his back against the wall. He started reloading his pistol, glancing around town in the process. He saw nothing, but noticed the horses were still spooked and preoccupied with something to the east. Jack fed in the final bullet and spun the cylinder. He took a breath, ran a sleeve over the sweat on his brow, then twisted around the corner and fired.

The shot echoed loudly off the adjacent buildings. Smoke from the discharge hung in a cloud before his face. His ears rang. But that was all. The small alley between the buildings was empty. Jack knelt to get a better view below the powder smoke, but there was nothing to see. He hurried back to the walkway.

Raymond groaned and straightened up. And then, before Jack could get back to him, he grabbed the bolt and jerked it from his shoulder. He rolled over, writhing and kicking the wall and floor. Blood spread across the walkway in smears wherever he moved. He eventually came to rest on his back, pounding the floor with his good hand and spitting curses through clenched teeth.

Jack moved beside him and inspected the wound. "We've gotta stop the bleeding."

"No time," Raymond breathed. His eyes were still closed, his breath still ragged. His hand blindly swept the walkway beside him.

Jack retrieved his pistol and laid it in his hand.

Raymond pushed himself up and leaned against the wall, blinking at the surroundings: the horses, the street, the woods across the way, and then at the primitive, blood-reddened weapon lying on the walkway beside him. His blood. He holstered his pistol and glanced at the corner of the building.

"Anything?"

Jack shook his head and helped him to his feet. Raymond started toward the horses under his own power.

Jack turned and scanned the walkway for Raymond's blade. His mind was still reeling, still struggling to process what had just happened. The speed of the stranger was like nothing he'd ever seen. It was inconceivable that anyone—

Sound erupted from the forest above the school. Jack whirled. Footfalls echoed from the east.

A door whined open somewhere.

Jack hurried toward his horse. Raymond was already mounted and staring off to the east. Jack followed his eyes to the far edge of town. Another gray-robed adversary stood at the end of the street.

Then a second joined from the woods beyond.

Jack picked up his pace. Another one appeared on the hill above the school, in roughly the same place as before. Jack moved to one side of his mare, using the animal as cover from the threat to the east. He watched the one standing on the hill, knowing if they were all like the one he and Raymond had just encountered, then there would be no chance to get his rifle, no chance to get mounted. No chance …

His heartbeat was nearly audible in his chest. Cold wind blew across his face, making sweat feel like ice water. It was a long way for a pistol shot. An awful long way. He dared a glance at Raymond, from the fingers dripping blood, to the intense stare. But if his friend had any ideas, he wasn't revealing them.

Jack had none. His mind was blank. For the first time in his life, he was totally unsure, completely at a loss. For the first time, he felt certain he was standing at death's threshold.

His hand moved to his pistol, fingered the grip.

The shadow on the hill tilted its head to one side.

Jack swallowed into a dry, swollen throat. He took a breath, held it, and then yanked his sidearm with all he had.

The terrible hissing sound came then, the uncanny sound of steel slicing and cutting the air.

The figure on the hill was gone, disappearing before Jack could even raise his pistol.

Jack's horse reared, and Jack stumbled back, nearly fell.

Raymond's rifle exploded above him.

Jack dropped to one knee and emptied his revolver into the wooded hill above the school. His horse reared again, screamed, and Jack was knocked down, hit hard by something. He heard more shots and Raymond screaming his name.

Jack sat up, feeling a dull throb in his ribs. He twisted around, searching the ground and scrambling for his dropped pistol. He saw his horse then, lying in the dirt beside him.

The mare was on her side, thrashing and kicking up dust. There were three bolts buried in her side: one in her gut, two others in the flesh behind her front leg.

Deathblows. All of them.

Raymond's voice came again, muffled and far away through the roar in Jack's ears. Jack got to his feet and looked east, saw nothing. The street was empty. He quickly wrestled his rifle and ammo pouch from the dying mare and then swung into the saddle behind Raymond.

As if knowing the danger, Raymond's wounded mare stretched out toward the broken church with the speed and poise of a healthy thoroughbred.

Jack looked back. Three gray-hooded figures were back in the street, hovering over his mare as she spasmed and sipped in her final breaths.

Jack's hands were full, his pistol empty, leaving him no way to defend them from behind. He screamed at their opponent in the street, but his voice came out raspy and incoherent.

Two more appeared to their left, standing on the slope leading into town.

Raymond's mare took the hill in front of the church in full stride, slowing only a heartbeat to leap the broken steeple. Shards of glass flew out from beneath her hooves as she raced down the length of the old cathedral. She reached the back corner of the church in a blink, and then reared and twisted to her left.

Jack was on the ground again, the quiet whisper of arrows filling his ears. He struggled to right himself, to find his rifle. He caught a glimpse of two gray cloaks fading into the forest.

Raymond's Winchester exploded again.

Jack crawled to his left, fumbling through the leaves for his rifle. He found it and turned just as Raymond's horse fell.

Raymond rode the mare down, bailing out at the last possible moment. He hurried to the corner of the church in a low crouch, slid up against the wall and looked back at his horse.

The mare rolled over, two bolts locked in her breast. She was screaming and pumping her legs, still trying to escape whatever was hurting her. One of her flailing hooves caught Jack in the shin. The pain was instant and tremendous.

Jack got to his feet and backed up to the wall. His lower right leg was ringing with pain, and his foot had gone numb. He swore and slammed the back of his head against the wall.

The mare was whining pitifully now. Her legs had slowed but her respiration had picked up. Only now, her breaths were quick and shallow, thick and slushy. She tried to lift her head but couldn't seem to manage it. Then Raymond's rifle popped again, and she was still.

Jack sighed. His breath misted out in front of him. The sounds were coming again: leaves rustling in the woods to the north, footfalls beating the ground in front of the church, the creak of the boardwalk back in town.

Jack tucked closer to the wall and aimed his rifle toward the front of the church.

Everything stopped. The sounds dissipated and fell away.

Jack tried to calm himself, to slow his breathing. His ears rang; arteries pulsed in his wrists and neck. His entire body seemed irrevocably tense.

The noise resumed to the east, followed by movement in the forest to the south, directly ahead.

Then nothing.

Jack noticed the tip of his rifle wavering.

They were surrounded, he knew.

And the net was tightening.

He took a long sidestep down the wall, careful to keep his rifle trained at the front of the church. He stopped beside one of the broken windows and peered inside, finding the act of tearing his eyes from the rifle's sights, even for a moment, difficult. The sanctuary was in ruins. All the pews near the entrance had been either overturned or reduced to so many broken planks and splinters. Glass was strewn everywhere. Jack leaned farther across the window, revealing more and more of the inside, and thought he noticed bloodstains in what had once been the main aisle, and more near the front doors. Then he saw the edge of the cloak.

The figure was standing in the center of the chapel, facing Jack. Staring at him, Jack knew. Though, like all the others, no eyes were visible behind the heavy gray shroud.

The figure tilted its head to one side.

Jack slid back against the wall. He looked down the length of the building at Raymond, who was peering around the back of the church but motioning for Jack to close the gap. Jack backed away, keeping his rifle level with the window. Walking was difficult now. Feeling had returned to his foot but only in the form of a queer tingling at the ends of his toes. The rest of his leg burned and throbbed, and each time he put weight on it, it reminded him with a stabbing pain that rose all the way into his hip. It had given him a limp. Running would be another thing, a greater challenge altogether.

"Just go," Jack said as he reached Raymond's side. "I ain't sure I can help you now."

Raymond ignored him. He glanced at the woods to the south, then around the corner again.

Something thumped against the wall to Jack's left. He turned to see the tip of a bolt no more than a foot from his head. Fine slivers of wood were collected on the point where the weapon had punched through the wall. The shiny tip glinted in the sunlight before it was jerked back inside the church.

Raymond grabbed Jack's sleeve and pulled him around the corner. They ran into the woods behind the church. Jack fell in behind Raymond, his shin now on fire. Leaves swished beneath their feet; sticks grabbed, bent, and broke against their bodies. Raymond's rifle came to life again as gray smears streaked in and out of sight to their left.

They were heading north again, making erratic course changes to avoid the denser woods. The forest seemed alive all around them: sticks breaking, leaves rustling, shadows moving, and the now sickening sound of a hundred vipers striking.

The woods parted and they were suddenly in a small open gap. Raymond hurried across, never breaking stride. Jack followed, dodging around an old, neglected well in the center of the clearing and toward the woods on the opposite side.

The bucket had been hidden from their view, lying on its side in the shadow of the well. The container was old, probably as old as the well itself, and wrought with cracks and fissures that had probably rendered it useless. Jack noticed all this a second before his foot tangled in the rope handle.

He sprawled on the ground, swearing and kicking. He looked back, saw nothing, but the noise was still everywhere. He heard Raymond's voice coming from somewhere behind him, then the report of his Winchester from what seemed like directly overhead. Jack freed himself and kicked the bucket away. He collected his rifle and darted back into the woods behind Raymond.

The forest quickly condensed again, but then gave way to another, much larger clearing. Under different circumstances, the beauty of the large grassy area would've given Jack pause. The edge of the forest wrapped around the flat, treeless landscape in a large, oval-shaped arc, then reconnected again behind a solitary cabin on the northernmost side. The cabin was small, with an equally small covered porch and window on the front.

They went for it.

Jack felt naked as they came out from the cover of the trees and into the clearing. His spine tingled, heart pounded, legs ached, lungs burned.

There was an empty wagon on its side twenty feet from the porch. The wheels were busted and unusable, one missing entirely. A horse lay toward the front of the overturned cart, long dead, but was facing the wrong direction to have ever been harnessed to it.

Raymond leapt the horse and ducked behind a support post on the porch. The column was small and frail, affording very little cover. He raised his rifle and took aim at something behind Jack, but the hammer fell on an empty chamber. He pushed away and turned toward the door.

Jack was already there. He kicked hard, barely slowing down. The door sprang open easily and he rushed inside.

The explosion was like thunder, instantly deafening him. The shotgun's muzzle-flash seemed as bright as the sun. The doorjamb immediately erupted in a hundred tiny splinters, spraying and biting into Jack's cheek and neck like needles.

Jack stumbled and dropped his rifle. His ears screamed; the room swam in little pinpoints of light. He slumped against the wall and raised his pistol at the shape in the far corner of the room.

The hammer dropped with a hollow snap.

Empty.

20

"**D**ear God!" The man in the corner dropped his shotgun. "Don't shoot!"

Raymond stepped inside and slammed the door. There was a long wooden plank leaning against the wall. He snatched it up and slid it through the iron clasps anchoring the door to the interior of the cabin.

Jack leaned his head against the wall, miraculously uninjured. He glanced at Raymond, who had moved to the far corner of the room and was peering out a small window. There was another small window beside it but on the adjacent wall. Both of them, the biggest in the house, were crowded together in the front corner of the cabin. The only other view outside came in the form of a yet smaller window positioned around eye level in the back. There were two crude cots tossed with dirty blankets in the little one-room structure: one in the back left corner, and another beneath the back window. A fireplace sat dark and cold in the far wall.

Jack unslung his canteen and slid to the floor. He emptied his ammo pouch. Six pistol and eight rifle cartridges rolled around at his feet. He reloaded his revolver and dropped the remaining shells in his pocket.

"Can I help you with that?"

Jack looked up. The voice had come from the man in the corner, who was still on his knees, hands wavering over his head.

Save for a few wisps of gray, the man's wiry, unkempt beard matched his thinning black hair exactly. His face was pale, his body lean and weak. He was looking at Raymond, whose blood was accumulating on the floor.

Raymond's eyes never left the window.

The man looked at the blood, then Jack.

Jack stood and holstered his pistol. He gestured for the man to lower his hands and pointed at the double-barreled shotgun. "How many shells you got for that scattergun?"

The man dropped his hands and rubbed his arms. "Just the one in the other side. I only fired one chamber."

Jack nodded.

"It's not mine," the man went on. "It was here when we got here. I looked around the place, but there doesn't seem to be any more ammunition for it." The man ran nervous fingers through his hair. "I've never even fired a gun before today."

Thank God, Jack thought. But he wondered if it might've been a better fate than the one waiting outside. The lesser of two evils. He saw movement from the center of the room and turned.

A little girl, no more than five or six, rose slowly from behind the second cot.

The girl's body matched the man's. Thin and fragile, perhaps more so. Sandy blonde hair hung stiff and oily over her shoulders, partially covering a slender, pale face. The flesh on her lips was dry and cracked and flaking away. Her dress was ragged and dirty. But despite her evident frailty and unhealthy pallor, her face was bright and alive. She was eyeing Jack's canteen.

Jack looked back at the man. "You're from Jones Mine?"

"No, no," the man said. "We were only just passing through."

Jack glanced at the girl, then back to the man. His eyes narrowed. "What's your name?"

"Tom," the man said. "Tom Morris."

"The preacher?"

Morris looked surprised. "Yes. Well, more of a missionary, really."

"You pass through Twin Pines?"

"Yes. Yes we did." Morris looked up at the ceiling. "I'm afraid I've lost track of time. I guess it's been more than a month, maybe a month and a half."

Jack shook his head. Maybe not *everything* Cavanaugh had said was a lie. The most effective deceptions often carried elements of truth. Maybe the old man had expected Asheworth to recover the preacher after he'd dealt with Raymond. Or perhaps he'd never cared one way or the other about Morris, but thought Jack would. Maybe he'd pinned his hopes on Jack's sympathy, figuring that would be enough to get him and, more importantly, Raymond into the empty northern forest, where they would just disappear like so many others before them, never to be seen or heard from again.

But the forest hadn't been empty.

"This is my daughter, Emma," Morris said.

The little girl smiled and waved, and Jack was struck by the genuineness of the gesture. It had none of the forced motions of a child simply obeying her parent's social graces, but real. Authentic. It was warm and excited, in fact, as if she'd been expecting them, like he and Raymond were long-awaited friends.

Jack touched his hat. "Emma."

Her grin widened at the sound of her name, and she came out from behind the cot.

Jack followed her eyes to the canteen. He picked it up and held it out to her.

"Thirsty?"

She nodded, came closer. The canteen was already half-empty, so she tilted it straight up. Jack noticed the tremble in her hands as she took in the water, and how each little swallow seemed to take effort. He could see bone and vein in the backs of her wrists.

Raymond watched from the window.

The little girl stopped, gasped in a breath, then went back for more.

"Emma." Morris's voice was gentle but firm.

Emma stopped and licked her lips. She handed the canteen back to Jack.

"Thank you."

Jack knelt. "You're certainly welcome," he said. "Take all you want."

Emma considered the canteen again but didn't reach for it. She glanced in Raymond's direction, seemed to study him for a moment. When her eyes came back to Jack, they were wide with delight, like she'd just remembered something. A bright, hopeful smile spread across her face and she leaned close to his ear.

"Are you heroes?"

The question came in a whisper, like she was asking to be let in on some grand, unfolding conspiracy. Her voice and countenance were charged with anticipation.

Jack's heart sank. He lowered his head, hoping to hide the dark truth that surely shone in his eyes, waiting for words that wouldn't come.

The girl's smile faded slightly but not completely. "Papa told me if we prayed really hard, then God might send us heroes, like in the old times."

Jack forced a smile. "How old are you, little miss?"

She held out a fist and extended all her fingers.

"Five?" Jack asked.

She nodded.

Jack gestured toward Morris. "I reckon it'll be no time at all before your pa here is beating the fellas away with a stick."

Emma grinned, apparently knowing she'd been complimented but clearly unsure how.

Jack was suddenly struck by how, even in light of everything that had happened, and was happening, this one little girl had so thoroughly wrestled his mind away from it all. If only for a moment.

He stood and laid a hand on her head, then looked at Morris. "I'm Jack Percy, and this here's Raymond McAlister."

Morris nodded.

"We're friends," Jack said to Emma.

Her eyes wandered back to Raymond. "Friends."

"Friends," Jack said again. He looked at Morris. "How long have you been here?"

Morris shrugged and looked at the floor. Aside from his physical erosion, the man also seemed detached, his mind elsewhere. "A month, I suppose, maybe longer."

Emma moved away from Jack, taking small, careful steps toward the window in the corner. The corner Raymond was occupying.

"I learned of Jones Mine from some of the locals in Twin Pines," Morris said. "So I decided to make the trip up here, hoping to acquaint myself with the townspeople before we moved on to the west." His eyes moved over the cabin's wooden floor.

"The town was abandoned and obviously had been for some time," he said. "So we were just going to go back. Back to Twin Pines, that is. But as we were leaving, we started seeing people, here and there, people in gray cloaks. I called out to them but they stayed away from us. They kept their distance. They just quietly looked on from the corners of buildings or in shadows at the edge of the woods. They never answered back; they just watched us as we moved north away from town. I'll tell you, Mr. Percy, I was already getting a bit spooked. And then, all at once, they attacked us. Just attacked. No provocation.

"I was hit in the leg, just a graze, but my horse was killed instantly." The preacher ran a hand down his face. "I managed to get on our second horse with my wife and Emma. I don't know how. I honestly can't even remember doing it. But then we ran, just ran. Wherever we could. Back through the forest and town and forest again. We saw more of them as we rode, but they left us alone until we reached this place. We came inside and locked up." He motioned toward the door. "That's when we heard our other horse screaming."

Jack thought of the dead horse outside. "Any idea who's out there?"

"None at all," Morris said. "I don't understand it, but they won't let us leave. It's like they want us to just waste away." He looked up. "We've barely eaten since we got here, and the only water we've had is rain we've collected in a cup."

Jack picked up his canteen and shook it. Only another swallow. He tossed it on the bed in front of Morris.

Morris limped out of the corner and sat down on the cot. He took the water slowly, closing his eyes as the liquid moved through his system. "God bless you."

Emma was beside Raymond now. She was watching the slow trickle of blood drop from his fingers. She looked about to reach for him, but hesitated. Finally, she gave his duster a quick tug.

He looked down.

"You're my friend?" she asked.

Raymond's eyes moved over the little girl: the straw-colored hair, the round eyes, the dirty face and dress. He turned away, back to the window. He said nothing.

"Emma." Morris's voice came with a parental edge the girl immediately recognized. She quickly retreated to the cot in the middle of the room, where she sat down and pulled a thin, threadbare blanket over her legs. Her eyes blinked curiously between her father and the strange man in the corner.

Jack glanced at Raymond and then around the cold one-room cabin. "We're part of a search party," he said to Morris. "We were sent to retrieve you and your ..." He paused and scanned the room again. "Where's your wife?"

Morris wilted like a great invisible burden had just fallen on him. He laid the canteen on the bed beside him and stared at his bandaged leg. "There's a well out front, at the edge of the woods."

Jack nodded. "Yeah, we saw it."

"Sarah went out early in the morning while I was sleeping, sometime before daybreak. She went for water, but ... well, she hasn't ... she never has ..."

Jack thought of the well bucket he'd tripped over. Something tightened in his chest. "In the morning? This morning?"

Morris answered without looking up.

"Five days ago."

Emma stood suddenly, a look of pure horror on her face. She ran to the front of the cabin and began wrestling with the board Raymond had used to barricade the door. It moved slowly, inch by inch, groan by little groan, until finally, with one measured thrust, the plank clattered to the floor.

Jack slid back into a sitting position by the door. He looked at Morris and their eyes met in mutual understanding, sympathy.

With some effort, Emma managed to get the plank standing in its place by the door. She backed up a step and brushed off her hands. "There now."

Jack awoke to muffled sound in the middle of the room. Whispers, it sounded like. It was dark now. Moonlight crept through the dirty windows like a strange luminescent fog, yielding just enough light to unveil the profile of Tom Morris kneeling beside his daughter's bed.

The wind came and went outside, whistling and pressing against the cabin's outer shell. The place creaked and whined like the turn in weather was causing it pain. But it was when the wind subsided that the muffled sound in the room became a whisper, and the whisper a voice. A little girl's voice.

"… which art in heaven. Hallowed be thy name …"

The wind gusted, snatching away the sound of Emma's prayer. Jack's mind was back in the forest again, thinking and worrying over CJ and the others. He was still glad he'd sent them south, glad they'd separated. He knew it had been their best chance. And if Ned had kept up, if Angelina hadn't slowed them, if they had kept moving like he'd instructed, they might have made it.

"… thy will be done …"

But had they? There were a lot of *ifs* in there. The question burdened him to his soul. And it was a question he might never know the answer to. He was certain that he and Raymond would try something, would have to. But he also knew there was nothing more he could do for the others. Regret swirled inside like fire. He had brought CJ along against his own better judgment. He didn't have to. He shouldn't have.

"… give us this day our daily bread …"

Jack lowered his head and stuffed his hands into his jacket. The cold air in the cabin was piercing. He felt the contours of the Indian relic in his pocket, remembered the condition they'd found it in, the blood on the leaves. Blood shed by the same evil awaiting them outside. He could still see the woman's face. The desperation, the terror, the face paint smeared by tears. The images were fixed in his mind like carved stone.

"… as we forgive our debtors …"

He'd seen something similar in Angelina that day on the hill—the day Eli had intercepted her tormentors. Similar, but different. The slave traders had already taken much from the young woman and were evidently not done. *They won't like you taking their prize.* They? Who? And exactly where had they been taking her? Here? To those bastards outside? There were so many questions. Why the squaw? And considering the kind of efficiency that could make an entire unit of cavalry disappear: how did Morris make it to the cabin alive? With two women? One just a girl.

"… but deliver us from evil …"

Jack squeezed his aching head. The squaw. Angelina. Morris's wife, Sarah. All of them so very different, all from different worlds. There seemed no connection between them, no common thread to bring them together. Except one.

They were all female.

"… amen."

Morris's cot creaked under his weight. It took him a long time to get stretched out and comfortable on the makeshift bed.

Jack watched Emma, the wheels in his mind still turning. She was already sleeping, no doubt exhausted from lack of nourishment. A wisp of her hair slipped off the edge of the cot. Her respiration was quick and abbreviated, and Jack wondered if she was dreaming. Her hands were still clasped together from the prayer.

Raymond was sitting in the corner beneath the windows, tying off his wound with a strip of fabric he'd cut from his duster. Jack watched him until their eyes met.

"I think I know what they want."

Raymond pulled the bandage and winced.

"Yeah."

21

Raymond was moving his left arm, stretching and bending it, testing its mobility. There wasn't much. He could raise it in front of his body, roughly parallel to the floor, but not much more. He finally laid his head against the wall and closed his eyes.

"Is it bad?" Jack whispered.

"Not as bad as whatever's out there."

A few hours had passed since the windows first began glowing with early morning sun. It had to be close to midday by now. The night had been uneventful, consisting mostly of broken periods of sleep for Jack. Morris and his daughter had slept soundly through the hours of dark, and still were.

"You have any water?" Jack asked.

"On the horse."

Jack nodded, sighed. "I reckon we oughta try and get it."

"Yeah."

"Think we can get there and back?"

"No."

Jack stood and crossed over to the windows where Raymond was sitting. Snow flurries were coming straight down through the still air outside. The precipitation was light and appeared to be tapering off even as he stood there. The ground was unchanged, however: brown grass and dead leaves blown in from the forest, not yet accepting any accumulation. But Jack knew it wouldn't be long. He looked down at Raymond.

"What about ammo?"

"Just what's in the pistol," Raymond said. "Rifle's empty."

Jack dug the extra rifle shells from his pocket and handed them to Raymond. He thought of all the ammunition they'd already spent throughout the forest and the town, all the rounds fired in haste as well as those precious few they'd taken time to aim. And apparently none had found a target. Not one.

Raymond rolled the eight cartridges around in his hand for a moment, thinking, then loaded six into his rifle. He handed two shells back to Jack. Jack started to object but Raymond pushed his hand away and stood. Jack saw his friend's eyes narrow as he looked at the door. There was life behind those blue ovals. There was hate there as well.

Jack dropped the two shells into his pocket and went back to the door. He picked up his rifle and checked the chamber.

Raymond took up position behind him, head down, rifle pointing at the floor.

Morris stirred and sat up in his bed. "What are you ... Wait, you can't—"

"There's food and water on our horses," Jack said. "We'll be back."

"But you can't," Morris stammered. "I'm surprised you made it in here at all. They'll never let you ..."

Jack stepped back and gave the door a gentle shove. The hinges creaked, and a slender column of light crept in around the jamb. He waited, listening, then pushed a little harder. The door swung away with a quiet whine, gradually revealing the bright world outside like an unfolding scroll.

Jack took a step onto the porch, one foot over the threshold. He saw his breath cloud ahead of him.

The sound of steel arrows filled his ears like rainfall. The noise erased all others, if there were any others, but only lasted a fraction of a second. Then the exterior of the cabin began to knock and clatter like a sudden hailstorm had erupted. The frame around the door splintered and cracked. Debris dropped and skittered across the porch, some spinning to rest on the floor inside.

Jack spilled into the cabin on his back, dropping his rifle. He rolled to one side and kicked the bolt-filled door closed.

Raymond went for the front window. It imploded, spraying broken glass across the floor. Two arrows lodged in the back wall above Morris's cot. Raymond dropped under the window and backed into the corner.

Then it stopped. Just like that. Leaving only the heavy breathing of the cabin's occupants.

Jack got to his knees and picked up his rifle. He glanced around the room.

Emma had taken refuge behind her bed as she had the day before. Morris was kneeling at the foot of his cot, squeezing the shotgun in trembling hands.

Jack looked back at the door, heart racing. He felt a cold sheen of sweat forming across his body. His mind reeled, desperate to find any other conclusion than the one presenting itself, any other word than the one pounding and throbbing in his head.

Trapped.

The group had followed CJ's lead, who, in turn, was following Eli's instructions. At least, he believed he was. But even he was questioning that conviction now. He was certain they'd done just as the scout suggested; they'd found the ridge to the west and had ridden south ever since. But it was taking so long, and there could've been a half-dozen ridges to the west. He had taken the first one they'd come to, and now, after riding through endless, unchanging forest for nearly two days, he wondered if he should've looked farther.

He was grinding his teeth, unconsciously giving himself a headache. They should be out by now. It should never have taken this long. Ned had already said it a couple of times this morning—had even written it in his godforsaken ledger. And all CJ could do was resubmit his confidence in Eli and trudge on.

Angelina hadn't questioned him, at least not outwardly. In fact, she had scarcely said a word. She was still bundled up on the back of his horse, still sheltering beneath the blanket. She still wept quietly every few hours, occasionally whispering her pa's name into CJ's back.

He had to get her out. Would get her out.

His chest tightened at the mere thought of failing this girl. The feeling was inexplicable but powerful, and gave him the sudden urge to kick Major into a gallop, to press harder.

But he didn't. He pulled up and stopped.

He recognized the new sound; he was certain of that, but found himself distrusting it in the barren forest. He turned an ear toward the familiar noise, but all he heard now were the dead leaves crunching under the hooves of Ned's mount.

Ned moved past, oblivious to CJ's stalled horse.

"Ned!" CJ said in the loudest whisper he could manage.

Ned rode on.

"Ned!" CJ tried again, this time louder than he liked.

Ned started as if he'd been asleep; probably had been. He stopped but didn't turn his horse, and only barely moved his head.

CJ resisted an impulse to throw something at him. Instead, he turned his attention back to the woods.

There it was again.

A dog. Yes, it was a dog. And judging by its long, drawn-out, half-bark, half-howl, it was no wild dog, but a hound. And there it was again, only this time it wasn't alone. This time there were two. At least two. And they were coming closer.

CJ's spirits soared. Warm relief washed through his body. Unless these animals were lost, they were the first sign of civilization in nearly a week.

"It's just dogs," Ned said.

"Yeah. And where there's dogs, there's people. And where there's people, there's ..."

The barking stopped.

CJ looked back to the forest. There was still noise out there. Only now, the long, persistent howls of hunting dogs had been replaced by a disturbance in the brush to the west. It was a careful, calculated stirring through the leaves and foliage, and it made the hair on the back of CJ's neck stand up. That warm relief turned cold. Something was wrong.

He slid from the saddle, mindful of Angelina, and drew his rifle from its scabbard. She looked down from beneath the blanket.

"Gonna have to get down for a sec," CJ whispered. "Ain't no problem, just gonna have a look around." He winked, trying to reassure her, then wished he hadn't. He flushed.

She looked down at him, unreadable, red swollen eyes locked on his. But she started off the horse.

CJ watched, concerned over the time this was taking. Her attempted dismount was awkward and clumsy inside the blanket, and he was suddenly afraid she might fall. But he was also terrified to put a hand on her. The noise was back again, though, behind him and sounding closer, so he placed a hand on her back and guided her the rest of the way. Angelina made no protest, no sound at all, but just quickly curled up under a nearby hardwood and disappeared under the blanket.

CJ turned. "Get down!"

Ned frowned. He was still mounted and apparently unconcerned with the latest unidentified noises. His eyes were bloodshot and barely visible through thin slits in his eyelids. He looked like a man coming off a hard night's drinking. Only Ned hadn't been drinking; he'd been deprived of sleep. And it was showing not only physically, in his eyes and slumped posture, but also mentally.

CJ turned away. The sound was divided now, coming from the north and west, louder from the north. He put his focus there. He dropped to one knee and steadied himself against a tree, then peered down the barrel of his rifle. He swept his sights over each piece of underbrush in his range, each tree, standing or fallen, any peculiar mound of leaves, anything at all that might conceal or camouflage. But he saw nothing.

He wanted to holler out, to yell for Eli, but he knew it couldn't be the old scout out there. Not even Eli could be in two places at once.

The noise was back in the west again. And this time, the clear, unmistakable sound of footsteps was easy to discern.

CJ lowered his rifle, preparing to swing around the tree and confront the possible threat to his left. He gave the woods to the north a quick last look.

And there it was. Someone, or something, crouching in the thicket not more than twenty-five yards ahead. It moved, and with the movement something glinted in the sunlight, something steel.

CJ stood up and took aim.

The footsteps from the west picked up. This time with no caution, no stealth.

This time they were running.

Whatever was in the brush to the north must've detected CJ's intentions, or maybe his rifle, because they suddenly bolted away from the bushes at a dead run.

It was now simply a matter of leading his aim and squeezing the trigger. CJ's target was in the open. It had its back to him.

It was a boy.

Angelina whimpered.

"Whoa, there, son." The voice came from CJ's left, from the west, and was followed by the distinctive click of a hammer being cocked. "Just take it easy, now. Ain't no one gotta get hurt here."

CJ's chest tightened. His target disappeared behind a tree.

"Ned?"

Ned started to speak but was quickly cut off.

"You ain't got nothin' to fear, boy. Long as you explain what you're doin' here on my property."

CJ lowered his rifle. The man beside him was holding a shotgun. The blued steel was as hard and oily as its owner's face. "Your property, sir?"

"You heard me right, son. This here's my property, legal and proper. And that one you was trying to kill is my boy, Elias."

CJ looked back at the young boy standing beside the tree to the north. He was also holding a shotgun.

"Name's Gabriel Ames. Came out to hunt squirrels today, or what's left of 'em. But that'll be enough about me. Now kindly state your business here."

CJ cleared his throat. "We're trying to get to Twin Pines, Mr. Ames. I need to find Sheriff Murphy and Doc Lewis somethin' desperate."

Ames came around the tree and looked down at Angelina. "What in hell?"

CJ gestured to the north and casually stepped into the gap between Angelina and the stranger. "I'm awful sorry, sir. There ain't no time to explain. There's been an attack and three of our friends are still up there. I've gotta get help."

"An attack? What kind of attack? Indians?"

"We don't know what it was, sir, or who. And even if we did, there ain't no time. I've got to find the sheriff."

Ames looked CJ over, likely appraising his sincerity. His gaze lingered uncomfortably long on the boy's eyes.

CJ waited as patiently as he could. A gray bluetick coonhound circled around his feet, sniffing, pawing, and slobbering on his boots. "They might be trapped for all we know."

Ames waved a hand at his son. "Go get your ma and sister. Tell 'em we got a sick girl up here." He turned to Ned. "You'll keep an eye on the little lady here, whilst me and …"

"CJ."

"Me and CJ fetch the others."

Ned nodded and then pulled out his journal and started writing.

Ames watched him curiously for a moment, then turned to CJ. "Twin Pines is a half-hour's ride. You might find the doc there, but I don't reckon Murphy would rouse lest the devil himself climbed in his britches. He's an old man and a hard sell." Ames ran fingers through his beard. "I hear tell there's cavalry stationed there. That might be exactly what you're after."

"There ain't no cavalry in Twin Pines, Mr. Ames," CJ said. "At least, none to speak of. It has to be Sheriff Murphy and any deputies he's got. I'm sorry, sir, but you'll just have to trust me."

"Go on, boy!" Ames screamed. "You waitin' to grow wings?"

CJ jumped at the outburst, but then saw Elias take off sprinting back through the forest to the west.

Ames shook his head. He pulled out a plug of tobacco, cut off a piece and set it in his jaw. He was giving CJ that appraising look again. He held it a little longer this time. "Say, you wouldn't be Jonas's boy, would ya?"

"That's right, sir. CJ Cantrell."

"By God, you do resemble," Ames said. "Ride southeast. Only a blind man could miss Twin Pines. Find the doctor, then head back this way." He looked at Ned. "Someone will meet you here and lead you and the girl back to my place. I'll get Murphy."

CJ looked at Angelina.

"She'll be fine, son. Got my word on it."

"Thank you, sir."

"Don't be thanking me, just be on your way."

With that, CJ pulled himself onto Major and bolted southeast. He had ridden only five minutes when he broke free of the forest and into the open countryside. The air had never tasted sweeter.

22

... They are the Watchers ...

Jack opened his eyes and the dream of the old woman vanished like smoke in a sudden wind. He lifted his head. The muscles in his neck were stiff and burned with the movement. He had fallen asleep on the floor, his back against the wall—a position, he was learning, one could never get used to.

Raymond was still to his left, still sitting in the corner, his head cradled in the seam of the two walls. He was staring at the ceiling, one hand pressed against his lower back, the other against the floor. The two windows above him were dark. It was night.

Emma was sitting cross-legged on her bed, examining something in her lap. A small candle flickered beside her, revealing a ghostly outline of her face and a silhouette of fine, sandy-blonde hair tucked behind each ear.

"Where'd you get the candle?" Jack asked.

Morris and his daughter looked up. "There's some in the closet," Morris said. He pointed at a little door by the fireplace. "There's a couple more in there, and a spade, but not much else."

Jack nodded.

Emma slid off her cot and started toward the front of the room. Her father looked up from his Bible and frowned at her bare feet.

Jack watched as she crossed over to him. She had gathered up whatever was in her lap into the fabric of her dress, and was clinching the improvised pocket with both hands, as if any wrong move might unsettle or loose its contents. She paused a couple feet short of Jack and grinned.

Her eyes were heavy, the flesh below them dark and swollen, and it looked like it was taking real effort to keep them open. Her lips were worse as well. They were still dry and flaking as they had been yesterday. But now there was a wet, cherry-colored split in the center of her bottom lip. It looked painful, likely was, but still she grinned.

She held out the makeshift pocket in her dress.

Jack leaned forward and looked in at a collection of marbles.

"Know how to play?" she asked.

Jack grimaced. "Well, it's been a while."

Emma bit her bottom lip. She glanced down at the marbles. "I could show you," she whispered.

Jack gave the floor a pat. "I reckon it'll come back. Let's give it a go."

Emma beamed. She carefully leaned down until the pocket of her dress was even with the floor. The marbles spilled out in front of Jack. He laid a finger on one that tried to escape. She smiled a thanks to him and then hurried back to her cot and retrieved a length of twine. She spread the string out in a circle between them and placed all the marbles in the center, save one.

"Wanna go first?"

"Nah, you go ahead. I bet—"

"Wait! Wait!" Emma made a quick adjustment to the twine, then leaned back and considered it for a moment.

Jack watched her eyes as they carefully surveyed each part of the circle, scrutinizing every edge of the curve. He chuckled and looked at Raymond, but his friend was still staring at the ceiling.

Emma put her hands in her lap. "Okay. It's ready."

Jack smiled at her—it was impossible not to—then picked up the shooter and thumbed it into the circle. The marbles broke apart gently, rolling, colliding, and mostly coming to rest on one side of the loop. One made it out.

Emma clapped. "Good job!" She rubbed her arms, half from cold, half from excitement.

Jack gave her a mock bow. He picked up the shooter and flicked it again, gentler this time, sending a few of the little ceramic balls scattering about, but none outside of the circle.

Emma looked up expectantly, brown eyes dark in contrast to her face.

"Looks like it's your turn," Jack said.

She snatched up the shooter and took aim. Her hand trembled as she focused on a mark. She bit her bottom lip again. The marble came out softly, missing her target but striking another and sending it out of the circle. She grinned and rubbed her hands together, but was obviously bothered she'd missed her real aim.

"Looks like I'm up against an ole pro here," Jack said.

She giggled.

Jack looked at Morris as she retrieved the shooter. "Seen anyone else out here?"

Morris shook his head. "No, no one else."

Emma flicked the shooter again. It bounced across the uneven floor and slapped into a tight cluster of marbles. Two went spinning out of the circle.

Jack rocked back and held his feet up. "Whoa!" he said. "That's some fine shootin'."

She laughed and tugged at his boot. "They won't hurt you."

He leaned forward slowly, pretending to be careful to stay clear of her aim, then turned back to Morris. "We ran into an old woman. Or rather, she ran into us. She was mostly rambling, out of sorts, I reckon. She called 'em the Watchers. That mean anything to you?"

Morris shook his head. "I'm afraid not."

Jack nodded and reached into his jacket pocket. He came out with the folded letter they'd discovered in Dr. Watts' office.

Morris laid down his Bible and slid to the edge of his bed. "She say anything else?"

Jack shrugged. "Don't really remember. She took us by surprise." He looked down and watched as Emma shot again, this time with no luck. He picked up the shooter and rolled it around in his hand. "She said we'd made 'em angry, or something like that, and were gonna pay for it. She said they were growing. 'The nefillum are growing,' I think. Something or someone had come, or was coming. I don't know. I could scarcely hear half of it."

"What was that last part?"

Jack thumbed the shooter unsuccessfully and Emma snatched it up. He looked at Morris. His concentration on the game had kept him from immediately noticing the change in the preacher's expression. The man's pale complexion was suddenly flushed. "That something or other had come. I'm not sure—"

"No, before that."

"Something about nefillum growing," Jack said, "But I suspect I'm not saying it right."

Tom Morris just stared, his eyes moving over Jack like he'd suddenly appeared in the room out of thin air. Then he turned away, looking genuinely puzzled, if not a little amused.

Jack waited, then said, "That familiar to you?"

Morris nodded. "Familiar, yes, but absurd. I mean ..." His voice trailed off.

Jack leaned back against the wall. "You'll understand, Reverend, it's always best to know your enemy. Now ain't the time for being silent if there's something—"

"No, no, Mr. Percy," Morris interrupted. "Heavens no, please forgive me." He shifted on the edge of his cot. "It's just ... are you sure she said Nephilim?"

Jack picked up the shooter. He grinned at his anxious opponent, who was waiting patiently on her knees across from him. "Yeah, I reckon. At least, that's what it sounded like to me." He glanced at Raymond, whose eyes were closed now. Jack rolled the marble.

"And the Watchers?" Morris asked. "She said, 'the Watchers'?"

"She said, 'They are the Watchers.' That much I'm certain of."

Morris stood, took a step to his left to avoid the window. He stroked his beard.

"Mean something to you?" Jack asked.

Morris shook his head. "Well, no, not really. I mean, I don't know what she was thinking, of course. It's just oddly similar to an ancient Hebrew legend, the terms you mentioned, that is. Just a strange coincidence, is all."

"Hebrew?" Jack asked.

Morris nodded. "Are you familiar with the Bible?"

"Not so much."

"Well, the Hebrews are the main characters, you might say. They are the people all the biblical stories are about. In fact, it is they who wrote the Bible, or most of it." He stopped, lost in thought.

Jack wasn't following. "What about the legend?"

"It's an obscure interpretation of a vague passage," Morris said. "I mean, most folks would know nothing of it, nor need they. But never mind someone in these parts. It's just—"

"What legend?"

"It's just coincidence," Morris finished. But there was something like doubt in his eyes, not quite doubt but something akin to it, more like confusion. He seemed distracted again, as if privately wrestling with some complicated riddle.

"What legend?" Jack repeated.

Morris looked at the Bible on his bed, considered it a moment, then finally leaned down and picked it up. He crossed the room, peeling back the first few pages, and laid it on the floor beside Jack.

"Chapter six, one through five."

Jack offered the preacher a puzzled look and then leaned over the Bible. It was open to Genesis.

1 And it came to pass, when men began to multiply on the face of the earth, and daughters were born unto them, 2 That the sons of God saw the daughters of men that they were fair; and they took them wives of all which they chose. 3 And the LORD said, My spirit shall not always strive with man, for that he also is flesh: yet his days shall be an hundred and twenty years. 4 There were giants in the earth in those days; and also after that, when the sons of God came in unto the daughters of men, and they bare children to them, the same became mighty men which were of old, men of renown. 5 And God saw that the wickedness of man was great in the earth, and that every imagination of the thoughts of his heart was only evil continually.

Jack looked up from the text. "I don't understand."

"You wouldn't," Morris said, "nor would anyone else, not laypeople, anyway. But that's my point. Folks don't see it, because it's not there, not openly." He paused. "What I'm trying to say is that it doesn't stand out. That's why this woman you speak of couldn't be talking about the same thing. It takes a great deal of reading between the lines, drawing from other sources, non-biblical sources. Ancient material that's only available in the academies. In Europe. And still, it's like forcing square pegs into round holes and swearing they fit. It's absurd, but people get excited over stuff like that, always have. It's how myths and legends are formed, how they persist. Just like this one."

Jack nodded, as if he were carefully following the preacher's logic, then said, "What's the legend?"

Morris sighed—not impatiently, but rather as though he couldn't believe what he was about to say. His lips tightened into a thin line. "It is thought by some that the 'sons of God' in this passage refers to angels. And to be fair, it seems that at least some of the Hebrews believed it as well. That ancient material I spoke of attests to that." He paused, thinking. "Those old, non-biblical writings tell us that a select group of angels was assigned to watch over humanity, to act as safeguards or protectors. Guardians, you could say. This group was called the Grigori, or the Watchers." He glanced at Emma, evidently choosing his words. "For certain reasons, these Watchers abandoned their posts and revealed themselves to mankind. It is said that they taught and exposed men to previously forbidden things. And also, as you can see from the biblical passage, they chose and took wives for themselves. The offspring from these unions would be the 'giants' of verse four. That word in the Hebrew language is Naphiyl, or Nephilim as plural."

"Plural?"

"More than one."

Jack cleared his throat. "What does it mean? What does Nephilim mean?"

"Fallen ones."

Morris walked back to his bed and sat down. He put a hand to his head, looking fatigued. "That's the legend, Mr. Percy, or at least a very brief sketch of it. But almost no scholar believes this interpretation. And how could they? I mean, how could such a thing work? The most accepted idea is that the 'sons of God' were descendants of Seth, that they were tempted by unrighteous women from other tribes, and that there's nothing at all supernatural happening in this passage."

Jack felt the fingers of an early headache tightening behind his eyes. He looked down at the Bible. "Giants?"

Morris nodded. "Yeah, some take it that way. But the term in Hebrew doesn't necessarily entail great size or stature. Remember, the passage describes them as 'mighty men' and 'men of renown.' So, it could be taken that they were *giants* in their craft, just as we would characterize great, and not so great, men of our own age."

"What was their craft?"

"The legend says they were experts in all the arts," Morris said, "not least of all war. It says they were daring but reckless, that they possessed extraordinary strength and control, skill and craftsmanship. It tells us they spread a wide void of devastation in their wake, eventually consuming all of mankind's resources, before at last turning on men themselves."

Jack glanced at Emma, who was waiting patiently on her knees. She smiled when he looked her way. He picked up the shooter and rolled it at one of the three remaining marbles. He missed.

"It's only legend, Mr. Percy," Morris said. "A myth."

Jack leaned back as Emma went to work on the marbles. "So you're telling me, whatever's out there waiting for us is really some kind of—"

"I'm telling you nothing of the sort," Morris interrupted. "I don't believe it for a second, nor am I proposing it. Remember, with all due respect, I was simply responding to your question about the legend. And that's all it is, legend. It's preposterous to even consider it, an entire waste of your time. I mean that sincerely, Mr. Percy." He gave a sigh of resignation. "I'll admit we can't be certain who the Nephilim were. There are real disagreements here. Aside from this passage, they virtually don't exist, biblically speaking. They are one of history's great unknowns. But just because we can't say who they are, doesn't mean we can't say who they are not."

"How'd she know about it?"

"Who?"

"The woman."

Morris started to speak, but then turned toward the windows. He said nothing.

Jack held up the letter they'd found in Jones Mine. "We found this in the doctor's office back in town."

Morris eyed the letter as if summoning the strength to get up again. But as Jack began to rise, Morris waved him back down and got up. He took the letter and returned to his cot. He unfolded the page and squinted at the script. His brow furrowed. "Sounds like they had some sort of communal disease, maybe even passed it on to their offspring. Makes sense, I suppose. It's certainly not unheard of—that is, a whole village contracting something by passing it on to one another." He scratched his chin. "In fact, it's happened quite often throughout history. A common thing, really. Do you have the rest of it?"

Jack shook his head and looked back at his playing partner. Emma's eyes were closed, her body swaying gently, balancing itself. There was one marble left in the circle. Jack reached over and touched her arm. Her eyes sprang open.

"It's your turn, little lady."

She grinned and blinked at the circle.

"How'd they kill 'em?" Raymond's voice came soft but clear from the corner of the room. He still hadn't moved, still hadn't opened his eyes.

Morris looked up, but seemed unsure how to answer the question. "In the legend?"

Raymond's eyes opened, blue and cold. "How did they kill the Nephilim?"

Morris glanced at Jack, then back to Raymond. "They didn't."

"Then what happened?" Jack asked.

Morris nodded at his Bible, which was still lying on the floor beside Jack. "God blotted them out," he said. "In the flood."

Emma thumbed the shooter into the circle and drove the final marble out. She looked up at Jack, little fists raised in silent triumph.

Jack removed his hat and bowed to her. "Well done, ma'am." He dug in his pockets until he found the Indian relic. He gave it a quick once-over to ensure it was clean—no evidence of the Sioux woman's terrible end—and then handed it to Emma.

"For the winner."

The little girl's whole body stiffened with excitement. Her eyes sparkled as she examined the relic's simple and unique beauty. She didn't immediately reach for it, however. Instead, she turned and looked back at her father.

Jack nodded to her. "It's yours."

She turned back and gently took it from his hand. "Thank you, Percy."

"You're very welcome, little miss."

She started back to her bed, holding her prize out in front of her as she went. She laid it on her pillow, then quickly came back and collected her marbles.

"Where'd you get that?" Morris asked. The preacher looked taken aback. Jack noticed he was also holding another piece of paper, a different piece.

"A Sioux squaw left it behind."

Morris shook his head. "No, Mr. Percy. An Indian would never leave that behind."

Jack glanced at Emma, then eyed the preacher. "She couldn't take it where she went." He waited until Morris understood, then said, "Why? What is it?"

"I'm no expert," Morris said, "but near as I can tell, it looks like a dream catcher."

"Dream catcher?"

"The natives believe it wards off bad spirits."

Jack stood up. He realized the new page in Morris's hand was the paper Ned had scribbled the Indian's words on. The small page, he figured, must've gotten inadvertently folded together with the doctor's letter. He walked over and stood beside Morris. "That's what she said to us. Some of it, anyhow."

Morris looked down at Ned's handwriting as Jack described their encounter. He told him everything, leaving out only what he deemed trivial, then watched the preacher's expression as he stared at the paper.

"Can you read that?"

Morris slid his finger over the first term. "*Wakhan sica, Wakhan sica.*" He said the words several times aloud, letting the terms hang in the air as he searched his memory. "I believe it means 'sacred bad.'"

Jack's mind rewound, replaying the image of the young Sioux woman screaming the words over and over to him, all the while shoving a finger at the forest beyond.

"It's their term for evil spirits," Morris said.

Neither man spoke for a moment.

"What about the other one?"

"*Okiya,*" Morris said. He grimaced and pointed at the page. "These things are tricky, Mr. Percy. Whoever wrote this down did a fine job, a fine job, indeed. But it's really hard to transliterate a word from a foreign tongue after hearing it only once."

Jack just stared at the man, waiting.

"What does it mean?"

Morris looked up at him. His face had turned soft, sympathetic.

"It means *help.*"

23

The next day's sun had come and gone before Jack noticed Morris stirring in his cot. His daughter, however, was still sleeping, her breathing quick and shallow. She was resting oddly motionless—no shifting, turning, or rolling over through the day; no coughing, or snoring, or any other sound. She just lay there, on her back, unmoving.

Jack didn't like it. And his sympathy for the Morris family was only intensifying as his own hunger pangs set in. His stomach burned, his head ached, and his tongue and throat felt strangely swollen.

He was tired as well. The night had been restless, allowing only intermittent periods of sleep. He'd listened silently through Emma's prayers with her father, had been moved by the little girl's plea for her mama's safe return, then heart-struck when she closed her petition by asking for the protection of himself and Raymond.

The cabin had been quiet then, but silence wasn't enough. Jack's mind refused to rest. He'd considered the idea of angels propagating with humans until the headache began. Fearing a migraine, he'd closed his eyes and cleared his mind, only to be jarred by every sound outside, real or imagined, every creak of the cabin against the wind, every footstep as Raymond paced the floor. And now the windows were darkening again, and night was descending once more.

Jack put his head on his knees. Aside from the occasional sniffling on the other side of the room, the place was still. His body and mind were finally beginning to relax, at last yielding to the weariness that had tapped him to the bone. The sniffling persisted, however, and the longer he listened to it, the more evident it became that the noise was not simply a product of the cold, but the mournful sound of a man weeping.

Jack raised his head, and Morris quickly looked away and dabbed a sleeve beneath his eyes.

"It's what makes you human," Jack said.

Morris glanced at his daughter and lowered his head. "I let her go."

Jack's pulse quickened. His eyes moved over the sleeping girl, taking in the rise and fall of her chest. "What do you mean?"

"Sarah," Morris whispered. "I woke up when she closed the door that morning, but I hesitated. Good Lord in heaven, I hesitated. I just couldn't wrap my mind around what she'd done. When I finally made it to the porch, I started calling out to her. God knows I shouldn't have. I wasn't thinking. It never occurred to me to stay quiet, to just pray. I kept calling and screaming her name until it finally hit me that I was giving her away. I gave her away."

The last part came out in an agonized whisper, and Jack saw a tear fall from the preacher's lowered face.

"I should've gone after her," Morris said. "I should've gotten her back inside while I still could."

"And leave Emma alone?"

"That was just it. I was so confused. I knew I couldn't leave Emma, but ..." He ran the sleeve over his eyes again. "God bless her. She went for water. Water for her daughter. Water for me. She risked everything for us and I failed her."

Jack sighed. He pried a splinter from the floor with a fingernail. "For what it's worth, I think you made the right decision, Reverend. The only decision. Our minds have a way of tormenting us when things go wrong. But if you had left the girl, or took her out in the open with you, then it's likely they would've ..." He stopped, reluctant to point out the obvious.

Morris nodded. He took in a breath as if restoring himself. "I appreciate the kind words, Mr. Percy. Now is the time to stay faithful, to trust the Lord, for he shall never forsake us."

"I don't see God out there anywhere." The voice came from the area beneath the windows, the corner where Raymond was slumped against the wall.

Morris looked around, surprised by the newcomer to the conversation. "I understand, Mr. McAlister. There seems only the devil out there. But that's because you're looking in the wrong place. We must turn inward to hear the voice of God, must learn to listen to the wisdom in our hearts. That's where God speaks, where he gives us courage and strength. That's where he shows himself because that's where he lives."

Raymond said nothing.

Morris coughed and cleared his throat. He tugged his blanket over his shoulders. "I've been thinking, Mr. Percy. The doctor mentioned signs of dementia—that is to say, a loss of certain cognitive abilities or brain function. But this would be highly unusual to find in a young person, never mind a village full of young people. If fact, it's just not going to happen, not the way I understand it."

Jack had no idea what dementia was, or cognitive abilities, or brain function, nor did he have the energy to absorb a lengthy explanation. What he did know was that the cause really didn't matter if it didn't help them deal with the effect. He nodded anyway.

"So maybe," Morris went on, "the populace of Jones Mine contracted some kind of rare or unknown disease, maybe some malady that attacks specific regions of the brain. Maybe this disease has stripped away a portion of their reason and conscience, while at the same time enhancing or stimulating physical ability."

"What about the old woman?" Jack asked. "How would she know about this legend?"

"I've wondered that, too, and I honestly don't know," Morris said. "But the letter makes mention of someone coming and going through the town. It suggests this had been happening for years." He held up a finger. "This may be important. Because this stranger, whoever he was, might have been the original carrier of a unique disease. He might have been from some foreign land, perhaps even suffering the effects of the sickness himself. This kind of thing happens. In fact, it has already happened to the natives in our own country."

Jack narrowed his eyes and grinned.

"I know it's a stretch, Mr. Percy, but it's more plausible than the alternative. Listen, a stranger with a strange illness shows up in a remote town, an isolated town. If his condition is contagious, then it's only a matter of time before at least a small segment of the population is afflicted, if not more. Moreover, maybe this outsider is familiar with the myth. Maybe he somehow persuades the townspeople that it's happening again. Maybe he believes it himself. I don't know, but it's not terribly hard to conceive. And it's certainly easier to swallow than the other option."

"I reckon the doctor would've noted that in his letter," Jack said.

"If he knew. And we don't have the letter, Mr. Percy, only one page of it."

Jack said, "If they were this legend—"

"They're not."

"—then how would we beat 'em?"

Morris rubbed his arms. "We wouldn't," he said, "unless the Lord delivered us."

Emma raised her head from her pillow, blinking tired eyes around the cabin. She grinned when she saw Jack and held up the dream catcher, but the grin receded as she took in the rest of the room.

She slid to the edge of her bed and patted the floor with her toes, as if she were testing the water's edge. She stayed that way a while, just staring aimlessly down, and Jack wondered if she was still asleep. He'd seen such a thing before, never in a child, of course. But then, he hadn't been around many children. He was about to call out to her when she hopped down and approached her father.

Morris was slumped on the edge of his cot, but he straightened as she drew near. She leaned in as if to confide in him.

"I've been praying, Papa," she whispered.

Jack felt suddenly intrusive, as it was clear the little girl intended a private conversation with her father. But the small room would allow no such luxury, so he just laid his head back and tried not to be distracting.

Morris clasped her hands in his and squeezed. "I know you have. And you're doing a fine job. Very fine. I'm mighty proud of you."

Emma grinned at the praise, but confusion clouded her eyes. She blinked and looked around, like she was having a hard time articulating what was on her mind.

Morris squeezed her hands again.

"But Mama said if we was ever apart, that I should pray real hard and she would too."

Morris nodded and leaned closer to his daughter. "And I'm certain your mama is too. I wouldn't doubt that she's praying and thinking of you right now."

Emma rocked on the balls of her feet. "But when's she coming back, Papa? How much longer?"

Morris frowned, though it was clear he was trying not to. "I know it seems like a long—"

Emma broke. She threw her face against his chest and wailed.

Morris pulled her in tight.

"I miss Mama."

"I know, I know. I miss her too."

"But she said—"

"I know, I know. And we will see her again. I promise we'll see her again."

"But, why—"

"*Shhh*. Hush now, don't cry. I know it hurts right now, but everything's going to be alright. Everything's going to be okay in time."

Jack closed his eyes. *Everything's going to be okay*. A lie as old and fallacious as man himself. An innocuous, false comfort that no one really believed but accepted anyway. Morris seemed to believe it, though. Real or imagined, Jack both sensed and felt the sincerity in the preacher's words, and probably his daughter did too. But for reasons he didn't fully understand, Jack found the preacher's conviction not inspiring, but sad.

Emma pled and questioned and sobbed into her father's chest for several minutes, each protest countered by a new assurance from Morris, each one ripping Jack's guts out.

Morris finally picked her up and paced the back of the room. He whispered to her, rocked her, sang to her, and then finally laughed with her. When they returned to her bedside, both father and daughter were visibly drained. They sat together on her bed for a time, whispering jokes and aligning her marbles by color. But it was plain by her inability to stay focused that Emma's limited energy was long spent.

Morris tucked her in and recited the bedtime prayers with her. He waited until satisfied she was resting, then retreated to his cot and held his head in his hands.

"I'm sorry," Jack said.

Morris looked up and nodded a thanks. "Me too."

"What'd you study in Europe?"

Morris held up his Bible.

Jack nodded.

"How'd you know about that?" Morris asked.

"We were told you're an important man, that you're even missed in Washington."

Morris looked surprised and a little entertained. "Really?"

"Yeah," Jack went on. "There's a federal reward out for your safe return. Five hundred dollars' worth, to be exact. I was told the president himself would consider it a personal favor."

The preacher leaned back, genuinely surprised now. "Well," he said, "we did get to spend an evening at the White House on our return trip from England. I had the honor of conversing with President Hayes himself, and then to pray with him later that evening." He smiled at the memory. "How kind."

Jack closed his eyes as Morris opened his Bible.

"Maybe they'll send the cavalry," Morris whispered.

Jack grunted, said nothing. He sat there for a long time, listening to the silence and the occasional flip of a page from across the room. Then sleep finally tightened its inevitable grip, sending him into glorious nothingness.

He awoke to a scream, the likes of which he had never heard or imagined. A scream of pain, he was sure. But even in the most intense suffering, nothing he'd ever heard had sounded this way. The scream filled the air outside and inside the cabin, exploding, echoing, ear-piercing, otherworldly, animal. And then nothing.

Jack's hand slid over his revolver. He struggled to focus through burning eyes. The cabin was moonlit and silent, but the terrible noise still rang distant in his ears. He could just make out Raymond's profile in the windowed corner, but his friend was otherwise invisible in the dark.

Morris lit the candle by his cot.

Emma was on her bed, her breathing steady. She had slept through it.

"Ever heard that before?" Jack asked.

Morris's eyes were wide and distracted, and he appeared to be holding his breath.

"Never."

Jack was awake the rest of the night, which wasn't long. It seemed like no more than an hour had passed since the awful scream, and then the light of dawn was streaming through the windows again. The light was bright and powerful, making it all the more difficult to keep his eyes open. He didn't resist. He was thinking again of how the daylight brought that false sense of security when something nudged his leg. He looked up to see Raymond standing over him.

"Better get up."

Jack rose slowly, using the wall to steady himself. He knew that look, the shape of Raymond's eyes, the set of his jaw. He hurried to the front window and peered out.

"Dear God."

He ran back to the front of the room and threw open the door.

Eli was coming toward the cabin from the western edge of the woods. He was staggering, running sideways, looking back over his shoulder at the forest beyond. He fell and rolled several feet.

Jack scanned the edge of the woods. He heard movement far off, deep in the brush, and registered gray in his peripheral vision. He ignored it, ran onto the porch and down the steps.

Eli got up, still trying to run but still reeling to one side. He fell again behind the overturned cart in front of the cabin.

Jack met him there.

The scout was trying to right himself. He was coughing and clawing at the dirt and grass. The sleeves and back of his jacket were soaked through with blood.

Jack slid to his knees and pulled him into his lap.

Eli cried out. His body stiffened and contorted. He winced, breathed, and then reached for his hat, which wasn't there.

Jack retrieved it from the ground and laid it on his chest.

Eli began wringing it weakly. He looked up through eyes deep with pain and regret.

"Sa-sa-sorry, Jack."

"*Shhh.* Don't talk now."

"They-they're ev-everywhere," Eli whispered. "S-s-so fa-fast." He swallowed, then coughed a thin, bloody mist onto Jack's sleeve. A slender rivulet of crimson crept from the edge of his mouth. "Na-na-not Indians."

"I know, I know. Just hold on. Try not to talk now."

"Yeah, Jack."

Jack's vision was blurring. He cupped away tears, but more were swelling and warming behind his eyes. The rise and fall of Eli's chest was slowing so fast. He could feel the scout's inhalations against his legs, feel them dwindling, feel the gap spreading between them.

"I ga-got one."

Jack noticed the empty knife casing on Eli's belt, remembered the terrible scream in the night. He shook his head in pain and wonder and tried to smile. "You did great. You're the best, my friend."

Eli grinned. And as his eyes wandered past the brim of Jack's hat, the grin stretched into a smile. "The sta-stars," he said. "They sh-sure are pa-purdy."

Jack looked up at the cold, dreary, gray sky, and then back to Eli. His chest was still, his eyes fixed. The old scout was gone.

Jack closed his eyes. "Not him," he said. "Oh, God, not him." Tears were coming freely now, cold and wet. He reached down and closed the old man's eyes. "Why didn't you go back, Eli? Why didn't you just ..."

Emotion after emotion came in waves: pain, pain, and more pain, tearing and ripping him apart.

And then hatred.

Jack placed Eli's hat over his face and slid out from under him. He felt nothing. He was numb. He stood up from behind the wagon and locked his eyes on the gray shrouded figure at the edge of the woods.

"You bastards!" he screamed. "Go back to hell!"

The hooded shadow tilted its head to one side.

Jack drew his sidearm and stepped out from behind the wagon. A searing, white-hot pain ripped into his leg. The impact knocked him back a step and he dropped his pistol. He grabbed the bolt, tore it from his leg, and threw it at the woods. He screamed again.

"Is that the best you got?"

Jack grabbed his weapon and ducked behind the wagon. He leaned out and aimed at the forest. The hissing returned, and the wagon absorbed a shot by his head with a loud thump. Another punched into his right arm, twisting him to the ground. His revolver spun to rest in the dirt beside him.

Jack rolled over and sat up. His chest was pumping; his ears rang. He spat and glanced at his arm. This time the arrow was absent, having passed through the flesh of his upper arm. He felt blood flowing warm inside his sleeve. But no pain.

"Bastards!" He snatched up the pistol and got to his knees.

A shot exploded to his right.

Then another.

Jack got to his feet but was immediately plucked backwards. He kicked and scratched and grabbed and fought against Raymond, who was dragging him up the steps by the back of his collar, all the while firing to his right.

"No!" Jack screamed.

Raymond pulled him inside and grabbed the door.

"No!" Jack jammed the door with a boot and kicked it open.

A gray figure was standing over Eli's body.

Jack fired. He scrambled to his knees and fired again. He screamed and cursed and cried, working the hammer until the pistol was empty.

A thick cloud of powder smoke rolled back into the cabin. Jack got up, coughing and waving a hand in front of his face. He stood in the doorway until the cloud dissipated.

Eli's body lay in the same spot, undisturbed and alone.

Jack stepped across the threshold, but Raymond grabbed him with a firm hand. Jack wrenched away and flashed a look of rage at the man.

Raymond returned it.

They stared.

A bolt splintered into the doorjamb.

A fresh tear spilled down Jack's face.

Then another.

Raymond shook his head, eyes never leaving Jack's.

Jack dropped the empty pistol and slumped to the floor by the wall.

Raymond jerked the bolt out of the jamb and slammed the door. He picked up the long board leaning against the wall and fed it through the first of the two iron clasps.

No, no, please!" Emma's pleading voice came from somewhere in the back of the room.

Raymond leaned against the door.

"Please don't! Please, please don't!"

Raymond stood there a long time, staring at nothing. He finally pushed off the door and went back to the windows, leaving the board hanging useless through the first clasp.

Morris rushed over to Jack.

"Emma!"

The girl looked around quickly, then grabbed a small wooden box and hurried to her father.

The preacher inspected the leg wound, opened the box and removed a long strip of gauze. He grimaced. "I'm going to have to synch this up, Mr. Percy."

Jack said nothing. His head was down, eyes closed, fingers digging at the wood beneath him.

Morris carefully wound the linen around the injury several times and then pulled it tight.

Jack swore.

"Now let's see that arm."

"It's fine."

"You're putting out a lot of blood, Mr. Percy. We should at least—"

"Get away from me!"

Morris backed off. He closed the box and put a hand on Jack's knee. He gave it a gentle squeeze and then walked away.

Jack flung his hat and slammed a fist into the wall. He raked his fingers through his hair until it hurt. "Bastards!"

He sobbed openly now, bitterly. The physical pain was starting, but he didn't care. Didn't care if it killed him. The images were already spinning through his head like a whirlwind, torturing him, blistering his mind. He clutched his head and screamed, wanting nothing more than to grab his rifle and bolt for the woods. He hit the wall again, feeling pain in his hand for the first time, and then spat in the blood collecting under his leg. He noticed the two bare feet then, and looked up.

Emma's eyes were wide and moist. She looked scared. But she put her arms around his neck and held on, squeezing, crying with him. She finally leaned back and wiped her nose with the hem of her dress.

"Don't cry," she whispered.

24

Emma was on her toes, fingers clinging to the wall. She looked prepared to scramble up the inside of the cabin like a spider if the need arose, or as soon as she discovered the trick of it. She was standing on a stool, peering out at the snow through the back window. The decrepit stool quivered and whined with each excited shift from the little girl.

Light snow had been falling for a few hours, but only a few scattered flakes remained now, drifting past the window here and there, now and then. Emma watched each one as they floated by. She followed the flakes as much with her body as her eyes, stretching, leaning, and twisting about, as if convinced that a sincere act of will could influence the course of the precipitation.

Her efforts to manipulate the weather didn't seem to be working. But she did have a catch. And that catch was the source of all the excitement—it would also be the end of the ancient stool if she didn't get down or quit wiggling.

Jack watched from across the room. The loss of blood had exhausted him. He'd slept several restless hours, but the pain from his leg and arm had limited the periods of sleep to only brief stretches at a time. It was during one of these cycles of half-sleep that he'd seen the little girl hop down and retrieve a discolored tin bowl from under her bed. She had jumped back on the stool, yanked open the window, and placed the little container on the ledge outside.

Jack hadn't understood it at the time, nor had he tried, but every time he'd awakened from that point on, Emma had been there by the window, watching, leaning, and talking to the weather outside.

He looked away. His thirst was incredible now. His tongue and throat were thick, dry, and scratchy. His insides felt raw. The earlier exertion hadn't helped, he knew. But all that, including the mounting pain from his injuries, was secondary now.

Try as he might—and he had tried—he simply couldn't force his thoughts away from Eli. He wished to God he could clear his mind, but that old trick wasn't working this time. The old man had meant more to him than he'd known. The scout had always amazed him, had always known the way, had always been one step ahead. How he'd ever been captured during the war was truly a great mystery to Jack, just as his treatment in the federal prison camp had been. And now it always would be.

The thought of Eli lying outside in the dirt and snow made Jack sick to his stomach. If anyone deserved better, it was that man out there. Eli had always been there when it mattered, his friends always coming before any thought of himself. As was clear today.

And that was exactly why Eli hadn't gone back, Jack now knew. Because he *couldn't* go back. He couldn't go back because his friends were here. And his friends needed him. Nothing more would've entered his mind.

Jack hated himself for not worrying more about Eli's whereabouts these last few days. But then, he'd never had to worry about Eli; there had never been any need to. He'd secretly hoped the scout had escorted the others back to the safety of Twin Pines. And now he wondered if he'd lost them too. Tears formed anew as he imagined the youngsters being surrounded by these demons of the forest. Their enemy had almost certainly sniffed out the misdirection and had no doubt given chase. Otherwise, he and Raymond would've never made it this far; they would've been killed in the cave, their bodies dragged off to God only knew where, and their weapons stacked neatly on top of one another, lost forever in this godforsaken wilderness.

He saw CJ's face, the way the boy had looked at Angelina. He knew that look, remembered it himself, and knew it only meant one thing. No other emotion was so transparent, so obvious, even in its attempts to hide.

The tears had formed but wouldn't fall. And Jack noticed something else—he felt no fear. Absent were the usual symptoms when he considered the reality opposite the door. There was no burning or tightening in his chest or gut, nor did anything stir inside when he considered his own imminent death. That part of him, he suspected, was already gone. All that remained now was anger. It wasn't so much that they were going to lose—he'd always known that day would come—it was that these cold-blooded bastards were going to win. According to Morris, it had taken divine intervention to stop them before. Of course, that assumed they were the mysterious, supernatural hybrids described in the legend, and not the disease-plagued monsters of the preacher's preferred theory. They'd never know the truth of either proposition. Nor did it matter.

Emma climbed down from the stool at the back window. She was obviously disappointed the snow had stopped, but also elated with her catch. She crossed to her father's cot on tiptoes and gently passed the bowl over to him. As Morris surveyed the contents, Emma slipped under her bed and retrieved two cups.

Jack watched as father and daughter leaned over the tin container and breathed warm air over the surface of the captured snow. Even from his position against the wall, it was easy to see how much progress they were making by the ever-widening smile on the little girl's face.

The process took only a moment to complete, and then Emma was arranging the two cups between them. The girl trembled with excitement as Morris lifted the bowl and carefully measured out a little in each cup. And it was little indeed.

In the flickering candlelight, Jack could see the once half bowl of snow was now only a small puddle of water, barely enough to slosh around in the bottom.

Morris turned up his cup with both hands, receiving every drop. He swallowed hard and deliberate, like the liquid had absorbed inside his mouth, leaving nothing to go down.

Emma cringed when the cup touched her dried lips, but just as her father had, she turned it up and swallowed.

They placed the two empty cups back on the floor and Morris divided up the remaining water.

Emma grabbed the bowl and hurried back to the window.

Her father looked on curiously.

"Just in case," she said.

Morris nodded.

Emma quickly reopened the window and slid the tin bowl out on the ledge. She shivered, closed and latched the window, and then hopped down from the stool.

Then, as if the world would end if she dropped them, she picked up the two cups and moved toward the front of the room.

Jack had to clear his throat twice. "You have mine, little lady."

Emma squinted at him like he was from another planet. "No, no, you have it. It'll help you feel better." She grinned and whispered, "Then maybe we could play again."

Jack tried to smile, wasn't sure if he managed it. He took the cup and tilted it back. The water trickled into his mouth. It couldn't have been more than two or three thimbles' worth, but it was cool and wet and felt good on his tongue. "Thank you, ma'am."

Emma giggled and started toward the corner of the cabin. She stopped short, however, about halfway there, blinking and glancing around the room as if something was suddenly different. She stayed there for a beat, in roughly the center of the cabin, puzzling over something only she was privy to.

Morris swiveled on his cot and looked about to speak. But before he could, the little girl crossed the remaining space to the windows and held the second cup out to Raymond.

When he made no movement she touched his knee.

Raymond didn't lift his head, didn't open his eyes. He simply shook his head.

"For you," Emma said.

Raymond shook his head again, this time laying his hat over his face.

Emma frowned. Her brow furrowed. She glanced down at the cup, picked a hair from its rim, crossed and uncrossed her feet—awkwardly waiting for the strange man in the corner. When Raymond still didn't move, she reluctantly turned and walked away, twice looking back at him over her shoulder.

She stopped at the foot of her cot, blinking and looking around like she had before, then finally knelt and set the cup on the floor. There was a brief hesitation as she started to rise, like she had a catch in her knee, or maybe a cramp in her leg. She placed a hand on the floor to steady herself.

Then she collapsed.

She rolled to one side, trying to regain her feet, and then Morris had her by the arm. There were tears in the preacher's eyes as he swept her up and laid her in the bed. He leaned over the cot, stroking her hair and whispering to her for a long time. She seemed okay, talking and responding to her father's questions. But Morris stayed, standing over her until Jack saw his knees start to tremble. The preacher knelt and did the best he could with the evening prayers before getting up and returning to his cot. Emma's quiet voice continued as he moved away.

The girl was hidden beneath her blanket now. But her raspy, muted voice went on, filling the small room with the quiet pleading of a little girl to her God. And then, eventually, silence.

Jack shook his head.

"Never underestimate the power of prayer, Mr. Percy," Morris said. "Especially those offered by a child. Miracles are made of such."

Jack glanced at the preacher, then away. He said nothing.

Emma coughed and coughed, dry and croupy. Her little body twisted about beneath the bedding, struggling and wrestling with the blanket like she was caught in the throes of a bad dream. Eventually, the coughing produced a fit of choking that forced her head up. She looked around, batting her eyes at the darkness and trying to clear her throat. She sat up slowly and then slid out of the bed.

Jack wasn't sure how much time had passed before Emma's coughing woke him, only that it was dark. But his stiff and aching body was telling him he'd been out a while. He noticed the moonlight reaching in through the cabin windows seemed brighter tonight. And then, upon a glance at the back window, he realized why.

The snow had come again, and was no doubt reflecting the moonlight outside, amplifying its luminary effect. It was also piled against the bottom of the back window, leaving only the rim of Emma's tin bowl visible from his vantage point by the door.

Jack stretched his leg out, then pulled it in. He shifted around for a full minute, searching for a position, any position, which might ease the pain. There was none.

Emma was still standing by her bed, staring off at the far wall, but apparently not seeing anything in particular. Jack wondered again if she was a sleepwalker. He whispered her name, but his voice was so hoarse and raspy he could barely hear it himself.

Emma finally knelt and picked up the remaining cup of water. She peered inside the cup, moved it back and forth in her hands. She tilted it this way and that, big, round eyes watching the liquid slosh from side to side. Then she tiptoed across the room and laid it on the floor by Raymond's feet.

Raymond made no movement, nor gave any other hint that he might be awake.

Jack watched his friend's silhouette beneath the windows as Emma silently returned to her cot. He thought of what the preacher had said earlier. If it was true that God made his dwelling inside folks, then, Jack figured, there must be one really big room inside that small, suffering child.

Jack cursed the pain and repositioned his leg. This time he knew not much time had passed. In fact, he felt like he hadn't slept at all. He laid his head against the wall and sighed. He could see the snow still coming down through the back window, still accumulating. Probably several inches on the ground by now. He imagined the pleasure it would bring Emma. She would have a big catch, indeed, and still more standing on the ledge.

He smiled at the thought, something he hadn't known he was capable of anymore. It felt good. It also felt wrong. It felt like a betrayal somehow, like by experiencing this brief and simple pleasure he was in some way turning his back on the others, on Eli.

But then all that was gone.

The face looking into the cabin was clear in the moonlight, and pale. Deathly pale. It had emerged behind the glass like an apparition, like a nightmare. It appeared as a young man, but too young, it seemed, to be attached to a body tall enough to see through the window. It stared, emotionless, no hint of thought or intention, completely lacking any evidence of fear, hope, desire, passion, or anything else common to man. There was only detachment in its eyes, disconnect. *They had lost that which made them human.* Jack knew he was seeing firsthand what the doctor had written about. The skin on the back of his neck tingled as he went for his pistol.

The intruder's watery gray eyes were fixed on the center of the room, on Emma. It seemed to be probing and analyzing the general area around her, scrutinizing the little girl as though collecting data.

Jack's hand found an empty holster. The pistol lay on the floor beside him, also empty. He spotted his rifle leaning against the wall a few feet away and went for it slowly, realizing for the first time he'd been holding his breath. When he stole a glance back at the window, the lifeless, pale face was turned toward him, looking into him with an emptiness that raised the flesh on his arms.

The face slowly turned to one side and stayed that way, motionless, for what felt like a long time.

Jack gave up on the rifle. He could feel his heartbeat throbbing in his neck, but he also felt the warm sensation of hate swelling in his chest.

The intruder straightened its head. The emotionless, blank eyes disappeared under the familiar gray hood. And then, like a drop of water into a black sea, it backed away and was swallowed up by the darkness.

Jack grabbed his rifle and laid it across his lap. He looked back at the window. It was empty, the ledge swept clean.

The bowl was gone.

"Damn you."

25

"When peace, like a river, attendeth my way,
When sorrows like sea billows roll;
Whatever my lot, Thou has taught me to say,
It is well, it is well, with my soul."

The preacher had been singing off and on throughout the day. But he recited this latest, unfamiliar hymn quietly, just above a whisper, like these particular verses were meant only for himself.

It was early evening and Emma still hadn't awakened. She was in real danger now, maybe on the threshold, and Morris obviously knew it. He'd been kneeling beside her cot for hours, moving from one painful position to another, praying and singing hymns to his daughter. The little girl had stirred only once, complaining weakly of a sore tummy, and Morris had caressed her hair and whispered reassurances until she was out again.

She hadn't opened her eyes after that, but her father remained beside her, head down, somewhere between exhaustion and collapse. He had held his composure. He had kept his faith. He whispered,

"… If Jordan above me shall roll,
No pain shall be mine, for in death as in life,
Thou wilt whisper thy peace to my soul.
It is well, with my soul …"

Jack had been dozing in and out all day—never long and never enough. His wounds had long since ceased bleeding, and even the pain had subsided a bit. But now he found himself hurting anew, hurting for a man who'd already lost his wife, and now, only a few feet away, was watching his daughter wither and slip away as well.

Morris placed a hand on the frame of Emma's cot and stood. He looked around and noticed Jack was awake. "You okay?"

Jack was surprised at the question. "I'm alright."

Morris reached for his bed and sat down. He let out a long, exhausted breath and rested his head in his hand. His eyes were sunken, tired, and bloodshot. The arm he was using for support was locked at the elbow and quivering.

Jack thought again of the various preachers and chaplains he'd encountered during the war. Their ability to sustain character, through even the worst hells this world had to offer, had always intrigued him. Even in their own deaths, some maintained a level of equanimity largely foreign to the rank and file they shepherded.

Jack remembered one particularly well, a young man, hit behind the lines by an errant minie ball. Jack had knelt beside the young cleric as he closed his eyes that final time on the battlefield, and it had not been unlike watching a man falling peacefully asleep after a hard day's work.

"How do you do it?"

Morris looked up. "What?"

Jack waved a hand at the room.

"What keeps you going?"

"I believe," Morris said. He cleared his throat and gestured at his daughter. "And so does she."

Jack said nothing.

"The Lord's will be done," Morris went on in a tired voice. "He puts men where he wants them to be."

"You think he put us here?"

"In a manner of speaking."

"Here? In this place?"

"Yes, but probably not in the way you're thinking of it."

Jack flexed his injured arm. He took in the cold, empty room and its four lost souls. "I just can't figure it."

Morris stared at the floor, nodded wearily. "Nor can I, Mr. Percy. But I trust him."

Emma coughed and rolled over on her cot.

Raymond stood, one hand on the wall, one on his lower back. He turned to the darkening window, tapped away a piece of broken glass and looked out toward the area in front of the house—the place where the wagon lay capsized. He stood there a while, occasionally glancing in the direction of the woods, but mostly just staring toward the wagon. Then he looked at Emma. It was brief, just a quick turn of the head and flick of the eyes, barely noticeable, and then he was back to the window, back to the forest. He finally moved out of the corner and began pacing the length of the cabin's front wall.

Morris leaned back on his bed and closed his eyes. There was obviously more he wanted to say, but he clearly had no energy to do so.

Jack got up. Though still throbbing, his leg and arm were functioning. The flesh around the injuries was pink and swollen, but there didn't seem to be any infection—which was typically the wounded man's real killer. He stretched and worked his limbs and then settled back down by the door. The whole effort did him good, got the blood moving, even cleared his head a bit. But it also drained him. He laid his rifle across his lap and rested his head on his knees.

Raymond went on pacing, floorboards creaking and whining under his feet.

Jack woke when something brushed against his leg. He couldn't remember falling asleep. It seemed like just a moment ago he'd been talking with Morris, but he could tell he'd been out for some time.

He looked around the room. Apart from the gentle footsteps and creaking floor, it was dark and quiet now. He could tell sleep wasn't going to return easily, so he moved around enough to get the tingling out of his legs, and then rested his head against the wall.

The footsteps stopped, then moved on.

They were softer than usual, like Raymond was making a conscious effort not to disturb anyone.

Emma coughed and sniffled in the middle of the room. It sounded like she was talking to herself, whispering, maybe praying again.

The footsteps stopped.

Jack wondered how much longer she had. He had no idea how long a man could go without food and water, let alone a little girl. He had witnessed death in many of its terrible forms through the years, but never by starvation, never from dehydration, not even during the war. He didn't want to know how it ended. He'd seen enough. Enough for a lifetime.

Emma's bed frame creaked like she was tossing around in the blanket again. Then more sniffling. It sounded like she was crying now, but the sobs were soft and muffled.

The footsteps resumed.

Before he realized what he was doing, Jack had withdrawn a cigar from his pocket. Old habits. He rolled the smoke between his fingers, examining its texture in the dark. He could tell without seeing that it was broken, snapped at an angle near the tip. He felt loose tobacco spreading in his hand. He held the unbroken portion under his nose. It smelled terrific, but it would be insanity to light up with nothing to drink, like adding fuel to an already raging fire.

There was another noise then, similar but different. It sounded muffled like before, but no longer coming from the middle of the room. It was hard to make out—not sobbing, but louder, more like a shriek. A scream, maybe, but far off. Both distant and near at the same time.

Jack laid the cigar down. The darkness in the room was near complete, but as he looked toward the windows, he could just make out the faint silhouette of someone beside him, someone standing at the door.

Opening the door.

"Ray?"

The door swung open with an audible whine. Moonlight flowed into the cabin, revealing a shadowy, hooded form in the doorway. The shadow stopped and tilted its head.

Jack sat up.

There was another muted scream. Emma's scream. She was pinned to the shadow's hip, kicking and flailing, trying desperately to latch her fingers on the doorjamb.

Jack stood. His injured leg seized. Pain rifled through his thigh like a bayonet thrust.

His Winchester clanged to the floor.

Jack dropped to his knees, ignoring the pain, searching and running his hands over the floor for the rifle. He found it, spun, and aimed at the door.

The doorway was empty.

The shadow was gone.

Jack got up, limped outside. He listened for sound, any sound. Heard nothing. The moonlight and snow provided better than usual visibility, but there was nothing to see, nothing there. He cursed and ran off the porch, plowing through the snow, rifle to his shoulder, spinning, searching.

Nothing.

"Ray!"

26

Emma struggled to get air. The hand over her mouth was locked down like an iron clasp, partially overlapping her nose and giving her a terrifying sense of drowning. Pressure throbbed below her left eye. She tried to scream, but the only noise she heard came muted from somewhere inside her chest and throat.

She pumped her legs furiously, kicking and stabbing her feet at dead, empty space. Her arms wouldn't move. They were jammed firmly to her sides. Her fingernails dug and scratched at the cold, damp fabric of her abductor's cloak, but already her energy was waning.

She was suddenly faint and lightheaded like before in the cabin. She felt like she was falling, spinning, turning around and around. Her tummy felt sick, legs went heavy, head lobbed back. Her whole body tingled. The wind bit cold and stung her face and neck. Trees blurred past. Her hair caught in a branch and snatched her head painfully to one side. A tear slipped from the corner of her eye.

There was a sharp, smacking sound and she was immediately jolted. The noise was familiar, like a slap against bare flesh, loud and wet, followed by wheezing and choking.

Then she was in the snow.

There was a thump on the ground behind her, and something brushed against her back. Then more wheezing, and a soft, muffled pop.

Emma pushed herself up. The snow was deep, well above her elbows. She came to her feet warily, struggling to keep her legs planted through the awful spinning.

She heard a crack then, a hard, splintering sound like wood against rock, and she was shoved back in the snow.

Her heart pounded. She jumped up and ran, but went right back down. There was another sound, but her ears were ringing too badly now to interpret the noise. She began crawling. Her fingers and toes didn't feel like they were there anymore. She was sure she was calling for her papa, but she couldn't hear anything, couldn't hear her own voice. She got back to her feet and managed a couple of steps, but the spinning was getting worse, pulling her to one side and another, and she just wanted to lie down, to let it pass like before.

Then she was scooped up from behind.

She tried to scream, but the strong hand clamped back down and she was in motion again, feeling the cold air rush across her body, watching the trees speed past on either side.

Jack dropped to one knee and took aim. The noise was dead ahead. A bending tree branch. A snapping twig. Silence. Then the sound of feet trudging through the snow.

An obscure shape was coming into view, coming closer, gliding through the darkness like a ghost.

Jack's finger tensed on the trigger. He placed the rifle's sights in the center of the approaching form, filled his lungs with air and held it. He waited. There would be no missing this time.

Closer.

His finger tightened; the trigger edged back. He could see it now. The shape was running, a cloak trailing out behind it. Why was it coming back? He held fast, rigid, rifle locked against his shoulder. The form was still coming. He heard Emma's muffled screams and elevated his aim.

Still kneeling, Jack waited until they were almost on top of him. Had to. He couldn't risk hitting the girl. Then he saw them, Emma cradled in the predator's arms. But instead of the familiar gray, the cloak was black. And it wasn't a cloak.

Jack lowered the rifle and exhaled.

Raymond bolted past him, Emma wrapped in his arms. He jumped on the porch and ran through the open door.

Jack followed, retreating backward on his heels. He heard noise to the west, rising and falling from various points in the woods, and then he was inside, slamming the door behind him.

Morris was on his knees in the center of the room. "Dear God." He brushed away tears and held out his hands. "Dear God in heaven, thank you."

Raymond laid Emma in the preacher's arms and backed away. He bent and put a hand on the wall, grimacing and grasping his lower back. A trickle of blood fell from a cut below his eye.

Morris stayed on his knees, cradling and rocking his little girl. Her body shivered and jerked as a rush of sobs took her. He nestled his head into hers. "*Thank you, thank you, thank you,*" he whispered. "*Thank you, Lord Jesus.*"

Jack stripped the blanket off Emma's bed and handed it to Morris. He looked over at Raymond, who'd slid to the floor under the windows. His friend was breathing hard, still clutching his side, and there was genuine pain in his eyes. He was looking down, not at the uneven wooden planks of the cabin floor, but at something else, somewhere else, someplace far off.

Emma stood and Morris draped the blanket around her and brushed snow from her hair. She trembled and shrugged underneath the blanket, legs unsteady. Her face was red and swollen, and there was a bruise forming on her left cheek.

Her eyes wandered to the fallen snow on the floor, and Morris quickly began trying to collect it for her. She watched her father, seemed to focus on his hands as they feebly swept and cupped the melting snow. She turned around, where more snow lay dirty and wet on the floor behind her. But when her slender, pale fingers appeared from under the blanket, they touched Raymond's knee instead.

Raymond looked up.

That was apparently all the little girl needed. Using his knee for support, she moved alongside and climbed into his lap. She laid her head on his chest and tucked her legs beneath her.

Raymond just watched her, his hands braced against the floor.

Emma closed her eyes and pulled the blanket over her face.

Jack fed the board through the iron clasps, sealing the door. He leaned his rifle against the wall and glanced back at the little girl.

Emma didn't move, didn't react to the barricaded door. Her body shivered beneath the blanket and she coughed once, but that was all.

Raymond continued to stare down at her. He watched as her small frame shuddered and stilled, watched as she coiled and twisted inside the dirty blanket. He touched his cheek and rubbed his fingers together, inspecting the blood in the trembling candlelight. He finally wiped his fingers on the floor and laid the edge of his duster over Emma's exposed feet. Then he slid an arm around her.

Dawn came an hour later, straining through the filthy surface of the cabin's one remaining front window in erratic, jagged patterns. Fog and wisps of snow drifted through the other. The wind rushed and swirled outside as if it were angry.

Morris slept, as did his daughter—still on Raymond's lap in the corner.

Raymond hadn't moved since the events earlier. He hadn't slept, hadn't closed his eyes. He'd just watched as the small girl cycled through periods of rest, to tossing and whimpering, through coughs, sniffles, and groans, and then back into deep sleep again. It was during those moments when she was still that his attention returned to that same unremarkable spot on the floor in front of him.

Raymond's head was down, the shadows and brim of his hat hiding his eyes. But Jack knew his lips were moving. He could see it now. But even before the gray dawn had illuminated the window, he had heard it, or thought he had. The strong wind had washed away all lesser sounds over the last half hour, but it was dying away now, coming in weaker, sporadic gusts. And in between were the whispers.

Whether his friend was talking to the girl or himself, Jack didn't know. But now as the wind paused and Emma was at rest, Raymond moved for the first time. He laid his head back and closed his eyes. His bloody cheek shimmered in the early light. He whispered, "*Not for me, but the girl.*"

Emma's head was tucked against his shoulder, but her arms and legs drooped like a wilted flower when Raymond stood, as though lifeless in his arms. He walked soundlessly across the room and laid her in her bed.

A groan of discomfort escaped her, but she didn't move or wake. Raymond stood over her for a time, looking down at her, just watching her. He brushed a gentle finger across her chin, clearing away a fleck of dry blood from her lower lip. Then he drew back her hair, leaned down, and kissed her forehead.

"I'm your friend," he said.

He straightened, twisted away, and returned to the corner. He glanced out the broken window, and then picked up his rifle and moved to the door.

Jack pushed himself into a sitting position.

Raymond stopped beside him, head down, rifle pointing at the floor. "This time I'm here."

Jack stood, favoring his wounded leg. "What are you doing?"

Raymond raised his head and looked at the door.

"The only thing I know how to do," he said. "I'm going to kill them."

27

Raymond slid the wooden plank out of the clasps and leaned it against the wall. The door creaked and light seeped in around the edges.

Jack looked back at Morris, who'd pushed up on one elbow and was watching them in silence. Their eyes met knowingly, but there were no words. Jack gestured at the board against the wall, indicating the preacher should put it back in place. Morris frowned but nodded. A sad and bitter smile tugged at the corner of his mouth.

Jack touched the brim of his hat. He picked up his rifle, tapped the stock twice on the floor, and followed Raymond out without looking back.

The world outside was quiet. Snow was still falling, and the accompanying cloud cover had kept the light, early morning fog from burning away. Visibility was nonexistent, and Jack quickly lost sight of Raymond as his friend dropped off the west side of the porch and advanced toward the forest.

Jack limped down the steps. That his heart rate was slow surprised him. His body was relaxed, ready for the worst, expecting the worst. Resigned, maybe, but not finished.

His boots disappeared in deep powder as he came off the last step. He noticed the sideboards on the overturned wagon were sagging under the weight of the snow. He also noticed the uneven mound on the earth beside it—a slight, irregular bump in an otherwise level landscape of white. The mass was unnatural, out of place.

Unforgivable.

Jack turned toward the woods. He had to lift his wounded leg high to clear the surface of the snow, and then stretch out in long, uncomfortable strides in order to make progress. He had done this only twice when a shot exploded somewhere ahead and right of his position. The unexpected blast ripped through the stillness, echoing through the trees and surrounding countryside.

Jack stopped. There was another noise now, also somewhere ahead, legs and feet treading snow, reacting to the gunfire. He still couldn't see anything, but he knew there was more than one of them out there. And they were moving in unison, with shared purpose.

He took another long step forward, and another shot rang out.

Hissing erupted throughout the forest. The sound arose like a sudden rush of air, like a soft, unexpected wind.

But there was no wind.

Jack raised his rifle and picked up his pace. The hissing increased, some of it sounding no more than a few paces away. Then another shot. And a scream.

The scream was loud and shrill, laced in agony. It was long and piercing, reverberating throughout the forest and back again, seeping into Jack's very core. The sound died away, slow and reluctant, dissolving like a living thing clutching to life.

Jack didn't realize he'd stopped again until the shriek had played itself out. There was a momentary hush then. Snow fell from a tree near the edge of the woods, and then something stirred in the forest to his left.

He moved on, rifle poised, grinding his teeth. One step, then another, quicker and quicker. The first few trees were coming into view, gray and white like sentinels at the forest's edge. Then something large brushed past him, bumping his arm.

Something gray.

Jack spun and fired, and something immediately buzzed past his right ear. He felt the air off the projectile below the brim of his hat, and then a pinch like a bee sting in the flesh of his upper ear.

He fired again, blindly. A gray shadow flashed through the falling snow to his right. The shadow was a blur, a brief smudge in the corner of his eye. There and then gone. Jack whirled again, searching, cursing, aiming his rifle into the snow and fog.

He saw nothing.

Everything went still. Even the noise in the forest stopped. Jack listened, strained against the thunderous silence, hoping for anything that might tip his opponent's next move. But there was only his own breathing now, and the light whisper of snow and freezing rain accumulating at his feet.

Then the rifle was knocked from his hands.

Jack jerked his blade and screamed. He lunged forward, stabbing, slashing, working the knife left and right. But there was nothing there, nothing but fog and emptiness. Then he saw it to his left, a gray blur, coming hard, moving fast. He twisted and swung the blade around with all he had, throwing his entire weight behind it. The knife came around in a wide and deadly arc, and again found nothing.

A sick feeling washed through Jack's stomach as the momentum from the reckless maneuver twisted his body halfway around before he could stop it. He felt a tingle in his exposed back and his spine ran cold.

He reversed the knife and dug in his heels. He pivoted and turned. And then something cracked into his jaw, something solid. The blow was rock-hard and painful, leaving one ear ringing and one eye watering. Jack landed on his stomach, vision swimming. He rolled. Something hit the ground beside him. He rolled again, and again. He heard footsteps, the swish of fabric, felt a gouge in the small of his back. He rolled again, dragging his hands through the snow behind him, this time coming to his knees with his rifle in his lap.

The shadow was there, five paces away. And it was just standing there, motionless.

It tilted its head.

Jack spat to one side.

The hood followed the marks of bloody saliva in the snow, then came back to Jack.

Jack eased his hand into the lever of the rifle; his finger slipped inside the trigger guard.

The shadow straightened its head.

And then the crossbow was coming up, coming up fast, impossibly fast. Jack saw the newly reloaded bolt, saw the twinkle of moisture on its razor-sharp tip. He closed his eyes, hoping to God he'd chambered another round, and pulled the Winchester's trigger without aiming.

The rifle bucked painfully against his lower ribs. There was a loud pop, a wink of light, and a cold slash at his right cheekbone.

Jack rocked back and caught himself with one hand. He levered in another round and aimed at the lingering powder smoke. He was breathing hard and trying to blink tears from his right eye. He could taste blood spreading in his mouth, feel it between his teeth. The gash below his eye began to leak, at first warm, and then cold on his cheek.

The smoke drifted aside. The shadow was on its back in the snow. It didn't move, didn't groan, didn't breathe. It lay still under a twisted bundle of gray cloth, gradually collecting snow, slowly receiving its due burial.

The awful hissing returned to Jack's ears like he was waking from a dream. He got up and limped to the woods' edge. He dropped at the base of a hardwood, tucked against it, then leaned out and fired at the closest noise. The fog and snowfall were lifting, stretching his range of vision. But still he could see nothing.

There was another scream from the woods to the west, and more crossbows came to life. Then running, footfalls all over the forest. Some distant, some close. Jack fired again, again with no result. He closed his eyes, mentally sifting through the noise around him, then rotated the rifle and fired at the nearest sound. He heard a clear thump in the snow, maybe fifteen yards away.

Jack leaned against the tree and moved his aim left. There were other footsteps there now, but these were slow and disciplined. They were approaching cautiously from the area around their fallen comrade. Jack listened, adjusted his aim to the sound of snow packing under their feet. One slow step, then another.

He squeezed the trigger.

The hammer fell and clicked.

He quickly worked the lever and tried again.

Click.

The footsteps stopped.

Jack shifted the rifle to one hand and went into his jacket for the two extra cartridges. He probed his pocket with numb fingers, then scratched and clawed. Finally, he just closed his fist and pulled it free. The first thing he noticed when he opened his hand was how badly it was shaking, then he saw the two rounds lying in his palm.

The footsteps were moving again, still slowly, still in his direction. Twelve yards. Ten yards.

Jack laid the Winchester across his lap and began to feed the cartridges into the magazine.

He dropped them. Both of them.

They fell and disappeared in the snow.

Jack slumped to his hands and knees, digging and scooping away snow, all sensation long gone from his hands.

Nothing.

The footsteps were no more than seven yards away.

Two gunshots went off, right together, again from deep in the woods.

The footsteps paused.

Jack shoveled away snow like a wild animal. He worked as fast and silent as possible, and had created a sizeable crater in front of him. But there was nothing there, nothing but endless white powder, now as great an obstacle as the ones standing merely yards away.

Another scream tore through the forest, a singular cry of pain, and then a high-pitched one right behind it.

The footsteps started again, still slowly, but now moving north. Away from Jack. They were turning toward the heart of the chaos. Turning toward Raymond.

Jack cupped his hands to his mouth and breathed into them. He dared a glance up. The snow and fog were retreating like a great white tide, revealing more and more of the forest, more and more trees and brush. And two crouching gray shadows creeping away to his right. He could see them clearly now, and if they only turned their heads, they would see him.

He looked at the hole he'd created, the new snow accumulating in the bottom. He reached to brush it away, to resume searching, but didn't. He leaned back and laid his head against the tree. He thought of his friend out there alone, thought of the preacher and little girl back in the cabin. He whispered, *"God, please help."*

Jack went back to the hole with both hands, scraping and pitching away snow in all directions. He didn't look up, didn't breathe, didn't care about the noise he was making. He dug and dug, eventually uncovering dirt and leaves, and then his fingers were raking uselessly into the frozen earth below. He placed his palms against the hard ground and dragged his fingernails through the dirt. A drop of blood hit the back of his hand. He swore aloud, surprised and saddened by the weakness in his voice.

And there they were, in the small bank of powder he'd shoveled to his right. Two brass casings glinting in the snow like stars in the dead of night.

He grabbed them up in a fistful of snow and fed them into the rifle. In one motion, he pulled the lever and brought the gun around.

The fog was gone; the snow had stopped. Two gray cloaks were slowly moving north, their deadly, primitive weapons held in front of them. One turned.

Jack took a breath. Anger and hate burned through him like wildfire. He thought of Eli, saw the old scout's face in his mind's eye. And fired.

The first one fell like a wet cloth, dead before it hit the ground. The unfired crossbow dropped harmlessly in the snow beside it. Jack chambered the second round and shifted his aim. The other one was already bringing its crossbow around, rotating in a tight, almost invisible arc. The two weapons discharged simultaneously. A small wisp of dust pitched off the front of the gray shroud, followed by a tiny shudder and a ripple of fabric. The bolt whistled past Jack's left eye and buried three inches deep in the tree beside him.

The shadow stumbled back and dropped the crossbow.

Jack lowered his rifle.

The cloaked figure touched its chest and glanced at the snow at its feet. The crossbow's handle was just visible above the surface. The shadow knelt to retrieve the weapon but then stopped and put a hand on a nearby tree. It touched its chest again, looked down where the red stain was spreading and deepening. It seemed to examine the stain, dab at it with its fingers. Then it staggered back, glanced off a tree, and fell and disappeared in the snow.

There was no scream.

Jack dropped his rifle and looked farther up the slope, deeper into the forest. He saw a man standing on the ridge in the distance. The man was looking into the woods to his left where most of the noise had come from. His coal-black hair was slicked back against his scalp, matching his clothing nearly perfect. The all-black attire exaggerated the man's already deathly-white pallor. At this distance, one might easily mistake the figure for a priest.

But not Jack.

The man took a step back. He looked up, then at the area around him, then up again. He went back another step, and his eyes briefly met Jack's.

"*I know you,*" Jack whispered.

The man tilted his head, that same quick, mechanical gesture. Then the snow was falling again, and the dark figure on the hill turned and disappeared behind a sheet of white.

Tom Morris was standing in front of the cabin when Jack emerged from the woods. He was gripping the double-barreled shotgun with one hand and holding the folds of his coat with the other. Snow was accumulating in his hair and he was visibly shaking. The tip of the big scattergun was submerged in the white powder below his knees. The preacher's eyes came to Jack with both question and surprise; then Emma was peeking out the door behind him.

It was over.

Jack rejected the notion as soon as it entered his mind, but as he stood there looking at the small, displaced family, something in his heart insisted. Whatever the case, he knew it had to be over. One way or the other, win or lose, there was nothing left to fight with.

Morris's head suddenly jerked to the right and he stumbled back a step and raised the shotgun.

Jack turned.

Another figure was emerging from the woods, but slow and gradual, stopping and starting. A long garment trailed out on the snow behind it. It moved from beneath the forest's canopy and into the shadow of the trees, then stopped.

Jack reached for his blade, but, of course, it wasn't there.

The figure was nothing but a vague silhouette in the falling snow, only a shape: tall and slender, arms folded as if shielding itself from the cold. It didn't come any closer, but just stood there, unmoving, shivering, looking around.

Jack saw the shiver, saw the gentle shudder through the figure's ragged dress. He saw the wet blonde hair, and the weak, early light playing off it.

Morris fell to his knees and screamed.

Sarah bolted from the woods at the sound of her name. She ran, dress hitched to her knees, bounding through the snow in long, clumsy strides. She didn't stop until the two collided and fell sideways in a long embrace. They rolled into the snow, shouting, weeping, not daring to let go.

Jack looked back at the forest's edge. Raymond was on one knee, leaning against his rifle, which was braced in the snow beside him. His eyes were on the reunited family in front of the cabin.

"Mama!"

Emma leapt off the porch. She stumbled and fell and popped up again, navigating the snow and ice like a tiny swimmer—all arms and legs and determination.

"Mama!"

Sarah rushed to her little girl. She scooped her out of the snow and lifted her high in the air. Emma clung to her mother's neck as Sarah spun her around and around, higher and higher, kissing and nuzzling and wetting her daughter's face with her tears.

Jack had never imagined he'd see Tom Morris beaming like he was now, would've never thought it possible. The preacher was still on his knees, hands clasped, watching a reunion that perhaps only he had believed possible. He turned and smiled in Jack's direction, and Jack was struck by how much he resembled a boy at that moment.

Morris's smile faded, however, as his eyes moved over Jack's shoulder to the forest beyond. His lips tightened, quivered, moved to speak, but nothing more.

Jack frowned as he read the change in the preacher's face. He followed his eyes back toward the line of trees.

Raymond was still there, still alone. But now he was leaning back against a tree, his body barely visible in the deep red snow around him.

Snow and ice flew around Jack as he struggled back to the woods and dropped to his knees beside his friend. His hands immediately went to work, throwing back the folds of Raymond's duster, probing and searching for the wound responsible for all the blood. But it wasn't just one wound. Raymond's entire upper body was soaked through in the same dark crimson as the snow around him.

"Oh, God, Ray."

The old soldier said nothing. His eyes were fixed on the little girl and her mother, watching as they laughed, cried, danced, and twirled about in the snow.

Jack tore a strip from the bottom of his shirt and pressed it on the worst of the chest wounds. Blood immediately seeped through the fabric and squeezed between his fingers. He tore off another strip and dropped it over the first, then another, and another. When he rocked forward to apply pressure, a hand touched his arm.

Raymond's eyes were weak and tired, and there was fresh blood at the corner of his mouth. "It's okay," he whispered. "It's a gift."

Tears streamed down Jack's face and neck. He pressed the saturated cloth harder into the wound. His vision clouded, voice broke. "I should be with you."

Raymond shook his head. His hand moved to Jack's shoulder and squeezed. "You still have something left to do."

The old soldier pulled his hat down then, and laid his head against the tree.

His grip weakened on Jack's shoulder until the strength in his fingers was gone. Jack sat with him as Raymond's energy silently drained away, until the swell and shudder of his chest ceased, until those cold blue eyes became fixed and still.

Finally, Raymond's hand slipped and fell into the scarlet snow beside him.

Jack put his face in his hands. Tears ran freely through bloodstained fingers.

28

Jack spent the rest of the morning and most of the afternoon burying his friends. Using the spade from inside the cabin, he attacked the rock-hard ground with an anger and hatred that left his fingers blistered and his palms smeared with blood.

He worked alone, as he wanted it, silently turning down multiple offers of help from Morris with either a shake of his head or gesture of his hand. Silently, because he didn't want to talk, wasn't sure he could, even if it was a simple *no, thank you*. Somehow just the notion of speaking, the thought of moving his lips, seemed impossible now.

He used the back of the spade to finish pounding in the second makeshift cross and then slumped down between his friends. He remembered Raymond telling him how a part of himself had gone into the ground at the burial of his own family, how whoever he'd been back then had died with them. Jack felt that now, a painful emptiness he knew would never, nor could ever, be filled.

There was also a strange and persistent sense that none of this was real, like he was somehow trapped in the cruelest sort of dream. But it was real, and the occasional sounds of the happy, reunited family on the other side of the cabin were the only consolation.

He heard footsteps round the corner behind him and turned, prepared to wave Morris away again. But it was Emma this time, looking on wide-eyed from beneath her blanket. She was holding the blanket with one hand and a disfigured snowball in the other. The snowball had little bite-sized wedges missing from it. Sarah stood behind her, hands resting on her daughter's shoulders, the picture of a guardian angel. The dirty blanket was draped over Emma's shoulders and had been fashioned into a hood to protect the young girl's head.

Her mom's doing, Jack knew, because only a mother could use a grimy, threadbare blanket in such a practical way. Only a mother would think to. A good mother. The kind all little girls needed.

Sarah looked down at Emma and then up at Jack. Her eyes were moist and apologetic, and tired, very tired. They wandered over the wounds on his face and ear, lingering on the blood dried to his cheek. Her lips curved into a sad smile and she swallowed.

Jack nodded to her, and she slowly removed her hands from her daughter's shoulders.

Emma dropped the snowball and walked toward him. She knelt by Eli's grave and laid two marbles on the mound of earth and snow. She looked at Jack.

"I reckon he would've liked those," Jack said.

Emma grinned. She stood and moved around to the cross marking Raymond's burial and hung the dream catcher there.

"For your other friend," she said.

Jack brushed away tears. "He was your friend too."

The little girl blinked, obviously bothered by his sorrow, then she looked back at the graves. She stayed that way for a time, frowning and studying the mounds of dirt. But when she looked back up, her eyes were different. They were bright, full of wonder and mystery, as if something had just occurred to her.

"He *was* a hero," she whispered. "Just like I prayed for."

Jack took a breath. "That he was," he said. "That he was."

They stayed there, Jack's head down, Emma in his lap. Neither spoke. Neither wanted to. And when Jack eventually turned and looked back at the corner of the cabin, Sarah had gone. He immediately understood the great compliment she'd paid him by leaving her daughter alone with him, but the thought struck only in passing, because the corner wasn't empty.

CJ was there now. He was on his knees, head down, shoulders slumped forward. The boy's cheeks were wet, and his raw, vacant stare revealed an inner torment that Jack not only recognized, but was intimately familiar with.

Jack was up and dragging the youngster to his feet before the boy could register what was happening. Jack hauled him up by the shoulders of his coat and hugged him, lost in the sudden rush of an unexpected joy. "Dear God," he said. "Dear God, I thought we'd lost you."

CJ broke. Jack felt his body sag against him, felt the wrack of sob after sob. "I'm so sorry, Jack. I tried. I shouldn't have stopped. It was just so far. Just so…"

Jack squeezed. "This ain't your fault. We— "

"I wanted Eli to stay with us, but … he wouldn't. He said he couldn't. Oh, God, I tried to get back. I tried to get help."

The boy's pain was piercing Jack's heart like white-hot iron. He'd never been certain that Eli had been with the others, but the revelation only confirmed that which his heart had known all along. It never could've been any other way.

Jack turned the teenager around so the boy could no longer see the graves. "What about the others?" he asked. "Ned and Angelina?"

"They're okay." CJ sniffed. "We're all okay. Eli got us out."

"How'd you get back here? Who's with you?"

"Pa … Mr. Ames …" CJ tried to think. "Some others." He turned and looked back at the mounds of dirt. "Oh, God, Ray. How could—"

Jack spun the boy again and walked him around the corner of the cabin. He saw Sarah jog past to retrieve her daughter.

There were strangers milling around out front now, and some heavily bearded men roaming the edge of the woods with rifles and shotguns. More than a few carried muzzleloaders. There were tracks everywhere.

A couple of them noticed Jack and turned to stare.

Jack stopped and faced CJ. "This ain't your fault."

CJ's eyes widened as if noticing Jack's bloody face for the first time.

"Listen," Jack said. "You did exactly what I'd hoped you would. There ain't a thing you could've done here, even if you'd made it back with all these boys."

CJ started to turn away but Jack grabbed him by the shoulders. "I ain't finished. You'll carry this the rest of your days, and it'll eat you like a sickness if you let it. There will be plenty of regrets in life that are all your own, but this ain't yours to bear."

CJ looked over Jack's shoulder and new tears dropped off his cheeks.

"Look at me," Jack said. "You're a bigger man than I ever was at your age. I mean that. I'm stunned you got back here at all, never mind as quickly as you did. You weren't supposed to come back. If you had mentioned it before, I would've scolded you for even thinking it."

CJ motioned toward the back of the cabin. "What was I supposed to do?"

"That's just it. I never expected to see you again, and here you are." Jack swallowed. "You did what any real friend would do. I don't know another man alive who could've gotten help this fast."

"It's too late." CJ cupped away tears. "If I hadn't stopped, then—"

"Then you and all these fellas would be dead," Jack said. "They would've been waiting for you. For all of you."

CJ shook his head and Jack hugged him again. "Don't you see, CJ? You did exactly what I asked. Exactly what I asked and more. And I'm so damned proud of you. So damned proud. Don't ever forget that."

"This ain't real," CJ said. He slumped into Jack's shoulder and wept. Jack let him, joined him, and then finally led him around to the front of the cabin, where the boy broke away and sat down alone on the porch.

Doc Lewis tended to the Morris family as a couple of other men inspected the overturned wagon. They had brought extra horses, food, and water.

Jack felt a hand on his arm and turned.

"Tom told us what happened," Jonas said. "I wish we'd got here sooner."

Jack shook Jonas's hand. "Good thing y'all didn't." He gestured at CJ, back on the porch. "Never seen a finer boy, Jonas. I mean it. I regret he had to go through this."

"I regret every bit of it," Jonas said. "I should've shot this Heminger kid and his bluebelly captain the moment they stopped at my gate."

Jack noticed Ned for the first time as the young man took a hesitant step back.

"Hardy had it coming," Jack said. "But I reckon Ned here was supposed to die in these hills with us."

Ned leaned forward and handed a brown envelope to Jack.

Jack opened it and withdrew a handful of money. He gave Ned a puzzled look.

"It's yours," Ned said. "One thousand dollars. There really was a federal reward for Reverend Morris's safe return. Evidently, Mr. Cavanaugh received the cash shortly after the telegraph arrived from Washington."

"Cavanaugh said the federals were offering five hundred," Jack said.

"One thousand," Ned said. "Saw the transcript myself."

Jack shook his head and stuffed the money back into the envelope. He glanced up at an approaching stranger.

"Hellfire," the stranger said. "Them there's just boys." He pointed at the woods. "They're healthy buggers, I'll give you that, big as mules, but boys all the same."

The newcomer was tall and thin. And like the men patrolling the edge of the forest, he sported a thick, greasy black beard.

"There's a handful of 'em at the trees there and several more deeper in to the west." The stranger looked at Jonas. "There ain't a one of 'em alive. All of 'em dead as hammers."

Jonas just nodded.

"You Percy?" the stranger asked.

"I am," Jack said.

"You had Ray McAlister up here with ya?"

Jack nodded.

"I reckon that explains these bodies, then."

Jack looked away, said nothing.

"Jack, this is Gabriel Ames," Jonas said. "He tried to get the sheriff to raise some boys and come up here, but—"

"But Murphy ain't nothing but a crusty ole turd now, undeservin' the star on his chest," Ames finished.

Jack extended his hand. "I'm much obliged."

Ames waved his hand away. "Ain't no need for that." He glanced back at the forest. "Can't get over the size of 'em," he said. "They're some corn-fed buggers alright, some of 'em thick as trees. But how were they livin'? We've been near a half-mile deep in all directions and ain't found the first shelter."

Jack just shook his head.

"And another thing." Ames pointed at the handful of men wandering the forest's edge. "I had near ten boys when we entered the woods at Twin Pines, and that's all I got left."

Jack glanced at the men. "I don't follow."

"I was hoping you'd enlighten me, Mr. Percy. You see, during our approach this afternoon, we came across several folk just meanderin' around the woods. Just wanderin' about like they was lost." Ames spat a stream of tobacco in the snow. "Damnedest thing I ever saw. It was like they didn't know where they was. Had to leave five boys behind just to collect 'em." Ames stepped closer and met Jack's eyes. "What happened in this place?"

"Women?" Jack asked.

Ames' eyes wandered away while he thought about it. "Yeah, several of 'em were. At least, the ones I seen, anyhow."

Jack nodded.

"Now might I inquire what in hell happened here?" Ames asked.

Jack took a breath, let it out. He looked out into the woods. The snow-covered ground and trees were truly a beautiful sight, a serene sight. It was a place that had been completely transformed in less than a day. It was the closest thing to a miracle he'd ever seen.

"A child's prayer."

"How's that?" Ames asked.

Jack motioned to the porch, where Tom Morris and his family were eating and listening to Doc Lewis. "I reckon you best be asking the preacher."

Ames gave Jack a long, questioning look, and then started toward the cabin.

Ned cleared his throat. "I want you to know I'm really sorry, Mr. Percy."

"Me too, Ned." Jack thumbed out a few bills of the reward money and slipped them into his pocket. He handed the rest to Jonas.

Jonas drew back, shaking his head, but Jack grabbed his hand and forced the money into it.

"I can't," Jonas said.

Jack ignored him and handed a bill to Ned. "I owe this to Randy Miller. See to it that he gets it, if you would."

Ned took the money and glanced at Jonas. "Yes, of course, Mr. Percy. But Mr. Miller's in jail right now."

"What say?"

"Yes, sir. He shot Mr. Cavanaugh."

"Shot him?"

"He didn't kill him," Ned said. "Just shot him in the leg. Both legs, actually. Heavy gauge shotgun." Ned looked at Jonas again.

"Blew out both his knees," Jonas said. "Bottom of his left leg came clean off."

"Yeah," Ned said. "You see, he found out Mr. Cavanaugh was behind the murder of his son, Brody. Set the whole thing up, I think, to secure his future ownership of the supply store. There's a young private from Pennsylvania backing the story. Says he's known about it for some time and couldn't carry the burden any longer. He confessed to Mr. Miller just as we were leaving Twin Pines."

Jack sighed, remembering the soldier entering Randy's shop as they left. "I reckon the old man's lucky he's still breathing."

"Lucky, indeed," Ned said. "And the charges against Mr. Miller aren't likely to stick. There's a lot of sympathy around town. He has the private's testimony, and now that it's out in the open, some others have come forward. Apparently, Sheriff Murphy is waiting for the marshal to decide how to proceed."

Jack nodded.

Ned held up the money. "But I'll make sure he gets it, nonetheless."

Jonas gestured over his shoulder. "We brought you a horse and more supplies. We'll be riding back presently."

Jack walked over to the horse and untied the canteen. He took a long, slow drink, and then just leaned across the saddle for a time. The world felt different now, both heavier and colder, and also smaller. But it wasn't, and he knew it wasn't. The feeling wasn't unfamiliar; he'd felt the same thing after the war. But he felt a permanence this time, like something known and understood had past away, and the ticking clock was both louder and faster than it had once been. He found himself wondering why he was still here, why he'd survived, whether any of it mattered.

"Let's have a look at that leg."

Jack turned his head enough to see Doc Lewis standing behind him. He ignored him and swung into the saddle.

"That's quite a limp, Jack. Let's at least have a look."

"It's fine."

Lewis stepped closer. "Such things are easy to treat sometimes, but if you ignore it and it turns gangrenous—"

"Then it'll fall off," Jack snapped.

Lewis slid back a step and held a hand up. "Your choice."

Jack swung the horse around to clear off the doctor. He took another long drink from the canteen and then looked at Jonas.

"You ain't coming with us, are you?" Jonas said.

Jack reached in his pocket and pulled out the old folded piece of paper. He stared at it a long time, massaging it between his thumb and forefinger, and then looked out at the blue-gray horizon. "You know, many a man went west huntin' gold," he said. "But one of 'em took mine with him."

Epilogue

Summer, 1882
Nebraska

The cowbell was loud and irritating, oversized. And that was the point, the very reason her husband had installed it. It was a prop, custom made—not from the usual tin, but heavy cast metal. The clapper was solid brass and had cost him a small fortune. But no one anywhere near Waters' livery stable could miss the jarring sound of the unique bell, whether in the sleeping quarters or the corral out back. It was her husband's way of preventing missed customers, as well as giving them something to talk about and play with. And it worked. It had served its purpose flawlessly.

But Mrs. Waters wasn't in the sleeping quarters or the corral behind the building. She wasn't in the private room or speaking with the hands outside. She was sitting at the desk by the front door. Her desk. The one the cowbell was mounted to.

Without losing her well-rehearsed, customer-friendly smile, she closed her eyes and took a deep breath. The noise was painful. It was like sitting inside a church bell tower on Sunday morning. But she refused to look away, refused to cover her ears, refused to give him that satisfaction.

The bell went on clanging.

Cyrus Kane laughed. He obviously knew it was getting to her. And she knew the only way to make him stop was to acknowledge that one simple fact. But she wasn't going to, not even if it meant carrying around a pounding headache the remainder of the day.

There were other men gathering outside, however. Waters could see them through the window now. That gave her pause. They were mostly lounging against the smaller corral out front, passing a bottle around, smoking and laughing it up. Heavily armed. They were with Kane, she knew. The same bunch that was giving Sheriff Jeb so much trouble. One deputy had already been killed, but knowing who was responsible and proving it were two very different things.

Kane grinned at her, his eyes roaming over the exposed skin at her neck and throat.

She looked down, pretending to busy herself with paperwork.

The bell went on clanging.

Eventually, the door opened and a slender Mexican woman stepped in. The little bell above the door rattled, but, of course, no one could hear it. The lady went straight to the cowbell and stopped it with both hands.

"*Detente! Vas a despertar a los muertos!*"

Waters didn't understand the foreign language any more than Kane did. But she was sure it was a rebuke. And the fact that the big man didn't slap the woman down right then and there surprised her. She'd seen him do it before, mostly to unwilling prostitutes who were fed up with his abuse. But he only gave the woman a cursory glance and then looked back at Waters.

He quit ringing the bell.

"That pony was lame," he said.

Before she could respond, the door opened again and another man slipped inside. This one looked haggard and had a slight hitch in his walk. He sat down in one of the chairs reserved for waiting customers and lowered his head. A war veteran, maybe. There were plenty around Nebraska. Probably a henchman now. Dangerous.

Waters' stomach started to burn.

Kane rapped his knuckles on her desk.

She jumped.

Kane tapped his chest. "Your business is here, Mrs. Waters."

Waters found she was gripping the edge of her desk. She let go and cleared her throat. "Business, Mr. Kane?"

Kane grinned as she collected herself. "That's right, business. Everything's just business. Sometimes you're collectin' a debt, sometimes you're owin' one. In fact, the way I figure it, that's the nature of life."

Waters said nothing.

"You agree with that?"

"You owe me a debt, Mr. Kane?"

Kane chuckled. "Nothin' gets my blood flowing like a spirited woman." He was probing her with his eyes again. "Even when it's just show."

Waters said nothing.

"Is yours just show, Mrs. Waters?"

Waters glanced at the man in the chair. He was picking at his fingernails, head still down. Her eyes stopped on a thin scar drawing back along his right cheek and disappearing beneath a graying, unkempt beard. She wondered if she could make the side door before he intercepted her. It would have to be quick. Everything would depend on her first move.

She inched her chair away from the desk. It scraped against the dirty wooden floor.

"That ain't the spirit I was referring to," Kane said. He chuckled again. "It'll do," he said. "Yes, ma'am, make no mistake, it'll do just fine. But allow me to be kind and let you in on a little somethin'. Among other things, me and my boys figured you might make a try at that side door. And you're free to do so, free to choose. But you should know, Mrs. Waters, there's only pain waitin' on the other side of that door, only pain and sufferin'."

Waters looked at the Mexican woman to Kane's right. The woman was watching her, studying her the same way Kane was. Her eyes were round and full, black as the night sky. But at the same time, they seemed to be twinkling, sparkling with anticipation. She was biting her bottom lip and there was a grin at the edge of her mouth.

"You can go on and make your play," Kane said, "or be civil and move your chair back where it belongs."

Waters scooted back to the desk. "That was a fine mare and you know it, Cyrus."

Kane smiled, held a hand to his chest. "I'm touched, Mrs. Waters. I sincerely am. But as a matter of principle, I consider it rude to address someone by their given name while conductin' business."

"There ain't a horse in this territory that could've made that jump," Waters went on. "Her busted leg is nobody's fault but your own. No one with ..." She stopped and looked away.

"Please speak freely, Mrs. Waters."

Waters set her jaw. "No one with half a wit about 'em would even try something so asinine."

Kane grinned. "Now, that's the spirit," he said. "Please understand, ma'am, a horse will do what I expect it to do, or I will put it down, plain and simple. Furthermore, I would expect a mare with her kind of breedin'—at least, the kind of breedin' you described to me—to be capable of accomplishing the simple tasks I require without a hitch."

"That's not—"

Kane held up a hand. "Please let me finish, ma'am. For I must tell you that I consider interruption to be rudeness of the highest sort."

Waters said nothing.

"Now, the way I see it," Kane continued, "is maybe you really didn't know what you thought you did about this horse's particular breedin', and therefore merely passed on the same false information to me that you received yourself." He paused as if waiting for a response.

Waters said nothing.

"Or," he said, "you were being deliberately dishonest with me for the purpose of profit."

Again he paused, this time a little longer.

Waters was silent.

"But, as I said before, I suspect that pony was just lame all along, and she simply put on a good show for me, for both of us. She had spirit, Mrs. Waters, like you. But, you know, the drawback of spirit is that it blinds us to our weaknesses. It makes us think we can do things we can't, makes us try things beyond our means."

"Philosophy doesn't suit you, Mr. Kane."

He smiled. "Maybe not. I'll allow for that. That's why I'm gonna give you a chance to prove me wrong."

"I'm not replacing that mare," Waters said. The defiance just leapt out of her, almost against her will. It always had. Her husband had once told her it was the quality that most attracted him. He had also warned her to be careful with it.

"Fair enough," Kane said. "That was option A. Shall we move on?"

"Just state your intentions."

"Right to the point," Kane said. "Just like I like it." He ran a hand over his chest and wet his lips. "Now we're gonna move our negotiations to the back room there." He gestured at the door behind her. "To your sleepin' quarters. We'll put your spirit to the test then. You may find it unpleasant, maybe not. But rest assured, before I leave, you will have worked off your debt in full."

Waters slid her chair back. Her arteries pounded. "Over my dead body," she said. But she noticed the edge had gone out of her voice. She glanced again at the side door.

Kane frowned and shook his head. "Sometimes it turns out that way."

Waters stood, but the man in the chair was already up and drawing his weapon. She looked back at Kane, who was now pointing his revolver at her face.

"Just take a horse and go," she said. "The pick of the lot."

Kane aimed his weapon at her leg. "That time has passed, Mrs. Waters. And if you try to run, I'll just cripple ya." He rubbed his chest again. "Now be a good girl and invite me into that back room."

Waters felt tears welling behind her eyes. She couldn't stop them now and she hated herself for it. She looked at the Mexican woman, desperate. But the woman had stepped back and was looking over Kane's shoulder. Waters followed her eyes back to the man who'd been sitting in the chair.

The tip of the stranger's revolver touched the side of Kane's head.

Kane's eyes widened.

"Kinda takes the excitement out of it, huh?" the stranger said.

Kane's jaw set. Hatred flashed in his eyes.

"I've been around animals all my life," the stranger said. "But I don't reckon I've ever come across one that spews as much shit as you."

"You have any idea who I am, mister?"

"I know what you are."

"You ain't nothing," Kane spat. He raised his pistol at Waters. "I can put her down right now."

"You'll be next."

"And my men will drop you where you stand."

"Then we'll die together," the stranger said. He leaned closer and whispered, "But know this: anyone makes a move on me or this lady here, my boys out there will cut you to pieces, literally. Every last one of you. That's a promise."

The Mexican woman turned and looked outside, as did Waters. The main street through town was a good distance away, but plenty of people were visible, either milling about or standing by storefronts. There were men mostly, some carrying rifles, but there were woman and children as well. The standard fare. Nothing out of the ordinary. Nothing remarkable.

Kane's men were all pointing rifles and pistols at the window.

The Mexican woman waved them back.

Kane saw the gesture from the corner of his eye and let out a breath. "What's next, mister?"

"Leave that Colt and be on your way."

"I won't be leaving this piece."

"I reckon you will."

"Ain't gonna happen."

The Mexican woman mumbled something in Spanish, then slowly turned and walked out the door.

Kane tried to turn his head as she went, but the stranger pressed his weapon deeper into his temple. "This pistol cost me nearly—"

"It'll cost you a lot more to keep it."

Kane hesitated. His gaze met Waters', and she saw no fear in his eyes. But there *was* something in those hollow ovals, something primal, something that scared her worse than anything had thus far. Her blood went cold. She tried to meet Kane's stare but wherever that earlier defiance had come from was empty now.

She started to warn the stranger—of what, she didn't know. But as her lips parted to speak, Kane lowered his revolver and eased the hammer down.

"Think of it as resolving a debt," the stranger said.

Kane laid the Colt on Waters' desk, then turned and faced the stranger. "You'll regret this, mister. Like nothin' you've ever regretted before. I never forget a face."

"Get a good look, then."

Kane spat on the floor between them, then turned and went out the door. The front wall rattled as he slammed it behind him.

The stranger picked up the Colt and spun the cylinder, checking the loads. He flipped it around and handed it to Waters.

"You'd be wise to keep it handy."

Waters was openly sobbing now. She couldn't help it; something had just broken loose inside her. She sat down and gestured at the pistol. "They'll come back for it."

The stranger set the Colt on her desk and looked out the window.

"You sure your men can handle them?" Waters asked. "I mean, they're as rough as they come. They've already killed a deputy sheriff."

"I ain't got no boys with me."

"Dear God. Are you mad?"

"Not presently."

Waters wiped her eyes.

"How many men does he have?" the stranger asked.

"A lot. But most of 'em rode out this morning. Word is they're headed back east somewhere. You think they'll turn back for this?"

"Kane's not the leader?"

"No. They call him Zee, or something like that."

"Then I doubt it."

"You don't know them, mister. Zee's worse than Cyrus. I wouldn't put anything passed ..." She stopped and wiped her eyes again. "Dear lord," she said. "Look at me. Please accept my apology, Mr.—?"

The stranger looked back out the window.

"I really owe you a debt of gratitude," Waters said.

"You owe me nothin'."

"No, really. Please, have a look at the corral out back. We keep the best back there. Take the pick of the lot, any steed that strikes your fancy. It's the least I can do."

"That's not necessary."

Waters dipped a handkerchief in a bowl of water she kept by her desk. She held the cloth to her eyes for a moment, then ran it over the rest of her face. Finally, she wet her hands and drew her fingers through her hair. She took a breath and exhaled slowly, collecting herself. When she looked back up, she saw the stranger watching her. She leaned back and smiled sheepishly, embarrassed.

A grin touched the corner of his mouth.

She examined the scraggly salt-and-pepper beard and the jagged scar just visible beneath it. She glanced at the lines drawing away from his eyes and his dusty brown hat. There was something about him, something inexplicable, something tickling the back of her mind. It was like being suddenly struck by a certain odor or scene that sent your mind rushing back to childhood or days gone by.

"Do you work in town?"

"I'm not from around here."

"Are you looking for employment? I mean, we could really use someone like you around. Not many will stand up to the likes of Cyrus Kane."

"You said they were headed out."

"There's always more."

"I ain't looking for work," the stranger said. He sat back down in the chair by the wall. "What about Mr. Waters?"

"I'm sure that's none of your business."

The stranger nodded.

Waters flushed. "Forgive me. I'm afraid my manners fled out the door with the trash." She grinned apologetically.

He grinned back. And there it was again, that queer sensation of familiarity, that forgotten name hanging on the tip of her tongue.

"What brought you here today?" she asked. "I mean, your timing is impeccable, Mr.—?"

"Not so much. I actually followed 'em here. Heard 'em mention your name."

"Do I know you?"

"I think I knew your father."

She nodded.

"Heard he went out west, though."

"Yes, well, that was his intention at one time. But that was years ago. Who told you that?"

"A friend. Years ago."

"Who was it?" she asked. "What was his name?"

"It was a girl."

She stared at him a moment, curious. "That was toward the end of the war, but this is as far as he ever got." She smiled and held a hand out at the room in general. "He got spooked by the Indian threat, and we've been in Nebraska ever since."

She noticed him watching her again, smiling when she smiled. "But I'm afraid I have to apologize. My father died a couple of years ago. I'm sure he would've been happy to see you, though, and grateful for your intervention."

"I wonder."

"What?"

"What happened? If I may ask."

Waters let out a breath. "He always insisted we take on cattle, 'branch out,' he would say. He swore there wasn't enough money in peddling horses, and if we only took in a few head of beef it would put us over the top." She shook her head at the memory. "He was never satisfied. So he reached out and made some contacts in north Texas. But his extras abandoned him for a better offer the day they were scheduled to leave."

The stranger nodded and lowered his head.

Waters sighed. "But my hardheaded dad went on without 'em. They say he made it to Texas without a hitch, and had driven the cattle halfway back before the Comanche came down on him." She paused and glanced out the window. "Our whole crew died that day, every man who worked here, my husband included."

"I'm sorry," the stranger said. "I shouldn't have asked."

"No need to be," she said. "I've told that story so many times since then, you'd think I'd be callused by now." She scratched at a stain on her desk. "Don't really work that way, though."

"There ain't no forgettin'," the stranger said.

She looked at him. The man's head was down like he was studying something between his boots, but his mind seemed far away. "You said you heard them mention my name?"

The stranger glanced up. "What say?"

"Kane's boys. You said you heard them mention my name."

"That's right."

"But I don't carry my father's name anymore."

The man said nothing.

Waters leaned back in her chair. She saw what he was fixated on now. There was a small folded piece of paper in his right hand. She watched for a moment as he stared at it and turned it gently between his fingers.

"Mister, could you at least tell me—"

The man stood. "I should go." He crossed to the door.

"At least tell me your name?"

He stopped in front of her desk and looked out the window. He watched the people on the far street for a minute, then took his hat off and ran a hand through his hair. He looked back at her, unsure.

Waters straightened in her chair. Her eyes moved over his face again. The beard. The scar. Dear God. No, it was the eyes. She covered her mouth. Fresh tears spilled off her cheeks.

"My name ain't—"

Waters stood and came around the desk. The man slid back a step. She stopped in front of him, placed a trembling hand on his face. It was the eyes, the eyes all along. Those same sad, brown eyes. The way they stared back at her, looked into her. The power they gave her. The power they took from her. The way they made her feel like the only person in the world. She put her arms around his neck. "Oh, God," she said. "Jack." She squeezed and leaned against his chest. "My Jack."

He slipped an arm around her, and she felt warm tears on her shoulder.

"Rikka."

Author's note

Like so many ideas, this story would've been no more than a quick spark or flash in the mind—alive and intriguing in one moment, only to be lost amid daily hassles in the next. Ideas come and go often like that for me. I wish I could remember just half of them. But this one wouldn't go away. It dogged me, demanded my attention. And when I had no time for it, no time to open that door, it would simply drag me away, kick the door down. It was threaded into every other song on the radio; it loomed in silhouetted strangers in the distance. At work, when I was fully preoccupied, it whispered in my ear. And during that mystical first draft when the story first began breathing on its own, it nearly killed me (and probably took years off my life).

That being said, the tale's nagging persistence isn't what ultimately gave it life. Nor was it necessarily the author—who, when he finally sat down to transfer the images playing about in his mind to the page, found he possessed no particular talent for writing. But it was my wife, who read the story piece-by-piece, chapter after completed chapter. It was her eagerness to see the rest of it, her insistence that I *"get back in there and finish the frickin' thing!"* I remember waiting for her input on a particular chapter in the final third of the book. She finished the piece, quietly thought about it, and then pointed at the office door at the end of the hall. "Go," was all she said. That stuff really kept me going. I know that now better than I did then.

The storytelling was fun, exciting, an experience like no other. But the writing was beyond complicated. I still shudder when I look back at it, even sections that have been revised ad nauseam. And it genuinely pains me that I was unable to do justice to what I thought was a really neat story.

I tried.

So who were they? Who were those gray-cloaked demons of the forest? Someone asked me that after reading an early draft, and at the time I had a definite answer. But not anymore. Now I'm not so sure.

In my original notes, I referred to them as *the unknown*. This was because I still wasn't sure who they were myself. I wanted that sort of insurmountable obstacle one sees in modern storytelling. Only, I wanted to set it in that particular historical period I've always been fond of. I decided I'd discover who the main antagonists were when the time came. The story grew from there, instructing and informing me more than I ever did it. Except for the ending. I definitely forced the ending in one direction in the first couple of drafts, and, in my mind, it never really worked or felt right. So I tried to let go in the later revisions, loosen the reins. I tried to let the story inform me as it had before. Two competing hypotheses arose, both of which you're familiar with now. There's the myth or legend (I took certain liberties here, of course, but the ancient interpretation isn't far from the way Morris explains it) and there's Morris's preferred theory: namely, a strange communicable disease. I think there's evidence to support both of these views, and frankly I'm fine with either of them.

It may be a bad sign that the book doesn't answer this question itself, but, in the end, the story seemed to demand a certain amount of ambiguity. After all, if the characters didn't know who they were, then how would I?

Be that as it may, the majority of first readers came down hard on one side, and without any input from me. And that's how it should be. It's not my story anymore; it's yours. So, where do you think the evidence points? Which of the two propositions do you think is more compelling? Is there a third? Drop me a line at www.estaylor.com/contact and let me know what you think.

Special thanks to …

Carol Davis, writer and editor extraordinaire – for contributing the experience, wisdom, and technical expertise I sorely lack (any structural, factual, or historical discrepancies are entirely mine).

Award winning author Teresa Hill – for her invaluable input and advice, as well as her willingness to meet with me.

Susie Sauvola – who gave the story perhaps its most unique and best compliment.

Donna Coponen – for reading a really awful early draft, and asking the kind of questions I never would have thought of.

Bob Dockery – whose sincere excitement made me believe there really was something worth working on.

My very great friend, Scott Reynolds – for a silent inspiration he's not even aware of.

Sharon – my best friend, sweetheart, and wife – for providing that immeasurable support and patience that any difficult project has to have.

And my nine-year-old daughter – who, after reading a selected (appropriate) piece of the work, said, "Wow, this sounds like a real book, like a real writer did this."

What better praise could a storyteller possibly hope for?

E.S. Taylor, 2015

Printed in Great Britain
by Amazon

20030226R00171